ASH OF THE FAE

Ash of the Fae

Modern Fae Book 5

E. Menozzi

For the Modern Fae fans.

1

THE thick wooden beams that spanned the infirmary ceiling made a beautiful cage overhead, but I was long past sick of staring at them. I rolled over, wincing only slightly in response to the ache of my still-healing ribs. My phone lay faceup on the small table next to my cot. The screen displayed the day and the time along with that annoying "no service" message that might as well have read, *Too bad about your career, Hannah.*

It had been six days since my last vlog. I knew this because my phone said it was Thursday, and for the past three years, I had been posting a new Fashion Friday video every week without fail. If the Faerie Queen didn't agree to let me out of her infirmary today, I was going to miss a week.

My followers would think I'd completely flaked. I'd already missed my chance to post the last few teaser videos I'd planned leading up to Morgan's annual Start the Summer weekend bash. After years of attending as Morgan's best friend, this year, she'd given me the coveted position of exclusive social media manager. I'd been planning for months. But that was before I found out that the person I'd thought was my best friend had been keeping a major secret from me. Not to mention the part where she nearly killed me.

Regardless, I'd seen social media icon after icon launch their career off the exclusive access to Morgan's annual party, and I was not about to miss my opportunity to do the same. I shot a glance at the tall Fae guard standing with their back to me by the door and considered my mental list of possible distractions searching for anything that might keep the guard occupied long enough for me to escape. There wasn't much I could do with my water magic, so it was a short list. I'd considered flooding the place, but that seemed too obvious. A mysterious drip from the ceiling might send the guard looking for a bucket, or someone to repair the leak. But there was always the chance that they just had the magic to counter whatever I attempted. It didn't seem worth the risk.

Besides, I didn't even know how to get home. I wasn't even really sure where I was, exactly. All I knew was that the Fae lived somewhere in England. Assuming I could find a way out, there was no chance of catching a flight back to Seattle. I didn't even have my passport with me. It's not like I expected to be whisked off to the Fae Forest after my former best friend accidentally hit me with a blast of magic.

At least, I hoped it was an accident. My fingers traveled to the tender skin on the back of my scalp and what was left of the lump. It would be a lot easier to believe that Morgan hadn't been trying to hurt me if I hadn't also been knocked out earlier that same day while helping Max, Angie, and Jayden with a secret project at the Silicon Moon offices. I still couldn't remember exactly what happened, but Morgan was one of only a few people who had access to the building and the motivation to keep me from getting in her way.

I closed my eyes against the warning pricks of tears I refused to shed.

What a mess. Once I got out of here, I'd deal with Morgan. She owed me more than an apology. Using her party to advance my career seemed like a good place to start getting even for the pain she'd caused.

Crying wouldn't help anything, anyway. It would only make my already wrecked skin get all puffy and blotchy. The Fae infirmary just wasn't properly supplied for mere humans who needed multistep skin-care routines to maintain a fraction of what came naturally to these effortlessly beautiful immortals.

Would it be too much to ask these Fae healers to restore my healthy glow before they released me? Sure, it would be embarrassing to be so admittedly vain, but it would save me having to book an emergency facial before the party this weekend. I made a mental note to ask Talie or Eira the next time they showed up to check on me. Until then, as long as I stayed calm, didn't start crying, and couldn't see how bad the damage was, I could fool myself into thinking that there was a chance I might be camera ready when they finally let me leave.

Gritting my teeth and mustering the reserves of my fortitude, I pushed myself up to a seated position so I wouldn't look like such a pathetic mess when Max arrived. I tried not to think about the fact that he'd been keeping secrets from me, too. He knew that his older sister was half demon.

At least he'd been making an effort to apologize. He'd come to visit me almost every day since I'd woken up. Sometimes he'd bring his fiancée, Angie, who was one of my top five favorite people in the world. And he'd promised me that he would convince the Faerie Queen to let me go home once their healers said I had recovered from my injuries.

I expected him to walk through the door at any minute and give me some good news. The only way in and out was at the opposite end of the infirmary, which was basically a long, narrow building lined with cots sticking out into the single center aisle like gap-toothed teeth in the mouth of a grimace emoji. I'd been assigned to a bed near the far wall. At the moment, I was the only patient.

When I first woke up, I'd had a roommate across the aisle. He was a big Fae with lots of scars, like he'd seen more than a few battles. I never did see his face, only his bare back. He'd been curled up, facing away from me, and he didn't answer when I tried to talk to him.

When I woke up again, he wasn't there. Since then, a few patients had come and gone, but they'd all been kept at the opposite end, near the door. Now it was just me and the guard.

I stared at the door, willing Max to make an appearance. The guard turned toward me and raised an eyebrow. Perhaps staring wasn't the best option.

I pulled my knees up, hugging them to my chest. A stab of pain shot through my lower rib cage, and I cringed. Deciding that wasn't going to work, I released my grip on my legs and crossed them like a pretzel instead. Then I let my head fall back until it rested on the wall at the head of the bed. My eyes fluttered closed, and I might have drifted off for a moment.

"Hey, Hannah!"

My eyes snapped open, and I turned my head toward the door. Angie was walking down the aisle holding up a brown paper bag. There were a few blotches on the outside where something greasy must have seeped through.

My mouth started watering. "Is that what I think it is?"

Angie nodded. "We come bearing treats."

I reached for the bag with greedy hands and peeked inside. The mound of plump, fried doughballs covered in powdered sugar made my mouth water. "Is this a celebration? Please tell me you got me these to celebrate my release back into the real world."

Max walked up behind Angie and wrapped his arms around her waist. She glanced over her shoulder at him, and they exchanged a look.

My fingers crumpled the top of the paper bag, closing it. "Come on. Just tell me. Am I dying?"

Angie's head swung toward me, her eyes wide. "No!"

Max scowled and shook his head. "Definitely not."

"Then what's the problem?" I glared at him, daring him to break the promise he'd made to me about getting me home today. "Spill."

"Fiona hasn't made a decision yet." He released Angie and held up his hands as I opened my mouth to respond. "She wanted to wait and discuss it when her Court meets today. We're going there next, but we wanted to come see you first. I promise we'll come back with news as soon as it's over."

"Max..." I hesitated. I didn't want to explain why I needed to be out today. Even though Max and I had been friends for nearly as long as I'd been friends with his sister, and he knew what my career meant to me, I couldn't be sure he'd understand. I had, in fact, been hoping that he'd forgotten about Morgan's Start the Summer bash. He avoided her Hollywood parties unless forced to attend. If I reminded him, after everything that happened, he might insist I stay away and probably tell Fiona to keep me here until it was over, just to be sure I didn't go.

Max cringed. "I know. I know. It's just... You don't understand how powerful Morgan is. She's always been barely able to control whatever magic is inside her, and now...if she's working with the demons...who knows what she's capable of."

"And I'm no match for her. That's what you're saying." My jaw clenched as I held my water magic in check. It would only prove Max's point if I let my emotions control me and geysers of water started erupting in the infirmary aisle.

"It's not that. It's just..." Max sighed. "Aside from my mother, I'm supposed to be the most powerful wizard in the Society, and *I'm* no match for Morgan, Hannah."

I tried to resist the urge to roll my eyes at Max's unjustified humility. He was nothing like me. He had control of two elements—something almost unheard of among humans—and both were more useful in a fight than my water magic. And he'd been taught to use them as soon as he'd shown an affinity, unlike me. Max and Morgan's mother was the head of the Wizard Society. Max's father was one of the wizards on the Council. My parents didn't even know they carried Fae blood, and they definitely had no idea that they'd passed that magical potential on to me. If it hadn't been for Morgan and her parents, I might never have realized I was a wizard, too. And I definitely wouldn't have figured out how to use my power.

What Max wasn't saying, but what he knew as well as I did, was that he could use his magic to protect himself against Morgan, if needed. Air and fire magic were both great for that sort of thing. Water magic, on the other hand... If Morgan tried to attack me again, what was I going to do, conjure up a wave and drench her?

I cringed and resorted to my backup reason for wanting to get home. "I get it, Max, but my agent probably thinks I'm dead. As much as she doesn't want me to be the center of some scandal, if she doesn't hear from me soon, she's probably going to call the cops, or worse...my parents."

Max frowned. He didn't want to explain magic to my parents any more than I did. "Okay. Okay. I'll get you out of here."

Angie sat down on my cot and set her hand on my knee. "I could stay, if you want? Keep you company while Max goes and pleads your case?"

I glanced back and forth between them for a moment, considering her offer. It would be nice to hang out with someone besides the infirmary guard who never spoke to me. But then I remembered Angie's superpower. She might be a human with no magic, but she was a lawyer and she'd always been way better at negotiations than Max.

I shook my head. "No. Go with Max. Leave me here with my consolation beignets. Just promise me that you won't let him take no for an answer. I am leaving here today. Got it?"

Angie grinned. "Got it."

Max groaned. "You can't promise her that."

Angie winked at me. "Don't worry. I've got this."

"Thank you." I clutched the paper bag to my chest, careful not to squish the contents as I watched them leave.

———

WITH Damir's return to the Fae forest, I'd lost my seat at the High Table. It had always been temporary. I didn't belong here. My place was back in the Dragon Fae clan's caverns, high in the mountains of Eastern Europe, at Damir's side, serving as his lieutenant and making sure the rest of the clan showed him all the respect he deserved as our new Alpha.

But Damir had arrived with Seren just before Fiona called

her Court to their seats at the stone table. There was barely time for him to greet me and ask how I was healing from the injuries I'd earned when I refused to swear an oath of loyalty to the previous clan Alpha.

At least I had good news to share on that front. "Talie says one more week and then I can try a transformation. He wants it to be supervised by him or one of the other Hands, but I think they worry too much. I feel great." I puffed out my chest in case he hadn't noticed that I'd barely lost a gram of muscle while he'd been off getting the clan sorted. Without anywhere to go or anything to do, I'd been getting in a lot of sparring practice with the Faerie Queen's Guard.

Damir nodded once. "Good. Depending on what Fiona has planned, I may have to stay here for a bit. If that's the case, I'd like to get you back to the caves to help Ivo. His strength has improved enough for him to take care of my day-to-day duties, but it will be a while before he's back in his dragon form, and I don't like leaving him alone with guards I don't know."

Our wing-mate had nearly died while challenging the previous Alpha of our clan, and it was my fault. I couldn't tell if Damir blamed me or not, but it didn't matter. If I'd kept my head down and held my temper in check, the previous Alpha would never have called me out. I wouldn't have been asked to swear my loyalty to the bastard who almost certainly killed my sire, I wouldn't have been nearly beaten to death for refusing, and Damir wouldn't have had to rescue me. I could have waited for Ivo to come around and agree to challenge for the title that should have been his. If I had, I would have been there to serve with Damir as Ivo's lieutenant. Damir wouldn't have had to protect Ivo alone.

The three of us should have been fighting side by side, the way we'd been taught by our sires since we were Fledgelings.

Instead, Ivo nearly died and Boro could have won, all because I'd been impatient and ended up stuck in some Forest Fae infirmary recovering from my injuries while my wing-mates faced an unfairly balanced challenge where they were out-numbered two to one.

Because of Ivo's injuries, Damir had to take on the role of clan Alpha. He'd made Ivo his first lieutenant in order to make sure that Ivo received the best care possible. As far as I knew, he had yet to take a second lieutenant. I hoped that meant he was planning to offer that position to me, but I worried that, since he hadn't said anything, he intended to offer it to someone he considered more dependable. I'd learned my lesson. I just needed a way to prove to Damir that he could trust me again.

I opened my mouth, the words waiting on my tongue, but Fiona called her Court to their seats before I could say anything.

Damir rested a hand on my shoulder. "We'll talk more after the meeting. Sit with Seren, for me?"

He motioned to the silver-eyed Fae who'd recently agreed to be his mate. She had been talking with the half demon I remembered from the only other Court meeting I'd attended. I'd failed to notice her approach. Either she was exceptionally sly or my skills as a lieutenant were extremely rusty.

"Of course." I dipped my head to him and signaled Seren to walk ahead of me toward the cluster of chairs that had been set at the far side of the High Table, just inside the stone circle.

Seren glanced back over her shoulder toward the table. I followed her gaze to the red-haired Fae who I remembered was the leader of the Elemental Faction. I'd forgotten her name, also. The dark-haired half demon was whispering something in her ear. I wondered why Seren appeared to be so interested in their exchange.

Just as the red-haired Fae's eyes lifted to look in our direction, someone bumped into my shoulder and immediately apologized.

When I turned, I found myself staring at a human that I recognized, but not because she sat on Fiona's Court. There were only two humans on the Court. One had no magic but served as Fiona's ambassador to the humans. The other was a wizard.

My Fae senses confirmed that the human staring up at me didn't have any magic. That made it odd for her to have slipped past the border between the Fae and human lands, let alone be present at a meeting of the Faerie Queen's Court. And yet, I was sure I'd seen her somewhere before.

I squinted at her, trying to place her face. Perhaps she was one of the young human women from the village who I'd bedded? That might make things a bit awkward since I made a point to never visit the same woman twice.

The human smiled and stuck out her hand. "I'm Angie. Hannah's friend? We met briefly in the infirmary when I was visiting her?"

She paused, waiting for me to recognize her. When I didn't say anything, she added, "You told me to *give the bloke a chance.* Remember?" Her eyes skimmed past me and landed on the wizard who had joined Fiona's Court around the same time I began sitting in for Damir.

"Right. Angie." My fingers closed around hers as the memories clicked into place.

"You must be Ved Ashwing. You're one of the Dragon Fae, right? Max mentioned that you had joined Fiona's Court." She glanced over her shoulder at the table. "How come you're sitting over here? Shouldn't you be at the table with the others?"

I forced a smile and hoped that it didn't look too much like a grimace. "No need. Our clan leader is here today. I only represent the Dragon Fae on his behalf."

"Oh." She turned her head to search out the unfamiliar face in the crowd. Once she found him, she returned her attention to me and gestured toward the chairs. "Mind if I sit with you, then?"

"Angie!" A petite woman came running toward us across the mossy clearing. "I'm so glad you're here!"

When the two women started to hug, I tried to escape. I was supposed to be keeping Seren company, not conversing with curious humans. I still wasn't sure why this Faerie Queen kept so many of them around. She fascinated me but refused every attempt I'd made at courting her, despite the fact that I'd promised her my seed. Of course, when I'd made that commitment, I'd been stuck in her infirmary, recovering with the help of her healers, and we'd thought my wing-mates, who also happened to be her cousins, might not survive their challenge and live long enough to produce the potential heirs they'd promised her.

I hadn't heard anything more about my promise since Damir had taken control of the Dragon Fae clan. I was beginning to suspect that Fiona had decided she didn't need to settle for my seed when she could have her pick from any of the eligible males in the Dragon Fae clan. As far as she was concerned, I was nothing more than Damir and Ivo's wing-mate. And if Damir chose someone else to serve as his second lieutenant, then I would truly be no one to her.

My pride refused to let that happen. Not because I wanted her as my mate. She'd made it clear that she planned to have lots of Faelings, and Fae males only carried one seed. That would mean she would have to carry Faelings from many sires. Dragon Fae weren't known for their ability to share, and I was no exception. If I ever took a mate—and I had no intention of doing so—she would be mine, as I would be hers, for life. And Dragon Fae lived a very long time. Which was why I wasn't inclined to settle for just one woman.

As though she'd read my thoughts, the only female who truly cared for me circled in the sky above the Court, then swooped down to land on my shoulder.

"Is that a faerie dragon?" The petite human stared at my familiar. She released Angie from their embrace and tugged on her arm to draw her attention to the small silver-and-purple-scaled dragon attempting to wrap herself around my neck like a fire-breathing scarf.

Angie lifted her hand and started to reach toward me but paused before completing the motion. "Can I touch him?"

"Her," I corrected. "Her name is Firrag. But don't reach out your hand like that unless you want to be bitten."

Fiona saved me from having to explain the best way to greet a faerie dragon. She cleared her throat and shot us a look that sent Angie and her friend scurrying for their seats. I sank into the last of the empty chairs next to Seren just as Fiona began to speak.

"Let's begin." A silence so complete that even the birdsong disappeared followed her statement and signaled that she had activated her wards. They cloaked the area, preventing the sound of our voices from escaping beyond the standing stones that circled us.

Firrag nipped at my ear and nudged my chin with the spikes on the top of her head, distracting me as Fiona asked for updates on preparations for the demon attack that, based on the half demon's spying, they expected would happen during the summer solstice festivities. I reached up and scratched Firrag under her chin as Arabella reported on how Seren and the half demon—Nigel, that was his name, not that it mattered to me, I was going home and wouldn't be around long enough to care what happened to any of these Fae—were training the Queen's Guard to fight demons.

Seren exhaled when no one commented on Arabella's report. She started to relax back into her seat, but then Gwawr began to speak, and Seren shifted forward again.

"Are you okay?" I whispered to her.

She waved a hand and shushed me, so I shrugged and focused my attention on Firrag. It was nice not sitting at the table. I didn't have to pretend to be listening when I was seated with the guests. I let my mind drift to more important things.

I had almost decided on, exactly, what I would say to Damir after the meeting to convince him I was a worthy lieutenant when someone at the table mentioned my name. I searched the faces around the table, trying to determine who had spoken, just as a robed Fae seated at Fiona's left responded.

"Now is not the time to be deciding such things as who will sire the queen's firstborn. We must focus on defeating the demons, first. Thanks to you, Damir, there are now two possible paths to succession, should we lose our queen. And, should Fiona take a seed now, she would not be safely through the Settling phase of the pregnancy before the demon attack. She will need her magic to defend herself should the demons breach the guards."

Thanks to Damir? What did Damir do to help ensure that the Faerie Queen had an heir? I tried to focus and follow the discussion so I could figure out what the queen's aunt was talking about.

"Fiona could wait out the attack in the caverns," Damir suggested. "The Dragon Fae would be honored to protect the Faerie Queen, especially if she is carrying the seed from one of ours."

Fiona placed her hands flat on the stone table. "Enough. I will not run in the face of danger. I will stand and fight with the factions. Sorcha is right. The Court can vote on any candidates proposed to sire my firstborn after we win this war. Unless there is anything else to discuss...?"

I tensed, only just then realizing the political implications of the commitment I'd made. Fiona was talking about me, about the possibility of me being the male who might sire the firstborn of the queen. And, as I suspected, it didn't sound like she was in a hurry to take me up on that promise. In fact, it didn't sound like she wanted a Dragon Fae sire for her firstborn at all.

Fiona's cousin, Arabella, was already carrying a Faeling, and so was their aunt, the robed woman who had spoken in favor of Fiona waiting to take a seed. But I'd heard that their aunt's Faeling could not be queen. Something about the heir needing to be the firstborn female of the next generation. Their aunt's Faeling would be Fiona's cousin. Damir and Ivo's cousin.

Wait. If Damir and Ivo were both High Fae, that meant if one of them produced a female Faeling, that Faeling could be the next Faerie Queen.

I glanced over at Seren. She was focused on whatever was happening at the stone table, so I allowed my eyes to drift down to her belly. If Seren were pregnant, why hadn't Damir told me? Why did everyone else in the Court seem to know what Fiona's aunt meant when I didn't? Damir was my wingmate. He should have said something. Unless I was right, and he didn't trust me.

The voices at the stone table began arguing over the safety of some wizard who was healing in the infirmary. I attempted to block the noise out so that I could further consider what Damir and Seren's Faeling might mean for my future, and for the future of the Dragon Fae. Then the human without magic who was sitting near me stood and addressed the Queen's Court.

Angie. I was pretty sure she'd said her name was Angie.

"My queen, if you will allow me to speak on Hannah's behalf?" Probably-Angie bowed her head and paused until Fiona acknowledged her. "The hundreds of thousands of humans who watch Hannah's videos know nothing of the world of magic. Her parents are also blissfully unaware. Unlike Hannah, they never discovered and never learned to use the magic they carry in their blood. If Hannah does not return to the human lands soon and resume her normal activities, it will be noticed, and it will be nearly impossible to explain where she is and why."

She paused briefly before continuing. "I agree that Hannah's safety is at risk because she knows the location of Emilio's boxes. And it is very likely Morgan will try to contact Hannah as soon as she sees that Hannah has returned. Morgan is—was—Hannah's best friend. However, they do live thousands of miles apart. Hannah's apartment can be warded, and if she goes out, she can keep to public spaces filled with non-magical humans where Morgan is unlikely to harm her. If that is not enough, perhaps you can spare one of the guards and assign them to keep an eye on Hannah for at least a few days until we see how Morgan reacts?"

The corners of Fiona's mouth turned down. She glanced away from Angie and appeared to focus her attention on the wizard at the opposite end of the table as though she planned to address him. To her right, Arabella, the commander of the Queen's Guard, moved her chin a fraction to the left before returning it to center. The slight shake would have been missed by anyone who wasn't watching closely. I had barely caught it, but Fiona must have noticed.

"Our guards cannot be spared." Fiona sighed. "If Hannah is released, it will fall on the wizards to protect her."

"But, Your Highness." The wizard at the end of the table leaned forward. "The wizards don't know about my sister, and I'm not sure we should risk telling them right now. It might divide our Society at a time when we need everyone focused on the true enemy. Focused on the goal of defeating the demons."

I glanced at the faces around the table, then up at Angie. Seren, who sat between us, moved one hand to rest on her belly. The gesture caught my eye, and I knew what I needed to do.

My mouth spoke before I could reconsider. "I'll do it. I'll guard the human."

It was time to prove my worth to Damir and to the queen. How hard could it be to keep one wizard safe from an untrained half demon?

2

B Y the time Max returned to the infirmary, I'd added five more items to my to-do list. Luckily, I could tell by the way Max was smiling that I was about to get good news. The guy was a terrible liar. If he was grinning, that meant I was getting out of here.

"You did it!" I swung my legs over the side of the cot and started to stand up. The sudden movement made me a little light-headed, but I grinned through it, unwilling to reveal any weakness that might make the Faerie Queen change her mind about letting me go. "Tell me you did it. You did, right?"

Max laughed. "There are some conditions, but yeah. You get to go home."

"Conditions? What conditions?" I glanced past his shoulder, searching for Angie, but she wasn't there. "Where's Ang?"

"She'll be here in a minute. She's waiting for your guard."

"My what?" I hoped it was just the fading lightheartedness that made me hear him wrong.

"Fiona wasn't convinced, so Angie suggested that she assign you a guard. For a minute there, I didn't think it was going to work." Max shrugged. "But it did, and I think it's a good idea. We don't know what my sister is capable of, and we are pretty sure she's working with the demons. I don't want anything to happen to you."

I squinted at him. "So, what sort of guard are we talking about here?" Morgan would definitely notice if I were forced to bring one of the Fae with me to her party. She would see right through their glamour. Not that I could use that as an excuse because if Max and Angie knew I was planning on going to Morgan's house, they would never let me out of here.

Max nodded. "The Queen's Guard is busy training to fight demons. They didn't have anyone they could spare to send with you."

I exhaled, hoping my face wasn't betraying my relief at avoiding that complication. "So, what, then?"

As soon as the words left my lips, I remembered the little corgi that had been a gift to Angie from the Fae. *Perfect.* I'd always wanted a dog but just couldn't justify getting one given my highly unpredictable schedule. "Is Angie lending me Salty? Please say that I get to take Salty with me..."

Max grinned. "Sure. If you want to take Salty for the week, I think Angie would agree to that."

I squinted at him. "Okay...but if you didn't mean Salty, then who did you have in mind?"

A deep voice spoke up from near the door. "Me."

I'd been so focused on Max that I hadn't noticed we were no longer alone. Angie had arrived, and she'd brought with her a massive Fae male. He filled most of the doorway with his broad shoulders. Whatever material his shirt was made from was getting tested to its limits as it stretched across exquisitely defined pectoral muscles clearly visible beneath the thin fabric. If I didn't know he was Fae, I'd have guessed he spent all his time at the gym. But given his heritage, it was much more likely he was born that way. His poor mother.

I tore my eyes from his bulk and glared at Max. "I thought you said no Fae?"

Max shook his head. "No. I said no Queen's Guard."

"So, who is that, then?" I gestured in the direction of the big male who was definitely not human. The way he was striding down the aisle toward us, with his confidence and his chiseled jaw and sharp cheekbones, the guy could be making millions modeling.

The Fae's lips pulled back into a feral grin, like he knew I was checking him out. "I'm your bodyguard. Name's Vedran Ashwing, of the Dragon Fae, but you can call me Ved."

Max wisely stepped aside as I pushed past him to meet the cocky Dragon Fae in the aisle.

"Look, Ved." My chin lifted and my neck arched as I was forced to look up at him. At almost six feet tall, that was not something I was used to doing, and I hated it. I flashed him my best camera-ready smile anyway. "Thanks. It was really nice of you to agree to this and everything, but I don't really need a bodyguard. Okay?"

He folded his thick arms across his chest, accentuating the bulge of his biceps as they emerged from the short sleeves of his shirt. "That's not what I hear."

"Is that so?" I shot a glare at Max before returning to my face-off with the Dragon Fae. "Honestly, now. Do I look like someone who needs a bodyguard?"

Ved's eyes raked over me from head to foot and then back up again.

I held myself very still and willed my body not to shiver,

but something about the way he took his time sizing me up sent my cheeks flaming.

When his eyes found mine again, his lips pushed out into a pout. "Honestly?" He shrugged. "Yeah. Since you asked."

The heat in my cheeks flared downward to fill my chest with righteous anger. "Wrong answer."

Max stepped forward before I could embarrass myself by drenching the hulking beast with my water magic. It would have accomplished nothing aside from proving him right. Still, an image of the big Dragon Fae with his hair dripping wet and that tight shirt clinging even more to his muscled chest flashed through my mind.

I blanked for a minute, only snapping out of it when Max turned to me as though expecting me to say something in response to whatever he'd asked. I tried to come up with a response that wouldn't give away the fact that I'd been fantasizing about wet T-shirts instead of paying attention.

"How long do I have to keep him around?" I asked.

Angie squeezed past the Dragon Fae so she could join the conversation. "Just until we get a better idea of what's going on with Morgan. Regardless, the summer solstice is in a few weeks. That's when the demons are supposed to attack. Worst case, you're stuck with him until then."

That wiped the smirk off the big Fae's stupidly attractive face. "A few weeks? I did not sign up to babysit wizards for a few weeks."

Angie pulled herself up to her full height. Even though she was still much shorter than me and had no magic, with her shoulders back and her hands on her hips, she looked fierce. "You signed up to protect my friend Hannah from anything or anyone that might try to harm her until the Faerie Queen's High Court agrees that she's safe. And that's exactly what you're going to do. Got it?"

Max and I watched with eyes wide and mouths gaping as a dark cloud of anger flashed across the Dragon Fae's face. For a heartbeat, I thought he was going to reach out and crush my defenseless friend. But he didn't.

The moment passed, and he just nodded. "Right. Of course, I'm going to guard Hannah. I just didn't realize it was going to take so long, that's all."

I snorted. "Like you have someplace better to be?"

His head swiveled toward me. "As a matter of fact, yeah. I do."

"Well, what are you doing here, then? Go on. Go. I can take care of myself."

"Are you so sure about that?" Before I could answer, he lunged at me.

I dodged out of the way just in time to slip out of his grasp. He followed me as I retreated between two of the cots, so I scrambled over the one closer to the door and hopped down on the other side.

"That's your strategy? Run away? I thought you had magic." He shoved the bed frame toward me, angling it so that it blocked my path into the main aisle and trapped me between him and the next cot. "Let's see it."

This was a waste of time. I was already winded from just that small amount of exertion. If I kept it up, Angie and Max were going to see exactly how weak I still was. I couldn't risk them reconsidering letting me out. Even if I had to accept this beefy bully as my bodyguard in order to do it.

I turned toward him with my arms raised, palms facing him. "Fine. You win. But before we go anywhere, I have a few rules for you."

Before he could respond, I started ticking things off on

my fingers. "You don't speak to anyone unless there is a life-threatening emergency. You don't touch me unless there is a life-threatening emergency. And you remain glamoured at all times."

When I paused to take a breath, he said, "Is that all? Because I have some rules, too." He cocked his head to one side. "Well, more like one rule. One really simple rule."

"What's that?"

"You do what I say when I say it."

"What?" I folded my arms across my chest. "No. Why?"

"Duck."

I glared at him. "I'm not going to just duck because you sa—"

Angie spoke over me. "No, really—"

Max made a strangled noise, something between a yell and a laugh. I turned my head toward them and got smacked in the face by something purple hurtling through the air toward the Dragon Fae.

"Ouch." Angie said what I was thinking.

I rubbed the side of my face.

Ved gestured at me, drawing my attention to him. "That's what I'm talking about. Now, are you going to agree to do what I say when I say it?"

The thing that had hit me in the face was perched on Ved's shoulder getting scratches under its chin. I wanted to be mad, but that was impossible once I got a look at the small silver dragon with purple-tipped wings. At least, compared to Ved's shoulders, it appeared to be small. Its lavender eyes locked with mine, and it cocked its head at me. After a moment of contemplation, it snorted smoke from its precious tiny nostrils.

I forgot all about the stinging pain on my cheek that probably meant I had scratch marks on my skin, or possibly a bruise. "That is the cutest thing I have ever seen. What is it, and where did you find it?"

"It's a faerie dragon," Angie nearly squealed, informing me. "Isn't she adorable?"

Ved folded his arms across his chest. "Firrag is not adorable. She is a fierce predator. She's dangerous, and you'd best keep your hands to yourself unless you want them bitten."

The faerie dragon preened at what appeared to be scales that covered the leading edge of her wing. Then she settled down and curled into a ball with her head tucked against Ved's thick neck.

Angie and I said "Aww..." at the same time.

"Stop that." Ved frowned.

"Is she coming with you, or are you leaving her here?" I asked.

"She goes where I go," Ved replied.

"Well, if she comes with, you're going to have to keep her in my apartment. You can't just walk around downtown Seattle with a small dragon on your shoulder. Humans don't think dragons exist." Perhaps this would be the thing that convinced him he didn't want this job, guarding me. "Hell, I'm a wizard, and I didn't even know dragons existed until one flew into my face. So, Firrag stays inside, got it?"

"Impossible. She needs to hunt."

I shrugged. "Then you can let her out very late at night when it's dark and no one is looking. But she'll have to be back before daybreak. Can you manage that? Will she obey you?"

"She's my familiar. She doesn't obey me."

"Well, if you can't control her—"

"Enough." Ved cut me off. "If you would just stop talking

for one minute and listen."

He paused to test me. Even though I wanted to tell him exactly where he could shove that attitude, something told me that wasn't going to help my cause. So I kept my mouth shut.

"She can understand you. And she's good at hiding and blending in. She's also good at detecting danger."

"All right, then." I looked at Firrag. "Keep away from the humans. Don't let them see you, please?"

Firrag stared at me. She snorted, releasing a puff of smoke, then closed her eyes. Somehow I got the sense she was laughing at me.

I frowned and turned toward Max. "If we're going, let's go."

Max shook his head. "Ved's going to take you home. I'm going to take Angie back to Lydbury to get Salty. Then we're going to get Jayden and Grace and meet you at your apartment so that we can set up some wards to keep Morgan out."

I clenched my teeth to keep from sighing and forced a smile. "Great. That sounds great."

When I turned around to face Ved, I found myself looking at his chest, which was only a few inches from the end of my nose. I stumbled a half step back and looked up. "You're creepy. Don't sneak up on me like that."

Ved grinned. "Shall we?" He cupped his large palm around my elbow and curled his long fingers around my arm.

"Do you even know where you're—" The transit void sucked the air from my lungs before I could finish my question. I pinched my eyes shut against the freezing cold.

I'd only traveled this way twice, and I didn't remember much about either occasion other than that I was not a fan. The first time was with Max, using the device his engineers had built so that wizards could travel like Fae and demons.

The second time was just a few minutes later, after Morgan had zapped me with her magic. On accident. Supposedly.

That second time might have been better than the first. The commander of the Queen's Guard had directed the transport instead of some beta-version Silicon Moon tech. But I didn't remember any of it because I was unconscious.

Maybe it was just because I wasn't ready for it, but, in addition to stealing my breath away, my third transport made my ears ring and my guts twist uncomfortably. I wasn't sure I was ever going to get used to the shock of being in one place and then being no place and then arriving someplace entirely different.

When the cold disappeared, I opened my eyes a fraction and squinted through partially closed lids, afraid I might puke if I opened them too quickly.

Something nearby screeched, then giggled. Ved released me, and I stumbled, slamming my shin against my coffee table. Wings flapped in my peripheral vision as Ved lunged toward the far side of the room.

"Damn!" He stood and turned toward me, arms empty. "Missed it."

———

HANNAH glared at me like she'd just caught me trying to pee on the carpet. "Missed what?"

I exhaled and shook my head. She must not have seen it. "Chaos demon. Probably been here a while, waiting for you to return. Likely run off to its master to tell them you're back. We need to get you out of here. It's not safe."

My nose itched. I rubbed it with the back of one hand as I started across the small room to collect my wizard charge so I could transport us back to the infirmary. Firrag cooed a warning at me, but I had no idea what she was trying to say. Then she disappeared.

"Where'd she go?" Hannah backed away from me.

"Probably to warn someone who speaks faerie dragon." I scowled, realizing that meant Damir, who was the last person I wanted to know that I'd failed to capture one irritating little orange demon. "Let's go."

Hannah twisted, avoiding my grasp. "Oh, no. I'm not going back there. I'm home, and I'm staying here."

"That was a demon." I pointed to the spot where the chaos demon had disappeared. "It's not safe here. What did I say about listening to me and obeying my commands when I tell you you're not safe?"

Hannah shook her head. "Max and the others will be here soon. They'll take care of my apartment. They'll make it safe. All you have to do is protect me until they get here. Are you incapable of doing that? Should I ask for someone else?"

"There is no one else, little witch. Just me. And I think we should go. Now." I reached out and caught hold of her hand before she could pull away.

Her eyes focused on something behind me just as another voice spoke.

"You're home! Sledge told me you were with someone, but I assumed it was just my brother. I've been so worried about you! Where have you been? Are you okay? And who's your friend?"

I turned around, angling my body so that Hannah was behind me. My first look at the intruder confirmed what I'd already guessed. "Demon."

The dark-haired woman shrugged. "Half demon, technically. But you can call me Morgan. And you are...?"

This was the evil half demon that the Faerie Queen's Court

was so worried about? Her head barely reached the center of my chest, and even though she was hiding her figure under a large hooded sweatshirt, the sleeves were pushed up. I doubted, based on her exposed wrists and forearms, that there was a muscle on her body. Sure, she practically hummed with barely contained magic, but she didn't intimidate me.

I narrowed my eyes. "I'm your worst—"

Hannah cut me off as she stepped forward to stand next to me. She set a hand on my bicep and leaned toward me. She squeezed my arm. "A date. Your brother set us up, actually. And I had my phone off. Sorry."

I stopped glaring at Morgan long enough to stare at Hannah, shocked at how easily humans could lie.

Morgan's eyes darted back and forth between me and Hannah. "Is he...? Are you...? His ears, are they...?"

Hannah nodded. "Pointy. Yeah. He's Fae."

I blinked down at Hannah. I supposed there wasn't any point in lying about that bit. I hadn't bothered with a glamour before I transported us. I didn't think it would be necessary. I wasn't planning on encountering other humans, and I certainly wasn't planning on standing around exchanging pleasantries with the half demon I was supposed to be guarding this human from.

"Max set you up with him? When? The last time I saw you, you were..."

Hannah's fingertips dug into my arm. "The last time you saw me, you zapped me with your magic."

Morgan winced. "About that... That's actually why I came. I wanted to apologize. And check up on you. I really was worried."

Hannah relaxed her grip on me, but her body remained stiff. "Thanks. You should probably go, though. Max is going to be here any minute now, and he's still really mad at you."

Morgan frowned. "Maybe I should stay and explain."

"How about later? We can talk more when I get to your place, and I'll help you figure out how to deal with Max. Okay?"

"Uh. Sure. Are you still coming? That's the other thing I wanted to find out. I thought you might need me to transport you to my place for the party. Assuming you can still make it?"

Hannah nodded. "Yes. I'll be there. At least, I'm planning on it. I also haven't checked my messages, but I'm looking forward to it."

"Great! I'll tell Brady. Do you need me to come get you?"

Hannah glanced up at me and smiled before returning her attention to Morgan. "I think I'm going to bring a date, actually. If you don't mind?"

"Oh. Sure." Morgan looked back and forth between Hannah and me. "Yeah. Of course. Sounds fun."

"Thanks!" Hannah grinned. "See you soon?"

"Yeah. Soon. Sorry to interrupt." Morgan's sleeve slid down over her wrist as she gestured between Hannah and me. "Glad you're okay."

Once Morgan disappeared, Hannah exhaled and backed away from me. "Before you say anything—"

"What was that?" I waved a hand toward where the half demon had been standing. "Did she mess with your head or something? You are not going anywhere. I am not taking you anywhere. Certainly not to her house. We need to get you back to the infirmary."

Hannah backed away from me, just far enough to be out of my reach. "Listen. We don't have much time."

I stepped closer. "Oh, no. Not a chance. I'm not listening

to someone who has been corrupted by a succubus spawn."

Hannah sighed. "Incubus. Morgan's mother is a wizard and also the head of the Wizard Society, in case no one told you that. So maybe don't be so quick with the insults." She lifted her hands so her palms were facing me. "I know what it looks like, but I'm not possessed. I'm a wizard, remember? I know how to guard my mind against demons."

"That is exactly what someone who has been possessed by a demon would say." I folded my arms across my chest.

"Can you not? I don't have time for this. I need to take a shower, get dressed, check my messages, film a video, get it posted, and then check off about a million more things on my to-do list. Max is going to be here any minute, and he can't know anything about any of this." Her hand traced a little triangle in the air connecting the points between where I stood, where she stood, and where Morgan had been.

"Too late for that." As if to illustrate my point, Firrag appeared at that moment. She flapped her wings once as she hovered in the air between us, then dropped down to land on the low table in front of Hannah's couch. "You told him, didn't you?"

Firrag cocked her head to one side and hissed at me.

"I don't need help." I wasn't sure exactly what Firrag was trying to tell me, but I could guess. She'd directed that hissing at me enough times that I'd come to associate it with the equivalent of a stern scolding. "If I can't handle a few demons, how is Damir ever going to trust me to be his lieutenant?"

Hannah edged closer to Firrag, which put more distance between us. "And what is he going to think if you take me back there, huh? It's just going to prove that you can't handle it."

I scowled. She had a point. Damir and the queen had their

own problems to deal with. I was supposed to be helping by keeping Hannah safe. "What do you propose we do, instead?"

Hannah grinned. "Easy. First, you make yourself comfortable while I go take a shower and charge my phone. Then, when Max and everyone get here, we tell him about the chaos demon, but that's all." She paused to glance at Firrag.

Firrag didn't know about Morgan. She'd left before the half demon arrived. Only Hannah and I knew about Morgan's visit, and if the wizards warded this place against future intruders, then they may never have to know.

"What about that other stuff you needed to do?" I asked, hoping she understood that I was asking about what she'd told Morgan and not about all that other stuff she'd been babbling about.

Hannah bit her lower lip as she considered my question. "We can figure that out after everyone leaves. All you need to do is make sure nothing happens until they finish getting the wards up. You can handle that, right?"

Firrag lifted her head and let out a short shriek.

I glared at my familiar. "Of course, I can handle that."

Hannah nodded. "Good. I'll be back in a half hour."

I lunged after her as she started to walk away. "Woah! Wait. Where do you think you are going?"

She stopped and turned her head to squint at me, then pointed down the short hallway that extended from the living room. There were three doors, two of which were open. Hannah's finger was aimed at the door at the farthest end of the hall. "I'm going to my bedroom, and then I'm going to the bathroom, where I am going to take off these filthy clothes and step inside this thing that sprays water. Are you familiar with the concept of a shower?"

I scowled. "I know what a shower is."

"Okay, then. Can I go? Or do you have any other—"

I pushed past her and started down the hallway.

"What are you doing?" Hannah stomped after me as I threw open the closed door and poked around in what turned out to be some sort of closet that held boxes of all different types and sizes, including two large white metal cubes with glass doors on the front.

There wasn't much room for anyone to be hiding in there, but I left the door open anyway so that I could make sure no one popped in without me noticing. Then I moved on to the first open door, which turned out to be the bathroom. It was also empty, but it had a small window above the toilet.

Hannah stood next to me with her arms crossed. "It's just a bathroom."

I pointed. "There's a window."

"I'm not going to sneak out of it, if that's what you're thinking."

I scowled. I hadn't been considering the idea of her sneaking out. I'd been more concerned about someone or something else breaking in, but I probably should have realized, especially after her exchange with Morgan, that she might just do something stupid like attempt to leave without me. "Leave this door open."

"You want me to shower with the door open? Creeper."

"I'm not going to watch you. It's for your safety. What if someone comes in while I'm out here?" I gestured toward the living room. "You could end up unconscious or dead or kidnapped, and I'd have no idea. Leave it open."

Hannah pursed her lips. She remained silent long enough that I thought she was going to argue. Then she said, "Fine, but you stay in the living room."

I shook my head and pointed to a patch of floor across

from the bathroom door. "I'll sit here."

She crossed her arms. "You absolutely will not."

Firrag cooed a warning before gliding past our heads and banking into the small bathroom. She perched on the sink, cocked her head, and squawked at us. I wasn't exactly sure what she meant by the interruption, but it was enough to give me an idea.

"All right. Firrag stays here. I'll wait in the living room."

Hannah frowned. "Fine."

"Good." I took a step toward her bedroom so that I could make sure there wasn't anyone lurking in there. Then I paused and turned back to add one more requirement. "And you have to make some sort of noise the whole time you're in there. Talk. Sing. Whatever. I don't care. Something so I know you're alive."

"You want me to sing in the shower? You're joking."

"Not joking. Deadly serious." I pointed to what I hoped was the very serious look on my face. "Apparently you don't understand what's at stake here."

Hannah sighed. "Morgan or some demon fiend is going to come and kidnap me because I know where Max is keeping the magic traps."

I shrugged. "Sure. That. But more importantly, if anything happens to you, there is no way that Damir is going to agree to let me be his lieutenant." I didn't add the bit about the Faerie Queen. Hannah didn't need to know about the embarrassing failure I was also hoping to fix with this mission.

"Just so I have this straight, you don't really care what happens to me. You just want to make sure you get this job you want?" Hannah cocked her head and squinted at me.

I almost nodded but caught myself. "No. I care about what happens to you because I need you to stay safe in order to get what I want."

Hannah shrugged. "Look. I get it. I've got career goals, too. That's why, after I get cleaned up, and after Max leaves, we're going to have a chat about this weekend. And as a gesture of good faith, I'll let your faerie dragon hang out in my bathroom and listen to me sing. Happy?"

"Thrilled."

"Great."

We both turned toward her bedroom at the same time. My arm collided with her shoulder before we sprang apart, back to our respective sides of the hallway.

"I thought we agreed. You're waiting in the living room. Which is that way." She pointed back down the hallway in the opposite direction.

"We did agree. But first, I need to check your bedroom."

Hannah rolled her eyes. "There's no one in my bedroom."

"And how would you know that? Did you know there would be someone in your apartment when we arrived?" I paused. When she only scowled at me in reply, I said, "See? Didn't think so."

Hannah shook her head. "Fine. Go. Check the bedroom."

It wasn't until I started walking toward the open bedroom door that I realized I had no idea what I would even do if there were someone hiding in there. Eira and Talie, the two healers that Fiona's Fae called Hands, had warned me that I still wasn't healed enough to safely shift into my dragon form, and I didn't have any magic that might help me against a demon. I would have to rely on my combat training because it would be embarrassing to ask Hannah to back me up with her magic. I was supposed to be guarding her, not the other way around.

Luckily, Hannah was right. There wasn't anyone hiding

in her bedroom. She collected some clothes while I checked under and behind her furniture for any traces of demon. Then I left her in the bathroom and made myself comfortable in the living room. I'd just plopped myself down on her couch and put my feet up on the low table when she started singing.

I cringed. Her off-key voice reminded me of the way she'd snored the few nights we'd spent in the infirmary together. When Firrag joined in with high-pitched whistles and warbles, I knew the Ancients were testing me. But I would prove my worth. I would persevere.

In spite of myself, I picked up on the chorus of whatever song Hannah was singing and started humming along. Then I caught myself and stopped. This was ridiculous. I had no idea what I was doing, and if I didn't pull myself together and figure out how to keep this human safe, I might as well not even bother returning to the clan. I wasn't anything if I lost the respect of my wing-mates.

My worried brain turned the problem over while I half listened to Hannah's terrible singing and waited for the water to turn off. I was so lost in my thoughts by the time Max arrived that I didn't even realize I had started tapping the toe of my boot to the wonky beat. Unfortunately, I was no closer to having a plan. I could only hope that I could reassure Max enough so that he wouldn't kick me off this assignment.

3

WATER magic can be useful, but a good hot shower can't be beat. If someone forced me to give up one or the other, I would probably choose to abandon my water magic. Especially after my stay in the Fae infirmary. Their freezing waterfalls were nowhere near as satisfying.

Maybe the Fae were immune to the cold. Or maybe they used fire magic to warm the water. Whatever it was, it didn't work for me. I could manipulate water, but I couldn't change its temperature, and I didn't know any wizard with only water magic who could. Maybe that was a trick that the Fae Elementals learned how to do, but it wasn't anything I'd been taught.

I chatted with Firrag as I toweled off and dressed. Ved had mentioned that she understood what we were saying, so while I had her alone, I figured it was worth a try to attempt to make her an ally. It would help if she was on my side when I told Ved about my plan to go to Morgan's house because I was not going to let anyone take this opportunity away from me.

"So, it seems to me that you are the brains of the operation, huh?" I thought starting with a little flattery might be a good strategy, given how much the little faerie dragon preened those luscious lavender chest feathers of hers. I longed to touch them and confirm they really were as soft and silky as I expected they were, but I could tell we weren't there yet in our relationship.

Firrag appeared to be ignoring me, but her eyes twitched in my direction when I asked my question, so I continued. "It sounds like that Damir guy is pretty important. Some sort of leader or something? Like a king?"

Firrag hissed but didn't turn her head toward me.

"Not a king, then. But someone important, right?" I decided that braiding my long hair and then pinning it up would be faster and easier than tackling it with a round brush and the hair dryer. My arms weren't used to this much exertion after almost a week in bed, and the noise from the blow-dryer would make it too hard to hear, let alone interpret, whatever noises Firrag was making in response to my comments.

This time, she chirped and cocked her head at me.

"Definitely important. Got it. And Ved seems to want to impress him pretty badly." A thought occurred to me, one that reminded me that Ved looked very similar to the large Fae who had been in the infirmary with me when I first woke up. That would be a strange coincidence, but it wasn't impossible. "Did Ved get in trouble or something?"

Firrag lifted her long snout up and squalled at the ceiling. Then she fluttered her wings and ducked her head down until her chin nearly rested on her chest.

I had no idea what all of that meant, but I got the impression there was a much longer story there. Unfortunately, I couldn't tell if knowing would help me convince Ved to go along with my plan or not. If he'd somehow injured himself badly enough to land in the Fae infirmary, it made sense that his familiar might not be so keen on approving another dangerous assignment.

On a hunch, I said, "You probably worry about him a lot, huh?"

Firrag's coo sounded almost like a sigh.

I decided I was on the right track. "Is that why you warned this Damir guy about the demons?"

Firrag hissed and snapped her jaw at me.

I took that as a warning. "All right. I get it. I'm not going to put your bestie in danger, all right? I just need answers—plus, I have my own Damirs that I need to please. Like hundreds of thousands of them."

Firrag snorted, then returned to preening her chest feathers.

I let her be for a minute as I allowed my arms to rest and considered what to do with my face. The doorbell buzzed, which meant that Max and Angie had probably arrived. Firrag's head popped up as she eyed the bathroom door.

I gestured to it. "You can go if you want. I'll be fine here."

A bit of smoke curled from her nostrils as she huffed in a way I interpreted as disbelief.

"Fine. Suit yourself." I shrugged.

Maybe I should have been more worried about demons popping in and kidnapping me, but after reassuring Morgan that I would be going to her house willingly, I didn't think they would bother. Filming and posting a video to prove to my fans I was still alive and definitely bringing them some killer celebrity content over the next few days seemed like a much more pressing issue. And I couldn't do that until

Max was convinced that this place was fully warded. Then he would leave and take everyone with him, except Ved, of course. I wasn't getting rid of Mr. Muscles anytime soon.

It finally occurred to me that I was planning on lying to my friends. If I did, I would be no better than Morgan. The thought was like a punch to my gut, and I cringed at myself in the mirror.

Whatever was going on out in my living room, the voices were getting louder and more intense. I decided I'd better hurry and reached for my small makeup bag. Just as I pulled the zipper open, a ball of fur came hurtling into the bathroom and slid across the tile behind me.

Salty scrambled to a stop and sat, staring up at Firrag with her mouth open and her tongue hanging out. The dog looked at me, then back at the faerie dragon. Firrag's eyes narrowed as she pulled her wings in tight against her sides.

I decided introductions were in order, hoping that a little calm might eliminate some of the tension and keep the fur and feathers from flying. "Salty, meet Firrag. Firrag, this is Salty."

Salty yipped, and Firrag didn't seem to be relaxing.

"If you're going to fight, take it outside." I pointed toward the living room.

"Oh! Hey! Good. You're dressed and everything." Angie paused in the bathroom doorway to catch her breath. She pointed to Salty. "Sorry about her. I let her off the leash, and she bolted straight down the hall. Now I see why."

"Ved insisted that Firrag keep an eye on me while I showered. Not creepy at all. Though, I will say, she provides excellent backup vocals." I grinned at the faerie dragon, then waved Angie inside. "I just need another minute. You can hang out while I finish up."

Angie squeezed past me and took a seat on the edge of the tub. "Thanks. Not like I'm going to be much help out there. It's just Max and Jayden, by the way. Varun is in London, Grace is at the Silicon Moon lab working on figuring out the boxes, and Callie was on her way to the hospital to start her shift. How are things going with Ved?"

"Fine." I shrugged. My eyes met Angie's in the mirror. That uncomfortable clenching feeling squeezed at my insides again. I didn't want to lie. I didn't want to hurt my friends like Morgan had hurt me.

I exhaled and started talking before I could change my mind. "I need your help."

"Sure. Anything. What's up?"

I glanced down at my makeup bag and started rummaging around for my favorite powder brush so that I could avoid having to make eye contact. Salty curled up at my feet and set her head down on the top of my bare toes. I chose to interpret the gesture as a show of support.

"You know about Morgan's party? The one she throws every year? Or, at least, every year since she married Brady and they bought that house in LA?" I glanced up to catch Angie's reaction.

She frowned and started fidgeting with the diamond engagement ring on her finger. "No. I've sort of been out of the loop on these things until recently."

"Right. Sorry." I winced at the reminder that we'd lost touch after she broke up with Max. It was such a relief when they got back together. Max and Angie had always been my power-couple relationship goals.

"Nothing to be sorry about." She shrugged. "What's the big deal with this party?"

I sighed. "Well, it's sort of this extremely exclusive event to kick off the summer season. I used to fly down early for it every year and help Morgan keep things managed. It started off small, but now getting an invitation is kind of a whole thing." I dusted powder onto my face as I explained.

"Okay?"

I opened my favorite palette of eye shadows and stared down at the comforting hues. I knew Angie watched my videos. She'd told me as much when she'd showed up out of the blue at Max's a few months ago. But I had been playing coy about the surprise I had in store for my subscribers, and if she didn't already know about Morgan's party, she probably had no idea what I had planned.

"This year, my invite to Morgan's wasn't just as her friend. Morgan and Brady wanted me to be the social media liaison." I paused to pick a base shade of eye shadow. "See, Morgan makes everyone lock up their phones for the weekend. Everyone except the official liaison, whose job it is to make everyone and everything look like absolute ideal perfection. This way, the guests can all have fun without worrying they're posting something they're going to regret later. It's a huge opportunity for me. See, I'm not quite making enough to quit and go full time yet. This party was going to change all that. *Is* going to change all that," I corrected myself as I darkened my creases.

Angie leaned forward. "What do you mean, 'is'?"

I switched to a highlighting shade with a little bit of sparkle before continuing. "The party is this weekend. Guests start arriving tomorrow. I was supposed to be down there already getting set up."

"You're not seriously thinking of going? After everything?" Angie stood. She took a step toward me and placed her hand on my shoulder.

I set my shadow palette aside and busied myself with locating my eyeliner instead of meeting her gaze in the mirror. "I told her I would be there."

"Do you want me to tell her you're not coming? I can totally help with that, if that's what you're asking."

"No." I set my makeup bag back on the counter with a little too much force and looked up.

Angie's hand slid from my shoulder. She stepped back.

"I'm sorry." Tears burned in the corners of my eyes, but I refused to let them fall. I did not have time to start all over on my makeup. I'd lost too much time already. I took a breath, instead. And then I took another.

"No." I managed to say it more calmly the second time. "I don't need you to do that because I literally just told her that I would be there."

"Just now?" Angie glanced down at my phone, where I'd set it on the shelf under the mirror, angled so that the time and date on the lock screen glowed at me.

Every minute I spent explaining was a minute I wasn't filming or packing or getting my story straight with Ved so that he could play a convincing boyfriend in front of Morgan. But if I wasn't going to lie to my friends, then I needed Angie's help. If I could convince her, it would take less time to get the others on board.

Firrag squawked. She cocked her head at me. Salty sat up, taking the warm, reassuring pressure of her head off my foot.

I glared at Ved's familiar. "No running off again. Got it?"

The faerie dragon blinked her vertical eyelids at me.

Without taking my eyes off Firrag, I started to explain. "Morgan was here. She showed up after the chaos demon disappeared. I'm pretty sure that the chaos demon was just assigned to watch my apartment and report back to Morgan when I returned."

"Morgan was here? In your apartment?" Angie sidestepped toward the bathroom door.

I moved to block her from leaving. "It's fine. She apologized and said she wanted to make sure I was still coming to her party."

"You're joking." Angie folded her arms across her chest and glared at me. "You don't believe her, do you?"

I shook my head. "No. Of course not. But don't you see? This is the perfect opportunity to figure out what she's really up to."

"Or...and hear me out on this"—Angie lifted one hand and held it up in the air between us—"she's luring you to her house so that she can kidnap you and force the Fae to turn over the rest of the wizard boxes."

"Sure. Maybe she is. But I have a bodyguard. And I have friends who can help me. We can make a plan. I'll be prepared this time. She isn't going to get away with what she's done." My fist clenched around my eyeliner.

"I don't think this is a good idea. You're talking about using yourself as bait."

"Not as bait. As a spy." I exhaled. "Angie, look. I really need this. I'm so close to being able to realize my dreams. The content from this party could seriously put me over the edge. I'd be able to do what I love full time. No more boring desk job. Please? Tell me you understand? Tell me you'll help me convince Max and Jayden to help?"

Angie shook her head. "For the record, I think this is a terrible idea. Do you even remember what happened in Italy? You almost died. Because of Morgan. Who has surrounded herself with demons. She has powers that even Max isn't sure he understands. And you're asking me to let you walk willingly into her house and make it that much easier for her to hurt you and control you?"

I swallowed. When she put it like that, especially with all the emphatic gesturing that accompanied her argument, it really didn't sound like a good idea. But it wasn't just the money. I wanted Morgan to pay for what she'd done to me. For keeping this enormous secret from me, for lying to me, and for turning her back on the Wizard Society.

"I want to try. I *need* to try. Will you please help me?"

AFTER letting Jayden, Max, and Angie in, I retreated to the couch. It seemed like the safest place to stay out of the wizards' way while they worked. With Angie, Firrag, and that faerie guard dog in the bathroom with Hannah, I didn't have much to do.

Jayden walked past me. "Living room and kitchen are warded."

Max followed him, and they both paused at the entrance to the hallway that led back to the bathroom and bedroom. Max glanced down the hall toward the bathroom before looking at me. "I wonder what's taking Angie and Hannah so long?"

I wasn't worried. It didn't matter to me if Hannah spent the rest of the day in that bathroom. Her absence was giving me time to think. Sure, it might look like I was just relaxing on the couch while the two wizards did their magic thing, but I needed that time to figure out what to do about this whole "going to the half demon's house" plan of Hannah's. Besides, I trusted Firrag to alert me if Hannah was in any danger.

I sat up and stretched. "Be sure to get the closets, too. Wouldn't want anything materializing in there and jumping out when we least expect it."

"I'm sorry"—Jayden crossed his arms—"what are you doing, again? Shouldn't you be guarding Hannah or something?" He gestured toward the bathroom.

I shrugged. "Hannah wanted privacy while she showered and dressed, so Firrag is watching her."

"Firrag?" Jayden scowled.

"His familiar. Faerie dragon," Max explained.

I nodded. "So, how about those closets?"

Jayden's eyes narrowed. For a moment, I thought he might lunge at me, but Max tugged on Jayden's sleeve and led him toward the first door in the hall. Before they could get started, the small ball of fur came bounding back down the hall, leading the two women.

Angie paused to say something to Max, but I barely noticed. I couldn't take my eyes off Hannah as she strode past everyone into the living room. Without even realizing it, I stood up.

She was wearing some sort of dress that wrapped around her long, lean frame. A fabric belt cinched the waist, and tall brown leather boots hugged her calves and tapered down to a low heel that gave her just enough additional height to look me straight in the eye. And those eyes. When mine finished traveling down her body and returned to her face, they were the first thing I noticed. Those wide hazel eyes of hers were now somehow artfully shadowed and highlighted in a way that made them seem larger and more intense than I remembered. She returned my stare and blinked at me with her long black lashes that curved up and out like delicate wings.

My mouth went dry, and I had to swallow before I could form words. "Where's Firrag?"

Hannah glanced back down the hall, and I followed her gaze in time to see my familiar gliding toward me. Angie and the two wizards followed.

"Let's all sit down for a minute, okay?" Angie posed her suggestion like a question, but it seemed more like a command to me.

Firrag settled on my shoulder as Angie led Max toward the couch. I stepped sideways to give them some room. If the wizards were going to have a little chat, I decided my body-guarding services were temporarily not needed. Rather than stick around, I headed toward the kitchen to see what there was to snack on.

Jayden's eyes followed me as he settled into a chair. "Where do you think you're going?"

I scowled at him. "Kitchen. I'm hungry."

"Sit down, Ved." Hannah sounded annoyed.

I turned in a slow circle until I was facing her. "Why?"

She tilted her chin up. "Or just stand there. I don't care either way, but pick one and be quick about it. We don't have much time."

I squinted at her, but she didn't seem intimidated by me in the least. She just widened her eyes when I didn't move and waved me back toward the other wizards. There wasn't any place left to sit unless I wanted to squeeze onto the couch with Angie and Max, so I relaxed back against the wall and crossed my arms.

Hannah leaned forward in her chair. She set her elbows on her knees and interlaced her fingers. As soon as I realized I hadn't heard a word she'd said and was instead staring at the curves and valley exposed by the deep V of her neckline, I shifted my gaze away until I found something else to study. The cutout pattern on the leaves of the plant sitting on the windowsill weren't quite as interesting, but they did help me focus.

It was bad enough that I was stuck guarding this human instead of Damir. I didn't need to go and complicate things by lusting after her. Especially when there were plenty of human women to lust after in the village near the clan's caverns. I just needed to do my job. Then Damir would make me his lieutenant, and I could go home and have fun with one of the village women. It wasn't like there was anything special about Hannah.

"What?" Max shifted forward. "You can't be serious. I mean, she's my sister and all, but that seems like a very bad idea."

"That's what I said," Angie muttered.

"I don't know," Jayden said. "I think it might work."

All the heads in the room swiveled toward him, including mine.

"Thank you. At least someone has some faith in me." Hannah sighed as she leaned back in her chair.

"It's not that, exactly." Jayden had one leg crossed over the other. His foot bounced in the air as he scowled and stared into the middle of the room, not meeting anyone's eyes. "It's more like...we need someone on the inside. We need to figure out what Morgan did with those boxes that she stole from us. They could be in her house. It's possible. Or maybe she handed them over to Lilium. But knowing for sure will make it so much easier to figure out our best strategy for fighting the demons. And if we can get the boxes back, that's a huge advantage. If we can't, at least we may be able to find out where they're hiding them."

"So, you want to use Hannah as bait? After what happened in Italy?" Max shook his head. "No. If anyone goes, I'll go. Morgan is my sister."

"And Hannah is her best friend." Jayden shrugged. "Or she

used to be anyway."

If they agreed to let Hannah attempt this scheme of hers, that was going to make my job as her bodyguard more difficult. Normally, I would be the first one running toward battle, but I wasn't being asked to fight. I was responsible for keeping one wizard safe, and what was safe was staying right here, in that wizard's comfortable, warded apartment.

I raised my hand. "Do I get a say in this?"

Hannah, Max, and Angie all glared at me. "No."

I sniffed. "Fine. Can I get a snack, then? While you all decide what to do without me?"

"No." Hannah's fingers dug into the arms of her chair. "I'm going to Morgan's party, and you're going with me. You're going to pretend to be my boyfriend while I get the views I need to skyrocket my channel firmly into the top tier, and we're going to find out what Morgan did with those boxes."

I smirked. "Oh, is that all? You make it sound so easy. Have you considered the fact that Fae can't lie?"

"I hate to say this, but I'm with the Dragon Fae on this one." Max leaned back and crossed his arms.

Angie exchanged a look with Hannah that I couldn't interpret. Then Angie set her hand on Max's thigh. "What if we just talked it through? Let's say it's not impossible. How would we do it? What do we need?"

Jayden stood and started pacing. "First, we need to know we can get Hannah out if things start to go sideways. She can't transport herself, and we're not sending one of those Silicon Moon transporter things in with her. It's too risky."

"I can transport her out." The words slipped out of my mouth before I realized I was speaking.

Jayden stopped pacing and faced me. "And what if you're not with her? What if she's attacked while in the shower?

What if something happens to you? What then, genius?"

My brain chose that moment to send a message to my fists, pointing out that Jayden had a really punchable face. My fists responded by clenching, but I managed to keep my hands at my sides. Barely. "Are you implying that I'm stupid?"

"Maybe you *should* go get a snack." Jayden scowled. "It might help you think."

Hannah stood up and stepped between us. "Stop it. Both of you sit down."

I stepped back and leaned against the wall without taking my eyes off Jayden, even after he sank back into his chair.

"Ved is the first line of defense, obviously." Hannah looked at me, staring until I quit glaring at Jayden and met her gaze instead. The tightness in my chest relaxed as soon as our eyes locked. "But Jayden has a point. What happens if I'm alone?"

"Is there some sort of a spell to yank her back to her apartment? Something one of you can initiate from here?" Angie asked.

It wasn't a terrible idea, but wizards didn't have that sort of magic. At least, as far as I knew. I wasn't even sure that the Fae could do something like that.

Max shook his head. "No. But maybe it would help if she had a way to call for help?"

"The blood coins." Angie breathed the words out like the answer was obvious. Judging by the looks on everyone's faces, they didn't understand any more than I did.

"What is a blood coin?" Hannah asked.

"You don't know?" Angie searched our faces. "The demons use them to communicate with each other. Arabella has some she got from Nigel. I used one once to communicate with her." She paused. "We may be able to get a few for Hannah to use."

"How do they work?" Hannah asked.

"They're preprogrammed somehow to return to a specific person. I'm not entirely sure how any of that works. But, when you need to send a message to that person, you sort of have to bleed on them. Then you can whisper your message, and the coin disappears and is transported wherever it's programmed to go."

"That sounds useful," Jayden said. "How do we get some?"

"I'll text Willow and see if she will ask Ari for a few." Angie pulled out her phone and bent over the screen.

"Okay, so if I get in trouble, I can send a message out with one of these coins. But who should I send it to? Arabella?" Hannah asked.

Jayden made a face. "Do we want to tell them what we're doing?"

"The Fae?" Max asked.

"Yeah." Jayden's foot started bouncing again.

Everyone else turned their faces in my direction.

"What? Why are you looking at me?"

"I believe they'd like your thoughts, genius." Jayden grinned.

My fingers curled into fists again. Firrag dug her claws into my shoulder, and I flexed my hand open. She was right, as usual. They were just a bunch of humans. I didn't need to get violent. That would only prove to Damir that I was impulsive and irresponsible. What I needed to do was think. I needed to be strategic. Unfortunately, that seemed impossible with all of them looking at me.

I picked a spot on the table to stare at and started talking. "They'll probably want to know whatever we find out about the boxes, but it sounded like the lot of them were pretty busy preparing for this war with the demons." As I verbalized my thoughts, it occurred to me how impressed Damir would be if I not only managed to keep the wizard safe but also got those magic boxes back. I glanced over at Hannah. "If we can handle it on our own, maybe we should."

"Can we?" Hannah turned away from me to make it clear that she was asking the others.

"Can we what?" Max responded.

"Handle it on our own." Hannah glanced at each of them in turn.

Angie's thumbs paused over the screen of her phone. "What do you want me to tell Willow? About why we want the blood coins?"

Hannah bit her lower lip. "You can tell her the truth. That I want a few in case I get separated from Ved and run into trouble."

"Who should be the one to receive the coins, if you have to send one?" Max asked.

Hannah rubbed the end of her fabric belt between her fingers. "Well...if I'm separated from Ved, and he's the one who's been assigned to protect me, maybe they should go to him. That way he knows where to find me?"

"But what if he's also in trouble? I think it should go to someone who isn't at Morgan's house," Angie said.

"I can't believe we're even still talking about letting you do this." Max shoved his hand into his hair.

Hannah leaned forward. "Max, listen. For months, we worked with you to help when you thought there was something or someone threatening the Wizard Society. Look how much we accomplished by working as a team. The Fae wouldn't have any of those magic traps if it weren't for us. Right?"

"That was different. We weren't sending one of the team

directly into danger. You have no idea what Morgan can do. I don't even know what Morgan is capable of, and she's my sister."

Angie set her phone down. "Willow is getting us some blood coins. She'll be here in a few hours to set them up and show you how they work."

"Who did you tell her to key them to?" Jayden asked.

"Hello?" Max waved his hands in the air. "Is no one listening to me?"

"I didn't. I told her we'd figure it out before she gets here." Angie directed her response to Jayden, then she twisted to face Max. She cupped his face with one hand and turned it toward hers. "Sweetie? Hey. Let's go in the kitchen for a minute and talk. Maybe we can find some snacks for everyone. We'll all think better with some food in our bellies."

Max frowned but followed Angie past me toward the kitchen.

Hannah stood up and straightened her dress. "I need to film a quick video before I lose all my light, and I need to pack. Can you two manage to not kill each other if I leave you alone together?"

Jayden stood up. "It's fine. He can have the living room. I need to ward the closets and the bathroom, anyway."

Jayden headed down the hallway, but Hannah paused. She looked back and raised her eyebrows at me. "Everything okay?"

I swallowed. "Sure."

Salty bounded after her. Then, before I even asked, Firrag took off after them. Once they were gone, I collapsed onto the empty couch, put my feet up, and rubbed the heels of my hands over my eyelids, hoping that Hannah hadn't caught me staring at her ass. I really needed to get my shit together.

Fast.

4

VED was totally staring at my ass. I fumed as I tossed clothes into my suitcase without bothering to fold them. Morgan would have someone on her staff who could get wrinkles out, if I needed help with that. Besides, throwing things, even if they were just balls of fabric, was helping to calm me down.

I thought I'd made it clear that he was only going to be pretending to be my boyfriend. I did not want to have to fend off a lusty Fae on top of everything else going on in my life. Maybe if I weren't trying to get revenge on my ex–best friend for nearly killing me, I might consider a Fae fling. But at the moment, I needed to stay focused on my career and Morgan.

I didn't really care how sorry she was. She had no business aiming any sort of destructive magic anywhere near me and her brother. I wouldn't have cared that she was half demon if she'd trusted me enough to tell me the truth. Instead, she let me believe a lie, and then went and sided with the biggest enemy of all wizards everywhere. The demons.

I balled up my favorite swimsuit and tossed it at my bag. Unfortunately, the lightweight two-piece didn't have enough heft. The bundle missed the opening and tumbled off the bed and onto the floor. I stepped forward to retrieve it, but Firrag swooped in, scooped it up in her talons, and deposited it in the bag before taking a perch on the edge of my desk. She cocked her head at me and blinked.

"I suppose you think this is a game?" Even though I wanted to continue feeding my frustration, the unexpected presence of the little lavender faerie dragon in my bedroom made that impossible.

Firrag tossed her head and cooed at me. Then Salty, not wanting to be left out, jumped up on the bed, spun around in excited circles, and collapsed next to my suitcase, panting while her tail swiped back and forth across my comforter.

"Listen, you two. I need to film a video, and you need to remain quiet and unseen. Got it? I do not need to be explaining to my subscribers that small, adorable dragons exist, nor do I want them asking when I adopted a dog. Okay?"

Salty set her head down between her front paws as though she intended to behave, but Firrag stretched her wings out and tossed her head again.

I took a guess about what she was trying to communicate. "Fine. I'll throw one more for you. If I miss, you can retrieve it. Then, if you stay silent and off camera like a good little dragon, I'll let you help me finish packing once I'm done."

I flipped through the hangers in my closet until I found the summer party dress I'd recently purchased just for this occasion. Instead of balling it up, I folded and rolled it. Then I launched it toward my suitcase. Firrag caught it in midair in her talons and dropped it neatly into the opening before circling back to her perch.

"Very impressive." I nodded and clapped.

Salty yipped.

"Yes, you can play, too. But after." I started setting up my camera and my lighting.

Once everything was ready, I shut the door to my room. As much as I enjoyed posting videos, I hated filming in front of an audience. Unfortunately, I was just going to have to deal with the watchful eyes of my two animal companions. I could have tried kicking them out, but no one had warded my room yet. It was probably safer if they stayed with me. Even though I didn't think Morgan would send any demons after me unless I completely flaked and didn't show up for her party, I wasn't going to let my guard down.

"All right. Quiet time starts now." I shot a stern look at Firrag and Salty. Firrag preened her chest feathers, and Salty swished her tail back and forth once.

I positioned myself in front of the camera, checked my shot one last time, then hit record. It took me a few false starts and retakes before I found my groove. Then I managed to film the whole short teaser in one go. I watched the playback to make sure that I was happy with the footage. Then I popped the card out and stuck it into my computer so that I could transfer the files, clean them up, add a thumbnail, and upload.

This video wasn't going to be perfect, and I was going to have to be okay with that. The footage that I'd get at Morgan's would make up for this compromise. Exclusive access to the hottest, most interesting celebrities would boost my numbers through the roof.

The only catch was that I had to convince them to trust me to make them look good in my videos. That's where Morgan and Brady were supposed to assist. I wasn't sure if I could still count on their help, but I'd spent the past week in the infirmary studying the guest list, and I'd made a short list of the ones I was pretty sure I could convince to collab with me, with or without the endorsement of the host and hostess. And if those videos did well, then more of the guests would be excited about getting on camera with me.

I finished packing with the help of my fur and feathered friends while my video uploaded. Then I took a few artful shots of my packed bags and posted them to my socials with a link to the teaser video. I had just hit the button to post when someone knocked on my door.

"Come in!"

Salty jumped up and ran to the door as Angie cracked it open and poked her head inside. "Are you ready?"

"Yeah. How's it going out there?"

"Surprisingly well." She stepped inside my room. "Willow's here. I hope you don't mind, but we decided to tell her what's going on. She's on board and says that Arabella will be fine with everything. The blood coins are all keyed to Ari's second-in-command. Her name is Brianne. You may not remember, but she was there in Italy..."

I jumped on Angie's awkward hesitation to try to smooth things over. "It's okay, you know. You don't need to be so nervous about bringing up what happened. It's not your fault. Morgan is to blame, and Morgan is going to pay for the choices she made that put me in that infirmary. You and me? We're cool."

Angie dipped her head, but I caught the warm flush rising up her neck. "Are you sure? I was worried. I mean, after Max found out about the Fae and then everything...I never really had a chance to apologize to you."

I shook my head. "I understand. You were trying to help us. Morgan is not. She chose the wrong side. And I want those boxes back. We worked too hard on that for her to just swoop in and steal them out from under us. Not to mention the fact that I still have no idea how I ended up drugged and dumped in the Silicon Moon offices. She was the only one who had access, so I have to face the fact that it was probably her. And even if she didn't do it herself, at the very least, she must have known about it. So, yeah. I may not be as powerful as Max, but I'm not letting Morgan get away with this. Not if I can do something about it."

Angie crouched down to scratch Salty between her ears. "Hey, at least you *have* magic. When Fiona sent me to find out what Max knew about the boxes, I was in way over my head. All I had was this little ball of fluff and a couple of blood coins. We're sending you in with all that plus a solid plan, a bodyguard, and your magic."

Firrag squawked.

I laughed. "And a fierce little faerie dragon."

"Right." Angie smiled. "We should get back out there so they can fill you in on the rest of the plan. Plus, Willow wants to add you to our group chat."

"She knows I won't have my phone on me while I'm there, right?"

Angie shrugged. "Max said the same thing. It's probably still worth it, just in case. You never know."

"True." There was a small chance I might be able to convince Morgan to let me have access to my phone if I could come up with an excuse, like I needed it for some social media management reason that couldn't be handled on my laptop. Then again, Morgan wouldn't be easily fooled. She'd been the one to help me get started, and she knew most of what I knew just from talking through strategy with me when I needed someone to bounce ideas off of.

My throat tightened from the pang of loss at the thought that those days were over. Her betrayal stung, and I hated it. Better to focus on action and keep moving forward. It hurt less.

"Do you want me to help you with your bags?" Angie asked.

"Sure." I grabbed my camera equipment and let her take the suitcase. "Hey, by the way, what do you know about that Fae they assigned as my bodyguard?"

"Ved? Not much. I talked to him once in the infirmary. He was there at the same time as you. I'm not sure why, though, and I don't think he actually remembers me." She paused and glanced up at me out of the corner of her eye. "He is pretty hot, even for one of the Fae."

I'd been trying to ignore that fact, so I focused on the other part of what she'd said. "I thought he looked familiar. I think he was there when I first woke up but gone after that."

"He seemed pretty confident when he volunteered."

I stopped walking. "He volunteered? You mean they didn't just assign him to me? He actually raised his hand and said 'pick me'? That's weird, right?"

"Well, it wasn't exactly like that, but now that you mention it...maybe? I don't know. He seems fine."

I rolled my eyes. I was trusting my life to someone who seemed fine. "Not exactly a ringing endorsement, Ang."

She turned to face me. "He's strong. He's good-looking. He may be more brawn than brains, but he's not a complete airhead, despite what Jayden thinks. And he was the only Fae available for the job. *And* the only way Fiona was letting you out of that infirmary. I did what I could. We're just going to have to work with it."

I cringed. "Sorry. It's just...I am pretty sure I caught him checking out my ass."

Angie shrugged. "You have a nice ass."

"Thanks. Not the point."

"Fine. So, what if he was? What's the worst that happens?" Angie flashed me a mischievous grin.

"Uh, he can't lie? And what if he starts taking this whole fake boyfriend thing a little too seriously, and then I have to figure out how to get him to back off without blowing our cover with Morgan?"

Angie sighed. "So set some ground rules. I mean, are you worried that he's genuinely into you? Would that be so terrible? Or are you actually worried that you might also be attracted to him?"

"Just so you know, I see what you're doing." I glared at her. "And, of course, I'm attracted to him. He's a freaking god. Look at him." I gestured past her to where everyone was gathered in the living room. Ved had taken over my couch and was sprawled across it like he lived there now. I had suggested he make himself comfortable, but, wow, was he taking that to heart.

Angie giggled. "So have some fun. Hook up with him, if you want. Who cares?"

"I care. First of all, he's Fae. And if that weren't enough of a reason—which it is—I do not need a boyfriend right now. Boyfriends just suck all your time and energy and keep you from achieving your dreams." I paused as I remembered whom I was talking to. "I mean, not everyone can be as lucky as you and Max. I think that's why it shook me so much when you two broke up."

"Well, that had very little to do with us and a lot more to do with this whole secret world of magic he was trying to hide from me. You don't have that problem. At least, not with one of the Fae."

"Sure. But he's immortal, and he can shift into a dragon. I mean, that's a whole other level of complicated." I snuck another glance at Ved.

Angie leaned toward me and nudged my shoulder with hers. "Then don't get complicated. Just have fun."

I sighed. "That's never going to work. Fun always gets complicated. You were right the first time. Best to lay down the ground rules now and then stick to them."

"Okay, but I'm still voting for fun. It's not like I am going to get to find out what it's like to make out with a ripped Fae who can turn into a dragon. I need to live vicariously." Angie tugged on the handle of my suitcase as she resumed walking.

I laughed. "You suck."

"That's what she said," Angie called back to me in a low voice.

I never thought I'd say it, but thank the Ancients these wizards were finally done planning so that we could leave. Their bickering about charms and spells and wards and such was making me want to scream, and they insisted I stay and listen to every word. I even had to skip my midmorning training session.

At least Hannah promised that Morgan's house had a gym. Not that I'd get a chance to go, either, as Max made it clear that I wasn't to leave Hannah alone for any reason except to use the bathroom, and even then, he wanted me to keep an eye on the door, just in case Morgan tried anything while Hannah was in there. I was regretting volunteering for this assignment more with every passing hour.

Once everyone got up and started heading for the door,

I sat up and stretched, beyond ready to be rid of the lot of them. Hannah showed her friends out and then returned to the living room but didn't sit down. Instead, she stopped on the opposite side of the coffee table and put her hands on her hips.

Happy to see that she appeared equally impatient to leave, I stood and faced her. "Right. I suppose you're ready to go now?"

She pursed her lips. Her eyes narrowed. "One last thing before we go."

I moved to sit back down, but she waved me back to my feet.

"This won't take long. I just want to lay down some ground rules before we get to Morgan's."

"I thought we already discussed the rules." I folded my arms across my chest and flexed my biceps for added emphasis. "I'm the bodyguard. I'm in charge of keeping you safe. You follow my instructions."

"Yes. If you say 'duck,' I duck. I remember." She glanced over at Firrag, who had made herself comfortable in the branches of a tall potted plant of some sort. "This is different."

"More rules?"

She nodded. "Rules to govern our fake relationship."

"We need rules for that?"

"I think we do."

"What sort of rules?"

She raised her eyebrows. "Rules to make sure that other people get the right idea—that we're genuinely dating and into one another—but also to make sure that neither of us get the wrong idea."

"And what would the wrong idea be, exactly?" I asked.

"That we're genuinely dating and into one another."

"I see." This conversation had taken an interesting turn, but I always did appreciate a challenge. I gave her the look that I knew usually set the village women's pants on fire. "So, you're saying that you're not into me."

Hannah bit her lip. "I'm saying that we are not actually dating, and there will be no kissing and no touching. Got it?"

She was definitely into me.

I grinned. "No touching, huh? I feel like that is going to make it rather difficult to convince others that I am 'genuinely into you.'"

She scowled. "Fine. Minimal touching. But not on any body parts that would otherwise be covered by underwear."

"What's underwear?"

"You're joking, right? Please tell me that's a joke."

I smirked. "I am familiar with the concept, but mostly as it relates to the most expedient methods of removing it."

She took a deep breath in an attempt to calm the racing of her pulse, which she probably didn't realize I could sense, given the fact that she was human and essentially prey. What she didn't know was that I had no intention of touching her unless it was to save her life. If I had to put on a show for this half-demon former best friend of hers, then I would. But there was no point in getting attached to a mortal.

Human women were for breeding purposes. Dragon Fae didn't take humans as mates. If she hadn't decided to make such a fuss about it, I would have told her as much. Since she had, I was going to enjoy making her squirm.

When Hannah spoke, her voice sounded strained. "Well, there will be no removing of any clothing. We're both here to do our jobs. You do yours. I'll do mine. We'll get out of this safely and maybe retrieve some boxes while we're at it. Then we will go our separate ways like none of this ever happened."

"From your mouth to the ears of the Ancients. Let it be so."

She squinted at me. "I'll assume that means you agree?"

"I agree. Now can we go?"

Hannah slung the strap of her camera bag over her shoulder, then picked up her equipment tote in one hand and her suitcase in the other. "Now we can go. Do you know where—"

I stepped around the table, scooped up the little dog, and put my hand on her shoulder. We were gone before she could finish her sentence. Firrag would follow on her own. She needed to stay outside the house until we knew where we would be sleeping. Then she would try to transport inside. That would be our first test of Morgan's security.

We appeared on the patio, near the back entrance, just as Max had instructed.

Hannah gulped in a lungful of air next to me. "You could have warned me."

"I could have. But would that have made it better?" I squinted at her until I sensed her pulse begin to steady.

She took a half step away from me. "How can you tell I don't like traveling that way?"

"I would think it would be obvious to anyone." Even without my ability to sense her vital signs, her physical reaction was hard to ignore.

Her lips twisted into a thoughtful scowl. "Max didn't seem to notice."

Max didn't strike me as the most observant of their little wizard group. That distinction would have to go to Jayden, not that I ever planned to say as much. Max seemed to only have eyes for Angie, so it didn't surprise me that he wouldn't have noticed Hannah's distress.

I shrugged. "Do we knock?"

The back door opened before we needed to decide. Morgan stood inside the small entry, bathed in bright sunshine from a skylight. "You're here. I'm so glad you're here!"

She lurched forward like she was going to give Hannah a hug, but Hannah took a half step backward, and I angled my body to shield her.

Morgan froze, then shrank back into her house. "Oh. Um. Sure. Why don't you come inside? Can I carry anything for you?"

"We have everything. Thanks." I released Salty, who promptly shook herself before circling Hannah's feet. Then I relieved Hannah of her equipment tote and her suitcase, leaving her with only her camera bag, which she hugged to her hip.

"What a cute dog!" Morgan reached out her hand but changed her mind before bending down to pet Salty. "What's its name?"

"Muffin," I said, speaking before Hannah could. I wasn't about to give a demon, even a half demon, a true name. So, I made up a nickname. Perhaps it was a bit superstitious of me, and I wasn't about to admit that I believed the rumors about demons, but Salty was a faerie dog, and she was meant to help me keep Hannah safe. I wasn't going to let a demon put some sort of curse on her.

"Is Muffin your dog...um, I don't think I ever got your name...?" Morgan squinted up at me.

"You can call me Ash." I couldn't lie, but I could give her the nickname that Damir and Ivo sometimes used for me. *Fire, Ash, Light. Wing-mates for life.* The three of us had always been a team. My impulsiveness had threatened that, and I needed to prove to them that I'd learned my lesson. Now every time Morgan used that name, it would remind me of what was at stake.

"I hope you don't mind that we brought Muffin." Hannah's voice stumbled a bit around Salty's new nickname. "It was short notice for Ash, and he didn't have time to find a sitter."

Morgan waved a hand. "Oh, it's no problem at all. Brady and I love dogs. We've been talking about getting one. Maybe having one around the house for the weekend will finally convince us to go visit the shelter. Come in."

Hannah followed Morgan inside. Salty trotted along beside her, and I followed, shutting the door behind me. The back entrance led into an enormous kitchen gleaming with stainless-steel appliances. I shivered. Man-made metals were no friend of the Fae. At least Morgan didn't live in a city like Hannah.

I could handle being around all those steel buildings for so long before they started to sap my power. It was better up on this hill without any close neighbors. But still, we'd only seen one room of this enormous mansion, and I could already tell Morgan's house wasn't built for dragons.

Morgan chattered as we passed through the kitchen and into the large dining room, pointing out features of interest and explaining which areas were going to be off-limits to the regular party guests but were open for us since we were friends.

Friends. I raised my eyebrows. I didn't know how demons did things, but Dragon Fae didn't go around blasting their friends with magic. We saved that for unnecessarily brutal Alphas and their slimy lieutenants whom we suspected murdered our sire and made it look like an accident.

It bothered me that Morgan was acting like she hadn't almost killed Hannah. I'd been there when they brought her in. I'd sensed how faint her life force had been before the Forest

Fae Hands managed to stabilize her. The sad excuse for an apology that she'd offered when she surprised us by appearing in Hannah's apartment didn't cut it for me.

Morgan continued to give us a tour of the rest of the house because, even though Hannah had visited and was already familiar with the layout, it was all new to me. Plus, she thought it might help Hannah consider her options for filming if she knew which of the areas open to guests were expected to be busy and which would offer a more private setting.

Even though Hannah appeared to be playing along, asking questions and holding up her end of the conversation, I could tell she was still seething. Luckily, our plan was for me to say as little as possible since I couldn't lie without ending up in very obvious and excruciating pain. All I had to do was remember to behave like Hannah's boyfriend, which sounded like it mostly meant showering her with lots of attention. At least I didn't have to pretend to like Morgan, too.

Morgan led us through the lower level first, guiding us past a hallway that seemed to lead nowhere. Max had said we should keep an eye out for Morgan's private office. He knew she had one, but he wasn't sure exactly where it was located in her house. Unlike Hannah, he'd only visited once since his sister had moved in.

I didn't get a good look down the suspicious hallway that Morgan failed to even acknowledge. Instead, she pointed out the game room, the movie screening studio, and the only thing I truly cared about outside of keeping Hannah safe: the gym. The fully equipped, well-lit, and blissfully ventilated suite opened up to a covered patio with all of my favorite toys. It made the gym in the clan cavern look like a stuffy and dark torture chamber, and it took all of my self-control not to drop Hannah's luggage and get to work.

"Are you coming?" Hannah called from the foot of the stairs where she had paused to wait for me.

"Yes." If I couldn't enjoy the usual pleasures I associated with human women, I would at least enjoy a good workout. I silently promised the beautiful oasis that I would find a way to return soon. Then I hurried to catch up to Hannah and Morgan.

Morgan explained that the main level would be open to all the guests, as would the gym and the game room, but the other rooms on the lower level would be closed off except for special events. The upper level would be where most of the activity would be.

One wall of the dining room was almost entirely glass and overlooked the city. The other side stepped down into an open living room that led to another patio. This one featured a pool with one edge that appeared to drop over the side of the cliff that the house had been built on.

Two halls extended out from the main room like wings. Morgan led us down the one closer to the dining room first. She explained that this was the guest wing. There were a handful of bathrooms, at least a half dozen small rooms that had all been set up as bedrooms, plus one large bunk room that usually served as their study but had been temporarily rearranged to serve as a crash pad for singles. The whole thing reminded me of the caverns, except with more windows and plusher furnishings. I'd never seen so many pillows in one room in my unnaturally long life.

After the guest wing, Morgan showed us to what she called the family wing. The master bedroom suite was located at the very end of the hallway. There were a few other rooms, most intended for children, but since they didn't have any of those, a selection of the more sought-after guests would be assigned to those rooms. And one of those rooms was where Hannah and I would be staying.

"Here you are." Morgan opened the door to our room and stepped aside so we could enter.

Salty ran inside and began sniffing everything. I set Hannah's bags down and noted the large window, the even larger bed, and the armchairs on either side of a glass-covered portion of one wall. There were a few other tables and a chest of drawers, but what interested me most was a partially opened door in one wall, which I hoped led to an adjacent bedroom.

"That's your private bathroom," Morgan said as I walked toward the door.

"This is"—I turned in a slow circle—"cozy." There was no couch and only one bed.

"I sort of consider this Hannah's room. It's where she usually stays when she visits."

"Thanks, Morgan," Hannah said, even though the chill in her voice reminded me more of the mountain peaks at home than the sunny warmth outside Morgan's windows.

"I'm glad you're here. And I'm hoping…" Morgan hesitated before continuing. "Ash, you won't mind if I borrow Hannah for a bit, do you? I was thinking we could relax by the pool and catch up for a bit while we wait for Brady to get home. It will be just the four of us for dinner tonight. The guests won't start arriving until tomorrow."

I locked eyes with Hannah in an attempt to signal that I did not think this was a good idea. We'd only just arrived, and Morgan was already trying to separate us. I thought Hannah would be sensible and agree with my silent suggestion.

Instead, Hannah said, "Give me just a minute to settle in and change into my swimsuit, and I'll meet you out by the pool. Okay?"

"Sure. Sounds good. I'll leave you to it, then." Morgan smiled and shut the door as she left.

"No." I whispered the word at Hannah in case Morgan happened to be lingering on the other side of the door.

Hannah lifted her suitcase onto the bed and unzipped it. "There's a glass door between the main room and the pool patio. You can keep an eye on me from inside."

"With a wall of glass separating us? That doesn't seem like a good idea."

"Fine. What do you suggest, then? Because I'm definitely not going to miss this opportunity to see what she has to say to me." Hannah retrieved two small scraps of brightly colored fabric from inside her suitcase and started toward the bathroom door.

"Where are you going?"

She paused and pointed toward the adjacent room. "To change. Did you want to inspect it before I go inside?"

"Leave the door open."

"No."

I crossed my arms. "Then sing."

Hannah groaned. "Fine."

She stomped into the small room, shut the door with a thud, and started humming a tune I didn't recognize.

"Louder." I sat in the armchair that faced the bathroom door and crossed my arms.

It didn't take her long to change clothes. When she emerged, she was wearing only the barest of coverings. Two small triangles covered her breasts, suspended by strings that tied around her neck and back. Her flawless golden skin practically glowed, and my traitorous hands itched to reach out and touch her. I swallowed the instinct down and gripped the arms of the chair instead.

While I was struggling to remember what we were arguing about a moment earlier, something tapped at the window. I tore my eyes from Hannah, only to discover that Firrag had found a perch on the tree outside.

5

THERE was only one bed, and the look on Ved's face when I stepped out of the bathroom reminded me of that fact. I'd been prepared to explain how I'd tucked one of Willow's coins inside the top of my swimsuit, just in case I needed it. And I was going to say that I planned to take Salty with me, but Firrag arrived before I could explain any of that, and she gave me an even better idea.

"Perfect," I said.

"Yes." Ved blinked at me. "Wait. What?"

I crossed over to the window and opened it. "Hey there, buddy. Perfect timing."

Firrag cooed at me.

"Can you find a spot where you can keep an eye on me at the pool?" I asked.

Firrag squawked and flapped her wings but didn't leave her perch.

I glanced at Ved.

"Don't look at me. She could be agreeing, or she could be

trying to tell you that it's impossible." He turned to Firrag. "Can you come inside?"

Firrag hissed. She tossed her head, then shivered, causing the feathers on her chest to ruffle.

"I'll take that as a no," I said. Then I turned my attention to Ved. "I'm going to go hang out by the pool with Morgan and see what she has to say. Firrag will keep an eye on me. Right, Firrag?"

Firrag cooed when I paused.

"Great. You"—I waved a hand in Ved's direction—"can go do whatever you want. Like, maybe visit the gym if that sounds like fun. Don't think I didn't notice you drooling over it."

"I wasn't drooling."

"Right. Well, you were definitely having a moment."

Ved snorted. For a second, I thought he was going to argue with me, then he sprung up out of the chair. "That's it!"

"What's it?"

"The gym. There's a patio there as well. It's on a slightly lower level, but I think it may be just below the pool patio. If I go out there—"

Firrag started squawking and flapping her wings.

Ved walked over to the window. He stopped next to me. Close enough that the sleeve of his shirt brushed against my skin when he took a breath but not so close that he was actually touching me. I didn't like the warmth that radiated up my neck when I noticed, so I tried to focus on what the faerie dragon was attempting to communicate and ignore the Dragon Fae next to me.

"I don't think she wants you to go outside," I said.

"Yeah. I'm getting that. Why not?"

"Maybe..." I paced away from the window. Walking helped

me think. "Maybe because of the wards on the house? What if...what if you step outside and the house won't let you back in again?"

"That's ridiculous. Didn't you hear what Morgan said? We aren't guests, we're *friends*," Ved sneered.

I grinned. "Yeah. I caught that. But you're not friends with her. I am—or was. So, maybe...I mean, she can't be too happy about having to host one of the Fae just because I decided that I was going to bring you as my plus-one."

"Your plus what?"

"Never mind." I shook my head. "My boyfriend. She's probably just as keen to separate us as you are to make sure that doesn't happen. Stay in the house."

"Don't go to the pool," Ved countered.

"I'll be fine. I have a coin with me." I tapped the fabric of my swimsuit top over the spot where I'd tucked it inside. "And Firrag is going to keep an eye on me. Just don't do anything stupid while I'm gone."

Ved frowned. "Can I still go to the gym?"

"Yes. Just stay inside. I don't want to have to figure out how to smuggle you back in again."

Ved turned toward the window. "Firrag?"

Firrag squawked, then took off, circling high up in the sky above the house.

I rummaged around in my suitcase until I found a scarf I could use as a cover-up. "Okay. I'm going now. Wish me luck."

"Don't die."

"Thanks. I'll try not to." I wrapped the scarf around my waist, grabbed my sunglasses, and hurried out the door before Ved changed his mind and tried to stop me. I only paused long enough to make sure Salty was following me.

Morgan was already lounging by the pool when I stepped out onto the patio with Salty—or Muffin, as Ved had dubbed her for unknown reasons—keeping close by my ankles. The moment the warm sun hit my bare skin, all my worries washed away. Whatever Morgan had to say, whatever information I thought I might be able to squeeze out of her, didn't matter, nor did the fact that I was sharing my room with a ripped and unnaturally gorgeous Dragon Fae and we still hadn't discussed who was going to sleep in that big bed and who was going to have to curl up and make the best of it on the floor. None of it mattered. I tilted my face up to the blazing ball of light in the cloudless Southern California sky and basked in the warm glow.

I hadn't had this much sunlight when I was cooped up in the Fae infirmary in wherever-the-Fae-hid England. And we didn't get this sort of bright heat during the winter in Seattle. Hell, we were lucky if we got any sunlight at all from November through March. But this? This was everything. And I needed more of it. Sunshine was just one of the many reasons I wanted to relocate to LA, and in order to do that, this weekend had to be a success.

"There you are!" Morgan called to me from her lounge chair, ruining the moment.

I blinked my eyes open and waved. I slid my sunglasses onto my face before making my way over to the chair Morgan had conveniently pulled alongside hers. That little bit of extra distance from what I expected was going to be a very difficult conversation made me feel more confident.

After reaching the lounger, just to make a point, I twisted it around so that my back would be toward the pool when I tilted up the end. This way, I would still be sitting next to Morgan, but I would be facing her, more like an opponent than an ally. Not to mention, the view from that angle would make it much easier to see if anyone left the house.

Not that I thought that Ved—*Ash*, I reminded myself that I needed to call him Ash—would leave. But there was always the chance that Morgan might be trying to distract me while someone else snuck up on me from behind. If I had to choose, having my back to the pool and the steep drop-off beyond seemed like the better option. Besides, I trusted Firrag would find a way to warn me, and maybe even intervene, if anyone tried approaching from that direction.

Once I'd arranged everything to my liking, I untied my scarf, draped it over the back and seat of the lounger, and sat down. "I forgot how warm it is down here, even this early in the summer. It's not even June yet, but Seattle doesn't get this nice until July."

"I love it here." Morgan stretched like a cat before curling her pale legs up underneath her and leaning forward to glance at the sliver of concrete between our chairs where Salty had decided to sprawl. "Ash's dog seems to like you. How long have you two been dating, anyway?"

I shrugged. "Not long. We're still getting to know each other. He wanted to use the gym, so I offered to take Muffin outside with me."

"I'm a little surprised you brought a date. You're always so anti-boyfriend. And I'm equally surprised that he's, well, Fae. But it is nice to see you with someone. Are you really giving him a chance? Or is he just arm candy for the party?"

I frowned. "Nothing's changed. I'm still anti-boyfriend, but after everything that happened, Max and Angie were encouraging me to have a little fun. They introduced me to Ash. I didn't expect it, either, but I suppose he is turning out to be more than just a pretty face."

I planned to stick to the truth as much as possible.

"I didn't know Max knew any Fae, let alone enough to find one to match you up with. Interesting." Morgan stretched her legs out and leaned back in her chair.

"I suppose something similar could be said about you. Since when do you know so many demons? What's that all about?"

Morgan sighed. "I wanted to tell you. Really, I did."

"Tell me what, Morgan?" I didn't bother keeping the ice from my tone. I wanted her to say it.

She stared at me silently for a moment. "Will you take those sunglasses off so I can see your face?"

"It's bright out here, and I already said I'm not used to this much sun. Why don't you tell me what you're going to tell me while I acclimate?"

Morgan pouted. "I thought you of all people would understand, but Mother made me swear never to say a word to anyone."

"A word about what?"

"I'm sure Max told you. He must have."

"I want to hear you say it. I think I deserve that much. Don't you?"

"Fine. I'm half demon. Elton isn't my biological father. My mother says she was seduced by an incubus. She said she didn't even know until after I was born and my magic came in...different." She waved a hand, and two small black horns appeared, one above each temple, right at her hairline.

I had to admit, they looked really cute poking out of her dark-brown pixie cut. "So, this is the real you?"

"Nothing's changed." Morgan tugged at the hem of her black long-sleeved sun shirt.

"Everything's changed. You lied to me. You lied to everyone. And you sided with the enemy. Does Brady even know?" I curled my fingers around the lounger's teak armrests.

Morgan groaned. "Of course, Brady knows. And you don't have to be so dramatic about everything. Are you even going to give me a chance to explain?"

"Please. Tell me. I am dying to know what made you think teaming up with demons was such a brilliant idea." I realized "dying" may not have been the best choice of word, but perhaps it would be another subtle reminder of what she'd done to me.

Morgan's face crumpled like my verbal jab had managed to land a hit. "I'm sorry. I really am. But can you please at least try to understand where I'm coming from with this?"

I wasn't a monster, and she wasn't an actress, so I decided to soften my approach a bit. "I'm listening."

Morgan nodded once. "Okay. So, imagine that you wake up one day, look in the mirror, and see these." She gestured to her cute little demon horns.

"Potentially traumatic, sure. But you've always been a bit goth, so kind of cool, too, right?" I asked.

Morgan grinned. "Fine. Maybe a little cool. But only after I got over the shock and stopped freaking out about the fact that my dad wasn't really my dad... I mean, he's my dad, but not my biological dad. And my mom swears she has no memory of my biological dad. So, there's that. And then there's the weird powers that I had no idea how to control, and my parents are the leaders of the Wizard Society, and they've always been so worried about how would it look if anyone knew, etc., etc."

I cringed. Max had explained most of this already, but it was different hearing it from Morgan. "I can see how that would be difficult."

"Yeah. It was. And I had no one I could talk to about it."

"You could have talked to me."

Morgan's eyes narrowed. "And risk the wrath of my mother? You've met her. Would you have crossed her?"

I cocked my head to one side. "I can name more than a few times that we disobeyed Mama Elle's rules. Shall I remind you about that misguided trip to the shore? Or the time you convinced me to get matching tattoos?"

Morgan's eyes drifted down to the single drop of water on my ankle. She lifted her foot and swung her leg over to tap her tiny flame against my drop of water and grinned. "Besties for life."

I frowned. "I'd thought so. But, come on. Sure, you were silenced and didn't know how to use your magic. But all of us went through that to some degree. I mean, you *have* met my magically clueless parents. When did you stop being my bestie and start making friends with the demons? And why, Morg?"

Morgan returned her leg to her own lounger and bent her knees so she could hug them to her chest. "One of them approached me. They offered to help. I hesitated at first, but eventually it got to be too much." She paused. "One day, I was at home studying by myself. I was writing a paper for Mrs. Bishop's class, remember her?"

"Sure." I nodded.

"Well, one minute I was there, and the next I was sitting at my desk in our empty classroom. It was nighttime, so the school was dark except for the emergency exit lights. It was so creepy, and I had no idea how I got there or how to get back. I thought I'd set off some sort of alarm if I tried to leave. I freaked out and started crying. The next thing I knew, I was home again, but I'd transported myself into Max's room. He didn't know about the horns or anything else yet. There was a lot of explaining and a lot of yelling. My mom refused to do anything about it. So, Max made it his mission to try to find help for me. A cure." She shook her head.

"Max wanted to cure you? Of what?"

She sighed. "Being a demon, I guess? It was all such a mess, and I remembered that demon who offered to help. I had no way of getting in touch with them. So, I just did what I always did when I wanted information. I started digging until I found someone who knew someone who could get me in touch with a demon. And that's when I started really learning. I learned how to control my powers, sure, but I also learned more about demons. Stuff that wizards like the ones on the Council don't want you to know."

"Stuff like what?"

"Like they're not all the same, for starters. There are different clans of demons, and they don't even all come from the same place. Some of them didn't even want to come here at all. To Earth, I mean. And a lot of the ones that want to be here are only here because they're running from something bigger and badder in their own realm. But they don't have magic here. On Earth. Only the Fae have magic here. The Fae and the wizards, their bastard, cross-bred, completely abandoned offspring."

Morgan gestured toward the house. "Which is to say, I could ask you the same thing, right? What the hell are you doing with one of *them*? One of the Fae? Aren't they just as much the enemy of the wizards?"

"I thought so, too. But it turns out we were wrong."

"Well, maybe the wizards are wrong about the demons, too," Morgan said.

"Maybe? But the Fae were never actively trying to harm

wizards. They just never helped us. They left us to fend for ourselves and never bothered to teach us anything about this magic we inherited from them." I allowed a small bubble of water to form in my palm and rolled it back and forth across my hand. My favorite party trick.

"The demons have been actively trying to suck that magic from us for centuries. Which, if they don't have any of their own, makes sense, I guess. But you teamed up with them against us. Not to mention put me in the hospital for weeks." I let the water bubble pop, allowing the moisture to evaporate back into the air.

Morgan cringed. "I didn't expect it would make sense to you just from me trying to explain. That's why I'm glad you decided to come. Now you'll get to see for yourself."

"See what?"

"There was some room on the guest list, so I invited a few of my new friends to the party."

"Demons? Here?" I fought the urge to run back to the safety of my bodyguard and took a breath. "But what will the celebs think?"

Morgan shrugged. "Nothing, I imagine. It's a closely guarded secret, but a few of the demon clans have made a home for themselves in Hollywood. You'll see. I think once you get to know them better, you'll understand. And then maybe you can help me get the rest of the Society on board."

"But the Wizard Council just approved an alliance with the Fae."

"Don't forget that the Council is led by my mother, and she will do anything to keep her secret shame from getting out." Morgan tilted her head to one side. "I really do hope your boyfriend doesn't mind. It might get a bit awkward, but I'm sure, given how obviously devoted he is to you, he won't make a scene." Her voice dripped with sarcasm.

I swung my legs over the side of the lounger. "Maybe we should go."

"He's welcome to leave any time if he's uncomfortable, but you signed a contract. I promised everyone that *the* Hannah Vos would be here, and they're all looking forward to collaborating with you. That's what you wanted, isn't it? Either way, you're here for the duration. I suggest you make the best of it."

"Wow. And here I nearly fell for your apologetic-friend act. Have you been taking acting lessons from Brady? I'm impressed. Truly." I pushed my sunglasses up on my head and squinted at her.

"It may not seem like it, but I did mean every word. I am sorry about what happened. And I'm sorry that I couldn't tell you. But you picked your side, and I picked mine. And now we're going to see how that works out for us. At least, as long as you're here, I can make sure nothing happens to you."

"That's really sweet, Morgan. But what about the others? What about Max and your parents?"

"I suppose that's up to you now, isn't it?"

AFTER my workout, I trudged back up the stairs. Hannah and Morgan were still sitting next to the pool, and Hannah seemed safe enough. The glistening blue water beckoned to me, but I'd promised Hannah and Firrag that I would stay inside the house. So much for a dip in the pool. A shower would have to serve as a substitute.

My eyes started itching as I made my way back down the hall to our room. The muscles in my neck ached. I was beat. Maybe I'd pushed it too hard? According to the Forest Fae

Hands, I was still recovering from my injuries.

I opened the door and nearly collapsed on the bed but dragged myself to the shower instead, hoping the warm water would loosen up some of my sore muscles. They shouldn't have been sore yet. They shouldn't have been sore at all. And I shouldn't have felt like I could barely keep my eyes open.

I glanced at my reflection as I waited for the water to heat up. The skin on my neck was blotchy. I sneezed. Then I sneezed again.

Maybe there was some artificial fragrance irritating me. I glanced around the bathroom and found a small bowl of what appeared to be dried leaves and fruit rinds that was giving the space a floral scent. But that was it. And my eyes had started itching back in the hallway on my way to the room. Whatever was in that bowl couldn't be causing this strange reaction.

I stripped down and stepped into the steaming stream of water raining down from the showerhead. It didn't take long for my muscles to relax, bathed in all that heat. A thermal pool would have been even better, but this would serve as a decent substitute until I got home. That gym more than made up for the lack of a soaking pool. I definitely needed to remember to tell Damir about it and the suggestions I now had to improve the fitness area in the clan caverns.

The warm water lulled me into a drowsy state. My eyelids dipped closed once, and then again, before I caught myself and twisted the faucet to create a cold blast. It wouldn't do to fall asleep when I was supposed to be guarding Hannah from demons. My eyes were so tired, though.

I rinsed one last time, turned off the water, and wrapped myself in one of the extra-large, plush white towels that had been folded neatly on a shelf over the toilet. I'd left the door to the bathroom open so that I would hear Hannah if she returned, but there were no sounds coming from the bedroom. Just in case, I wrapped the towel around my waist.

The bathroom mirror was too steamy to get another look at the blotches on my neck and chest. So, I didn't bother to check. I laid down on the bed, instead, just for a moment, to rest. I closed my burning eyes to see if that helped. The next thing I knew, the bedroom door slammed shut, and I jolted awake.

I tried to sit up, but it felt like pins and needles had been lodged under my skin. Everything hurt, my lips felt swollen, and my eyes still itched like mad. I rolled onto my side and moaned.

"What the—" Hannah's shocked voice worried me more than the fact that my vision had gone fuzzy. "What happened to you? You look like someone beat you, but you somehow managed to shower afterward?"

I groaned. It must be worse than I thought. When I tried to reply, I found my tongue was taking up way too much room in my mouth to form words.

Something, probably Firrag, tapped a frantic beat on the windowpane. Hannah's footsteps retreated in that direction. A blast of air and the beat of wings reassured me that the silver swirl outside was just my familiar and not a hallucination. Then it disappeared, and I reconsidered.

"Filag?" I couldn't seem to make my mouth form an *r* sound.

"She took one look at you and left." The bed shifted. "Seriously, Ved, what happened? Who did this to you? I was hurrying back here to warn you that we were right about Morgan not wanting you here and trying to get me alone, but I didn't think she would have tried something already. Not when she was out there attempting to win me over with her just-a-misunderstood-half-demon sob story."

I tried to sit up, but Hannah placed her hands on my chest and pushed me back down.

"Wow. Your chest is on fire." She placed a cool hand on my forehead. "You're burning up. Are you sick? Can you talk?"

I swallowed and forced my tongue to obey. Fire was something I could work with. Dragon Fae weren't afraid of a little heat. With extreme effort, I managed to get two words out. "I'm. Fine."

"Um. I beg to differ."

"Where? Firrag? Here?" I blinked up at the ceiling, trying to clear my vision.

"Okay. Now you're freaking me out. Firrag isn't here. She was banging on the window, trying to get in, but I couldn't get the screen off. Then she just disappeared. Probably went to tell Damir and Fiona, and I can't say I blame her this time. Whatever Morgan did to you, she did a good job. I don't think we have a choice. We need to send you home."

"No. No. Fine. Staying." My control over my tongue was too clumsy to communicate to her that I had no home unless I could prove myself, and the only way to do that was to stay here and keep her safe.

"You are really not. You're no good to me like this. If Firrag isn't back soon, I'm going to send one of these coins to Arabella." Hannah walked over to her suitcase and started rummaging around.

I swung my legs over the side of the bed, but they wouldn't hold my weight. The towel shifted and slid off my hips just as Hannah turned around.

"Woah." She spun so her back was facing me. "Um. Can you... Where are your clothes, anyway?"

They were probably still lying in a damp, sweaty heap on the floor of the bathroom. I didn't have clothes for this party. Jayden and Max promised that they would have something delivered to the house for me. It was part of the plan. "Need. Some. Remember?"

Hannah snapped her fingers. "Right. Damn. Well, I guess you won't need them now. Just wrap that towel around your-self while I get a message to Arabella."

She held something gold in her hand. It glinted in the sunlight coming through the open window. Even with my blurred vision, I knew what it was and what it meant for me. "No. Please. No."

Hannah glanced over her shoulder at me. "You can't stay here like this. I know it's too late to get another bodyguard, but at least I have a better idea of what Morgan is up to now. I don't think she'll hurt me. You can just go back to the Fae, and—"

If the tapping at the window hadn't interrupted her, I might have frightened her with the primal roar that had been building in my chest. Firrag's return, and Hannah's attempt to retrieve whatever it was that Firrag carried in her talons, gave me enough time to return to my senses.

"I need something to cut the screen." Hannah glanced around, then hurried over to her suitcase. She needn't have bothered.

Firrag stretched out one of her talons and sliced through the mesh with her razor-sharp claws. She tapped on the win-dow again to get Hannah's attention.

"Clever girl. Thank you." Hannah retrieved the strip of parchment that Firrag offered. She unrolled it, read it, then sighed. "They're sending help."

I groaned and flopped back onto the bed.

Hannah rushed over. "Are you okay? Hang in there. Did you hear what I said? They're sending help." She pressed her cool hand against my forehead again and muttered, "Though I'm not sure what that means, exactly."

My eyes itched, my throat felt like Firrag had scratched it out with her claws, everything ached, and now Damir and Fiona knew that I'd failed. A thought poked through the haze of pain in my head. Unless Firrag hadn't gone to Damir and Fiona. Only the wizards and Arabella knew where we were.

"Who? From?" I croaked out the words. The little faerie guard dog jumped up onto the bed and sniffed at me.

"Let me get you some water." Hannah lifted her hand off my face. "The note is from Max, if that's what you're trying to ask."

Her response gave me enough of a boost that I managed to raise myself up on my elbow so I could take the glass she offered and tilt some water into my swollen, dry mouth. "Better."

A knock on the bedroom door startled both of us.

"Be right there!" Hannah called. Then she lifted the glass from my hand and whispered instructions. "Roll over so that you're facing away from the door. I'm going to cover you with a blanket and say that you're sleeping."

I rolled away from her as she set the glass on the small table by the bed. Salty curled up next to me. Then something soft and light settled over my shoulders, and I closed my eyes. I listened to Hannah's soft footsteps as she walked to the bedroom door.

"Hi." She whispered the greeting. "Did you need something?"

"I have a delivery for Vedran."

I tensed at the sound of my name in a low voice that I

didn't recognize. I wasn't in the best state to fight, but I'd been worse after a few rounds against Boro's lieutenants, and I still managed to make at least one of them suffer worse injuries than I'd ended up with.

"I'm sorry, do you mean Ash?" Hannah kept her voice neutral and polite, but I could smell her fear even if I couldn't seem to sense her vitals through the haze of my own pain.

Salty lifted her head to sniff the air. Then she stood, placing her front paws on my hip to look over my body toward the stranger at the door.

"May I come in and set these packages down, please?" the low and unfamiliar voice asked.

"Ash is sleeping, and I didn't order anything. Are you sure you have the right room? Who sent you this way?"

Salty yipped and bounded over me. She dropped down off the bed and scampered over to Hannah. I didn't dare roll over to look and lose the element of surprise. Salty's toenails clicked against the wood floor when she reached the bedroom door. Judging by the rhythm, she was moving fast, but the sound didn't seem to be getting louder or quieter.

"Sorry about..." Hannah paused. "Oh. Um. Why don't you come in? You can set those down over there."

"Thank you." The door clicked shut a moment later.

"Who—" Hannah's voice cut off midquestion.

"One moment," the stranger said.

I counted my breaths in the silence as I listened, waiting, curious but not sure if I should move. Then the stranger spoke again.

"There. I've warded your room to keep others out. This should offer Vedran a safe place to recover."

"Recover? You mean you're not taking him back with you? And who are you anyway?"

I rolled over so I could get a look at our visitor. I couldn't make out any of their features, but the thrum of magic coming off them gave them away. It was stronger than what a wizard usually gave off. If Salty had signaled Hannah to let them in, then they weren't likely to be a demon. I couldn't get their ears to focus, and I couldn't taste their magic, but I was pretty confident what they were.

"Fae." My swollen tongue formed the word well enough to be understood.

"Rogue." The stranger corrected. Something about their appearance shifted, and then it was easier to make out the pointed ears rising up on either side of their hairless head. "You can call me Bryn."

"How did you...?" Hannah's voice trailed off as her hand waved in the air between them.

"Shae-shiter." My mouth wouldn't quite cooperate with me on that one.

"Rogues are shape-shifters. I can take the form of any human I touch. The one I borrowed happened to be having a smoke outside the kitchen."

"Did you—?"

"Kill her? No. She will recover." Bryn stepped closer to the bed. Their large black eyes looked down at me. "It appears that the Dragon Fae Alpha was right."

Hannah's face appeared next to Bryn's above me. "About what?"

"The Dragon Fae have evolved a severe allergy to demons. Especially those from the Cubus clan. It is meant to be a natural defense mechanism to warn them away from succubus who might attempt to seduce them. Since Dragon Fae breed almost exclusively with human women, greedy succubi proved to be enough of a threat to the future of the clan that they developed this survival response."

"So, it's a feature, not a bug." Hannah frowned.

"Yes. One that Damir might have warned you about if you had bothered to inform him of your plans."

I winced.

Bryn noticed. "No need for concern. He is unbothered. When your familiar informed him of your situation, he contacted Fiona and insisted the Hands produce an antidote. They crafted a solution, and they selected me to deliver it. I was the only one with the right skills based on what little Firrag could tell us of Morgan's defenses."

"You can communicate with the faerie dragon?" Hannah asked.

Bryn retreated and returned with a small vial. "Drink this," Bryn told Ved. "All of it."

I propped myself up and tilted my head back so Bryn could tip the contents into my parched mouth. At first, I tasted nothing. Then, I nearly gagged on the awful rotten sweetness covering my tongue.

Bryn pressed my jaw closed. "Swallow."

I choked the last of the antidote down, then I collapsed back onto the bed. "Water."

"Is he going to be all right?" Hannah asked as she propped me up again to offer me some water.

"He should be much improved by morning." Bryn paced away from the bed and out of my line of sight.

Hannah squinted down at me and held the glass while I sipped water from it like a Fledgeling. "We're supposed to have dinner with Morgan and Brady. Should I tell them that he's sick?"

"You shall tell them nothing," Bryn said.

Hannah set the glass down, then turned to face Bryn and

gasped. "You—you look just like him. How?"

When I turned my head, it was as though I were looking into a mirror. I knew that it was impossible, because I was lying on the bed, but there I was, standing in the middle of the bedroom. "Shape-shifter." This time, the word came out as intended.

"My powers are not limited to adopting only the forms of humans. I can also take the form of some Fae. Gnomes, pixies, and sprites are a bit more difficult to manage, but those similar in size to my natural form are quite easy to adopt."

"Can you take the form of a demon?"

"I've never tried, and I'm not sure it would be advisable. Demons are from a different realm. Their shapes, though they may seem similar to ours on the surface, are actually quite different. However, half-demon, half-human forms are within my capabilities."

"I see now why they sent you."

"Yes. I may not be much help in a fight, but I can serve in other ways."

"Then tonight I'd love it if you'd serve as my date."

"To be clear, I am happily mated, and we are expecting a Faeling very soon."

Hannah laughed. "Thank you for clarifying, but I only meant, I'd like you to pretend to be Ved, who is, as you seem to already know, pretending to be my boyfriend while actually serving as my bodyguard."

"I am afraid, as I said, I won't be much help as a bodyguard, but I will happily pretend to be Ved pretending to court you. Though, you said he is going by Ash?"

"Demons." I hoped the one word would be enough to get my reasoning across since I hadn't yet recovered enough to sit up and participate fully in the conversation. At least I could see clearly, and my Fae senses were returning. That was an improvement.

"Ah, yes." Bryn nodded. "A safe precaution to not give them your true name, though I don't believe there is any merit in the rumors."

I cringed. *Did I really look like that when I spoke?*

"What rumors?" Hannah asked.

"Makes it easier for them to steal your soul, corrupt you, seduce you, curse you, whatever sort of mischief that the clan in question specializes in." Bryn waved my hand through the air, and I had to look away or I was going to be sick. It was too much.

"Oh," Hannah said.

"Perhaps you should get dressed for this dinner. I also brought clothes for Vedran. I'll help him into something warm and comfortable. He'll appreciate that when the shakes start."

I grumbled. Of course, whatever antidote those Forest Fae Hands came up with, it would be worse than the thing they were curing.

"Shakes?" Hannah asked. "Are you sure he's going to be okay in here by himself?"

"He will be fine. My magic will alert me if there is any cause for concern, and the worst of the side effects won't start until later this evening. I'm sure we will be back from our dinner by then."

6

BRYN was dressed and Ved was asleep when I emerged from the bathroom in my new navy sundress. Since I had time, I decided to go live while doing my makeup and film a quick getting-ready chat. These types of posts boosted the number of subscribers who signed up for notifications so that they wouldn't miss the event premier. It had also been enough of a distraction and ego boost that I'd almost forgotten about Ved.

Poor Ved. I crossed over to the bed to check on him before digging my tan sandals out of my suitcase, slipping them onto my bare feet, and securing the thin straps around my ankles. "How is he?"

"He will be asleep for a while, I believe." Bryn gestured to the window. "Firrag is keeping watch. We will take the faerie dog with us."

"Muffin. We're calling her Muffin in front of the others. And you're Ash, not Ved, remember?"

Bryn was no longer wearing Ved's face, and those all-black

eyes were creeping me out. The completely hairless head didn't help. I'd seen a few Fae who looked like this in the infirmary, but none of them had ever spoken to me, and I'd never seen any of them shape-shift.

As though Bryn had guessed what I was thinking, their face and body shifted. The clothes that had been a bit too baggy now stretched across the muscled chest of a creature that looked identical to the Fae that had been assigned as my bodyguard. I couldn't decide if that was more or less disturbing than those Rogue Fae eyes.

"A bit of instruction before we go, if you don't mind?" Bryn said.

"Of course. It's probably best if we get our stories straight. Morgan and Brady don't know anything about Ved—I mean, Ash." I shook my head. "This is going to get so confusing."

"That is what I wanted to say. In your mind, you must think of me as Ash, exclusively. Do not think of me as Bryn, or as a Rogue Fae. Be on guard in case there is any chance that Morgan, or anyone in this household, can infiltrate your mind. Once we leave this room, I am Ash, and only Ash. Understood?"

I nodded. My mind reeled back, trying to remember if I'd thought of Ved as Ved while I'd been with Morgan. I suppose it didn't matter as much as tipping off Morgan that another Fae had infiltrated her defenses. Especially not one who could take on the form of any of her staff, giving them access to her entire home. A brilliant idea popped into my head. "Hey!"

"Hey?" The eyebrows on Ved's face lifted.

Ugh. I was really going to have to work to think of them as "Ash's eyebrows" because Bryn didn't have eyebrows, and Bryn was only borrowing Ved's for the evening. I closed my eyes and took a deep breath. *Ash. Only Ash.*

When I opened my eyes, I forced myself not to see anything other than the Fae form standing in front of me, and I named him Ash in my head. "Sorry. Just getting used to thinking of you as Ash. And I had an idea, but maybe we should talk about that after dinner. Otherwise, we're going to be late."

Ash nodded and offered me his arm. "Shall we?"

I laughed. "You are not that chivalrous."

Ash smiled. "Well, if our hosts don't know that, I won't tell."

"Ved is going to have quite the act to follow once he's better." I glanced over at the sleeping Fae sprawled out on the bed.

Bryn appeared to have clothed Ved in some sort of thermal long-sleeve shirt and pajama pants, though how the Rogue had managed to wrestle the much larger Dragon Fae into sleepwear, I couldn't imagine. At least Ved was no longer naked. Even with the blotchy rash all over his chest, it had been hard to ignore that full-frontal glimpse I'd gotten of what I would not be enjoying this weekend. I pushed those thoughts out of my head and put my game face on so that I would be ready to sit down with Morgan, again.

I linked my arm with Ash's, and he led us to the door. Salty jumped off the bed where she'd been curled up near Ved's feet and followed us.

Dim lights lit the hall leading back to the main room, even though the final rays of sunlight were still streaming through the floor-to-ceiling windows that opened out onto the pool deck. The orange-pink glow from the sun setting over the city cast the entire room in a rosy hue. As many times as I'd enjoyed this view, it still took my breath away and made me wish I hadn't left my camera in my room.

I was debating going back for it when Morgan stepped out of the shadows at the top of the steps leading into the dining room. The way she smiled made me hesitate. I wasn't going to leave Ash alone with her.

"Don't you two look lovely," she said.

"Thank you." I gestured to the sunset. "Ash and I were just admiring your magnificent view."

"It is stunning, isn't it?" Morgan made her way down the steps. "I'm so glad that you *both* decided to stay and enjoy it. I promise it will be an enlightening weekend."

I winced at the emphasis she'd put on the word "both." Then I mentally kicked myself for neglecting to fill B—Ash in on the details of my conversation with Morgan by the pool. "Where's Brady?" I asked. "I thought he was joining us for dinner."

The corners of Morgan's mouth turned down ever so slightly. It was so brief a moment that I could have imagined it, if I didn't know her as well as I did. She quickly recovered her hostess smile. "He was running late. He's in the shower. Can I get you a drink? Ash? What will you have?"

I tensed. What if she tried to poison Ash? She'd made it clear she didn't want him here.

Ash patted my hand as though he knew what I was thinking. "I would prefer water, if you don't mind."

"No problem at all. Sparkling or flat?" Morgan reached under the bar and extracted three wineglasses.

"Flat is fine." Ash paused before adding, "Your gym is spectacular, by the way."

"Thank you. It's really more Brady's baby than mine. Nearly all of that downstairs suite is, actually. His job is very demanding on his physique, and movies are his passion. He loves watching them over and over, especially with his friends." She shrugged as she filled one of the wineglasses with water from the cold glass bottle she retrieved from the bar fridge. "What about you, Hannah? Your usual? Or would you prefer wine tonight?"

The sweet tang of a cocktail sounded more appealing, but I didn't want to give her any excuse to be playing mixologist. It was much more unlikely that she would be able to tamper with a corked and sealed bottle. "I would love a glass of wine."

Morgan raised her eyebrows but didn't comment. "Red or white?"

I waved a hand. "Whatever you're having."

Morgan hummed to herself as she scanned the bottles. "I think I'm in the mood for a red tonight."

"Hannah!" Brady's voice boomed down the hallway. He stretched his arms out as he approached. "How are you? You look great. The picture of health. And I was so worried."

I allowed him to hug me and kiss my cheek. "I'm much better now. Thank you."

"Morgan was a wreck for weeks after." He shook his head, then appeared to notice Ash for the first time. Neither Morgan nor Ash had bothered with a glamour, so her horns and his ears were on full display. "And who's this?"

A glass shattered, and our heads all turned toward Morgan. Large and small bits of broken wineglass glinted in the final rays of the sunset.

"Babe. Are you okay?" Brady took a step closer to the bar, then looked down at the ground. "Let me get something to clean this up."

Morgan sighed. "I'm fine. It's fine. I've got it." She bent down to rummage under the bar and surfaced with a rag in one hand and something about the size of a Frisbee but thicker. She flicked a switch, and a series of lights cycled on the domed top. Then she set it on the ground.

Salty yipped at the robo-vacuum, and I scooped her up before she ended up with broken glass in her paws.

"You sure you don't need any help?" Brady asked.

Morgan wiped up the fragments with the rag. "I've got it. Hannah, why don't you introduce Brady to your new boyfriend while I finish pouring the wine?"

I grimaced. Something was bothering her. I could tell. Rather than push the issue, I took her suggestion, odd as it felt.

"Brady, this is Ash. Ash, Brady." I'd never had to introduce someone to Morgan's husband before. Pretty much every human in the country, and many beyond our borders, knew who he was and rushed him for an autograph when they caught him out in public. But Ash was Fae, and based on what I'd seen, Fae didn't have television. They were purely an "entertain yourself" group of creatures.

Ash only knew Brady was Morgan's husband, and that was the important thing to him, and to the rest of the Fae. They didn't care that Brady Killigan's face had been plastered on movie posters and big screens for years during his run as the handsome yet shy and studious wizard in the most talked-about and argued-over love triangle ever to drag out over seven seasons of television drama. It didn't matter to them that even people who didn't watch the show recognized Brady's face. Nor did it matter that Brady had played several minor roles in big movies but hadn't yet managed to land a lead. Not that the pair of them needed the money. Between what he made off the reruns and merchandise from his hit show, and what Morgan stood to inherit from her parents, they were set.

What mattered to the Fae was that Brady was an actual

wizard, and that he had married a half demon who was working for the leader of the demon clans. To Ash, Brady was an
enemy. And given how wizards generally felt about the Fae,
I expected Brady to feel the same and tensed for his reaction.

"Hooked up with one of the Fae, huh? Nice. I wondered
why Maxie was hanging out with them. Makes sense now."
He eyed Ash's muscles and nodded approvingly.

"Max was the one who supposedly introduced them," Morgan said. She handed Brady a glass of red wine, then extended one toward me. "Isn't that right?"

I took the glass from her. "It is."

"How long have you two been together?" Brady asked before taking a sip of wine and smacking his lips. "Ooh! I like
this one, Morg. Good choice."

"Not long." Ash lifted the glass from my hand. "May I have
a sip?"

After the broken glass thing, I had changed my mind about
drinking anything Morgan poured for me, even if it did come
from a sealed bottle. "Sure."

Ash inhaled the aroma before he took a sip. Then he nodded and handed the glass back to me. "I think you'll find that
very drinkable."

The robo-vac beeped a series of descending notes. The
lights on the top blinked off, and it remained still.

"Are all the Fae wine connoisseurs, or is that just a hobby
of yours?" Brady asked.

"No, and most assuredly it is not," Ash replied as I set Salty
down and stared at the dark-red liquid in my glass. "I happened to apprentice with a pair of twins who enjoyed a good
vintage. They were rather important, as Fae politics go, and it
was my job to make sure that no harm came to them."

"So, you were sort of like a poison tester?" Brady shook his head. "That's messed up. Do the Fae attempt to poison each other a lot?"

"Not usually, no." Ash smiled at Morgan, and I realized this was all for her benefit. He was giving her a subtle warning not to try to mess with us. Interesting.

"Perhaps we should move to the dining room?" Morgan suggested.

Brady slung an arm across Ash's shoulders and led the way. "So, what sort of magic do you have? I've got a little Earth magic, myself. But I wasn't trained well. Maybe you could give me some pointers while you're here?"

I caught Morgan rolling her eyes toward the ceiling as she turned to follow them. I paused, alone in the living room, to take one last look at the sunset and sip my poison-tested wine. This was going to be a very long dinner, but Brady was right. The wine was delicious.

HANNAH and Bryn were trying to keep their voices down, but they were arguing about something, and I wanted to know what. I blinked my eyes open and grinned as I realized that everything was back in focus again. Even my tongue felt a size smaller as I pushed it around my extremely dry mouth.

Salty hopped up on the bed and panted hot dog breath in my face. The smell made me think that my mouth tasted like she'd been licking the inside of it. I wrinkled my nose at her.

"Vedran is awake," Bryn said, cutting off whatever point Hannah had been trying to make. "Let us ask what he thinks."

"Could I have some water first?" I rolled onto my side and pushed myself up on one elbow.

"Hey! Welcome back to the party." Hannah retrieved my glass and hurried into the bathroom to fill it with water.

"Dinner went as well as could be expected. I will need to transfer some impressions into your mind before I leave so that you don't contradict anything I have already said. But first, I am going to have a look around while everyone is asleep," Bryn said.

I glanced at the window. Someone had pulled the shades, so I couldn't tell what time it was. I sipped my water and swallowed. My throat screamed for more, so I took a few long gulps.

"I don't like the idea of you wandering around out there." Hannah stood with her hands on her hips, facing Bryn. "What if you get caught? They'll figure out what you are and throw you out. Then what good will you be to us?"

Bryn dug around in the packages and lifted out some sort of amulet dangling from a cord. They tossed it at me. "Put this on."

"All right." I set the glass down so I could get a closer look at the amulet. "What is it?"

Bryn frowned. "Some sort of protection spell from the wizards. The antidote I gave you will reduce your sensitivity to demons. That means it will be difficult to sense their magic. This is supposed to warn you if there are demons about, in case it is not obvious. I am unsure it will work."

"I suppose it can't hurt." I tied the wizard amulet around my neck. "Aside from this argument about creeping around, which I'm all for, by the way. What else did I miss?"

Hannah shook her head. "Morgan has it out for you. She wants you gone. But much to her annoyance, Brady is ready to make you his new best friend."

I managed to pull myself up to a seated position. Salty wagged her tail, danced in a circle, then lay down alongside my leg with her head in my lap, drawing my attention to the clothes that now covered my upper and lower body.

"What are these?" I pulled at the fabric.

"Pajamas," Hannah said. "You wear them to sleep."

I locked eyes with her. "I wear nothing to sleep."

"Well, you do when you're sharing a room with me." Hannah turned her back on me and focused her attention on Bryn. "I think you should stay here."

"There is nothing for me to do here." Bryn's features shifted through several faces before settling on the face of an extremely handsome man. "If I can locate Morgan's secret room, then I will be able to see how it is secured."

"Did you touch the half demon?" I asked. Bryn's shape-shifting was much more impressive when I could see clearly and was sure I wasn't hallucinating. "Can you make yourself look like her now?"

"No." Hannah shook her head. "We decided it was too risky. We don't know enough about her powers."

"When I touch a human, I can sense their mind," Bryn explained. "If Morgan is half incubus, as she believes, she might have inherited the Cubus clan's mind-control powers. Even if Morgan cannot read my mind or control it, she may be able to see through my disguise if I touch her. I decided it was better if I did not risk it."

"I don't think you should run around looking like Brady, either," Hannah said, gesturing to Bryn's current form. "If you're going to do this, you should make yourself look like one of the staff."

Bryn's face contorted again, this time shifting into an older woman with short, curly brown hair. "Better?"

"I still don't like it, but yes. Better. Do you even know the woman's name?" Hannah asked.

"I know many things about this woman." The wrinkles on

the woman's face creased when Bryn frowned.

"Rogues eat lies," I explained, leaning forward. I'd only heard of Rogues. I'd never seen them up close. Their magic was fascinating.

Hannah's features scrunched in a look of confusion. "I don't think I want to know the details."

"Do not worry. Your lies are safe with me." Bryn's words coming from the older woman's mouth made Bryn seem like a wise elder.

"Wait...you...did that...to me?" Hannah took a step back.

I wondered what had her so worried.

Lies, like Rogue magic, were foreign to me. I'd been taught that Rogues couldn't feed off other Fae because Fae couldn't lie. They needed humans to feed. Because of that, for centuries, Rogues were one of the only factions of Fae that were allowed contact with humans. I only knew this because Dragon Fae also had a similar exception, though ours was for breeding purposes. I didn't know the specifics about how Rogues fed, but I knew that whatever they did, the human supposedly never remembered the encounter.

Bryn shrugged the old woman's shoulders. The gesture didn't look quite right because, from the neck down, Bryn still wore the body of a young, muscular man. "All humans lie. Especially to themselves. I did not take your lies from you, though I will, if you would prefer that."

Hannah tried to back up another step, but her legs hit the mattress. Her knees buckled and she sat down on the bed near my feet. "I don't think so?"

Bryn shifted from the neck down, taking on the rest of the old woman's physique. "Let me know if you change your mind. Most humans experience the reconnection with their truth to be a relief."

"I'm good. Thanks." Hannah shifted farther away from me, closer to the end of the bed, but didn't get up.

Bryn nodded. "Stay in the room. There is always the chance I will need to borrow your face, or pretend to be Ash again, should the situation arise. It would be inconvenient if there were two of us walking about."

"Be careful," Hannah warned as Bryn slipped out the door, shutting it without making a sound. "Are the Rogues all so serious? Or is it just this one?"

"I haven't met many, but from what I've heard, they're all like this."

Hannah twisted her body to face me, pulling her knee up onto the top of the mattress and tucking her foot under her opposite leg. The motion drew my attention to the fact that both legs were bare, and she was wearing a thin dress that clung to the curve of her hips.

"How are you feeling?" she asked.

I tore my eyes away from her long legs and lifted them until they met hers. "I would prefer not to have to fight any- one this evening, if it could be avoided, but my eyes are no longer itching." I ran a hand over my lips, then reached down to lift the hem of my shirt up so I could inspect the skin on my chest.

Hannah turned her head to the side so that she wasn't looking at me. "Could you please just leave that on?"

After determining there were no more blotches, I pulled the shirt back down. "If I didn't know better, I might get the idea that my bare skin makes you uncomfortable."

Hannah groaned. She picked up the water glass and re- treated into the bathroom. "I think I liked it better when you were snoring."

"I don't snore. You snore," I called after her with all the

maturity of a Fledgeling going through power surges.

Hannah returned with a full glass. "I do not snore."

I laughed because she was very, very wrong. "Oh, you most certainly do. You woke me up with your snoring more than once in the infirmary."

Hannah paused next to the bed. She squinted at me. "So, it *was* you in the infirmary. Angie said you were there, but why? What were you doing in there? More allergies?"

"Ha ha." I took the glass from her. "It's a long story."

She returned to her seat at the end of the bed. I did my best not to notice the way the hem of her dress crept up her thighs.

"Well, we'll be here for a while, so let's hear it. I'm going to guess it has something to do with that Damir guy. Am I right?"

"Yes and no." I leaned back against the headboard. "I got into a fight. Not with Damir, though."

"With who?"

"Three Dragon Fae."

"Three?"

I nodded. "There may have been four at one point, but that's not really relevant."

"It's not?" Her eyes widened. "Seems relevant to me, but fine. Why take on three—or maybe four—Dragon Fae? That seems a little misguided."

I snorted. "Damir and Ivo would very likely agree with you about that. But they weren't there, and it wasn't their sire who was murdered."

"These Dragon Fae killed your sire? Why would they do that? And if they did, why weren't they in the Fae equivalent of jail, whatever that is?" The bridge of Hannah's nose wrinkled when she frowned.

"You really do sound like my wing-mates." I shook my head. Words tumbled from me unfiltered. I blamed it on side effects from the antidote. "Maybe I truly am the odd one. Maybe they're right. I'm just impulsive and reckless and spoiling for a fight."

Hannah's scowl softened. "I don't know. Jayden was really pushing your buttons back there in my apartment, and you didn't attack him."

"I thought about it."

Hannah shook her head. "Tell me about what happened with these Dragon Fae murderers."

"I couldn't prove it. I wasn't there. They said they'd been out hunting with my sire. That was hard enough to believe. They weren't friends of his. They'd been stirring up trouble in the clan, pushing for a Challenge, and my sire was Velibor Lightwing's lieutenant."

The way Hannah cocked her head to one side reminded me of Firrag. "What does that mean?"

"Velibor was the clan Alpha and Ivo's sire. Every Alpha names two lieutenants. My sire and Damir's sire were his."

"Lieutenants. That's what you want to do, right?" Hannah shifted farther onto the bed so she could curl both legs underneath her. "What do lieutenants do?"

"They protect the Alpha and the clan, and they fight at the Alpha's side if there is a Challenge."

"All right." Hannah sighed. "What's a Challenge?"

"It's what happens when one of our clan calls out the Alpha. There is a Challenge for leadership of the clan. It's a fight to the death. Whoever wins becomes the next Alpha."

She recoiled. "That's harsh."

"It's our way." I reached for the glass and took another sip of water.

"So, Dragon Fae murdering other Dragon Fae is okay as long as it's part of one of these Challenges?" Hannah asked.

I nodded as I set the glass down. "You could say that. Yes."

"But that's not what they did. They killed your sire while they were out hunting. Why would they do that? Because he was Velibor's lieutenant?"

I shouldn't have been surprised that she was paying such close attention to the story, but it had been such a long time since I'd had anyone besides Damir and Ivo to talk with. Anyone who actually paid attention and appeared to care. It only made the next bit, which still hurt too much to think about, harder to tell. I glanced down and focused on the subtle pattern in the stitching on the blanket rather than meet Hannah's intense gaze.

"It wasn't an accident. My sire was the best fighter in the clan. He taught all the Fledgelings to fight, but he gave Damir, Ivo, and me special lessons. They knew if they took him out, it would be easier to defeat Velibor and Milomir. And that's exactly what happened. They paved the way for the biggest bully in the clan to Challenge for Alpha.

"When Boro named his two lieutenants for the fight, they were two of the three who were supposedly hunting with my sire. Milomir couldn't hold them off alone. It was two against one. They murdered him and Velibor and took over leadership of the clan."

I glanced up to make sure she was still listening, caught the look of sympathy on her face, and shifted my gaze toward the curtain-covered window. "Ivo, Damir, and I were gone at the time. We'd made a trek to the Fire Isle to see if we could attract faerie dragon familiars like Damir's grandsire did centuries ago. When we returned, we were expected to pledge ourselves to the new Alpha. Ivo fled. Damir avoided the caverns and kept to the village where he was responsible for retrieving any male Dragon Fae offspring and returning them to the clan to be raised in the crèche."

"And you decided to fight," Hannah concluded.

I shrugged. "I shouldn't have tried to take them on alone."

"But you didn't Challenge?"

I shook my head. "I'm not Alpha material. Ivo should have been the one to Challenge. Especially after what Boro did to his sire. Damir and I would have fought by his side. We would have made him Alpha."

"But Ivo left."

"Ivo left." I reached down and scratched Salty behind her ear. "And I refused to bow down to Boro. So, when his lieutenants came for me, I fought them. But they had me cornered, and more kept coming until I fell and couldn't get back up. They took me to a cell and chained me to the wall. They refused to treat my wounds or feed me until I agreed to pledge my oath to the new Alpha. Luckily, Damir found out what was happening and rescued me."

"And took you to the infirmary."

"To his mother's kin. The Forest Fae. He didn't know they would help me, but he didn't know where else to go. If he took me with him back to the village, they'd just come after both of us there. And he didn't want to Challenge for Alpha any more than I did."

"But he's Alpha now, isn't he?" Hannah asked.

I kept my eyes down so I wouldn't have to see her reaction when I told her my greatest shame. "Ivo came back. He said he would Challenge Boro. But I was in no state to fight. Damir and Ivo had to Challenge Boro alone. Without me. They defeated him, but Ivo almost died in the process. So, Damir became Alpha."

"Hey." Hannah leaned forward and tapped my knee with her hand. "Look at me."

I shook my head. "It's my fault that Ivo almost died."

She scooted forward until she could reach out and lift my chin. "But he didn't die. And it's not your fault."

"If that's true, then why hasn't Damir named me as his lieutenant?"

Hannah released my chin and cocked her head to one side. "That's why you volunteered. You think that by showing him you can keep me safe from some demons, he'll make you his lieutenant."

I looked past her shoulder toward the window. Even though the shades were pulled, I could sense Firrag out there. If I could speak with my faerie dragon like Damir could speak with Sillag, then maybe she could reassure me. "He thinks I'm impulsive. Irresponsible."

"Then we'll just have to prove him wrong."

My eyes met Hannah's. "What are you saying?"

"I'm saying that we're a team now. You're helping me get what I want, and I'm going to help you get what you want."

"You think Damir is going to listen to you?"

"I think that by the time we're done, Damir is going to be ready to put a medal around that thick neck of yours."

"You've been checking out my neck, huh?"

"You wish."

I grinned. Her face was so close, I could count the freckles on her cheeks. Or kiss them. I sensed her pulse rate increase as the moment extended, our eyes locked, waiting to see who might make the first move. And would that move be to close the distance between us or to shift away?

The door creaked open, breaking the spell.

7

B RYN stepped inside and shut the door. "Good. You are both still awake."

Thank the elements for Bryn's timing. That had been a close call. I slid away from Ved, back down to the end of the bed, where I would be much less tempted by his lips and his soft heart.

I focused on Bryn, who was still wearing the face of the curly-haired woman with the wrinkled skin and hunched shoulders. "Did you find something?"

"I think I have discovered the location of Morgan's room." Bryn's face shifted back to the more alien-like hairless Rogue. "It is not on the lower level as we thought."

"Did you get inside?" I asked.

"No. I did not. There are wards, but there is also a device that leads me to believe that the security works something like the blood coins. If that's true, Morgan has probably been working with the demons for longer than we thought."

"What I don't understand is why she would go to them for

help and not someone like that half demon on Fiona's Court," Ved said.

"Nigel?" Bryn asked.

"He's the one who's partnered with the leader of the Elemental Faction, right?" Ved asked.

"Yes." Bryn pressed the tips of their fingers together. "You bring up an interesting point. Nigel is also half wizard and half demon of the Cubus clan. Though, he was raised by his demon mother, so he is much more knowledgeable about demon powers."

I stared at Ved, not because I was surprised by the fact that he had suggested something so brilliant—though it was a bit shocking how quickly he'd recovered from his demon allergies. I was more concerned about the fact that no one had told me there was a half demon, half wizard on the Faerie Queen's High Court. Why hadn't Max already tried this?

"Do you think Nigel could help Morgan?" I asked. I doubted, based on what she'd said at the pool, that we could succeed in luring her loyalty back from the demons. But if this Nigel had changed sides, and he already knew about the nuances of the various demon clans and where they came from and why, then maybe he could convince Morgan that she had it all wrong.

"It might be worth a try. Though I am not sure it would be safe to send him here," Ved replied.

"Why?"

"He's been working as a spy for the Fae, and his mother is the one uniting the demon clans against Fiona's kin," Ved explained.

"If you think they will not come for all the Fae once they have control of magic here, you are fooling yourself, Vedran. The demons pose as much of a threat to the Dragon Fae as they do to 'Fiona's kin,' as you say."

"All right," I interrupted before Bryn and Ved could waste time on a pointless argument when we needed to be working as a team to evolve our plan. "Let's think this through. This is a party for celebs and influencers. Morgan said there would be some demons here. She said that some of the clans had infiltrated Hollywood as a way to survive in this realm. But I've seen the guest list. I know all the names on there. So, either some of them are actually demons, which is possible, I guess? Or there are demons coming as guests of some of those celebs. Regardless, how likely is it that anyone at this party is going to know who Nigel is?"

Bryn's face showed no sign of emotion, either positive or negative. "I can ask Nigel and see what he thinks about this idea."

Ved leaned forward. "I think it's worth a try. If we can convince Morgan that it's madness to trust the demons, there's a chance she'll hand over the boxes she has willingly."

"Assuming she still has the boxes and has not yet given them to Lilium and the other demon clan leaders," Bryn said.

"It's more than just knowledge she wants," I said, interrupting to keep the pair of them from bickering. "Morgan thinks that the demons are misunderstood. She's a long way into justifying this to herself."

"I will speak with Nigel and send a message to let you know what the High Court decides." With that, Bryn disappeared.

I continued to stare at the space where Bryn had been, even though I knew that they weren't going to reappear there. Bryn had already determined that there was no way to transport into Morgan's house. Out, yes. But not in.

"We should probably get some sleep," I said, still not able to look at Ved, especially now that we were alone again.

"I can take the floor, and you can have the bed." Ved shifted his weight toward the edge of the mattress, sending me sliding toward him.

I stood. "No. I'll take the floor. You're still recovering. You should take the bed."

"I'm fine, and I'm used to sleeping on the floor. Take the bed."

"No, really. I couldn't." I walked over to my suitcase so that I could find my pajamas.

While I was preoccupied, Ved snuck up behind me and set his too-warm hands on my bare shoulders. He nudged me to turn around. When I did, he gestured to the fact that he was standing and said, "See. I'm fine. Take the bed."

I pressed the back of my hand to his forehead but avoided meeting his gaze, not willing to risk getting caught in his eyes again. "You're still burning up. You must still have a fever. I can't let you sleep on the floor."

The corners of Ved's mouth pulled up into a grin. "That's just me. Dragon Fae are naturally hot."

I groaned. "You can't be serious. Does that line even work on women?"

Ved shrugged. His hand slid from my shoulder, nearly taking the strap of my sundress with it. "I don't know. I've never tried it before. What do you think?"

I rolled my eyes. "I think it's cheesy. I'm going to pretend that you're still loopy from the medicine Bryn gave you."

Ved chuckled as he walked into the bathroom and shut the door. As soon as he was gone, I buried my face in my hands and screamed silently. *Whatever you are thinking, you must stop!*

I pulled on my pajama shorts before taking off my dress and putting on the matching tank top. Only then did I remove my bra. I was not going to give Ved the opportunity to see me naked. I searched the closet and the dresser drawers until I found an extra blanket. Then I grabbed a pillow off the bed and set it down in front of the glass fireplace.

"What are you doing?" Ved stepped out of the bathroom and stared at me.

"Sleeping on the floor."

Ved shook his head. "Don't be stubborn. How about this? What if we share the bed? Look at it. It's huge. You stay on your side. I'll stay on mine. It will be fine."

I looked at the bed. I doubted it was big enough to keep me from getting pulled toward him in the middle of the night. "I thought you said I snore."

"It's fine. I'm used to it." Ved sat down on the side closest to the bathroom. "Come on. I promise. No touching. Just sleeping."

I picked up the pillow I'd tossed onto the floor and dragged it with me over to the opposite side of the bed, all while holding the blanket I'd found up to my chest as a shield.

Ved leaned over and pulled the blanket out of my hand. He stretched it down the middle of the bed, bunching up the sides so that it provided a barrier between us. Then he gestured to the two halves. "See? My side. Your side."

I pulled the barrier closer to me. "That's not fair. You're bigger than me, you can have more room."

Ved snorted. "Just get under the covers and go to sleep already, will you?"

I pulled the duvet back. As I slipped underneath, I was reminded that even the sheets in the guest bedrooms in Morgan's house had a higher thread count than the ones on my bed in my apartment. I squirmed against them and grinned. Heaven.

I popped my head up to peek at Ved, only to realize he'd stretched himself out on top of the duvet. "What are you doing?"

He turned his head to the side to look at me. "Going to sleep."

"You're going to sleep on top of the blankets?"

He grinned. "I'm hot, remember? I don't need blankets."

I set my head down with a thud and squeezed my eyes shut. "Ugh. Good night."

"Sweet dreams, water wizard." Ved's low voice, so close in the dark room, sent a jolt of awareness through me.

I opened my eyes. Even though it was too dark to see anything, I stared up at the ceiling, trying not to move, much too conscious of the Dragon Fae body making the mattress dip on the other side of the bed.

Ved didn't seem to have any problem falling asleep, though. His breathing evened out almost immediately. I listened to him not snoring until I was sure he wasn't awake. Then I closed my eyes and tried to relax. I needed sleep. There was only so much I could do with makeup to cover up a restless night, and I did not want Morgan and Brady drawing their own conclusions about why I wasn't well rested in the morning.

I ticked through my to-do list in my head, trying to remember everything I needed to get done, in the order I'd listed them on the notepad in my bag. I'd copied everything down on paper since Morgan would be confiscating phones. So, it was all fresh in my head. Usually, the process of listing things lulled me to sleep, but it wasn't enough of a distraction. I switched to thinking through who was on the guest list and wondering which of them might be demons.

Eventually, I must have drifted off, because the next thing

I knew, Salty was panting in my face with her paws on my shoulder. I blinked my eyes open and confirmed it was the little faerie dog's hot breath and warm paws I'd registered in my half-awake state. Once I remembered where I was and whom I was with, I sat up with a start.

"Good morning." Ved was already awake and dressed. He handed me a steaming coffee mug.

"You're up." I was brilliant first thing in the morning so long as I didn't have to speak.

"Got up early, so I went down to the gym. Grabbed some coffee on the way back. Wasn't sure if you liked coffee or not, but I've heard that's what humans drink in the morning." Ved took a sip from his own matching mug and swished the liquid around in his mouth before continuing. "Interesting. It's terrible, and yet"—he took another sip—"I still want more."

"Sounds about right." I happened to love coffee, and this particular blend smelled great—plus, it would help wake me up. I closed my eyes and savored my first sip.

Ved had added a touch of cream and a little bit of sugar. It was almost perfect. Not that I was going to be picky. I would have drunk it plain out of a mug the size of my head if that had been on offer. But too much coffee on an empty stomach wasn't a good idea, either.

I set the mug down and pushed the covers back. "Have you seen anyone else?"

Ved lifted one shoulder in a half shrug. "Met that woman Bryn impersonated. Her name is Louise, and she works in the kitchen. Set me up with coffee and these." Ved stepped to the side to reveal a basket of muffins and doughy pastries that he'd set on the top of the dresser.

My mouth watered. "So, Louise is okay?"

"Seemed fine to me." Ved picked up a muffin and sat down

in one of the armchairs. "I also saw Brady but didn't talk to him. He was just heading down to the gym as I was leaving the kitchen. I had a mouthful of biscuit, so I waved, but I don't think he saw me."

"Okay. Well, I need to shower and get dressed, and then I'd like to scope out the areas of the house that I think are going to work best for filming. And, if we get the all clear from Bryn, I want to see if I can convince Morgan to invite Nigel. Sound good?"

"You should eat one of these muffins while they're still warm. They're delicious. This part of human food I could definitely get used to." Ved finished off the last of his muffin and licked his fingers.

He caught me watching him and raised an eyebrow.

I sprang up from the bed, grabbed some clothes, and mumbled something about wanting to get moving so I didn't miss all the morning light. Then I closed myself in the bathroom and exhaled. That Fae was too hot, and he knew it. Worse, he knew that I knew it. My shower would have to be a cold one this morning because I had to wash these thoughts out of my head, fast, before I did something very foolish.

———

FOLLOWING Hannah around turned out to be more interesting than I'd thought it would be. By lunch, I'd learned how to use her camera equipment, and I'd been briefed on photo composition and how to capture Hannah at just the right angles to make sure she looked just as stunning in two dimensions as she did in three. She'd even posted a few of the photos I took to her social media accounts, whatever those were.

I liked that my competence seemed to make her happy, and it gave me a legitimate excuse to follow her around. Which didn't appear to be necessary, because we hadn't crossed paths with Morgan or Brady all morning. I was beginning to suspect that Morgan, at least, was avoiding us. I kept sensing someone nearby, but when I turned to look, there was no one there. I didn't bother mentioning it to Hannah because she seemed pretty focused on her work, but it was beginning to creep me out.

I almost thought that I was imagining things, but Salty's ears perked up whenever I got that strange sensation of being watched, and she always turned her attention in the same direction. Every time she noticed something, I snuck her a bit of sweet bread from my pocket as a reward. Hannah finally caught me and started to scold me for giving the dog human food until she remembered that "Muffin" was supposed to be my dog, not hers.

Morgan finally showed herself just as my stomach was beginning to rumble. "Guests will start arriving after lunch, and I don't want to make more work for the staff. So, Brady is going to run out and grab some burgers, and we're going to eat out on the patio. Do you want to join us?"

Hannah looked from Morgan to me and back again. "The patio?"

Morgan waved a hand. "It's fine."

"This isn't a trick to get rid of him?" Hannah asked.

"Get rid of who?" I asked, even though I knew the answer, and Hannah knew that I knew. I couldn't lie, but I could play dumb, especially when everyone seemed to think I was all muscle and no brains.

Morgan crossed her arms. "Brady will be pissed at me if I do. So, no tricks. Do you want a burger or not?"

"What's a burger?" I asked, at the risk of actually sounding dumb. I assumed it was another sort of human food, but I truly didn't know what kind.

Hannah sighed. "Have Brady just get two of whatever he's having, and I'll take a salad."

"They have veggie burgers." Morgan held up her phone screen to show Hannah whatever was displayed on it.

Hannah shook her head. "No, thanks. A salad is fine."

"Suit yourself." Morgan shrugged. "Oh, and after lunch, you have to turn over your phone. Don't forget."

Hannah groaned as soon as Morgan was far enough away that she probably wouldn't hear. Although Hannah probably hadn't factored in the fact that Morgan was half demon and very likely had extra-sensitive hearing.

"Really. What's a burger? And why don't you want one?" I asked.

Hannah stared at me. "Meat on a bun, and I don't eat meat."

"You don't?"

Hannah shut off her camera and handed it to me. "Can you take all this back to our room? I don't want to leave it around in the main area of the house. I'll go talk to Morgan, and you meet us out on the patio."

"I'm not leaving you alone." I nestled her camera back into its cushioned bag.

"I told you, she's not going to do anything to me." Hannah picked up her notepad and checked something off her list. "She's already promised all her guests that I'm going to be at this party."

"Sure. You can be here." I gestured to my body. Then I pointed at my head. "And not be here."

"I told you. I can shield. She's not going to take control of my mind." Hannah lowered her voice to a whisper. "Plus, maybe you can get a look at the security on *that thing* while I'm talking to her."

It took me a moment to realize she was talking about Morgan's secret room. Bryn had told us where to find it, but the entrance must have been really well hidden in the wall because we'd walked around that area and spent nearly an hour taking photos, and neither of us had spotted anything. Hannah was right, I might have better luck if I could get a closer look without worrying that Morgan was going to sneak up on me.

"Take Muffin with you," I said.

"Be careful with my equipment," she countered.

"Don't worry. I'll make sure it gets all of my attention." I grinned.

Hannah closed the distance between us in two steps. She locked eyes with me and paused. Her lips hovered close to mine for a heartbeat. Then she leaned forward, skimming past my mouth to brush her lips across my cheek. She stepped back, out of reach, then bent down to pick up Salty and stood with a snap.

In a too-sweet voice, she said, "See you on the patio, babe."

I swear she put some extra sway in her hips as she walked away just to torture me. I wondered how much was for show, in case anyone was watching, and how much was because she knew I was watching. Either way, it didn't matter to me. Appreciation of Hannah's body was well within the fake-boyfriend job description. So, I let myself savor the view before returning to my assigned task.

Once she was gone, it didn't take long to gather up the equipment bags and carry them back to the relative safety of the room. Bryn had done a very nice job with the wards. Dragon Fae didn't have that sort of magic. The High Fae did, though.

Bryn's wards were similar to the ones that Damir's and

Ivo's mothers put in place to protect our clan's caverns centuries ago. Not that any demon had ever been foolish enough to transit into the labyrinth of tunnels crawling with Dragon Fae. We still appreciated the extra measure of safety, especially since that made the cave mouths the only way in or out, and those were located high up in the mountains and nearly inaccessible by foot.

Just the thought of home made me want to fly. After setting everything down, I stretched my back muscles. I'd been itching to transform for days. The Hands had said I needed to wait a bit longer, but the phantom ache of wings that had gone too long unused was like an itch I couldn't reach to scratch.

I knew they didn't really ache. They couldn't. It wasn't like they were inside me, folded up and waiting to emerge through my skin. That would be incredibly uncomfortable. With effort, I could transform an individual body part without making a full transformation, but there was no equivalent of wings in my Fae form. I couldn't just sprout them without shifting fully into my dragon form. Still, I ached to fly.

As though she'd heard my thoughts, Firrag appeared at the window and cooed to get my attention.

"What are you doing here? Shouldn't you be keeping an eye on Hannah? She's out there alone on the patio with that half demon." I scowled, remembering that I also had something else I should be doing.

Firrag lifted one talon, drawing my attention to the rolled-up piece of paper she held there. I shoved my hand through the slit in the screen, and she dropped the message into my palm. I unrolled it to find a note from Damir.

Ash, If you let Firrag scratch Hannah, it should give her truth sight. Will help her see through demon glamours. Stay safe. ~D

I glanced at my familiar. "I'm sure that will go over well."

Firrag squawked.

"Don't try it until after I talk to her. I don't want her to think you're trying to attack her."

Firrag ducked her head and hissed at me.

"If you're implying that you'd never, I know you better than that. Keep your talons to yourself for now. All right?"

Firrag flexed her wings, then refolded them neatly at her sides.

"Show-off." I grimaced. "Rub it in, why don't you? Or better yet, make yourself useful and go look after Hannah."

Firrag stretched her long neck toward the window and tilted her head to one side. I reached out and scratched behind her horns.

"I know. I miss you, too." I slid my fingers down to scratch under her chin. "Let's get back to work so we can get out of here, okay? If the demon allergies don't kill me, the effort it's taking to keep my hands off this woman might."

Firrag nipped at my fingertips when I tried to pull my hand away.

"At least someone wants me to touch them," I grumbled, giving Firrag one more caress before shutting the window. "Time to go find Morgan's lair."

I lurked around in the hall, reaching out with my senses, trying to find the seam, the place that wasn't a wall but an opening. Bryn had said it was near the end of the hallway that led to the family wing. This close to the main room, there was a lot of traffic. Staff was coming and going from the dining area and kitchen, out to the guest wing, and back again.

The longer I spent pacing around the area, the more suspicious I was going to look. Or lost. Someone might think I was turned around and come try to help me. I found a chair that had a view of the end of the hallway, then I picked up one of the books displayed on a low table and took a seat.

I glanced down at the cover before flipping it open to a random page. There were barely any words, just a few large images. I turned to the next page. The glossy sheet showed a pair of attractive movie stars locked in an embrace with large letters looming above their heads. A pair of names appeared in smaller print near the bottom of the image. On the opposite page, a man in a trench coat holding an umbrella gripped a lamppost in the rain, but he looked happy. I shook my head.

I pretended to read until the last of the staff left the area. Then I lifted my head and stared at the hallway. If I were in my dragon form, I'd have been able to see heat signatures, but that wasn't something I could do in my Fae form. A ball of dust near the baseboard caught my attention.

Morgan had said she didn't want to make more work for the staff before the guests arrived. It was probably safe to assume that the whole house had been cleaned thoroughly already. Someone had either missed that spot, or that bit of dust came from somewhere else. Somewhere that probably wasn't cleaned as frequently.

The opening to the door had to be there. I scanned the wall just above that spot, searching for the panel that would open to reveal a bio-reader like the one Bryn had described. There was a painting, but Bryn hadn't said anything about a painting. It had to be something in the wall.

The light in the room dimmed, and I turned toward the window. A cloud had passed over the sun. I couldn't see Hannah or Morgan from where I sat. So I returned my attention to the hallway. The cloud had moved on, and a bright beam of sunlight now added extra definition to every shadow in the house.

There it was. I snapped the book shut.

"Hey, man! You hungry? Just wait until you taste these burgers, bro. The best." Brady walked in front of me and held up a cluster of paper bags. "Huh. Come to think of it, do Fae even eat burgers?"

I didn't want to take my eyes off the spot I'd found on the wall, but there was nothing I could do. I stood and inhaled the rich scent of grilled meat. My mouth watered. "I suppose there's a first time for everything."

"Seriously? You've never had a burger? This is epic." Brady handed me one of the bags. "I promise, you will not be disappointed. These things are insane."

"Morgan and Hannah are out on the patio," I said, half hoping he might go ahead and leave me alone to investigate. My other half was fixated on lunch.

"Sweet. Let's get out there so we can dig in." He gestured toward the patio door with his head since his hands were full of paper bags.

I took the lead, opening the door for Brady and pausing briefly before stepping over the threshold and onto the concrete pool deck. Brady had turned right and was headed to a long outdoor dining table that ran parallel to the one inside the dining room, on the other side of the glass. Either I hadn't noticed it during the initial tour, or it had been recently added in honor of the party.

Morgan stood as Brady greeted her. She locked eyes with me over his shoulder. When she realized I was hesitating, she grinned. There was a challenge in her eyes, and it drove me out onto the deck. I closed the distance between me and Hannah in a few long strides. When I reached her, I set my hand on her shoulder.

Morgan could threaten me all she liked, but I wasn't going

anywhere. If I had to, I'd tear her down so I could bring Hannah, and those boxes Morgan was hiding, home to the Fae. She'd realize soon enough that she was no match for me.

8

THE warmth of Ved's hand on my bare shoulder made the sun seem like a very distant star. I looked up at him only to find his eyes locked in a glaring match with Morgan's across the table. She'd done something, and I wanted to know what. Except I couldn't ask in front of Brady, who was checking the contents of each paper sack and handing them out to the appropriate person, all the while babbling about how these were the best burgers on the planet. He waited to hand me my salad, in the clear eco-friendly clamshell, until last.

"I can't believe you didn't want a burger," he said.

"Brady, I'm vegetarian, remember?" I popped open the clamshell, only to realize I didn't have a fork. "Did they give you any utensils?"

Brady smacked his head with the heel of his hand. "I knew I forgot something."

"No problem." Ved squeezed my shoulder. "I'll go grab you a fork from Louise in the kitchen."

Morgan had been just about to sit down. She stood. "I'll get it."

Her phone buzzed, and she paused to check it before leaving the table.

"I'm the jerk who forgot. I'll get it." Brady gestured at the paper bag he'd set in front of Ved. "Man. Seriously. You got to try it before it gets cold. Sit and eat."

"Go ahead. Don't wait for me," I said, reaching over to steal one of Brady's fries. "Additional forgetfulness tax."

Morgan ignored us as she tapped out a response on her phone.

Ved lifted his wrapped burger out of the paper bag and set it on the table. "I have some of those fried sticks as well."

"If you don't want them, hand them over," I said.

Ved bit the end off of one and chewed. "Not bad. I like it better than coffee."

Morgan laughed.

Ved and I both looked up and stared at her, surprised that she'd actually been listening.

Morgan slid back into her chair and placed her palms down on either side of the wrapper she'd unfolded to make a plate. "Maybe you're right."

"About coffee?" Ved asked.

I shot him a glance out of the corner of my eye.

Morgan laughed again. "Not about coffee. You can pry my coffee out of my cold dead hands."

I set a hand on Ved's thigh under the table before he could respond. Both of us were practically vibrating with the urge to take her up on that invitation. But I had a feeling I knew what she was talking about. I just wasn't sure why she'd changed her mind. Or why she'd laughed at Ved. I thought she hated Ved and wanted him gone.

"You'll reconsider?" I'd mentioned Nigel to her before the guys joined us, trying to be casual about it, just in case the High Court decided it was too big of a risk to let him come. I'd been hoping that knowing there was someone else like her, half wizard and half demon, but raised by his demon kin and who still decided to align with the Fae, might open her mind to the possibility that she'd been too hasty about choosing sides.

Morgan rubbed the skin at the base of her horn. "Maybe it wouldn't hurt to hear what this Nigel has to say. Go ahead and invite him."

"Oh." Ved realized what we were talking about.

"Really? What made you change your mind?" I slid my hand off Ved's leg and gripped the side of my chair. The teak wasn't nearly as warm and nicely muscled, but it was a whole lot safer.

Ved stuffed another fry into his mouth. If he'd noticed either the presence or the disappearance of my hand, he didn't let on.

Morgan waved in the air. "You. Him. My stupid brother. I don't know. If there's some piece of this puzzle that I'm missing, I want to know what it is. I want the whole picture. So, invite him. For the day. Figuring out sleeping arrangements was enough of a nightmare. I'm not about to go back and shuffle everyone around again. Not when people are going to start arriving in..." She paused to check her watch. "Crap. Less than an hour."

"I'll text him after lunch. Before I give you my phone."

"Text who?" Brady waved a shiny silver fork and knife in my direction. "Your cutlery, my lady."

"Turns out that Hannah has a friend who is half wizard and half demon," Morgan explained.

"Wow! There's another one? Huh." Brady unwrapped his burger and lifted the dripping mass up to his mouth. "Come to papa."

I focused on my salad, stabbing a mix of lettuce and other vegetables with the end of my fork. Next to me, Ved mimicked Brady's actions. Out of the corner of my eye, I watched him open his mouth and take a bite.

"What do you think, bro? Good, right?" Brady nodded and grinned as he watched Ved chew and waited for a response.

"Fascinating." Ved took another bite.

"Told you you'd love it." Brady put his arm around Morgan's shoulders. Then he leaned over and gave her a kiss on the cheek. "Hey, babe. How was your morning?"

Morgan twirled a fry in the puddle of ketchup she'd made on one corner of her burger-wrapper-turned-plate. "Good. I think everything is ready to go."

"Sweet. I'm pumped. This is my favorite weekend of the year." He nuzzled the side of Morgan's face. "My wife throws the best parties."

Morgan tilted her head to lean against his. He kissed her temple, right below her horn, and then retreated so he could take another bite of burger.

It didn't matter how cute the two of them were together. I was still hurt that Brady had known about Morgan this whole time but had never told me. I frowned at my salad and stabbed a few more pieces. Sure, she'd agreed to talk to Nigel, but she still hadn't given me a good answer as to why she hadn't been honest with me. I wasn't buying her claims of unquestioning obedience at Mama Elle's swearing her to secrecy.

"Wow, Hannah, what did that poor salad do to offend you?" Brady asked.

I looked up. "What?"

He mimed a stabbing motion.

I pushed my chair back from the table. "I think I'm just not really hungry. I'm going to go text Nigel and then I'll bring you my phone."

I was really going to text Willow, Angie, and Eve on our group chat. I didn't have Nigel's number, but I was pretty confident that they would be able to get him a message from me. I also just wanted to be alone for five minutes. Once Morgan's guests started arriving, I would have to have my game face on, and at that moment, Brady was right, I did want to stab something.

Before anyone could convince me to stay, I put the lid on my salad and headed back inside the house. I didn't even make it to the family wing hallway before Ved came jogging through the door after me.

"Hannah, wait." He fell into step next to me.

"You didn't need to follow me. I am perfectly capable of making it to our room without getting killed. Go back and enjoy your burger."

"If that's the best that burgers have to offer, I don't think I like burgers. I think I'll just stick to muffins. And biscuits. The biscuits were good, too."

I couldn't tell if he were serious or not, and I almost didn't care. I just wanted to be alone. "You seemed to like the fries," I grumbled.

Ved held up his small container of fries and shook it so that the smell of crispy fried potatoes wafted up at me. My mouth watered, but I refused to be lulled with comfort food. Why couldn't he understand that he'd been glued to my hip all morning and I needed some space?

Sure, he'd been an exceptionally fast learner. He'd shared a bed with me and kept his hands to himself. He'd brought me coffee. He'd probably located the entrance to Morgan's secret room, too. He was perfect, and if he didn't get out of my face soon, I was going to end up kissing him.

"Are you okay?" he asked, lowering the little paper cone of fries.

"I'm fine." I bit out the words.

"Oh. You're *fine.*" Ved was unfamiliar with human food like burgers and coffee, but apparently the air-quote concept and voice had transcended the boundary between the Fae and humankind.

"I am. I am fine. You should go hang with your new best bro or glare at Morgan or go lift some weights or whatever it is that's not following me around like—" I froze. *Salty.* "Where's S—Muffin?"

I spun around, searching the floor around me, up and down the hallway, tracing the path I'd walked back through the main room to the patio door, but Salty wasn't there. Ved started back down the hall, and I followed, calling out the nickname that Ved had given her, even though I didn't think she would actually respond.

But she did. Ved and I followed the bark around the corner and up the steps into the dining room, only to find Salty sitting at the feet of Justin Lee. With the expensive leather duffle bag slung over his shoulder, his expertly tousled dark-brown hair, and the sleeves of his button-down rolled up, he looked like he'd just stepped out of a Calvin Klein poster.

"Hannah?" His eyebrows shot up when he saw me.

I smoothed my hands over my dress and smiled. *Shit.* How had I missed his name on the guest list? "Hey, Justin. How are you?"

"Great! Is this your dog?"

Ved stepped forward and scooped up Salty. I silently thanked the elements that he had glamoured his ears so they appeared human. Then I noticed that the amulet Bryn gave him was glowing through the fabric of his shirt.

I blinked at Justin, searching his head for horns, even though my brain refused to believe that this ex-costar of Brady's who I'd met at last year's party and then dated for a few months could possibly be a demon.

"She's Ash's dog, actually." I took a tentative step forward. "Ash, this is Justin. Justin, Ash."

Justin held out his hand. Ved glanced at it, hesitating before seeming to crush Justin's long fingers in his strong grip.

"Hey. Nice to meet you." Justin smiled. The way he was studying Ved's features, he appeared to be sizing Ved up and trying to figure out if he'd seen his face anywhere. Either that or he was a demon, and he could see right through Ved's glamour. Regardless of which it was, I could tell Justin was trying to determine what Ved was doing at Morgan's party.

Since Ved couldn't lie, that left me to explain. I forced a hopefully convincing smile. "Ash is my boyfriend."

Justin looked at me, then back at Ash. "Boyfriend. Wow. That's...new."

Internally, I cringed. I heard what he wasn't saying because I remembered what I'd said when I was breaking things off with him. I didn't have time for a boyfriend. It was true then, and it was still true, but I couldn't explain that to him. I had to maintain appearances.

"Yeah. It just sort of happened." I stepped closer to Ved and linked my arm through his before continuing the polite small talk that I was in no mood for. "How have you been?"

"Um. Fine. Good. I've got a new movie coming out next year." Justin looked past my shoulder toward the main room.

"Is Morgan around? I should probably let her know I'm here and get settled."

"She was out on the patio with Brady. They were just finishing up lunch." I glanced through the wall of glass that separated the table inside the dining room, where we stood, from its mirror image on the other side of the glass, but Morgan and Brady were no longer there. "I didn't hear them come inside, so maybe they're over by the pool?"

"Great. I'll just poke my head outside and check." Justin adjusted the strap on his bag, shifting the weight on his shoulder. "See you later?"

"Definitely. I want to hear more about that movie." My eyes followed him down the steps.

I could tell I'd hurt Justin, but I couldn't apologize, at least not in front of Ved, and it wasn't like my big Fae bodyguard was going to leave me alone anytime soon. Especially not if Justin were actually a demon.

We hadn't even been at Morgan's house for a full day, and already I'd had enough. I was supposed to be enjoying this weekend that I'd been anticipating for so long. But Morgan had ruined everything by lying to me and nearly killing me with her magic. And now that my big career break was here, instead of savoring it with my best friend, I just wanted to get it over with.

I let go of Ved's arm and stared at the lump under the collar of his shirt. "Your amulet was glowing."

He looked down. "Really?"

I gestured toward the place where Justin had been standing. "Did you notice anything?"

"On that guy? No." Ved's eyes narrowed. "Who was he, anyway?"

"He was Brady's costar in that show..." I started to explain before I remembered that Fae didn't watch serial dramas. "Never mind."

"I'm not stupid. I gathered that he was some sort of movie star or something." Ved's eyes narrowed as he studied my face. "What was he to you?"

I groaned. "Nothing. We went on a few dates. That was it."

Ved scowled. "Didn't seem like nothing to him."

"Whatever." I lifted Salty out of his arms. "I'm going to our room to text Willow and relax for a little bit. Alone. Can you...I don't know...find somewhere else to be for a little while?"

"I don't think—"

I held up my hand. "I don't care. You can watch me walk down the hall. You can watch the door while I'm in there, if you want. But I need some time by myself."

I didn't wait for him to answer before stomping down the steps and turning into the hallway toward our room. I didn't look to see if he was watching. I didn't want to know. I had work to do, and I wasn't going to let him, or anyone, get in my way.

I watched Hannah walk down the hallway and into our room. She was right. She was safe in there, but she also hadn't given me a chance to tell her about Firrag. It would be a lot easier if at least one of us could identify which of the guests were demons. If the antidote Bryn gave me was preventing me from being able to see through their glamour, then she needed that truth sight.

I started down the hall toward our room. Then I reconsidered and circled back to the main room. I thought about sitting down in that chair with a view of the hallway and pretending to read, but more guests were starting to arrive.

Morgan opened the patio door and stepped inside, laughing with Brady and that Justin guy. Her good mood fizzled when she spotted me. "Where's Hannah?"

"She went to our room. She'll be back in a bit." I shoved my hands into my pockets.

Brady put an arm around Morgan. "Hey, I was just going to take Justin down to my office and show him this new project I'm working on. You want to come? You have to swear not to say anything to anyone about it until it's all officially announced, though."

I glanced at Justin and noted that he didn't seem particularly thrilled by the idea of me joining them. "I was just going to hang out here and wait for Hannah."

"No, man. That's lame. Come hang out with us. Justin's going to go drop his bag in the bunk room, then he'll meet us down there. Right, J?"

Morgan slipped out from under Brady's arm. "I think I'm going to skip this so that I'm available to greet the guests, but you guys go have fun."

"All right, babe. I promise we won't be long. I just want to show J that he's not the only one with a soon-to-be block-buster in the works." Brady caught Morgan around the waist and gave her a quick kiss. "Do I have the best wife ever, or what?"

Morgan fought the smile that was forming. She held out her hand. "Phone, please."

"Right." Brady dug into his pocket and extracted a slim, rectangular device. "Here you go."

Morgan turned to me. "I am going to assume that you don't have one of these?"

I shook my head. "No phone."

Justin squinted at me as he handed Morgan a device nearly identical to Brady's. "You don't have a phone? Who are you?"

Brady saved me from answering. He slapped Justin on the shoulder. "Come on, man. Hurry up. Go drop your bag off. You're lucky you're the first one to arrive. Let's do this before someone else shows up."

Justin started down the hall to the guest wing, and Brady waved me toward the stairs. "Let's go get something to drink."

"Hang on a sec." Morgan's voice made me pause. "I'd like a word with Ash. Go on down. He'll be there in just a minute."

Brady shrugged and took off down the stairs.

Once he was gone, and Justin was out of earshot, Morgan said, "I noticed that you've glamoured those ears of yours, Ash. Should I take that to mean that you'd prefer our guests didn't know about your heritage?"

"It sounds like some of your guests may notice what I am, glamour or not."

"True."

"Then I suppose we should leave my identity to the observant."

Morgan shrugged. "Have it your way." She started toward the dining room, then paused. "Oh, and because I don't want to fight with Brady, I've decided to allow you access to the paved areas outdoors. But, set one foot out of bounds, and you're out. Got it?"

"Understood."

"Good. Also? Just so you know, your shirt is glowing." Morgan pointed at my neck, then stalked up the steps into the dining room and disappeared around the corner.

I waited until I was sure that she was gone before tugging the amulet out. I stared down at it. That was twice, at least, that I'd missed the signal. What good was a demon-alert charm if you had to wear it around your neck where you couldn't see it?

I untied the leather strap and wrapped it around my wrist, crisscrossing the ends and looping them around a second time until there was just enough left to tie a knot. The only problem was I couldn't tie a knot one-handed.

I was still standing there struggling with the loose ends when Justin returned.

"Hey. I thought you went with Brady?"

"I got a bit delayed." I glanced down at the amulet I was attempting to secure to my wrist. It wasn't glowing. "I should be on my way down there now, but I could use a little help. You mind?"

Justin walked over to where I was holding the ends of the necklace pinned to my wrist. "Sure. You just want me to tie a regular knot?"

"That would be great. Thanks." I released my grip on the ends of the necklace.

"So, how did you and Hannah meet?" Justin tied the ends together. He tugged on them, then asked, "Too tight?"

"No. That's great." I examined his work. The amulet still wasn't glowing. I hoped I didn't have to be wearing it around my neck for it to work. Since I couldn't exactly test it out until I found myself a for-sure demon, which apparently wasn't Justin, I shoved my hands back into my pockets and ignored it. "I met Hannah through one of her friends."

"So, you haven't known each other long?" He started toward the stairs.

I followed. "No. She mentioned that you two dated for a bit."

He turned his head to grin at me. "Before or after you met me?"

"After." I laughed.

"Yeah. Sounds like Hannah. She's great, but...well, I was just surprised to hear her call you her boyfriend. You guys must have some kind of insta-hot connection or something. We dated for months, and she still refused to use that word."

I didn't know how to respond. I knew she was lying about our relationship, but still. She'd introduced me to this guy as her boyfriend. Part of me wanted to roar with triumph, the other part wanted to pound this guy into a wall. Neither reaction made any sense. How could I be jealous of a guy for having a relationship with a woman I hadn't so much as kissed?

That swirl of confused thoughts ended when he asked if I was a model.

I snorted. "No."

"I feel like I've seen your face somewhere before. You must have been in something I've seen, but I can't think of what it was." He paused at the door to Brady's office. "I'm going to feel like such a fool when you tell me."

"Hey, what is taking you two so long? Get in here and shut the door!" Brady's eagerness saved me from having to explain that I hadn't been in anything and he was most likely mistaking me for someone else. Someone actually famous.

Brady's office had a similar view as the gym, which made sense because they were right next to each other and on the same side of the house. I wasn't sure why he called it an office, though. The room looked more like a smaller version of the main room upstairs. There wasn't even a desk.

Brady was lounging on one of the large brown leather chairs clustered in the middle of the room. He had his feet up on a low table that also held a large silver bucket filled with ice and glass bottles. Once we were inside with the door closed, Brady pushed a button and shades rolled down to cover the wall of windows overlooking the city.

"Grab a drink and take a seat." Brady pointed a remote at a wall covered with a series of framed posters, each featuring a younger version of Brady and Justin along with a young woman. In some of them, Brady and Justin faced off while the woman stood in the background. In others, she was at the center and they glared at each other behind her back. As a screen descended from the ceiling, blocking the view, my eyes found a favorite. In that one, all three were riding dragons and brandishing swords with the woman leading Brady and Justin.

"Who's that?" I asked.

"Kayla," both men said at the same time with slightly different tones. Brady sounded almost nostalgic, while Justin sounded like his familiar had just died.

"Have you seen her lately?" Brady asked Justin.

Justin frowned. "She auditioned for the movie I'm in."

"Did she get it?"

Justin shook his head.

"Too bad."

"Yeah..." His voice trailed off before he resumed with renewed enthusiasm. "But wait until you see—"

Brady waved a hand. "In a minute. My house, so I get to go first. Come on and sit."

The glow from a projector hidden in the wall opposite the screen was the only light in the room, but it was enough to catch the grimace on Justin's face. I glanced at the bits of the first and last poster, just visible behind the screen but now cast in shadow, searching for a hint about the strange dynamic I sensed between these two guys and the woman on the posters.

Justin and I slid into the chairs on either side of Brady.

Justin leaned forward and grabbed a bottle out of the bucket. He offered it to me. When I shook my head, he shrugged and popped off the metal cap.

"All right, bro. Let's see what you've been up to." Justin sat back in his chair and took a long sip from the bottle.

"Okay, Jeannie, roll tape." Brady spoke the words out into the room.

I glanced around to confirm there wasn't anyone else in the room, confused about whom he was speaking to.

"AI assistant. I named her after that old sitcom." Brady grinned. Then his mouth scrunched as he attempted to wiggle his nose.

I stared at him, still confused.

He shrugged and pointed at the screen. "Check it out."

A series of colored blocks appeared on the screen, followed by a close-up of Brady's face. As the camera panned outward, the orange swirl behind his head began to resolve into some sort of fire coming from an old wooden building. Screen Brady scowled into the distance as he put a cowboy hat on his head.

The bits of film had been roughly cut together without any narration to explain what was going on. I was enjoying making up my own story in my head to explain the bizarre series of clips that included aliens and vampires as well as some sort of space travel and a lot of longing looks between various pairings of actors. I was trying to determine if Brady's character was lusting after the male vampire decked out in space-age battle armor or if that was supposed to be his enemy when a face I recognized appeared on the screen.

It was only for a moment. So fast that I nearly missed her. But there in the back of a shot from the cockpit of a spaceship was Nigel's mother, the succubus who had managed to rally the heads of all the demon clans to join her fight to steal Earth's magic from the Fae.

I set my hands on the broad leather armrests and leaned forward in my chair. Out of the corner of my eye, my amulet started glowing. At first, I thought it had something to do with Lilium's appearance on the screen, but that didn't make any sense. Then something moved in the corner near the window. My eyes fixed on it.

What came into focus caused a rumbling growl to form low in my throat. Justin and Brady both turned to me, but I wasn't going to let that little demon out of my sight. With the supernatural speed of a Dragon Fae on the hunt, I leapt out of my chair and across the table. That demon, or one who looked nearly identical, had slipped from my grasp once in Hannah's apartment. I wasn't about to let it happen a second time.

As my fingers wrapped around the demon's neck, Brady started laughing so hard he nearly fell out of his chair. Justin just sat there with his mouth wide open, staring at me.

"Got you," I whispered to the little demon.

The demon blinked up at me, smiled, and disappeared.

"What. Was. That?" Justin asked.

Brady wiped his eyes. "That was epic, bro."

"Where did it go?" I spun around, searching the dark corners of the room.

"No. Seriously." Justin scooted forward in his chair. "What was that thing?"

"Chaos demon." Brady shrugged. "You'll get used to it. The house is practically infested with them these days."

Someone knocked on the door, and Brady groaned. "Okay, Jeannie, tape off and reset."

The images on the screen stopped, then disappeared. The

screen retracted into the ceiling, and the shades began to lift.

"Come in," Brady called.

The door opened, and three guys walked in. One tall and lean, one of medium height with a more muscular build, and one short and wiry. Behind them trailed the little chaos demon.

9

THE High Court had met. Nigel was on his way. My camera batteries were all charged and ready to go, and it was time to get out there and mingle with the guests. The only problem was, Ved had actually left me alone, like I asked. I was starting to feel a little bad about how I'd treated him, especially after Firrag showed up at the window trying to get my attention.

"What's up, buddy? Something wrong?" I asked after opening the window.

Ved had removed the screen at some point, but Firrag still refused to come inside. I couldn't say I blamed her.

Firrag cocked her head at me and lifted up one leg. She stretched her talons toward me, then set it down again on the branch where she'd perched.

"I don't have a message for you. I just used my phone." I held up the device, only then remembering that I was supposed to bring it back to Morgan.

I glanced down at the screen. Max had given me instructions about how to secure the device, just in case Morgan had someone who could hack into my phone. Not that there was anything there to retrieve. Still, I ran through the list of steps I'd jotted down in my notebook. Then I extracted my data card and slipped it into a secure pocket in my camera case. I powered the device down and slid it into my back pocket before returning to the window.

"I suppose I should go find Ved now, huh?"

Firrag stretched her talons toward me again.

"What are you trying to say?" I looked around to see what she might be pointing at, but there wasn't much else in the room besides our clothes and my camera equipment. My eyes landed on the empty basket of muffins and scones. "I should probably take that back to the kitchen, huh?"

Firrag squawked when I looked inside the basket.

"There's nothing left." I held my hands out, palms up.

Firrag stretched her talons out a third time.

I walked closer, extending one of my arms toward her, very slowly. I couldn't remember what Ved had warned me about trying to touch the little faerie dragon. Was I supposed to reach out with my palm up or down?

Firrag watched me from her perch. She didn't snap her beak or back away, so I continued reaching toward her. Then, when my fingers were almost touching her chest feathers, she swiped at my hand with her talons.

I pulled my hand back. Sure enough, there were three welts striped across my palm. As I watched, the middle one started to bleed.

"Ouch." I sucked on my hand. "I thought we were friends. What did you do that for?"

Firrag blinked her vertical eyelids at me and bobbed her head.

I had no idea what that was supposed to mean, but my hand was still bleeding. "I should probably wash this out."

Firrag cooed and squawked and danced on the branch, flapping her wings.

"Fine. All right. I won't wash it. But I can't just be bleeding on everything." I dug around in my bag until I located the little first-aid and mending kit that I always kept in my suitcase. I found a bandage to cover the section that was bleeding and managed to get it stuck on with only one hand.

"There." I held my hand up for her to see. "Happy now?"

Firrag cooed, then took off, circling high in the sky.

I watched her go until I could barely see her against the bright sky. I sighed. "Weirdo."

After one more look at my hand, where the blood from the scratch marks was already starting to dry, I checked my makeup and my outfit, grabbed my camera bag, and left everything else. I'd ask Ved about whatever just happened with Firrag and then wash my hands in one of the guest bathrooms and toss the Band-Aid.

But first, I had to find him. He wasn't in the main room or anywhere on that floor, inside or out, but I spotted Morgan out by the pool with a few of the eager early-arriving guests. One of them was at the top of my list of people I wanted to convince to do an interview with me.

Morgan spotted me and waved. She yelled something about karaoke and told me to find Brady and tell him to get everyone out onto the patio. I gave her a thumbs-up. Then I held up my phone and made a show of sliding it into the locked black box that she'd set on a table next to the patio door.

Once that was done, I hurried back inside. In addition to the million other reasons I needed to find Ved, I wanted to apologize before everyone else arrived and things really started to get busy. While I was looking for him, I'd keep an eye out for Brady so I could deliver Morgan's message.

I made my way downstairs and found it to be nearly empty. That's when I started to worry that maybe Morgan had found a way to kick Ved out while we were separated. My heart started racing, and I scolded myself for letting my guard down.

I sped past a couple who had already found a dark corner where they probably thought they could have a private moment. The lights were out in the gym, and the door to Brady's office was closed, but there was a light on in the game room. I cracked the door open and poked my head inside where I was greeted with hysterical laughter.

I stepped inside to get a better look at the occupants and see if any of them happened to be my missing Dragon Fae. Or rather, the Dragon Fae who was supposed to be guarding me. He wasn't mine, I reminded myself. But he was there, so I relaxed.

"Here you are. I've been looking all over for you." I took a step closer to the poker table, where Ved was laughing it up with three nearly humanoid demons, while a fourth, smaller one with pink-orange skin lurked near the pool table.

Ved turned his head toward me and waved me over. "Oh, hey! Sorry. I made some new friends. Come over, and I'll introduce you."

I let my eyes flick down to the collar of the Henley he had chosen from the stack of clothes Bryn brought, but he wasn't wearing the amulet. It wasn't until he moved his hand on the table that I spotted it wrapped around his wrist and glowing. I wondered if he even realized that he was playing cards with a bunch of demons. It wasn't like they were hiding their horns. If I could see them, then he must be able to as well.

I stopped close to Ved, making sure to position myself so that the littlest demon wasn't behind me. I didn't like the look of its mischievous grin. Then I turned my attention to the ones sitting at the table, greeting them with a small wave and a polite smile.

"Guys, this is Hannah. Hannah, this is Never, Ever, and Nope." He pointed to each of the demons in turn.

I was surprised that these were faces that I recognized, without the horns, of course. The names Ved had used to introduce us didn't match the ones I knew, the ones that were also listed on the guest list. The demon that Ved had called Never had a huge following in the online gaming community. The one he'd called Nope ran a small start-up that Max had been trying to buy for the past year. And the shortest one of the bunch, the one that Ved had called Ever, had played a bit part in the television show that made Brady famous. I shrugged off the obvious nicknames as another Ved demon superstition thing and decided to follow his lead.

Ever was so busy counting the enormous pile of chips in front of him that he didn't look up right away. But I was pretty sure that Never recognized me because he flashed me a sly grin and nudged Ever, prompting the smaller demon to lose count and hiss at his larger friend.

Nope looked over at me and said, "Hey." Then he returned to shuffling the cards. If he knew who I was, he didn't show it.

"You guys seem to be having a good time," I said.

Ved nodded. "Oh, yeah, and I almost forgot to introduce Bins, over there. He doesn't like poker."

Never and Ved started cackling again, Nope and Ever just grinned. Whatever the joke was, I'd missed it.

I placed one hand on Ved's shoulder. "Morgan is trying to rally everyone for karaoke."

"Oooh. Yeessss." Bins crept closer to the table. "Let's sing."

Never groaned. He eyed Ever's stack of chips. "Let's play another round first."

Nope tapped the deck of cards on the table. "You know what would be fun?"

Ever glanced at the littlest demon and grinned the most impish grin I'd ever seen on any creature. "Shots."

"Karaoke is always better with a little chaos." Nope aligned the cards into a neat stack, then pushed it, facedown, toward the center of the table.

The stack of cards disappeared, and four small glasses on a small wooden tray appeared in its place. The clustered glasses began to fill with a bright-pink liquid. A shiver ran down my spine. I squeezed Ved's shoulder, but he ignored me and reached for one of the glasses.

"What's this?" he asked.

"Chaos brew." Ever giggled. "Bottoms up if you want to be a karaoke star."

"Is it liquor?" I'd never seen pink liquor before, and I was pretty sure this was some sort of potion, but I hoped I was wrong.

Never reached for a glass. "No. This is a specialty of our friend Bins, here."

"What does it do?" I asked, willing Ved to put the glass down and back away from the table.

Nope, the only one who hadn't picked up a glass, tilted backward in his chair until the front two legs lifted up off the floor. He folded his hands behind his head. "Makes you want to sing."

"And dance!" Ever cackled.

"How long does it take to kick in?" Ved asked, staring down at the glowing pink fluid he was busy swirling around the inside of the glass.

"Depends." Never tilted his head back, poured the contents into his mouth, and swallowed. He set the empty glass down on the table with a thunk. "Who else is in?"

Ever sipped from his glass as Nope leaned forward. He picked up the last glass and stood. "I'm waiting until we get up there."

"Don't let Morgan see you," Never said, falling into step with Nope. "You know she hates it when we cheat."

Ever took another sip, set his half-full glass on the table, then hurried after the other two demons. The little pink-orange demon disappeared.

"Ved. Don't drink that." I reached for the hand holding the glass, but he moved it away.

"Why not?" He turned his face toward me. "I thought you didn't need me hovering around you all the time. What does it matter if I have a little fun?"

"I'm sorry, okay. I shouldn't have said that. We're a team. I was a jerk. Just...those guys were demons. Didn't you notice? You have no idea what's in that glass or what it will do to you."

"Entug demons. I know." He looked at the glass in his hand. "They drank it. How bad could it be?"

"What if you're allergic?" I asked.

He glanced up at me, tilted the glass to his lips, and swallowed the pink stuff. "Then I guess we'll find out."

I ripped the glass from his hand. "What are you doing?"

Ved stood. He closed the distance between us, lifted the glass out of my hand, and set it on the table. "I need them to trust me. Just like I need you to trust me."

"And you think this is going to help?"

"It's just chaos." He shrugged, grinning. "How bad could it be?"

"I guess we're about to find out." I waved a hand toward the door.

Ved caught my hand and turned it palm up between us. He lifted the edge of the Band-Aid to look beneath. "What happened?"

"Firrag scratched me."

"Oh!" Ved's eyes met mine. "Good!" He peeled the Band-Aid off and crumpled it up.

"Good?" I stared down at my hand, but the scratch mark had disappeared.

"Yeah. Damir sent a message. Faerie dragon venom has some sort of truth serum in it?" He slid the pad of his thumb across my palm. "That's probably how you knew those guys were demons."

"I just thought they weren't bothering with a glamour, but I guess maybe you're right. What is up with the little one with the orange-pink skin and big floppy ears?"

"That's a chaos demon. Like the one that was at your apartment, though Morgan called that one Sledge, and the one who was here is called Bins." He shook his head. "Brady said the house is crawling with them."

"Weird. I wonder why?"

"That's what I've been trying to figure out." Ved rolled his shoulders. He tilted his head from one side to the other like he was trying to loosen up some muscles in his neck. "I think I feel a song coming on. Maybe we should get upstairs."

Of course, I didn't trust the demons. I may not have been able to see through their glamours—whatever antidote Fiona's Hands had brewed up to minimize my demon allergies came with an annoying side effect that completely dulled any sense of their magic or their true forms—but the amulet helped. They knew that I knew what they were.

After I'd tried to strangle their little friend and Brady stopped laughing, he remembered he was supposed to be greeting guests upstairs. Justin also found an excuse to be elsewhere, leaving me alone with the lot of them. At first, I'd thought it was a coincidence, but every time I tried to leave and return to our room or try to find Hannah, they found another excuse to keep me with them a bit longer. Once I realized that they had probably been sent, on purpose, to keep Hannah and me apart, I dropped the charade and started asking more direct questions.

"Turns out that the Entug demon clan is at the lower end of the newly united demon clan hierarchy," I explained to Hannah as we made our way back upstairs. "According to my new friends, the Goriston clan and the Fendal clan are at the top. But, given their difficult to disguise demon features, they weren't invited to Morgan's party.

"The Entugs were perfectly happy about that because their clan shares a realm with the Goristons, and the Goriston clan has been trying to crush the Entug, whom they see as competition for scarce resources. The Entug are weaker than the Goristons, so that wasn't working out well for them until they found their way here.

"In this realm, the Baylord clan, which apparently rules Hollywood, took the Entug under their wing. The Entugs don't want to return to their realm. They want to get what's left of their clan—the ones that are still stuck there—here and convince the Goristons to go home. They seem to think that they'll be able to negotiate that once they've successfully helped the other clans defeat the Fae."

"They told you all this? Even though they knew you're Fae?" Hannah sounded surprised.

I shrugged. "They were apologizing. Said they didn't have anything against me or my kin. It wasn't personal. They were just trying to survive."

"How...thoughtful of them?" Hannah shook her head.

"I get it. There are Fae factions scattered all around this world. The Dragon Fae don't get along with all of them. Any of them, come to think about it. Not until Damir brought me to Fiona and begged for her help. And he only did that hoping that it would mean something to her that their mothers were sisters. Hells, from what I understand from the brief time I spent among Fiona's alliance of Forest Fae, those factions don't all agree or get along. I get the impression that the High Fae are holding on to Fiona's throne with the claws and talons of their animal forms and not much else."

"High Fae can shift into animal forms?"

I nodded. "Usually predators. But each one develops a different form. No two who walk the earth at the same time are ever the same. It's not like our clan." I glanced over at her. "You don't know much about Fae, do you?"

Hannah paused at the top of the stairs. "Why would I? They left us to fend for ourselves and retreated to the forest centuries ago."

"Well, as much as I hate to admit it, Morgan may be right about the demon clans. The Entugs also said the Baylord clan only agreed to join Lilium's alliance because they believe she kidnapped their king." I rubbed a hand against my throat. "Where is that music coming from?"

Hannah glanced around. "Music? I can't hear anything.

But it looks like there are a lot of people out by the pool. Maybe that's where it's coming from."

I hummed a few bars of something. Not a song I knew, but something. Then I grabbed Hannah's hand and pulled her outside.

As soon as we stepped out onto the deck, whatever song was playing grew louder. The sound resonated in my bones and made my feet want to tap out a beat. Never, the largest of the Entug demons, stood on a platform next to the pool, gripping a black cylinder in his hand that was somehow amplifying his voice.

"Wow." Hannah stared at Never with wide eyes. "That guy can sing."

Ever slid up next to Hannah and whispered, "Chaos brew."

She jumped, closing the distance between us. I put an arm around her. "How does it work?"

Ever cackled. "You'll know when you know."

He slid through the guests who were clapping and swaying along with the music, cheering as Never held a long, low note. Then Ever disappeared for a moment in the crowd. He resurfaced at the foot of the platform, climbed up next to Never, and started dancing. At first, it was just a frantic motion of hips and arms, then it turned into something that moved with the music, picking up where the lyrics in Never's song trailed off and filling the gap until Nope hopped up on stage and took over from Never.

The guests whooped and hollered, loving every minute of it. Their energy charged something inside me. A vibration was building, and an instinct told me to go up there and take the black cylinder from Nope. It was an impulse, and part of me warned that being impulsive got me in trouble. But I suddenly couldn't resist the urge to sing.

I let my arm slip from Hannah's shoulders and started forward.

"Where are you going?" Hannah asked.

I didn't respond. My focus had narrowed to fixate on the platform and the cylinder and the song that was building inside me. Hannah tried to grab my hand and pull me back, but I evaded her and continued to make my way toward Nope.

He spotted me and grinned before belting out the final line of lyrics. He bowed as the music faded. Ever did a little jig, then took a running jump off the platform directly into the pool. Everyone clapped and cheered.

I reached for the black cylinder that Nope held out to me, then I stepped up onto the platform. Never whispered something to the woman wearing headphones at the back of the stage, then he and Nope retreated into the crowd, leaving me up there alone. My fingertips pulsed against the smooth black metal. I stared down at the domed mesh end and took a breath.

A heartbeat later, what I assumed to be the chaos magic surged through me. The first few notes of a simple guitar melody repeated. I didn't recognize the song, but it didn't matter. I opened my mouth and a line of lyrics tumbled out. They weren't my words, but they were sung in my voice, and they were tumbling out of some place in the center of my chest.

Morgan's guests sucked in a breath after that first line. After the first few lines, I leaned into the words, swaying my hips in time to the rhythm. I found Hannah's eyes at the back of the crowd, and suddenly the words started to make sense. All the longing and the tension that had built up between us curled out as lyrics to a song I'd never heard before but that made perfect sense to me in that moment.

Maybe I should stop. I couldn't stop. The beat sped up, and my words along with it. The crowd jumped up and down, cheering and singing along with the chorus. But I barely saw them. I kept my eyes locked on Hannah, not that I had much choice. The chaos magic had its grip on me, and at the same time, none of it was a lie.

That little shot of potion had erased my inhibitions and, along with them, released the one thing that was certain to make a complete mess of the situation I'd found myself in. But it didn't matter. There was nothing holding me back from making a complete fool of myself for this water wizard in front of everyone. And somehow, I didn't care.

My eyes locked with Hannah's as I repeated what I somehow knew were the final lines of the song, building to that last note. Morgan's guests had figured out whom I was singing to back during the chorus and parted to make a path between Hannah and me. They kept glancing back and forth between us, but I barely noticed. There was only me and Hannah and the words I was repeating. She wrapped her arms around her waist as the song ended, and the crowd turned to stare at her.

As that final note lingered in the air, I set the cylinder down and jumped off the platform, walking through the guests on the path they'd made for me, directly to Hannah. The effects of the potion were starting to wear off now that the song was over, but it still had a grip on me. I stopped in front of Hannah, took her hand, and twirled her around, only to catch her and dip her over my arm. As the last of the chaos drained out of me, I leaned over and kissed her.

To my surprise, she kissed me back. Her hands slid up my shoulders and wrapped around the back of my neck. My hand splayed against the small of her back as I pressed her more firmly against me. The other hand cupped the back of her head, buried in her soft hair.

I'd almost forgotten that we were surrounded by people. Then everyone started clapping.

My eyes blinked open as my lips separated from hers, only to find that her eyelids were still shut and her lips still parted. For a moment, I wondered if maybe she hadn't been pretending. Was it possible that she'd wanted to kiss me as much as I'd wanted to kiss her? Unfortunately, this wasn't the place to try to find out.

I lifted Hannah back to standing, our bodies still pressed together. The music had started again. Someone else had started singing, taking some of the attention off of us.

Hannah's hands slid down to rest against my chest. "You can sing."

"Your turn?" I suggested with a grin, trying to make light of the situation, even though I had no interest in letting her go now that she was in my arms. I wanted to forget about everything we were sent here to do, lift her up, and carry her back to our room.

"I don't think so. You've heard me sing, remember? I can't do that." She lifted her chin toward the platform behind me.

I hadn't forgotten about her shower duet with Firrag. If she weren't interested in singing in public, maybe she would consider going back to the room. We could try a different sort of duet. "I was thinking—"

A voice nearby interrupted before I could finish that thought. "Hannah? Your friends are here."

Brady walked up to us, followed by a dark-haired and scowling Nigel wearing his usual tailored suit. Beside him was a lean, muscular woman with close-cropped hair.

Hannah took a step away from me. I released her from my arms but caught her hand in mine. She surprised me again by not pulling away.

"Uh, hi!" Hannah waved at the couple with her free hand.

Salty ran up to Nigel and the Fae woman. She wagged her tail as she danced around their feet.

Brady slapped me on the shoulder, distracting me. "Hey, man, I missed it, but everyone's talking about your performance. Sounds like it was epic!"

I needed to get rid of him because I could tell that Hannah didn't recognize Nigel, and I had no idea who this Fae female was other than that she was definitely one of the Faerie Queen's Guard. Introductions would be awkward since Brady expected that Hannah already knew them.

"Thanks. You should get up there and try it." I nudged him toward the platform where a beautiful woman was belting out the lyrics to a heartbreaking song.

Brady nodded. "I'm on my way over there now. Stick around and check it out."

"I cannot believe I agreed to this," Nigel said after Brady left. "There are demons everywhere, and one of them is almost certainly going to recognize me."

I turned to Hannah. "This is Nigel."

"Oh! Right." Hannah's posture relaxed. "I should have guessed. Thanks for coming."

"It appears they sent you with your own bodyguard," I added, nodding to the Fae female.

"Yes." Nigel gestured to his companion, who was too busy scanning the crowd to pay any attention to us. "Have you met Brianne? Not the first time she's been assigned to keep an eye on me."

Brianne waved a hand at us, but her attention was on the woman singing. "Fendal," she said.

I glanced down at my wrist. Sure enough, my amulet was glowing. Which made sense because I was standing next to a half demon. This demon allergy thing was getting increasingly frustrating. How was I supposed to keep Hannah safe if I couldn't identify which of the guests were demons?

Hannah blinked at the platform. "Is she...half snake?"

Nigel grimaced. "Yes. I really shouldn't be here."

Hannah set a hand on Nigel's sleeve. "Let's find Morgan. After you talk some sense into her, get out of here. We've got it under control."

Nigel raised an eyebrow as his eyes flicked between us, lingering on our joined hands. "Yes, you two really are selling it, aren't you?"

Hannah tried to slip her hand out of my grip. I let it go but moved closer so I could put my arm around her shoulders instead.

Nigel's eyes focused on my wrist. "What's that?"

I followed his gaze to the glowing amulet now resting on Hannah's shoulder. "Demon-alert bracelet. The wizards made it for me to compensate for side effects from the anti-allergy potion."

Nigel leaned forward to study it. "Interesting. I have one just like it, but mine must be broken."

"I think I see Morgan over there." Hannah pointed toward a cluster of lounge chairs along one side of the pool. The group was close enough to hear the singers but far enough away that their chatter wasn't distracting from the performances.

Hannah looked at me. "You can stay here if you want to watch Brady."

"I'm not leaving you alone again," I said, keeping my voice low. I didn't want a lecture from Nigel or Brianne, or any questions about why I'd let Hannah go off by herself.

Maybe it was because of their presence, but Hannah didn't argue. She just nodded, then started toward Morgan, pausing only to let me take her hand and to make sure that Nigel and Salty were both following.

10

NIGEL was right. There were demons everywhere. Now that I could see them because of whatever venom was in Firrag's talons, I couldn't help but agree that this place was not safe. Not for him, and probably not for me or Ved. That was enough of a shock by itself, but then there was Ved's voice, singing to me up on that stage. Singing about how it would be all right if we let go and took it way too far.

Just the thought of it sent a shiver down my spine. And that kiss. I could not think about that kiss. I needed to stay focused on Morgan. Convince her to talk with Nigel and then get Nigel out of here before something terrible happened.

Ved mentioned that Nigel had been spying on the demons for the Fae. If the demons knew that, and if anyone here recognized him... I didn't want to think about it. He was taking a huge risk on the small chance that Morgan might come around.

"Hannah!" One of the women who had been sitting with Morgan bounced up from her chair and gave me a hug. It was

Lexie. The actress at the top of my list for possible collabs.

"Hi!" I hugged her back like we were friends, even though I'd only met her once, briefly, at last year's party. Justin had introduced us. If I remembered correctly, she was friends with Kayla.

Lexie tucked a curl behind her ear and grinned at me. Her brown skin glistened in the afternoon sun. "I'm so excited that you're here. I really want to do one of those 'what's in my bag' features with you. What do you think?"

I tried not to gape at her. Lexie Robbins wanted to work with me, and I didn't even have to ask her. "Of course! That sounds great."

I clutched the strap of my camera bag just to make sure it was still there. Then I glanced over at Morgan and back at Nigel before returning my attention to Lexie. "Let me just introduce Morgan to my friends, and then we can work out the details. Okay?"

Lexie's eyes slid past me to Ved. "Maybe you can introduce me, too?"

I groaned. Of course. It wasn't me she was interested in. It was the swoon-worthy guy who had been singing his heart out to me. Apparently, I hadn't been the only one he'd charmed. "Sure."

Ved put his arm around my shoulder as Nigel stepped up alongside us. Brianne lingered behind him. Morgan tilted her head in my direction and slid her sunglasses down her nose so she could squint at Nigel over the top of them.

"Hello." Nigel stepped forward and extended his hand toward Morgan. "You must be Morgan."

Morgan took Nigel's hand and used it to steady herself as she set her feet on the ground and stood to face him. "You must be Hannah's friend. Nigel, was it?"

He smiled. "Indeed. Pleasure to meet you. I can't say how thrilled I was to receive an invitation. And on such short notice."

"A friend of Hannah's..." Morgan let her voice trail off.

"There was something I was hoping to discuss with you. Perhaps we could take a bit of a walk?" Nigel waved a hand toward the far side of the pool, away from the larger clusters of guests.

Morgan lifted her cocktail off the table and took a sip through the striped straw. "Let's do that."

Lexie and the other two women watched Morgan saunter away alongside Nigel. The three of them shared the same confused yet fascinated look as Brianne followed the pair, staying a few steps behind.

"Who is he? Some sort of agent?" Lexie asked.

"You could say that." Ved's low voice so close to my ear sent a spike of awareness to my core.

"That accent, though." The blond woman next to Lexie fanned herself. "Is he British?"

The petite Asian woman with the pink hair ignored her friend and shifted her attention to Ved. "I didn't know Hannah Vos had a boyfriend. Especially not one who can sing."

And I didn't know this pop star even knew who I was. I swallowed my fangirl moment so I could introduce her. "Ryko, this is Ash."

"And what do you do, Ash?" Lexie asked.

"Aside from Hannah." The blond woman whispered her remark, though not quite low enough to prevent us from hearing, which seemed to be her intention based on how she was giggling into her drink.

"Amber, would you mind getting us another round of drinks? It looks like we're out." Lexie drained the remaining liquid in her glass and held it out to the blond.

"I'm a bodyguard," Ved responded as Amber stalked away.

"That checks out." Lexie raised a perfectly shaped eyebrow. After a quick glance to make sure Amber was gone, she leaned in and rested the tips of her fingers on my arm. "Ignore her. My makeup bag is in my room, but I can grab it and be back out here before you're done setting up your camera, if you want to do this now."

I glanced over at Morgan and Nigel. They'd be talking for a while. I had some time, and this would give Ved and me an excuse to hang around and keep an eye on them. Plus, the sun was low enough in the sky that the lighting would be great. "Sounds perfect. I'll set up over here."

Ryko crossed her arms. "I want in on this. What are you doing?"

Lexie waved a hand. "Hannah does these segments where she talks about what's currently in her makeup bag, or she interviews a guest and they talk about what they're using. I have wanted to do one with her for so long," Lexie squealed. "Be right back."

I tried not to remain calm about the fact that one of my favorite actresses not only watched my videos but had been wanting to collab with me. Inside, my arms were flailing, and I was screaming like a preteen at a K-pop concert.

As Lexie ran off toward the house, Ryko eyed my camera. "When you're done with Lexie, do you want to film my turn at karaoke? I'm thinking I'm going to start with a fake-out cover of one of Neil's songs and then test out my new single."

I nodded. Rumors were flying around that Neil, who'd recently performed with Ryko at an awards show, was obsessed with her, but she was playing hard to get. Choosing one of his songs to cover was a genius maneuver to make sure that the post would go viral.

"Sure. It's probably not enough for my channel, unless you want to do an interview as well, but I can definitely post it to my social accounts," I said.

"I'd love to collab, but my agent will kill me if I let you have an interview without talking to him first, and you know how Morgan is about phones at her party." Ryko tossed her long ponytail over her shoulder.

"Totally understand." I unzipped my camera case and fiddled with the settings. "Let me just get a couple of teaser photos. Have a seat and look casual."

Ryko kicked back on a lounger just as Amber returned with a refresh on her drink. While Ryko posed, I found an angle that allowed me to get her in the foreground of the image with a blurry shot of the stage in the background.

After a couple of photos, Ved sat down next to the pool at the foot of her lounger and faced away from the camera like he was watching the performance. He was a natural. It made me want to kiss him again.

"This is great." I showed Ryko the pictures.

"Yes. I love it. You're good." Ryko glanced over at Ved. "So are you. Are you also a model or something?"

"Everyone seems to be asking me that. Maybe I should give it a try." Ved angled his chin up so that the sun highlighted his profile.

I couldn't help it. I snapped a few shots and didn't stop even after he turned his head to smile at me.

Ryko shielded her eyes with her hand so she could look up at him. "If you want, I'll get you a meeting with my agent. With that face and that voice, you could do more than model. Just ask Justin."

I'd forgotten that Justin had started off as a singer in one of those popular boy bands before he became Brady and Kayla's costar. As though fate were determined to remind me, Justin chose that moment to take the microphone on the karaoke stage.

"Speak of the devil." Ryko picked up her glass and swirled what was left at the bottom, which sounded like mostly ice. "Gone already? Damn. All of a sudden, I'm parched."

Up on the stage, Justin crooned into the microphone like it was his baby or his lover. His hips were swaying in preparation for the beat change. Then he broke into one of his routines as he sang the first chorus.

I'd forgotten how well he could dance. The post-karaoke compliment I'd given him last year had led to the conversation that had started whatever had happened between us and ended six months later, with me explaining it wasn't him, it was me. I expected to feel something watching him perform, but it was nothing like watching Ved.

He must have noticed me watching Justin's performance because he stepped in front of me and lifted the camera out of my hand. "You want me to film?"

I blinked at him. Did he mean Justin? I'd clearly forgotten what we were supposed to be doing.

I'd been thinking about that kiss and how I wanted to curl myself around my fake boyfriend again just to make sure I hadn't imagined that spark of something. And then there he was, in front of me. But he was talking about filming. Nothing made sense. Especially not this idea that was forming in my mind about taking Angie's advice and having a little fun.

Ved gestured toward the steps that led into the shallow end of the pool just a few feet away from where we stood. "If you two sit there, I can stand over here and get a pretty good shot with the city view in the background."

My brain snapped out of lust mode and back into work mode. The interview with Lexie. Ved had a good eye. As though it weren't enough that he could sing and sweep me off my feet with a scorching kiss, my fake boyfriend and very real Dragon Fae bodyguard was picking up this whole influencer-boyfriend thing like he was born behind a camera. And he hadn't once tried to tell me that I should be paying more attention to defeating the demons than to advancing my career.

I could get very used to this, if I weren't careful. "I like it. Good idea. Let me just—"

The crowd around the stage screamed their appreciation, swallowing the rest of my suggestion. I turned toward the performance to see what had caused all the commotion and realized that someone who looked a lot like Ryko had stepped onto the stage and was about to start some sort of dance-off with Justin.

I glanced over to where Ryko had been sitting to confirm that she wasn't there. "Shit."

I grabbed for the camera, but Ved already had it pointed at the stage, and the little red light was on, confirming that he was recording. "I've got it," he said.

Damn, he was good. I only had a moment to appreciate him before Salty nudged my ankle to get my attention. I bent down to see what she needed, and she bounded off toward the house, then circled back to me.

I glanced over at Nigel and Morgan, who were still talking at the far end of the pool. Their postures were relaxed. From this distance, it seemed like everything was fine, and they were standing in the opposite direction from where Salty waited for me.

Up on the stage, the song had just ended. Ryko and Justin

were hugging it out, and he was handing her the microphone with a deferential bow. Had she won, and I'd missed it? I guess I'd have to watch the video like one of my followers.

Ryko bent over to say something to the DJ, who grinned and nodded. Then the first few bars of Neil's hit single started, and I knew we couldn't leave now, regardless of what was bothering Salty.

Ved glanced over at me and raised his eyebrows.

I shrugged and shook my head. It wasn't worth trying to explain over the music and the cheering.

Salty started another run toward the house. She paused when I didn't follow and trotted back to me. I bent so I could slide my hand down her back and stared at the house. The fur on the back of her neck was standing on end and wouldn't lay flat however many times I smoothed it down. Whatever was going on, it had her spooked.

I straightened and stepped closer to Ved so I could whisper in his ear and hope that the microphone on the camera wouldn't pick up my words over the music coming out of the speakers. "Something's up. I think she wants us to follow her inside."

Ved looked down at Salty, then back at the stage, before meeting my eyes. He raised his eyebrows in question. Up on the stage, the music had shifted into something with a fierce beat. A moment later, Ryko's voice sang out over the top of the track.

"Keep recording," I whispered to him. There was no way I was missing this. Once people started realizing what they were hearing, they went wild.

Ryko sang through the first break, held a long note, and then the music cut. She folded at the waist in a dramatic bow. Everyone was screaming and clapping. I reached over and hit the button to stop the recording.

"Come on," I tugged on Ved's arm.

———

HANNAH took the camera from me, secured it inside her bag, and started toward the house. Salty took the lead, trotting just ahead of us.

"What about the interview?" I asked, then glanced back over my shoulder. "And Nigel?"

Hannah kept walking but turned to look behind us as well. "Nigel looked fine last time I checked. They're still over there, right? And Brianne is with them?"

"Looks like it."

"All right. Let's leave Nigel to Brianne for now until we figure out what's got Salty all bothered." Hannah set a hand on the patio door.

The woman Hannah had been planning to interview appeared on the other side. She pushed the door open. "Sorry that took so long."

Salty took a few steps back and started growling.

I squinted at the woman, then looked down at my wrist. The amulet wasn't glowing. Not a demon, then. But maybe possessed by one? I glanced at Hannah.

Hannah ignored the look I gave her. "No problem. You just missed Ryko up on the stage, though. I promised her I'd upload a couple of clips. Do you mind if I do that real quick and then meet you back by the pool?"

I scooped up Salty as Lexie stepped outside. "Sure. Same spot?"

"Sounds good." Hannah nodded, then stepped aside so I could get past without having to squeeze between her and Lexie.

Almost all of Morgan's guests were out by the pool, and those who weren't were heading in that direction. That meant Hannah and I had the main room almost entirely to ourselves.

"Why is she acting like that? She was fine with Lexie before." Hannah reached over to pet Salty, who was still shaking in my arms.

"Maybe we should take her back to the room," I suggested.

Hannah nodded and led the way down the hall. "I need to upload those videos, anyway. But we probably shouldn't be gone for too long. I don't want to lose track of Nigel and Brianne, and I really want to get that interview with Lexie before she changes her mind."

"Or implodes," I muttered.

Hannah shot me a look out of the corner of her eye. "Why would she do that?"

"Call it a hunch." I scratched Salty under her chin. That always worked to calm Firrag down.

Hannah opened the door to our room, then shut and locked it once we were inside. "Explain."

I set Salty down on the bed. "My amulet wasn't glowing when we ran into Lexie just now, so it isn't likely that she is a demon."

"Was it glowing before?" Hannah asked.

"I couldn't tell with Nigel and Morgan there. Then, after they left, I didn't have a chance to look. It definitely wasn't glowing when we were alone with Ryko, though."

"Okay." Hannah extracted a small card from the camera and inserted it into her computer. "What are you saying, then?"

"Maybe a demon got to her sometime between when she left us and when she returned to the pool deck."

"You mean, while she was getting her makeup bag in her room?"

"Sure. It's possible."

"It is possible. And maybe Salty was attempting to warn us? That's why she started trying to run back to the house?" Hannah glanced over to the patch of carpet in front of the glassed-over portion of the wall.

Salty had hopped off the bed and settled down between the chairs like nothing was the matter. Technically, we were safe here because of the wards Bryn had cast. So, she was probably right to be relaxed.

Hannah was bent over the table in the corner where she'd set up her computer. She sucked in a breath. "Wow! This is great."

My view of her ass from this angle was pretty great, but I didn't think that was what she was talking about. "What is?" I asked.

"The video you took of Ryko." She glanced over her shoulder at me. "Are you sure you've never held a camera before this weekend?"

I walked over to stand next to her so I could see her screen. "First time for everything, I guess."

She hit a few keys and clicked through some menus on her laptop. Then she straightened and turned to face me. "About that..."

I stared at the spot where she'd caught her bottom lip between her teeth. "About what?"

Her pulse sped up. "How much of that was you and how much was caused by whatever those demons gave you?"

I took a step closer until we were almost touching. "It was all me. Just me without inhibitions."

"I'm not looking for a boyfriend." Her hands gripped the

table behind her.

"I'm not interested in taking a human as a mate." I leaned closer.

"As long as that's clear...then I suppose we could make a few slight alterations to the rules." She cocked her head to one side.

"Like it might be all right if I touch you." I let my palms hover over her bare shoulders.

She licked her lips and nodded. "And you should probably kiss me again."

My hands brushed against her skin, skimming down her arms before finding their way around her waist and tugging her closer. Her head tilted back, and her nose slid against mine as our lips crept closer. Every move was in slow motion.

"Are you sure?" I asked.

"Yes." She breathed the word against my mouth as she leaned in to capture my lower lip between her own.

Then everything disappeared except the points where my body pressed against hers. My fingers crept up her back until they found the zipper at the back of her dress. "Can I?"

"Yes." Her hands wrapped around the hem of my shirt. She pulled up as I pulled down.

Her dress slipped off to pool around her ankles, and my shirt landed in a crumpled heap next to it. I lifted her up, hugging her to my chest, warming her smooth skin with my heat. Her legs wrapped around my waist as her lips devoured mine.

I stepped forward, over our tangle of clothes, so I could press her up against the wall. Her head tilted back, giving me the opportunity to explore her neck with my mouth.

"More." Her legs tightened around me. "Don't stop."

With one hand curled around her ass to hold her up, I let

the other slide up her side until it found the curve of flesh hidden under the thin scrap of fabric covering her breasts. She arched against me when the pad of my thumb traced a circle around her nipple through the fabric.

Her lips skimmed the point of my ear, reminding me that I'd never done this with a human who knew what I was. The women from the village didn't see past my glamour. As though my water wizard knew what I was thinking, Hannah's hands splayed across my shoulder blades. Her fingers were like wingtips dancing along my spine and down until she found the waistband of my trousers.

Two could play that game. I hooked my thumbs under the elastic that stretched around her chest. I hesitated only a moment, shifting my focus to the tips of those two fingers. The healers had said I shouldn't attempt a full shift into my dragon form, but they hadn't said anything about a partial shift. With a satisfying tear, my talons shredded the fabric, leaving Hannah's upper body bare.

"Neat trick." She grinned against my mouth as she reached back to grab my hand, pulling it forward so that she could examine the sharp keratin hook that had replaced my humanlike thumb. She brushed her fingertips along the outer ridge, and I shivered. "Can you feel that?"

I swallowed. No human had ever touched me in my dragon form. "A little."

She slid her fingers down, closer to the base of the talon, where it connected to the flesh of my hand. "How about here?"

My breath caught in my throat. I leaned my forehead forward until it touched hers. Together, we stared as her fingers caressed the spot of transition between my Fae and dragon forms. I slid my other hand down her side and over her hip until she caught that one as well and brought both of my hands to her mouth.

Her lips pressed against the very tips of my talons. Her eyes locked with mine as she began to kiss her way toward the base of my thumbs. My hips surged forward, pressing her firmly against the wall. In that moment, there was nothing I wanted more than all of her. Always.

I reminded myself that this didn't mean anything to her, and she didn't know what it meant to me to let a human see me this way. To touch this untouchable predator part of me. The part that had been trained by my father to kill. To dominate and destroy anyone who might try to harm my Alpha or my wing-mates.

A frantic tapping pulled my attention to the window. Hannah unwrapped her legs from around my waist. I helped her onto her feet as she attempted to cover her chest with her hands.

"It's Firrag," I grumbled. My faerie dragon familiar had impeccable timing.

Hannah bent to retrieve her dress from the floor. "I guessed that much. Go see what she wants."

As soon as I opened the window, Firrag took off, circling up into the sky. Salty put her paws on the windowsill and watched with me as Firrag headed toward the skyline.

"We should go." I caught the shirt that Hannah threw at me and pulled it over my head.

Hannah checked her computer, retrieved the little card, and slid it back into place in the camera. She didn't wait for the camera to settle in her bag before hurrying to meet me at the door. Salty ran out of the room after us, her toenails clicking on the wood floors as we rushed through the silent hall.

The main room and the dining room were empty. There

was no music when I shoved open the patio door. All the guests appeared to have left, or perhaps been relocated to some other part of the house.

Morgan, Brianne, and Nigel were still there, but a woman stood with them, and the small orange-pink demon that the Entugs called Bins lurked nearby.

"Oh, good. Just in time." The woman stretched her arms out as she turned toward us. "Now that we're all here, we can get to the point."

11

I'D never seen the woman in the long red dress before, but somehow I knew exactly who she was. I cursed and checked the shielding on my mind.

"That's right. Protect yourself, wizard. It won't do you any good, but it does make it more fun for me." Lilium grinned like someone had just served her favorite dessert.

Firrag exhaled smoke from her perch on Ved's shoulder. Salty pressed her body against my ankle and growled.

Nigel stepped forward. "Perhaps we could leave them—"

Lilium twirled a hand and pointed it in Nigel's direction, cutting him off as though she'd wrapped her fingers around his throat. "Perhaps you should have thought of that before you defied me."

Nigel choked. Brianne lunged forward to help, then froze like she'd hit a wall.

"No heroics, Fae," Lilium sneered at Brianne. "Or I *will* banish him."

Morgan stuck her hands into the pockets of her signature black jeans and strolled over to intercept me and Ved. I wasn't sure if the gesture was meant to reassure us, or if she was really that relaxed about having Nigel's evil mother in her house. Unless she'd arranged for this. Which meant I'd invited Nigel right into her trap. *Oh, no.*

Morgan must have understood the look of horror on my face, because she shrugged. "Sorry, not sorry?"

My fists clenched and my water magic surged as I lunged toward her. "You monster. How could you?"

Ved's hand clamped down on my shoulder, holding me back.

Morgan shook her head. "See. I knew it. You think I'm a monster. And there you were just yesterday trying to make me believe that I could have come to you. Trusted you. That you would have accepted me and tried to help me."

"I would have. It didn't have to be like this." I nearly growled the words at her as I tried to channel my power and debated who to attack first.

Morgan shrugged. "Yes, it did. You would have been just like my brother. Trying to save me. He didn't understand, either."

"And Lilium does?" I asked, glancing over to where Nigel's mother stood, grinning.

"Oh, I do." The self-appointed Demon Queen wrapped her magic around Nigel and Brianne so she could pull them along in her wake as she sauntered closer. "Morgan is the daughter I never had. And so much more loyal than my true offspring turned out to be."

Lilium hooked a finger under Morgan's chin and turned Morgan's face up toward her own. She looked at Morgan with pride. "She's managed to bring you all here, just for me: my traitor son so he could be punished; one of the wizards who stole my boxes from me and knows where they're being hidden; and two Fae to drain for their magic, which will help us defeat their own kin."

Salty growled but her body had started shaking.

"Is that the little faerie dog? Muffin, is it? Come to Mama, Muffin." Lilium curled a finger at Salty to draw her from my side, but Salty didn't budge.

The pleasant look on Lilium's face turned dark. "Oh, someone thinks they're clever, don't they?"

"Sorry, not sorry?" Ved offered.

"I suppose your name isn't Ash, either?" Lilium glared at him. Then she sniffed the air and shifted her attention to me. "You may be clever, but I suspect I know how to break you. The same way I broke Liam. What is it with you Fae males and your weakness for helpless little humans?"

Ved stepped forward, angling his body between mine and Lilium's. "Hannah is not little or helpless."

It was true that I was nearly as tall as him, but who was he kidding? I was a water wizard. What good was my single element magic going to do in this situation? It wasn't like we were facing off against the Wicked Witch of the West. She wasn't going to melt if I summoned a tidal wave up from the depths of the pool to dump down on her head.

Though, the thought did give me a thrill, and I savored the fantasy for half a minute before setting the idea aside so I could try to come up with a real plan. One that wouldn't end up with all of us dead just because I'd let my guard down for a hot minute. And it had been a very hot minute. One that continued to prove that men were a fatal distraction for me, and immortal Fae males were no exception.

The earth shook as though trying to wake me from my reflections and remind me that now was not the time. At first, I thought it was just a well-timed earthquake. We were in California, after all. Morgan may have thought the same thing, but Ved and Lilium weren't fooled.

Lilium turned to confront Brianne, who had used the Demon Queen's distraction to unleash her earth magic in an attempt to free herself and Nigel from Lilium's grip. Ved, in turn, decided to use Brianne's diversion to escape.

Firrag leapt into the air as Ved wrapped an arm around me. The next thing I knew, all the air had been sucked from my lungs. Just as I started to panic, oxygen returned. I blinked at our new surroundings, which didn't look that different from where we'd been a moment earlier, except I could no longer see Lilium and Morgan, or Nigel and Brianne.

"Where are we?" I whispered.

Ved held a finger to his lips.

Lilium's voice cut through the silence. "Enjoy your small victory, clever Fae. I know you're still here. I can sense your presence, as well as the wizard's. I will find you, and when I do, you will pay."

Someone grunted. A soft thud followed the sound.

"In the meantime," Lilium said, "I'll entertain myself by making your friends suffer. Morgan, bring me the box."

The soles of Morgan's favorite Chucks slapped against the concrete in a beat that signaled she must have set off at a jog toward the house.

"If you want the other boxes, you don't need to torture the Fae or the wizard," Nigel said. "Let them go, and I'll tell you everything I know."

Ved growled.

I set a hand on his shoulder and whispered, "He's lying. He can do that, remember?"

"He better be. If he's not, I'll tear his throat out myself."

Ved's shoulders remained tense, but his face softened.

Firrag appeared with Salty clutched in her talons. The little dog was almost too heavy for the faerie dragon, who hovered briefly before dropping lower and releasing Salty from her grip.

"No." Ved's eyes locked on his familiar, his voice low but firm. "I think it's time for you two to get out of here. Go warn Damir. Tell him that as soon as we figure out how to extract Brianne and Nigel, we'll return."

Firrag snorted twin puffs of smoke. She settled on the edge of a nearby table.

As my eyes adjusted to the light, I realized that Ved had transported us to the backside of the karaoke stage. That's why we could still hear Lilium but couldn't see her. And that's why it was so dark. We were sandwiched between the raised platform and the sound baffling that had been erected behind it.

Firrag didn't budge.

"Sure. Now you decide to stick around." Ved shook his head.

Firrag nipped at Ved's sleeve and tugged.

"I think she wants you to go with her," I whispered.

"We can't just leave Nigel and Brianne out there alone." Ved tilted his head to one side and paused to listen.

Something scraped across the concrete, like a chair being dragged. Then there was silence, followed by another soft thud a few moments later.

"If you aren't careful, you'll break her neck, and then, poof, there goes her magic." Nigel sounded unbothered.

"Nigel, do shut up. I've had just about enough from you and your ridiculous scheming. Did you really think I wouldn't figure out exactly what you were up to, you silly boy? It's a good thing I found Morgan when I did. The girl has more potential in her little finger than you do in your whole—" Lilium's voice cut off as, somewhere in the distance, the whoosh and click of a sliding door shutting and the slap-slap-slap of shoes announced Morgan's return.

"And I thought my parents were bad." I sighed.

Ved gripped my shoulders and turned me to face him. "Listen. I need to get Brianne out of there before Lilium can use that box thing on her. In order to do that, I need to trust that you are going to stay here. Got it?"

"What if she figures out where I am? Can I move then?" I scowled. I never did like following orders, despite the fact that I was scared out of my mind and had absolutely no intention of running out there and trying to be a hero.

Ved raised his eyebrows. I barely registered that the corner of his mouth twitched up before he pressed his lips against mine in a quick kiss.

He looked at Firrag. "If anything happens to me, get her to safety."

I almost stumbled backward when he disappeared, but I caught myself. "That stupid, impulsive, irresponsible Fae."

Firrag nudged me with the horns on her head and stretched her wings.

"Oh, no. You're not going to leave me here, too."

Salty stared up at Firrag and rumbled her displeasure.

Firrag lifted her head, then cocked it to one side. We all fell silent and listened.

"What do you want me to do?" Morgan asked. "How does it work?"

Lilium's heels clicked against the concrete. "Wake her up first. She'll need to put her hands onto the metal, and I want control of her mind when she does so that she doesn't go running off with my prize like last time."

Judging from the plink of metal that followed, Morgan must have set the box down on the pool deck.

Then Nigel said, "Mother, I was wondering…" But I didn't catch whatever he said after that over the sound of some sort of scuffle.

Lilium started yelling, and then there were so many sounds all at once, it was hard to tell what was going on. I held my breath and waited for it to make sense.

Then Firrag disappeared. A moment later, silence.

Fear flooded my veins. *Shit.*

I stared down at Salty. She set a paw on my foot as though I were really going to try to go out there. I wasn't. What was I going to do? Flood the place? I didn't even know for certain that anything was wrong. Firrag could have left for any number of reasons. It didn't have to mean that something had happened to Ved.

I shivered and clutched at the strap of my camera bag like it was some sort of safety blanket. If only I could see what was going on. But I'd promised Ved I wouldn't move unless they found me. I listened for approaching footsteps and waited.

———

I didn't go far on my first transport. I only needed to get somewhere with a better view of the patio. I'd chosen the roof of the pool house because I didn't remember there being any lights on over there, and with the sun going down, it was getting dark.

Crouched low on the edge of the tile roof, I had an excellent view of Brianne slumped awkwardly in a lounge chair. Lilium stood nearby, about halfway between Brianne's unconscious body and Nigel, who was floating with his feet hovering just above the ground. A golden ring of energy swirled around his waist, pinning his arms to his sides.

Morgan crossed the patio, walking toward Lilium with a metal cube in her hands.

I needed to move fast if I were going to transport down there, grab Brianne, and get out before Lilium could get her claws into me. I hoped that Morgan's return would distract her long enough to give me an advantage.

Just as I was about to go, Nigel's voice stopped me. *Wait. New plan.*

It took me a minute to realize he was speaking to me inside my head. While I stared at him from the rooftop, confused, Morgan reached Lilium, held up the box, and asked her what she should do.

Nigel sent me his idea. *Grab Morgan and the box and take her somewhere safe.*

But what about Brianne? I had some experience speaking mind to mind. It was how Dragon Fae communicated while in their dragon forms. I didn't think I could send Nigel my thoughts while in my Fae form, but I hoped he could at least read what I was thinking if I made the thought clear enough.

She'll be safe if you get that box out of here. And I can handle my mother, alone, but not both of them at once. Nigel sounded confident, but I knew Bins was still lurking down there somewhere, and the chaos demon wasn't the only demon in the house.

Are you sure?

Wait for my signal, then go. Fast.

Morgan walked over to Brianne and set the metal cube on the ground.

"Mother, I was wondering..." Nigel said, causing Lilium to

turn toward him and away from Morgan and Brianne. *Now.*

I didn't hesitate before transporting myself down to the patio, landing neatly between Morgan and the box. As soon as my feet touched the ground, I reached for the box with one hand and wrapped an arm around Morgan from behind, covering her mouth with my hand. Then I was gone.

I transported us to the first safe place that came to mind. The mouth of the Dragon Fae caverns. Because of the wards, I couldn't transport us directly inside. I could have carried Morgan through the tunnels. Instead, I made another impulsive decision, shifting into my dragon form just as we landed on the stone ledge of the West Mouth.

Clutching Morgan and the cube in my talons, I flew through the wide tunnels, straight down to the arena. My body was so full of adrenaline that I didn't feel the shift. I tried not to think about it, not that I would have been able to focus on anything besides the shriek coming out of Morgan's mouth now that I no longer had a hand covering it.

She pummeled and scratched at the scales covering my chest, twisting and turning, trying to free herself. Luckily, it was only a short flight to the arena. I glided in and dropped her down on the dirt-covered floor but kept the cube gripped in my other talon.

The Dragon Fae guards standing at the door to the Alpha's chamber scrambled to attention. "Who dares disturb—"

The door to the Alpha's chamber opened, and Ivo stood framed in the doorway. I hadn't seen him since he'd left me in the Forest Fae infirmary to go off with Damir and Challenge Boro. He was thinner than I remembered, with a streak of gray striping through his dark hair and a scar slicing down the side of his face and neck before disappearing under his shirt. Both the gray and the scar were new, but he was still

Ivo, alive and breathing, and a band of tension released from around my heart at the sight of him.

"Ash? Is that you?" He stepped forward, but the guards blocked his way.

I reached for the magic that would transform me back into my Fae form, but it kept slipping from my grasp. I tossed my head in frustration, which only had the effect of setting Ivo's guards on edge.

"Stand down, you fools." Ivo pushed forward. "And send for the clan medics."

The guards flanked Ivo as he made his way toward me. Then he spotted Morgan lying in a heap on the dusty ground and pivoted toward her. The guards hesitated, unsure if they should keep their focus on me, the big, threatening dragon, or guard Ivo as he wandered toward what appeared to be a helpless, unconscious human.

I realized that my impulsiveness was about to put Ivo in mortal danger once again. I roared a warning, but it didn't help. To make matters worse, my reaction only caused the guards to swing around and point their spears at me, leaving Ivo to defend himself.

Ivo's magic would be no match for Morgan's, and he was clearly in no state for a physical fight. He looked like he would struggle to take on a batch of Fledgelings in their first year of guard training. This was a disaster.

I groped for my magic, trying to shift so I could tell him to stay away. The more I writhed and roared, the more agitated the guards became.

Then, just steps away from Morgan, Ivo turned around to face me, putting his back to the half demon. I sensed the spike in her pulse and the change in her breathing as her eyelids cracked open. She was waking up. Either that, or she'd been awake this whole time and had only been pretending to be unconscious.

I grabbed for my magic and tore. Nothing happened.

Morgan's body flickered as she attempted to transport herself and realized that was impossible here, inside the Dragon Fae caverns. Once she realized she couldn't escape, she stirred, freeing her hands from where they'd been pinned under her body. One of Ivo's guards caught the movement and yelled something, but I was already moving.

Fire blazed from Morgan's palms, singeing my scales as I arched my tail up to block the path of her flames. The guards finally sprang to action, pointing their spears at Morgan while I shielded Ivo with one wing.

Morgan realized she was outnumbered but didn't appear to be giving in. She dropped her hands to the ground so that she could use them to push herself up. But she must have been injured when I tossed her down because one wrist wouldn't hold her weight. It bent with a sickening crack, causing her to cry out.

The guards hesitated, but I doubted that she would let such a small thing prevent her from fighting her way free. I slapped my tail down and swiped her body away from Ivo, pinning her against the wall with the spikes that ran down the ridge of my tail.

She squirmed and pushed against me, but I held her there. Ivo yelled something to the guards, and they rushed forward, only to falter and fall back as three pairs of wings circled Morgan's body, blocking her from seeing well enough to cast her magic.

The flurry of faerie dragons around Morgan caused the guards to back up, and that only brought them closer to me. They were not thrilled about that. Even though I was clearly one of them, they still hadn't identified me.

Then Damir's grandsire appeared on the upper balcony of the arena, flanked by the other Dragon Fae medics. His voice boomed down to me from above. "Vedran Ashwing, what do you think you're doing? You were told not to attempt a shift."

Two of the medics hurried down the steps to the main level.

"Ved brought someone. I think she may be hurt. But Tarmog and the others won't let me near her," Ivo yelled back. He tried to step around my wing, but his faerie dragon familiar diverted from his flight path to intercept Ivo.

Ivo stared at Tarmog, then said, "Oh."

Thank the Ancients. Ivo could communicate with the faerie dragons. Firrag must have told the others who this was, and Tarmog must have explained it all to Ivo.

"Guards!" Ivo shouted. "We have a half-demon prisoner who needs to be detained."

Word traveled fast through the caverns, and soon guards were rushing in through every entrance to the arena. They assembled, shielded themselves, and then advanced as a team. Once they had the steel restraining cuffs on Morgan, I pulled my tail back and curled it around my feet. I wasn't sure that the cuffs would prevent Morgan from accessing her magic in the same way that they worked on Fae, but at least they knew what she was and that would help them figure out how best to detain her.

While I was distracted, watching the guards, one of the medics stabbed me with a needle. I lashed out with my tail and then fell to the ground with a thud. My eyes remained open, but my body wouldn't respond to signals from my brain. I couldn't move my head to watch the guards escort Morgan from the arena. I didn't feel them pry the metal cube from my talons. I only knew they had taken it when one of Ivo's guards walked into my line of sight and handed it to Ivo.

Now that Ivo was safe and Morgan was secure, I calmed enough to listen to the little voice that had been nagging me about something I'd forgotten. *Hannah.* If Firrag was here, who was guarding Hannah?

I moaned, but it came out as a puff of smoke. Then another needle plunged into my neck and my world went dark.

12

THERE were no footsteps, but Nigel's grunts and groans broke the silence. Then some creature shrieked and another responded from somewhere closer to me, sending shivers down my spine.

"What did you do?" Lilium asked, her voice low and menacing.

"Nothing," Nigel wheezed. "I had nothing to do with it."

"You would lie to your own mother?"

Nigel moaned. I closed my eyes, even though I couldn't see whatever it was she was doing to him. If only I could shut the sounds of pain out of my ears as well. But if I covered those, I wouldn't be able to hear what they said, and I needed to know what was going on out there.

"Where did he take her?" Lilium asked.

Did she mean Ved? Did that mean he'd succeeded in getting Brianne out of here? If that were true, it wouldn't be much longer before he came back to get me. I crouched down so I could rest my hand on Salty's warm, furry back.

"You really do like her more than you like me, don't you?" Nigel sneered the words at his mother.

I frowned. What he said didn't make any sense. Lilium had been praising Morgan. She didn't even know Brianne. *What did Ved do?* I resisted the urge to poke my head up over the stage and confirm my suspicion that Brianne was still here and Morgan was the one Ved had whisked away.

"She delivered you to me, didn't she? And what did you do? Hmm? Sell me out to the Fae? And for what? What did they give you that convinced you to turn your back on your own kin?"

Nigel groaned.

"Leave him alone." Brianne's voice echoed across the patio.

I sighed. *So much for sticking to the plan.*

"Look who decided to wake up." Lilium's heels clicked against the concrete. "Is it you? Are you the one that convinced my son to side with the Fae? You're not the type he usually goes for, but who knows? His father wasn't really my type, either, but the heart wants what it wants, doesn't it?"

Nigel started laughing. His hysterics kicked off a bout of coughing.

"You find this amusing?" Lilium asked.

Once Nigel stopped coughing, he managed to choke out an explanation. "Oh, Mother. You could not be more wrong if you tried. Brianne is not my lover."

"And why should I believe you? Of course, you would lie to me to save her. It doesn't matter. That clever Fae may have run off with my box, but I have others. I'll drain this one of her magic while you watch. Then I'll banish you back to the hellish realm I escaped from. We'll see how you like it there, you ungrateful bastard."

Whatever shred of hope I'd been holding on to, whatever silly wishful thinking had led me to believe that we'd get through this without disrupting Morgan's party, evaporated in that moment.

This wasn't some small obstacle, easily overcome. Lilium had Nigel and Brianne, and it was all my fault. Between the chaos demons creeping around and the celebrity demons Morgan had added to the guest list, the house was crawling with Lilium's minions. Once they helped Brady find some excuse to get rid of the rest of the guests, they'd be out here looking for me. And Ved, once he returned.

I fingered the pocket in my camera bag where I'd stashed a couple of the blood coins Angie had given me. If Ved had taken Morgan back to the Fae, maybe he'd already warned them. Or maybe that's where Firrag had gone when she'd disappeared. Either way, it wasn't worth wasting a blood coin yet.

Something sparked. Then another quake shook the patio, followed by a whoosh that almost sounded like a wave crashing against the shore.

I needed to resist the temptation to pop my head up and see what was happening. My fingers dug into the fabric of my camera bag as I hugged it to my chest. Then I remembered. I didn't have to put my head up to look.

I unzipped the bag and pulled out my camera, hoping that the small amount of noise I was making wouldn't be heard over the commotion happening on the other side of the stage. Then I folded out the view panel on the back and adjusted it so I could see what was going on when I raised the lens above the surface of the stage.

It took me a moment to get the camera pointed in the right direction. At first, I didn't know what I was looking at. Then, as I began to make sense of the image, I stared, mouth gaping, at the cone of water swirling above the surface of the pool. I snapped a couple of pictures, then I hit record.

The deck around Lilium glistened in the porch lights like it had been soaked, but the water was receding. Sure enough, the growing vortex started rising and whirling back toward the Demon Queen like it was going to suck her inside and trap her there.

Lilium fought back with her own magic, but it cost her control over Nigel. He slumped to the ground. His knees and hands hit the concrete, hard. I winced as his muscles responded just in time to stop his skull from cracking down on it as well.

Brianne stomped her foot and sent a fracturing seam directly toward where Lilium stood as she focused on keeping the fierce cyclone from advancing any closer. Brianne's elemental magic was impressive and inspiring. It also made me a little mad that the Fae had abandoned the wizards without ever teaching us to use the magic we'd inherited from them properly. Watching Brianne, I could understand why Callie's family, along with some of the other prominent wizard families, were skeptical of the deal Max had made with Fiona.

Even though I'd only spent a little time with the Fae, it was enough to know that I preferred to never spend another minute in their infirmary, trapped on their side of the wards that separated the Fae lands from the humans. But it was also enough to believe that they would follow through on their end of the bargain. If we helped them, they would help us. And if this demonstration of elemental water magic was any indication of what was possible for me, I wanted to learn how to do what Brianne was doing, and whatever else they could teach me.

In the meantime, from where I stood, hidden behind the stage, after having promised Ved I wouldn't rush out and attempt to be a hero, the best I could do was try to help. I just had to do it without revealing where that help was coming from or drawing attention to myself. So, I stopped recording, tucked my camera away, and prepared to use my power to boost Brianne's cyclone.

From a standing position, my eyes were level with the stage platform. It was risky exposing myself, but necessary. And, technically, I was still honoring my promise to Ved, even though he hadn't returned, and I was beginning to worry.

I reached for my magic, letting the power swirl to the surface of my skin, then directed it through my fingertips, which I kept hidden behind the stage. As my support boosted the speed of the cyclone, I caught the moment Brianne noticed someone was helping. Her body tensed with realization, but she was smart and didn't look around. She just nudged my power with hers, guiding and directing me as to how I could help her more efficiently.

Then Firrag appeared, distracting me. The cyclone faltered for a moment, and Lilium was able to push it back out over the pool. But Brianne compensated for me and held it steady. While I reached for the scrap of paper Firrag clutched in her talon, Brianne sent the cracked slab of concrete under Lilium's heels tipping toward the pool.

I unrolled the paper and read the word scrawled across the page. *Stall.*

"Not helpful," I grumbled, crumpling the paper and dropping it on the ground. "Where is he?"

Firrag stretched her wings out and snorted smoke. Whatever that was supposed to mean.

"Any ideas?" I gestured toward the fight raging over near the pool.

Firrag took to the sky, circling up until she blended into

the sunset colors, leaving me to figure it out on my own.

I checked on Brianne. Her body was shaking with the effort of holding off Lilium. If we didn't get help soon, she was going to fall.

Nigel had managed to raise himself up onto his knees. Whatever he was doing was taking all of his concentration. He'd squeezed his eyes shut, and his fists were clenched at his sides. I couldn't tell if he were somehow attempting to boost Brianne's magic or if it were taking all his focus just to try and fight off the control his mother had gained over him. She was a succubus. Those demons were especially skilled at infiltrating and corrupting human minds. And Nigel was half human.

Stall.

What did he want me to do? Ved didn't want me to run out there and do anything stupid, but he'd gone and changed his plan without consulting me. Perhaps he meant for me to throw myself into the fight. Didn't he know that my magic was basically useless? Unless he meant for me to hang tight and continue hiding?

A crash followed by a bang shook the foundation of the stage and put an end to my attempt at interpretation. I had just enough time to scramble back, behind one of the enormous speakers, before a blast of magic shattered the stage, sending pieces of scaffolding flying. Salty pressed against my ankles, herding me closer to the relative safety the speakers provided.

From where I stood, even with my back pressed up against the wiring, I had a partial, unobstructed view of the pool. The cyclone was gone. Or at least it was no longer suspended over the now tranquil waters.

The sky flashed bright and something crackled. Lilium

barked commands. It took me a moment to realize that she must be directing those instructions at someone. In order to see who, I was going to need to stick my head out from my hiding place.

I glanced down at Salty. "I'm going to do something stupid."

She didn't put her paw on my foot. I took that as a sign of approval of the tentative plan forming in my head. In my mind, stalling meant helping Brianne and Nigel so that Lilium didn't win. Even without Ved's terse note, I knew that was the least I could do. Especially since I'd gotten them into this mess.

I knew my magic was no match for Lilium and however many of her minions had joined her. So, I was going to have to rely on distraction and a little bit of luck, and hope that would be enough to accomplish my goal. *Stall.*

Taking inspiration from Brianne, I reached out with my magic and grabbed control of as much pool water as I could handle. Then I crept around the side of the speaker until I could see the rest of the patio.

There were demons everywhere. At least, that's what it looked like until I realized that it was really only the same three that kept appearing and disappearing. Every time Brianne directed a blast of magic at them, they'd transport themselves out of the line of fire. They weren't throwing any magic back at her, though. Dodging appeared to be their sole defense.

Meanwhile, Lilium was trying to make her way over to Nigel. He'd pushed himself up to standing, but his eyes were still squeezed shut and he wasn't stable on his feet. He didn't seem to be having much success shaking off whatever Lilium was doing to him.

I decided helping him was my first priority. With a mental heave, I flung a blast of water into Lilium's eyes and hoped that Morgan's pool had been recently refreshed with chlorine in preparation for the party.

Since Lilium's physical shielding was focused on covering her backside against Brianne's blasts of elemental magic, she wasn't prepared for a strike to her face. Her hands wiped at her eyes as she stumbled back a few steps, twisting her ankle when her heel caught on a piece of mangled concrete.

Nigel's eyes flicked open and locked with mine across the patio. *Don't,* his voice warned in my head. *Help Brianne. Leave her to me.*

From where I stood, that didn't seem like a great plan, but Lilium was starting to look around, searching for who had dared to assault her. I sucked in a breath and cowered behind the speaker, hoping her eyes were burning badly enough that she hadn't seen me.

"The wizard is out there somewhere. Get her," she yelled to her horned minions.

One of them released a high-pitched screech followed by a babble of words in a language I'd never heard before. I concentrated on my breathing, trying to slow my racing heart so I could focus on helping Brianne.

Next to me, Salty's body stiffened. She growled. The hair on the back of her neck was standing on end. I pushed myself up, out of my crouched position, just as a demon blinked into existence right in front of me.

I froze. Everything appeared to be moving in slow motion. I had enough time to register that, up close, these demons looked more human than I'd realized. The one facing me had horns and scaly skin like the others, but otherwise, it was shaped like a muscular human. Sure, its eyes were orange and the teeth that showed when it snarled at me were pointed. There were claws at the end of the fingers on the hand it raised to strike me with. But other than that...

My vision faltered, and the world seemed to sway beneath my feet, like I was standing on the deck of a ship in a storm. My stomach rolled. I felt like I might faint or hurl. Then Salty rushed at the demon, and I snapped out of it. Angie's dog was about to get killed trying to protect me, and here I was just standing there swooning like a fool.

I reached for the pool water, intending to blast this demon like I'd done to its leader. I didn't want to die in a stupid war over magic, but if I had to go, at least I'd die fighting.

———

My eyes blinked open, and I found myself staring up at a wall of rock. I flexed my hands and feet, registering that they were no longer wingtips and talons. I had somehow returned to my Fae form. And Hannah was alone. Unguarded.

I sat up and my head spun. I closed my eyes.

"Woah, there." Hands steadied my shoulders.

I turned my head and found myself looking into the eyes of Damir's grandsire. "What happened?"

He chuckled. "I was going to ask you the same thing. You brought that young woman here along with some sort of metal cube?"

I nodded. That wasn't the part I was having trouble remembering. "I couldn't shift back."

His lips pursed. "Mm-hmm. That will happen when you don't follow the medic's orders."

"It was an emergency."

"I gathered as much." He held up a hand. "But before you start explaining, let me get Ivo in here. He's been waiting for you to wake up."

"I owe him an apology."

Grandsire Firewing paused at the entrance to the small cavern where I'd been resting and peered at me out of the corner of his eye. "Do you? For what?"

"I nearly got him killed. Again." I stared down at my clenched fists. "I'm impulsive and irresponsible."

Damir's grandsire crept back into the room. He placed a hand on my forearm. The weight of it relaxed the muscles in my arms. "That's enough of that."

I looked up to meet his worried gaze. "It's not even close to enough. And then, as though it isn't enough that I've put my own wing-mates in danger, I've left the human I'm supposed to be guarding alone with a raging demon who has a record for leaving dead wizards in her wake."

"Ah. Yes. Firrag told me about your Hannah."

"She is not *my* Hannah. Not even close. And you talked with Firrag? Of course, you did. Everyone seems to be able to talk with my familiar. Everyone except me." A part of me realized that I was having a bit of a meltdown, but I couldn't be bothered to stop. "Honestly. My sire would be ashamed of me."

"Now that is quite enough." Grandsire Firewing pinched my chin between his fingers. "Your sire trained you to act, and that is what you do. In the face of danger, you assess and react at a speed others envy. Why do you think Boro and his lieutenants targeted your sire and then you so aggressively? They were scared of you. And as for your familiar, I didn't know you couldn't speak with her. I can help you with that. You only needed to ask."

"Wait. What?" I blinked at him.

Damir's grandsire released my chin. He snatched a scrap

of paper and a bit of charcoal off a nearby table and handed them to me. "Tell your Hannah to hold tight. We are coming to help her. Hurry now. Firrag will take the message to her while you brief Ivo and the clutch of guards he's sending back with you."

I wanted to remind him that she wasn't my Hannah and tell him I didn't need a clutch of guards to help me protect one human wizard, but he was right. I needed to hurry if I wanted to get her a message before she did something dangerous. Or worse, before she gave up hope that I was coming back for her.

"How long have I been out?" I asked.

"Not long. We only needed to sedate you long enough to get your body to relax. It knew what to do once you stopped fighting it."

My hand gripped the charcoal but hesitated over the paper. If I told her to stay and she wasn't safe where she was, I would be putting her in danger. I needed to trust her, but I also needed her to not get herself killed. If Ivo was going to send me back with trained Dragon Fae guards... I scribbled a single word on the page and handed it to Grandsire Firewing.

He rolled the paper and nodded. "Let's go. Faster if you can follow me."

He had already ducked out the door and shuffled halfway to the bend in the cavern passageway before I caught up with him. He whistled, short and sharp. Ahead of us, Firrag banked as she glided around the corner to meet us.

She landed on Grandsire Firewing's outstretched arm. He tucked the note in her talon, and she took off, back the way she'd come with only a small nod in my direction.

"First lesson," Grandsire Firewing said as he continued to lead me through the tunnels, back toward the arena. "What is

Firrag's favorite treat?"

It took me less than a heartbeat to answer. "Pear. She loves fresh pears."

Grandsire Firewing nodded. "Picture it in your mind."

I tried to imagine the curved piece of fruit with the dull, mottled skin that hid the juicy flesh that Firrag found irresistible. The image kept slipping in my mind. It took all my concentration to hold the entire pear, fully formed, in place. Then, it was gone, replaced with another image. This one of me feeding pear to Hannah. Something I'd never done.

"What?" I must have spoken the word aloud because Grandsire Firewing answered.

"Tell me what you saw."

"I pictured a pear. One pear. Then it was gone. Replaced with something else." Even though I'd never had that thought before, now that it was in my head, I wanted to do that.

"Faerie dragons communicate in images, not words."

"Are you saying that Firrag wants me to feed Hannah a pear?"

"Is that what she sent you?" Grandsire Firewing cackled. "Don't tell the others, but little Firrag has always been my favorite. She reminds me so much of my Dormog."

"How would Firrag know if Hannah even likes pears?" I grumbled. Not that it mattered. Once this was over and Hannah was safe, I wasn't ever going to see her again. She was a human, and Dragon Fae didn't take humans as mates.

"She may not." Grandsire Firewing shrugged. "You know Firrag better than I do. She is your familiar, after all. But, if I had to guess, based on the little I have communicated with your faerie dragon, I would assume that she is using a pear as a metaphor. She knows how much she likes pears. You give her pears. It makes her happy. She wants you to give Hannah pears and make Hannah happy. Whatever that means to you and Hannah." Grandsire shot me a sly grin.

Who would have guessed that my familiar would have such a filthy mind. *That's my girl.* I grinned. Did this mean that Firrag liked Hannah? We were approaching the lower entrance to the arena, the one closest to the Alpha's personal lair. So, I tucked that thought away for later consideration.

"Ash!" Ivo stood when I stepped through the archway into the Alpha's lair.

I hadn't been inside the space since it had belonged to his sire. As I stood there, cataloging the differences, Ivo approached. He opened his arms and enveloped me in a hug.

"It's so good to see you up and around. And shifting! Good for you. They won't let me try it yet. But it's nice to see you back in action again." Ivo grinned at me.

I sniffed. Words clogged my throat. I had been so worried about him, and here he was, standing, hugging me, acting like nothing had happened. I didn't deserve this.

"Are you all right?" Ivo asked, squinting at me when I didn't respond.

I nodded. "I'm just... I'm sorry."

Ivo's eyes widened. I couldn't help but notice the shadows around them and the way his cheekbones cut stark lines under his skin. He looked like he hadn't been eating well, or perhaps hadn't been able to eat at all for a long period of time. Regardless of what Grandsire Firewing said, what happened to him was all my fault.

He shook his head. "For what? Bringing that wizard here? Where else would you have taken her? To the forest? Damir may think our cousin, the Faerie Queen, can do no wrong, but the caverns are much better equipped to keep a prisoner like her. And Sillag took the box we had to pry out of your paralyzed talons to Damir. So, that's safe, too. There's nothing to be sorry about."

I glanced at Grandsire Firewing, who only raised his eyebrows in response. Ivo didn't understand and there wasn't time for lengthy explanations. If I wanted to prove myself, I needed to finish the job I'd been assigned, and that meant getting back to Hannah.

"I should go," I said.

"I'm sending a clutch with you. They're assembling at the West Mouth. You can meet them there. I've told them that they are under your command as lieutenant."

"But I'm not..."

Ivo's brow furrowed. "You're not going back without backup. I've heard enough about Lilium and these demon clans to know that they're dangerous. Oh! And they've all been inoculated against that pesky demon allergy you had the pleasure of experiencing. Thanks for reminding us about that. Good thing our medics have long memories." He nodded at Grandsire Firewing.

"Will you shut up for one minute?" I shoved a hand in my hair, ready to rip it out in frustration.

"All right." Ivo took a step back. "What's wrong?"

"Damir never named me as lieutenant, for one. And you're just sending a clutch of guards off with me to do what, exactly? Don't you want me to brief you? Don't you want to think about this? Take some time to come up with a plan?"

"Of course, you're Damir's lieutenant. 'Fire, Ash, Light. Wing-mates for life.'" Ivo blinked at me. "Are you sure you're all right? Did that demon woman get into your head?"

"No." I held back the roar building in my chest. "I'm fine."

Ivo's words were nice, but I needed to hear that from Damir. He was Alpha now, not Ivo, which was also my fault.

I needed Damir to tell me that he still believed in "Fire, Ash, Light."

Ivo waved his hand toward the door. "Good. Then get going. I don't want you to miss your chance to capture Lilium and take her down. Let's end this war so that Damir can come home and Seren can have that Fledge of theirs here in the caverns where it belongs."

I'd been right about Seren. It hurt that Damir hadn't told me. That the Faerie Queen knew, and I didn't. All Fiona wanted was an heir. Damir was my family. "What if it's a..."

Ivo grimaced. "Fiona claimed your seed. That doesn't mean she gets to raise all the High Fae offspring as Forest Fae, even if Damir and Seren do produce a female. But we can fill you in on those plans later. Damir and I have been discussing this for weeks. We'll deal with the politics, and you take care of the enemies. Just like old times."

Ivo grinned at me. He was enjoying this. Damir may be Alpha, but Ivo was clearly the one in charge. He still thought of me as part of the team, but apparently neither of them trusted me enough to tell me everything.

"Just like old times," I said. It was true that I had no patience for politics. I never had. Part of me loved that I didn't have to worry about navigating alliances between Fae factions, but the other part ached at being left out.

"Good hunting," Ivo said.

I nodded, thanked him, and ducked out of the smaller room. As soon as I stepped out into the arena, I took a deep breath, letting the damp mineral smell of the rock surrounding me mix with the dusty musk of the packed earth floor that had witnessed centuries of challenges, feasts, and festivals. My lungs filled with home, family, loss, and celebrations.

If I wanted to find my place here, I had to prove my worth.

Even as sire to the Faerie Queen's firstborn, I would just be a pawn in the political games of those who ruled. If I wanted a true seat at the table, I had to make a name for myself.

I could do more than just keep Hannah safe. I could do what I did best. Fight. And destroy the enemy of the Fae.

13

SALTY snarled and snapped at the demon's calves, distracting it while I prepared to blast it with a chlorine water bomb. Just as I wrapped my magic around a bubble of pool water, the sky exploded with fire.

Five huge dragons flapped their wings in the sky above us. Each of them roared flames down onto the patio, aiming for anything with horns. The demon who had been about to kill me a moment earlier paused to glance up. In that moment of hesitation, Ved appeared at my side. He lifted his arms and swung the sword he gripped with both hands at the demon who was still looking up. By the time the demon realized we had some beefy sword-wielding company, Ved had sliced its head clean off.

"Are you okay?" he asked.

I released my grip on my magic and shook out my hands. "Great. I'm great. That thing nearly killed me, but other than that, yeah. Everything's going just great."

"Good job stalling." He turned toward the pool as one of

the dragons swooped down, breathing fire at the demons attacking Brianne.

"Thanks?" I wasn't sure if he were being serious or sarcastic.

Lilium glared up at the dragons, then stalked toward Nigel, who was standing with his arms still pinned to his sides. Before she could close the distance between them, one of the dragons swept in to block her. It roared, sending her stumbling back. Then it exhaled a wall of flame, separating her from her son.

"How long can it keep that up?" I asked.

"Long enough. I hope," Ved responded as more demons began to materialize on Morgan's patio.

The new ones with purple skin had horned brows that curved up on the ends. They looked like a cross between a goblin and a bull. There were at least a dozen of them, and they were joined by more that looked like the one who had been about to attack me. And all these new arrivals carried battle-axes.

"I brought some friends," Ved said. "But it looks like Lilium also called for backup."

I stared up at the five circling, swooping dragons. Each of them was nearly as big as Morgan's pool, and that wasn't even including wingspan. They looked fierce, with spikes running down their spines and sharp claws at the tips of their talons. A couple of them had horns. Even against the dark sky, I could tell that their scales were all different colors, no two the same. It made me wonder what Ved looked like as a dragon and why he wasn't up there with them.

Ved glanced at me. "Ready to take out a few demons?"

I recoiled. "Hold on. You want me to help? You aren't going to insist that I just hide back here and wait for you and your buddies to take care of this?"

One corner of Ved's mouth lifted in a sly half smile. "Weren't you the one insisting that you could protect yourself?

"Well, yes, but..." My voice trailed off as I gestured toward the battle going on. He wanted me to go out there, in all that, armed with just my water magic, against two dozen or so muscular demons wielding axes?

"Come on, water wizard. Let's see what you've got." Ved gripped his sword and marched toward the nearest demon.

I pulled the strap of my camera bag over my head and set it down on the ground, tucked up against the back of the speaker. Then I looked at Salty. "Stay. And keep this safe."

Salty yipped, then sat down next to my camera bag.

"Good girl." I took a breath.

This was such a bad idea, but it was either go out fighting or stand here waiting for something to come kill me. So, I flexed my fingers as I turned toward the fight. *You can do this.*

By the time I located Ved, he had already sliced through another demon neck and was moving toward the next one. I started after him just as one of the purple mono-horns materialized behind his back.

I yelled to get his attention, knowing there was no way he'd be able to hear me over the roaring and screeching. At the same time, I gathered a wave of pool water and directed it at the demon.

Ved turned at the woosh of my magic aimed in his direction. He raised his arms without hesitation and followed the splash of my wave with a sweep of his sword. The water confused the mono-horn, but it recovered fast enough to duck, and Ved's blade bit into the demon's horn instead of its thick neck.

I kept moving forward as I gathered the water that had crashed to the concrete and brought it swirling up. The demon roared, trying to free its horn from Ved's blade. I silenced it with a blast of water to the face. It sputtered and spat as Ved wrenched the sword free.

I pinched my eyes shut so I wouldn't see the killing blow. Then I realized how ridiculous it was to close my eyes in the middle of a battlefield, because that's what Morgan's patio had become. I was almost glad she wasn't here to see the carnage.

The demon's lifeless body was still crumpling to the ground as Ved started toward the next one. As much as I admired his obvious desire to decapitate them all, he was moving farther away from Brianne. Couldn't he see that we needed to get to her and work together? Murdering demons was fine and necessary, so long as they were standing in our way, but rescuing Nigel from Lilium was the goal.

I ran to catch up to Ved, feeling uncomfortably exposed in my sundress and sandals. This was one time when I had to admit that something like Morgan's signature dark jeans and sneakers would have been a much wiser choice in wardrobe. A corner of my mind started brainstorming ideas for a video focused on magic battle fashion as one of the dragons glided above me, heading in Brianne's direction.

There wasn't time to stop and see what was going on because I was starting to realize that approaching a Dragon Fae warrior while he was focused on slicing off demon heads was a little more complicated than I'd anticipated.

"Hey! Ved! Hey!" I yelled as I approached.

Rather than turn, he charged at the next closest demon, who raised their axe to meet him. The pair clashed weapons and another demon turned at the sound. Then it raised its ax, preparing to join them.

Shit. I stopped in my tracks and glanced around to make sure nothing was about to attack me as I reached for my water magic. Since it worked so well the first time I tried it, I sent a blast of pool water straight at the advancing demon's face. It shrieked and faltered long enough for Ved to notice that he had company.

Unfortunately, after shaking off the water, the demon charged at Ved. I should have been grateful that it didn't seek me out and come after me with its battle-axe, but I was too busy freaking out that Ved was now trading blows with two demons. Their fight had attracted more attention, and I scrambled to conjure up another cyclone to block more of the demons from joining in.

Just as I got a wall of water up and spinning, Ved sliced through the first demon. He pressed the second one back toward my cyclone with every blow. More rushed forward to join, but they had to break through the water storm in order to get to him. It was enough to slow the advance to a manageable demon beheading pace for Ved.

Just as he got into a rhythm, a woman's cry, followed by a hiss and a string of cursing distracted me, dividing my attention between Ved and whatever was happening on the other side of the patio.

After a few quick glances, I determined that Nigel must have broken free enough to attempt escape. His body was frozen in midlunge, and Lilium's hands were in the air. She directed twin bolts of energy at her son's torso, blasting him backward. He crumpled to the ground in a heap.

Brianne ran toward them, then disappeared. She reappeared on the far side of Nigel, but Lilium had already cast some sort of a field around him, preventing Brianne from getting any closer.

I yelled to Ved to get his attention and pointed toward where Brianne stood facing off with Lilium and her two demon guards, unable to break through whatever magic Lilium had cast to imprison Nigel.

Ved sliced through the last of the demons and roared at the sky. He signaled something to the dragons, then disappeared. When he reappeared a moment later, at my side, I nearly jumped out of my skin. He managed to grab hold of me. Then we were both gone, and I was gasping.

We reappeared behind Lilium, opposite Brianne. I sucked in a breath, torn between drawing attention to myself and filling my lungs with large gulps of sweet, life-giving air.

Above us, three dragons circled. I wasn't sure where the other two had gone until Ved took a step forward, sword gripped with both hands and pointed at Lilium. The other two Dragon Fae appeared then. Transformed into their Fae forms and holding one of the abandoned demon battle-axes in each hand. They fell into position, flanking Ved as he advanced on Lilium and her guards.

The muscular bulk of the three Fae blocked my view, but their mass also stood between me and the wrath of the remaining demons.

"So sorry, boys, but I think it's time for me to go," Lilium said, in her too-sweet voice.

Lilium's comment was followed by a curse and a scuffle. The Dragon Fae raised their weapons to respond. I blinked my eyes shut against a flash of blinding light. When I opened them again, the Dragon Fae had lowered their weapons and parted formation enough for me to see that Lilium and her minions were gone. And so was Nigel.

It was over. For now. What remained of Morgan's patio was an uneven pile of scorched rubble. Her pool had been reduced to a half-filled rectangular pit. It was a good thing she was safely trapped in the Dragon Fae caverns so she didn't have to see this mess. Not that I felt too bad for her. She brought it on herself when she called Lilium.

Brianne stalked toward me, through the scorch marks that surrounded the place where Nigel had been standing, trapped by his mother.

"No. No. No." Hannah rushed forward, closing the distance between us. Her hand grasped my forearm. "He's gone. She took him."

I signaled the three Dragon Fae guards who had been covering us from the sky, and they transformed, appearing next to their wing-mates at my side. After scanning Hannah and reassuring myself that she was fine, I surveyed the clutch to check that none of their injuries needed urgent attention. Then I instructed them to go collect the weapons that had been left behind.

"I need to report back," I said to Brianne when she joined us.

Brianne's fists clenched. "*You* need to report back? *I* need to report back. Let the other dragons report for you. You were assigned to guard Hannah."

"And I did." I gestured to the dead demons littering the ground. "Hannah is fine. And now there are no demons left to attack her. Morgan is chained in a cavern. And Lilium is gone."

"With Nigel," Brianne said, eyes narrowing. "Which you might have been able to help me prevent if you weren't so busy with your killing spree."

"I was protecting Hannah." I growled the words at her.

"Enough!" Hannah stepped between us. "I am not a child. I don't need a babysitter. I'll be fine with Salty. We'll go figure out what happened to the rest of the party while you two report to your commanders or whatever. I can take care of myself, remember?"

She crossed her arms and glared, clearly directing that last word at me.

I stared back at her, confused. I was her bodyguard, assigned to keep demons from killing or capturing her. Killing demons was my job. What were they both so mad about?

I glanced at the other Dragon Fae and reconsidered leaving. Brianne was right. They could report back without me. But if they returned and I stayed, would Ivo think I was prioritizing Hannah over my kin? If I was a lieutenant, then I needed to act like one.

"I won't be gone long," I said, mostly to Hannah, willing her to understand.

Then I turned to Brianne. "I'll have Firrag take a message to Damir so he knows what happened and can inform Fiona. That way, you can stay here. With Hannah."

It was a good thing Brianne didn't have fire magic, because the look on her face made it clear that she would have hit me with a ball of flame if she could have. I took a step back, just to be safe.

"I will stay here long enough to clean up and repair the damage so that none of the humans find out what happened, but then I am leaving," Brianne said. "Nigel is my responsibility. Hannah is yours. You have your orders, just as I have mine."

"Wow. I'm really feeling the love here, friends," Hannah

muttered.

I couldn't give in to fond feelings for a human. Not over loyalty to my wing-mates and clan. "That may be true, but I also have a responsibility to my clan."

"Let me be perfectly clear, Dragon Fae." Brianne pointed a finger at me. "If I return without Nigel, my commander will set the rest of the Guard on me, and when they're done beating me senseless, the Elemental guardian herself will have a go at me for losing her mate. How is it you think my responsibility less than yours?"

"It isn't." The clutch of Dragon Fae guards returned with their arms full of battle-axes. I took one and handed it to Brianne. "Take this, and I'll help you get Nigel back as soon as I return."

"I don't need your help, Dragon Fae. I need you to do your job." Brianne hefted the axe I'd given her, then reached over and took a second one.

"You said you were going to repair the damage before you go. Just don't leave until I return. I'll be right back." We were wasting time arguing. I could have been there and back already.

Before Brianne could respond, I signaled the others that we were leaving and transported myself back to the caverns, intending to make my report and return as quickly as possible.

Ivo and our three faerie dragons were waiting at the West Mouth when we arrived. I relaxed a bit when I spotted them, thinking that this would speed things up considerably. Before addressing Ivo, I ordered the clutch that had been assigned to me to visit the medics and get some rest while they could. They would be needed again—soon.

"What happened?" Ivo asked after I'd dismissed them.

I shook my head. "It wasn't good. Lilium has Nigel. We have no way of knowing where. At least we killed the demons who arrived to help her, but there are sure to be more."

"And the wizard you were assigned to guard? Where is she now?"

"Still there. With the Fae who was assigned to guard Nigel. I told them we'd send a message to Damir so that he could inform Fiona."

Ivo nodded. He whistled, and Sillag circled down from the sky to land on his outstretched arm. While Ivo communicated with her, I tried to imagine a pear.

Firrag swooped down to land on my shoulder. She nudged my cheek with her horns before curling against my neck. An image of Hannah throwing a pear at my head replaced the juicy pear I'd been concentrating on.

I scratched the scales under Firrag's chin. "I know."

Sillag flapped her wings once as she leapt from Ivo's arm. Then she was gone.

Ivo gestured to me. "Walk with me. We'll wait in the Alpha's lair where it's more comfortable. This cold wind has nearly frozen me to the bone."

"How long have you been waiting for us?" I fell into step beside him, even though I knew I should be leaving.

"Not long. Your Firrag returned to let me know that the fight was over. Her warning gave me just enough time to walk up to meet you." Ivo wrapped his arms around himself and rubbed his palms against his biceps.

"How are you?" I asked, thinking I would stay only until Damir arrived. I understood now why he didn't want to leave Ivo alone.

Ivo shrugged. "Improving. That's what the medics say."

I took a breath, preparing another apology, but he spoke

before I could.

"It really isn't your fault. If it's anyone's fault, it's mine. I knew what needed to be done, and I ran from it. I was scared." He glanced at me out of the corner of his eye. "Did you know that I've always secretly wanted to be more like you? Brave. Running into the fight instead of away from it. Fiercely protective of my kin."

My mouth gaped. Words stuck in my throat. Ivo wanted to be more like me? "Impossible."

He laughed. "It's true. When your sire would train us, he always went easy on me and Damir. He knew we weren't natural fighters like you. I envied the way he pushed you and how easy it seemed for you to master skills he never bothered to teach us. We knew that you were the best. I should never have left you to fight Boro alone."

I remembered how my sire had pushed me, but I'd never realized that it hadn't been the same for my wing-mates. It hadn't occurred to me to question why I'd always been the one to take point, even though I had thought it unfair that I'd been punished for not covering their backs as well as my own, while they'd only been scolded for form or speed.

I had imagined it was because Ivo's sire was our Alpha, and their mothers were High Fae sisters of the Faerie Queen, while mine was just some long-forgotten human woman from the village. All this time, I'd thought that was why he'd pushed me harder. Why it had been easier for them. I'd never considered that he saw potential in me that he didn't see in them and that was why he expected more.

"It's done and behind us. We can leave it there." I slung an arm around Ivo's shoulder.

"Yes. And now Damir is Alpha. Can you believe it?" He grinned at me.

"Poor Damir. He only ever wanted to escape the caverns, and now he's in charge of them."

Our laughter echoed through the tunnels. It really was like old times until Ivo had to stop so he could catch his breath. He leaned one hand against the wall and pressed the other to his chest.

"Are you all right?" I asked, unsure what to do or how to help him.

He lifted his hand and waved it at me. "Fine. I'm fine. Come on. We're almost there."

His eyes scanned the tunnel, and I knew he was checking to see if anyone had noticed his moment of weakness. He may not be Alpha, but he was Damir's lieutenant. If Damir had potential challengers, they might see this as an opportunity. I didn't need to be an expert in clan or Fae politics to realize that we were crossing very thin ice on the path to what I wished to be the long history of Damir's reign as Alpha.

Damir had a mate and a Fledgeling on the way. If he were killed, and a new Alpha took over, Seren would be banished along with their Fledgeling. Her ties to her own kin were tenuous at best. They'd cast her out for having what they considered to be cursed magic. What would happen to her without Damir? Even if he survived a Challenge, Ivo and I would likely die trying to protect him, given our current weakened states. Then Damir would need to find new lieutenants. And after so many years in the village, how would he know whom to trust?

Without Damir as Alpha, the Dragon Fae would never consider helping Fiona's kin. Brianne didn't understand what was at stake. Without Nigel, the Forest Fae might still win the war against the demons, but not if the Dragon Fae didn't come to their aid.

"Tell me about this wizard you've been guarding while I let my breathing settle," Ivo said, interrupting my thoughts.

"Her name is Hannah," I said. "Hannah Vos. She's a water wizard."

"And?"

"And what?"

"And I can tell that there's more to it than that. What aren't you telling me?" Ivo elbowed me in my ribs.

I sighed. "She's...intoxicating? Infuriating? Stubborn and fierce—"

"And she's set your pants on fire?" He laughed.

"Shut. Up."

"You finally found a human who isn't prepared to just rip all her clothes off and climb on top of you, and you find that irresistible. Am I right?"

"You are insufferable," I growled. "Dragon Fae don't take humans as mates."

"Who said anything about taking a mate?" Ivo feigned a shocked expression.

I shook my head. "Nice try."

Ivo swatted my shoulder. "What I don't understand is what you're doing here when you should be there?"

"What happened to 'of course, you're a lieutenant, Ash'?" I shoved him back, then winced when he faltered and nearly tripped, reminding me that he wasn't as strong as he used to be. I gripped his elbow to steady him.

"The clutch could have reported back for you. Tell me why you're really here, because this looks like a first for you. I didn't think Vedran Ashwing ever ran from a fight."

"I didn't run."

"You didn't?" Ivo stepped into the empty arena.

I followed him across the dirt floor to the Alpha's lair

where a pair of guards stood waiting for his return. "I'm going back."

Once we were both inside the small room, I shut the door.

Ivo collapsed into the largest of the three chairs positioned around the small circular table. He leaned his head back until it rested against the carved wood frame, then he closed his eyes. "Good."

"Are you sure you're all right?" I asked.

He opened his eyes a crack. "I'll be better after a short rest. Can you ask the guards to send for food, and maybe also Grandsire Firewing?"

I nodded, but he'd already closed his eyes. I retraced my steps to the door and swung it open, only to find Damir standing on the other side with his fist raised as though he'd been about to knock.

"Oh, good. You're both here," he said.

"Why are you knocking on your own door?" I asked.

He ran a hand through his hair, then waved me back inside. I relayed Ivo's request to the guard, then retreated.

Damir joined us, shutting the door behind him. "There's been an unfortunate development."

14

*A*FTER Ved disappeared, Brianne sighed. "This is why we don't associate with Dragon Fae."

She waved a hand. The dead demons crumbled to dust that was absorbed by the concrete as the cracks leveled out and sealed themselves shut. Slowly, the pool began to refill. Even though it was hard to be sure in the dim patio lighting, most of the evidence of our battle seemed to have disappeared. The damage that remained—demolished stage, broken furniture, collapsed bar—resembled the aftermath of an extremely rowdy party.

A twinge of envy pierced my core. "Hey, um...do you think you could teach me how to do that?"

"Earth magic?" Brianne asked.

I shook my head. "I can't control earth. Only water. But you have both, right? That cyclone was impressive. I just never thought my water magic was good for much, but there you were using it to fight Lilium, and maybe if I knew how to do that, I wouldn't need a bodyguard? You know?"

Brianne's eyes narrowed. "I can see why you'd want to get rid of that Dragon Fae, but water magic alone won't be enough to take on Lilium."

"But it could protect me from her minions, right?" Sure, Ved had done all the actual demon killing, but I thought I'd held my own in the fighting. I could do better with proper training.

Brianne frowned. "The only way to be sure you're rid of a demon is to cut off its head. For that, you will probably need some skill with a sword. But you could use your magic to hold them off. To stall long enough for help to arrive."

Stall. That was what Ved wanted me to do. He believed I could hold off a demon with my magic even before I did. Maybe he didn't think I was completely helpless. If he did, he would never have assumed I was going to join him in the fight.

I filed those thoughts away to consider later. At that moment, I was still angry about the fact that Lilium had gotten away, and she might not have if we'd all been working together. Like a team. I thought we were, but then he disappeared with his Dragon Fae buddies and left us here to clean up.

I supposed Ved had every right to be done with teamwork. He'd captured Morgan, and we'd managed to get one box back. Once I was back in my warded apartment, I'd be safe enough on my own. He didn't need me.

I should have been happy to be rid of him. It was what I'd wanted. But whatever I was feeling, it wasn't relief or joy.

"Then will you teach me?" I asked, ready to be focused on anything else but this tangle of emotions in my chest.

Brianne paused in repairing the demolished stage to consider me. "After I get Nigel back."

I nodded. "Of course. Definitely."

She glanced toward the house. "Where do you think they went?"

"The rest of the party?"

Brianne grunted as she refocused her attention on repairing broken patio furniture.

"That's a really good question." I turned to stare at the house. "Maybe downstairs? I wonder what Morgan and Brady told them to get them off the patio so fast. It wasn't like Ved and I were gone that long."

The memory of how his talon had shredded my bra, and how he'd held me effortlessly while he kissed me like he never wanted to stop, sent shivers through my core. After our brief encounter, and then the further reminder of the power hidden beneath his Fae exterior, I had to admit that Angie was right. I was glad I'd given in to my attraction to him, especially now that he was gone. He'd left me wanting more, but I knew where that would lead. It was better this way.

When I turned around, Brianne was already halfway across the patio, heading toward the remains of the stage. I jogged to catch up to her and remembered I'd abandoned Salty. And my camera. My jog turned into a run as I sped past Brianne, cutting around the broken platform to the speakers.

Salty yipped and wagged her tail when she spotted me.

"Good girl!" I bent to pet her, scooping her up into my arms. "Such a good girl!"

Aside from a scattering of ash covering the canvas, my camera bag appeared untouched by the fighting. I breathed a sigh of relief that both it and Salty had survived the battle unscathed. Then I dusted off my camera bag, slung it over my shoulder, and carried Salty over to where Brianne stood piecing things back together with her earth magic.

"Do you want to go inside and see if we can find them?" Brianne asked. "Then we can get you packed up and back to your apartment. At least you'll be safe there while I hunt down Lilium and stop her from continuing to torture her son."

"I can't leave." I set Salty down and clutched the strap of my camera bag.

"Of course, you can leave. Morgan's gone. Once the guests figure that out, there isn't going to be a party. You might as well wait it out somewhere safe. I'd offer to take you back to the Fae, but I wasn't kidding about showing up without Nigel. Arabella won't kill me herself, but my close call with mortality will be at her command."

I cringed. "How about we just see where everyone is, first, and then decide?"

I wasn't ready to explain or try to convince her that leaving would mean accepting the death of my career. It wasn't the same as facing my own mortality, but at that moment, it seemed equally bad. The stupid shred of hope I'd had that Lilium would leave and things would go back to normal had resurfaced when she'd disappeared. With it came my hope that I could salvage something out of this wreck of a house party.

Brianne flicked her hand in the direction of the stage, putting the final touches on her repair. She glanced around to make sure she hadn't missed anything, then looked at me. "All right. Good enough. Let's go see where everyone is hiding first."

When I started toward the house, Salty bounded ahead of me. I paused, remembering what else might be waiting for us inside. "There were these chaos demons lurking around before the party. I didn't see any of them join in the fighting, and I am beginning to suspect that they report to Lilium, not Morgan. But if we see any short demons with pink-orange skin; big, floppy ears; and a long, hooked nose—"

"Off with their heads." Brianne nodded, retrieving the pair of battle-axes she'd taken from the Dragon Fae. "Got it."

Despite my growing sense of dread at the absolute silence inside the house, no demons jumped out at us as we checked the rooms on the main floor. But there were also no guests, which was equally disturbing. So, we made our way downstairs.

On the lower level, we stopped to check the game room first. The door was already open, and there were plenty of people inside, but they all appeared to be asleep. A group that had been playing cards was slumped over, heads resting on the table or tilted back against their chair back. Someone was lying draped over their cue on the pool table. More were curled up on the floor around it. Others had collapsed near the arcade games.

Something cackled from the shadows, but when I turned to look, there was nothing there.

"You heard it, too?" Brianne asked.

I nodded.

"I have a feeling I know what's going on here, but let's keep looking. I want to find Brady." Brianne backed out of the room and waited for me to join her.

At the end of the hall, the door to Brady's office was half open. "Let's start there, then work our way back to the viewing room."

Brianne nodded. Her feet made almost no sound as she crept forward, positioning herself ahead of me. She pushed the door open the rest of the way, and we stepped inside.

Brady was sprawled out on the floor in front of the windows. He didn't look comfortable. It was more like he'd either passed out or fainted and just crumpled to the ground. While

Brianne checked his pulse, I stared at the large wooden box on the coffee table.

"He is breathing but asleep." Brianne stood. She wiped her palms on the hem of her tunic. "This is no natural sleep, though. Based on what Seren and Nigel have been teaching us about the various demon clans, and knowing that you've seen some in the house already, I'd say this is almost certainly the work of chaos demons."

"How long until they all wake up?" I asked.

Brianne shrugged. "I don't know."

I glanced at the box on the table. "Can you use your magic to open that?"

Brianne studied it before replying. "What is it?"

"Morgan makes everyone put their phones into a locked box for the duration of the party, and that's it." I pointed. "My phone is in there. If we get it out, I can use it to text Max and Angie to let them know what's going on."

Brianne rolled her shoulders, then lifted both hands, palms facing the box and fingers spread. When she slid her hands apart, the sides separated from the top panel and fell open, revealing a mound of rectangular metal and plastic devices. Most were black, but a few colorful cases stood out, including mine.

I reached in and plucked out the one with the lime-green case. It wasn't my favorite color, but it did make my phone stand out in a crowd. The case had been included in a goodie bag from a club opening my agent had insisted I attend in Seattle—back before Morgan had almost killed me. Between helping Max and Angie hunt for the magic traps and ending up in the infirmary, I hadn't had time to change it for something different.

I dug the memory card out of my camera bag and peeled

the case back so I could reinsert it. Then I powered up the phone and stashed it in my camera bag. "Okay. Let's go."

"We should get out of here." Brianne started toward the door. "Chaos demons aren't really fighters like the Goristons and Drudens we were dealing with outside, but they are sneaky, and they can still cause a whole lot of trouble. Keep your eyes open and don't eat or drink anything."

Too late for that. I thought of the shot Ved had taken before karaoke as I followed Brianne back down the hall. Salty hurried after us, nails clicking on the wood floor.

On the way back up to my room, we peeked into Brady's viewing room. On the big screen, I recognized a scene from one of the first movies Brady landed a supporting role in. The explosions on the screen flashed across the sleeping faces of the dozen or so guests sprawled in the large reclining red velvet viewing chairs.

I recognized Lexie's face among them. She had dozed off with her head leaning toward Justin, who was in the chair next to her. They looked so cute together, with their heads almost touching and the light from the movie screen washing their faces in a riot of color. I reached for my camera to snap a few photos before backing out of the room.

Brianne waved me on before I could tuck my camera back into its cushioned nest. I placed the strap around my neck and followed her up the stairs. At the top, I led the way down the hall of the family wing to the room I'd been sharing with Ved. When I stepped inside, Salty bounded past and scouted the perimeter of the room.

While Salty sniffed everything, Brianne stayed at the door. "As long as I'm here, I'll go check out that secret room Bryn found while you pack up. You'll be safe in here. Just don't leave the room until I get back."

Once she was gone, I collapsed on the bed and released the frustrated scream I'd been holding back for hours.

Salty jumped up on the bed and licked my face.

"Ew." I wiped my cheek as I rolled away from her. "Thanks, though."

She pounced on me. Then jumped over my body so she could pant in my face.

"I know. I know. I should be packing. But everything suuuuuucksssssss," I moaned and pushed myself up to a sitting position.

A quick glance around the room confirmed that, even after only about twenty-four hours, we'd managed to get stuff everywhere. My clothes were heaped around my suitcase, at least. It wouldn't take long to stuff them all back inside. Except for my bra, which was still lying, shredded, on the floor over by the wall where Ved had pinned me.

I slapped a palm against my cheek. "Focus, Hannah."

Heading to the bathroom first, I collected my makeup and toiletries. Next, I shut down my computer, collected all my cables, and stuffed everything into one of my equipment bags. Everything else got shoved into my suitcase. Then I scanned the room to see if I'd missed anything.

The only thing left that wasn't already there when we arrived were the clothes Bryn had brought for Ved. I debated packing them up and bringing them with, then remembered that I said I would text Max and Angie.

I slid my phone out of my camera bag and entered my code. Then I stared at the group chat in the message app, trying to decide what to type. Before I could craft a message, Brianne returned.

"We have to go," she said, slipping inside and shutting the door behind her.

I gestured to my bags. "I'm packed."

She glanced around. "What about the rest of this?"

I shook my head. "Bryn brought it for Ved. I think it was mostly a cover for Bryn to get inside the house. If Ved wants any of it, he'll have to come and get it."

Something scratched at the door. Brianne and I both turned to look. While I stared, Brianne raised her hand and spread her fingers. The gaps between the door and the wood trim disappeared until the whole thing was just a solid wooden slab.

"That will slow them a bit." Brianne grabbed Salty off the bed.

I slid my phone into the pocket of on my camera bag, slung the strap across my shoulders, then gathered up as many of my bags as I could hold. Brianne got the suitcase.

"Ready?" she asked.

I nodded and sucked in a breath. Whatever was on the other side of the door had moved on from scratching. The slam and scrape of angry claws that probably belonged to one of Lilium's demon minions sent a shiver down my spine.

Just as the wood began to splinter, we disappeared.

When I opened my eyes, gasping and shivering, we were back in my apartment. I let my equipment bag slide to the floor before falling back into one of my chairs. I hugged my camera bag against my chest and closed my eyes, dimly aware of Salty running circles around my living room.

"I should go," Brianne said. "I need to find Nigel. Are you going to be all right here by yourself?"

I opened my eyes. Before I could answer, my phone vibrated. I pulled it out and glanced down at the missed messages and notifications that had been rolling in. My phone was finally catching up after being turned off.

I started to set it down on the table next to me when I noticed that the most recent message was from Callie. "Weird."

Brianne waited while I opened the message.

OMG!!! What happened?!?

A moment later, another message appeared below her words. It was a picture.

"Oh, shit!" I slapped a hand over my mouth as tears welled in my eyes, making the image blur and wobble.

Salty jogged over to me and sat next to my feet. She raised a paw and set it on my leg.

"What is it?" Brianne asked, taking a step closer so she could see the screen I held up.

"Silicon Moon. That. That was—" I choked on a sob. "That's Max's building."

Brianne said something in a language I didn't understand, but the meaning was clear enough.

I closed the message application, opened my contacts, and pressed a finger to Max's face on my screen. While the phone was ringing, I flipped back to the message application and typed a reply to Callie.

Is Grace okay? Was anyone in there?

Max picked up just before it went to voice mail. "Hey. I thought Morgan didn't allow phones at that party."

"Where are you? Are you okay? What happened?"

"How did you find out so fast?"

"Callie just sent me a photo. I think she's there? Where are you?"

"I'm home with Angie. The police just called. I don't think anyone was in the office, which is—"

"Good but also very bad?" I finished his sentence for him. "Yeah."

"Yeah." I locked eyes with Brianne.

"Are you still at my sister's house?" he asked.

"About that..."

"What happened? Are *you* okay?" he asked.

"Short answer? Yes. But some stuff happened, and...I'm back at my apartment. With Brianne." I sighed.

"Hang on. We'll be right there."

———

DAMIR explained that the demons had destroyed the building where the wizards were testing two of the magic traps so that they could steal them, giving the demons a total of three of the six boxes that had been found. After he finished filling me and Ivo in on what happened, he added, "As though that weren't bad enough, a faction of the Forest Fae is pushing to abandon the wizards, and all of humanity. They're saying that protecting magic is more important than protecting mortals."

"They're not wrong," Ivo said, giving voice to what we were all thinking.

"But the wizards can't fight off the demons alone. They were managing all right when the demon clans weren't all working together, but now that they are..." Damir shook his head. Since taking Seren as his mate, he'd become quite the expert on demons. Killing them for the humans had been how Seren managed to survive after her own faction cast her out.

That thought gave me an idea about who might be behind the push to abandon the wizards. "It's the Elementals, isn't it?" I asked.

Damir glanced at me with wide eyes. "How did you guess?"

He didn't have to act so surprised. If Seren's faction had been awful enough to kick her out for not having the right kind of magic according to some ancient legend of unknown origin, then they were probably also the ones behind this shortsighted decision. You didn't have to be a political genius to figure it out.

I shrugged. "Lucky guess."

"It's not all of them," Damir explained. "Their new guardian doesn't agree, but she's being pushed by their Elders."

"She's the one who took that half-demon spy as her mate, right?" I asked. Thinking of Nigel reminded me that I'd told Brianne I'd help her save him before Lilium succeeded in torturing him to death. I felt worse knowing his mate was fighting with her kin to keep the Fae from abandoning the wizards while we sat around, snug in our little cavern, discussing things.

I stood. "I need to go."

"Where?" Ivo asked.

"Back. I need to help Brianne rescue Nigel." I didn't bother reminding them that I was supposed to be guarding Hannah, as well.

Damir stood and stepped in front of me, blocking me from leaving. "Wait. Fiona called a Council meeting to decide what to do. I'm on my way back there now. Stay with Ivo, and I'll let you know what she decides."

I shook my head. "I'm not waiting."

"Then go with him," Ivo said. "Plead your case to Fiona. Regardless of what they decide, I'll have our best guards ready and waiting for your signal."

Damir frowned. "We can't do that."

"What do you mean?" Ivo said. His hands gripped the arms of the Alpha's chair.

Damir squared his shoulders. "As Alpha of our clan, I have pledged our loyalty to Fiona. If she decides in favor of the Elementals, then we will have to abide by their decision. If we don't..."

He didn't need to finish that sentence. Ivo and I both knew why. Fiona had gone against the Elementals and guaranteed Seren's safety when Damir chose her to carry his seed. If anything happened to Damir, Fiona would be the only one with the power to make sure no one tried to separate Seren from their Fledgeling. Especially if that Fledgeling turned out to be female and the heir to the Faerie Queen's throne.

My loyalty was sworn to Damir and Ivo, not Fiona. But that didn't make it any easier. Because of Damir's promise, if Fiona sided with the Elementals this time, helping Hannah and her wizard kin would mean turning my back on my wing-mates and my clan.

"Let's go," I said.

Damir turned to Ivo. "Will you be all right—?"

"Stop it." Ivo waved a hand. "The medics fuss over me enough. I don't need both of you doing it, too."

I stepped past Damir and started toward the door, but Damir didn't follow. When I turned around, he was still standing there. He'd crossed his arms over his chest and appeared to be in some sort of silent stare down with Ivo.

"Keep that chair warm for me," Damir said.

Ivo grimaced. "Go on."

Damir uncrossed his arms. "Regardless of what happens with the Council, I'm bringing Seren home."

Ivo nodded. "I'll inform the medics and her guards."

Damir nodded and turned to face me. "We can go now."

"Good hunting," Ivo called to us as we made our way across the arena.

All three faerie dragons were waiting for us at the West Mouth when we arrived.

"Why isn't Tarmog with Ivo?" I asked.

Damir snorted. "Well, Ash, when a male dragon loves a

female dragon very much—"

"Ugh," I groaned, cutting off the rest of his explanation.

Then it hit me, and I froze. "Wait. Sillag, right? Not Firrag."

Damir laughed. "Sillag."

I sighed with relief. "Good." Let Damir have all the Fledgelings. I had no interest in that sort of responsibility. I could barely manage to keep one human wizard safe.

The thought of Hannah and the wizards made me anxious to get moving. "Lead the way."

Damir whistled to the faerie dragons. They changed course and banked toward us. Sillag and Firrag stayed with us. Tarmog circled the cavern entrance once, then zipped past us down the tunnels, heading back toward Ivo.

"He's going to be all right?" I asked, watching Tarmog go.

"Ivo? He'll be fine for now, but I don't want to leave him long. Let's go." Damir clamped his hand down on my forearm, and we disappeared into the void.

We arrived to find a group of squabbling Forest Fae. Arabella had one hand on her sword, her body tense, as she watched Liam arguing with two Fae I didn't know. One had long brown hair adorned with colorful leaves. The flowing dark-green gown she wore appeared to be formed from similar foliage, all layered on top of each other. The other Fae had a wavy mass of short red hair. The neck of his white tunic gaped open to show off his broad chest, and a jeweled scabbard hung from the belt around his narrow waist.

Fiona stood nearby, listening. Bryn was next to her and nudged her when Damir and I arrived. Fiona's eyes landed on us. She clapped her hands together, and the red-haired male stopped talking to stare at her.

"We're all here." Fiona gestured to the stone table. "Take your seats, please."

I glanced around as everyone made their way into the stone circle that surrounded the High Table. Max wasn't here, nor were any of the other wizards. The only human present was Liam's mate, the immortal human named Eve. Apparently, Fiona had only invited the Fae portion of her Court to this meeting.

Since there were no chairs for guests, I remained standing when Damir took his seat at the table. Even though Nigel's and Max's chairs remained empty, neither of the two Elemental Fae who had been arguing with Liam moved to take those seats. Instead, they stood at the other end of the table, opposite Fiona's seat at the head.

"We're here to decide what to do now that the demons have possession of three of the magic traps."

"Three?" the red-haired male asked. "Don't you mean four? Lilium had one, then they found another. If they took the two from the wizards, they should have four now."

"The Dragon Fae have one," Damir explained. "Vedran took it when he captured Morgan."

"Thank you, Damir. And Vedran." Fiona nodded at us before turning her attention to the red-haired male. "Barrfhionn, I invited you and Anwen to this meeting because you insisted that you did not trust your guardian to speak on your behalf due to her...how did you put it? 'Compromised position'? I believe that was it. I ask that you remember you are a guest of the High Court. You will only speak if asked. If you find yourself compelled to interrupt again, I will not hesitate to have you removed. Do you understand?"

"Apologies, my queen." The jerk whose name was apparently Barrfhionn bowed his head.

"While I appreciate your apology, I asked you a question, and I expect an answer. Do you understand your role here?"

"I do."

"Excellent. Then do any of my Court have thoughts on this matter?"

Damir leaned forward, preparing to speak, but Gwawr's soft voice stole everyone's attention before he could begin to make his case.

"We should protect ourselves," she said.

Liam swung his head around to stare at her. "But—and I cannot believe I am about to say this—what about Nigel?"

Gwawr wrapped her arms around her body and leaned back in her chair. Her jaw was set, even though her eyes glistened with unshed tears.

Eve set her hand on top of Liam's. "I agree with Liam. If the Fae retreat, the demons will use this opportunity to prey on the wizards. They will fill their boxes with the magic drained from those wizards, and then they will come after the Fae."

Sorcha exchanged a look with Bryn before speaking. "Our illusions will keep us hidden. The demons would have to find us if they hoped to destroy us."

"But that would mean closing ourselves off from the humans. Completely." Liam's eyes locked with Eve's.

"So, we have a decision to make." Fiona spread her hand flat on the stone table. "Defend the wizards as we have promised and continue to fight off Lilium and the demon clans until they have all been killed or banished from Earth. Or... retreat. Allow the demons to plague the human lands until either they grow bored and leave or kill all the humans. Have I missed anything?"

Fiona's words made me think of the Entugs I'd met, and the things that Morgan had told Hannah about the demon clans. I opened my mouth, caught Barrfhionn looking at me, then shut it and leaned over the back of Damir's chair to tell him my thoughts, rather than get called out for being impulsive.

"Not all the demon clans will leave, and some may try to bring their wars here. It will be worse than she thinks," I whispered to Damir.

"If you have something to add to this discussion, you may share it with everyone, Vedran." Fiona's golden-brown eyes met mine.

"Apologies, my queen." I bowed my head.

"Speak," she said.

"I met some of these demons. There is a very precarious relationship between the clans. Some are serving Lilium only to avoid a worse fate. Perhaps we might be able to exploit that in our favor. The human is right. The demons will only grow stronger if we retreat and do nothing."

Barrfhionn gripped the back of one of the empty chairs. Anwen reached out to hold him back, but he brushed her hand away.

"Yes, Barrfhionn?" Fiona said. "I get the sense that you have something to add, even though your guardian has delivered the decision made by your Elders on behalf of your faction. Is there something else you would like to say?"

"If what the Dragon Fae says is true, then all the better." Barrfhionn grinned. "Let the clans fight among themselves. Perhaps they will destroy each other without the Fae having to lift a finger."

I glared at him. "That isn't what I meant. They are being coerced. They can't fight back. If we offer to help them—"

"Help the demons?" Barrfhionn cut me off, dismissing my explanation with a wave of his hand. "Your mind must have been corrupted during your encounter with them. Demons are the enemy of the Fae. All of them. And anyone who thinks otherwise is certainly ensorcelled." His eyes fell on Gwawr.

A growl rumbled at the base of my throat. I nearly lunged at him but caught myself when Anwen's eyes widened. Whatever she saw on my face had frightened her enough to make her take a step back, away from her companion.

Then Fiona spoke, and I reigned in my impulsive desire to stretch my claws out and slit the throat of that male for his refusal to see reason, not to mention his cruelty to Nigel's mate.

"I think that is enough discussion. I will now go around the table and ask you each to state your position on this, not personally but in the role that you serve on this Court. I will start with Arabella." Fiona turned to Arabella, who was seated at her right hand, as befitted her second-in-command. "Are you, as commander of the Guard, in favor of assisting the wizards in their fight against the demons, or do you think we should retreat and isolate?"

Arabella sighed. "As commander, I want to fight and destroy the demons. But the Guard isn't ready yet. We thought we had until the summer solstice to be prepared for war against the demons. We need more time. I say we retreat until we are trained and ready."

"Your position is noted." Fiona nodded. She focused on her next closest cousin, who was sitting to the right of Arabella. "Liam, what is your decision as representative of the small Fae factions?"

Liam cringed. He glanced at Eve, who sat on his other side before responding. "I believe that we should stand against the demons, but the Small Fae Faction is united in their desire that we retreat. As their representative, I must vote according to their wishes."

Fiona tapped her fingers against the stone table. "Evelyn?"

she asked.

Eve patted Liam's hand before releasing it. She slid her hands off the table and into her lap. "As ambassador to the mortals, I beg the Faerie Queen not to abandon the humans. Please help us fight the demon clans."

"Your plea is noted." Fiona nodded to Eve. Her eyes skipped the empty chairs as she turned her attention to the Elemental guardian. "Gwawr, what have the Elementals decided?"

Gwawr's jaw twitched from clenching it so tightly. She sucked in a breath through her nose and exhaled. "The Elemental Faction believes we should retreat."

Fiona tapped her fingers on the table again but said nothing in response. She didn't even nod before turning to Damir. "And, Damir? As Alpha of the Dragon Fae, what do you think?"

Damir leaned forward. "I think we should fight. The Dragon Fae will stand shoulder to shoulder with your Guard against the demon clans. We cannot let them prey on the humans. Not only must we honor our promise to the wizards, but the Dragon Fae depend on human women to produce our Fledgelings. Without them, we would go extinct."

Fiona scowled. "What of you and Ivo, then? Your mothers were High Fae, not human. The Dragon Fae could mate with Fae. They just choose not to. You yourself took a Fae female as a mate."

Damir shifted in his chair. "That is true, but it is only recently that our clan has been in contact with our more distant Fae kin."

"And now that you have sworn your oath and pledged your clan's loyalty to me as Faerie Queen, you wish to allow your clan to continue preying on unknowing village women? To continue the barbaric practice of stealing away their male offspring to be raised as Dragon Fae?"

Damir squirmed. "We have not had a chance to discuss this, my queen."

"No. But we shall. And I will not accept your clan's previous dependence on human women as a reason why we should put all Fae, and the very existence of magic, in danger." Fiona raised her eyebrows as though challenging him to argue. Her fingers tapped a beat on the stone slab.

"Yes, my queen," Damir replied.

I stared daggers at the back of his head. This wasn't working.

Bryn stepped forward, out of the shadows near the standing stones. "My queen, though you may find issue with the Dragon Fae Alpha's claim, as High Rogue, I will remind you that the health of the Rogues *are* dependent on the humans. We vote to fight."

"Noted." Fiona nodded to Bryn. "That leaves Sorcha, my master of illusions."

"My queen and niece, I would not be able to fulfill my responsibilities as master of illusions without access to my Rogue powers. I am also dependent on the humans and think that we cannot abandon them. But, if our commander thinks that we are not ready to fight and need more time, I can defend our lands until we are ready."

"All right." Fiona folded her hands in her lap. "Based on the feedback from my Court, I choose to order all Fae to remain inside the safety of our warded forest. No contact with any humans. This order extends to all factions, including the Rogues. All Fae may have until sundown tomorrow to settle their affairs in the human lands. At sundown, the borders will be closed. Humans in our forest will be required to stay here for the duration. Fae left outside will be closed off from their kin. Is that understood?"

Around the table, heads bobbed to a chorus of: "Yes, my queen."

Gwawr pushed her chair back. "Excuse me, Your Highness. I have things I must see to." She didn't wait for approval before tugging the hood of her patchwork cloak over her head and exiting the stone circle.

A look of sadness crossed Fiona's face as she watched Gwawr go. It was the last thing I saw before I disappeared. I, too, had things I needed to do, and there was no time to waste.

15

MAX and Angie were the first to arrive at my apartment. Brianne waited until they were inside before leaving. It wasn't until she was gone that I realized I didn't know if she were planning on going back to the Fae or heading out on her own to look for Nigel.

"You don't think she'd go after Nigel by herself, do you?" I asked.

"What is she even doing here?" Max asked. "And where's Ved?"

Someone knocked on my door.

"Hang on. I'll be right back." I left Angie and Max sitting in the living room, still in full view of the door, while I squinted through the security porthole.

Callie and Grace stood side by side, both with their arms crossed, facing the door.

I scowled, then flipped open the dead bolt to let them in. "Are you two all right?" I asked as they filed past me.

Grace, who entered after Callie, waved a hand in the air.

"Fine."

Callie didn't seem fine, though, as she stomped over to Max. "We need to talk."

"That's why we're here, isn't it?" Max scooted forward on the couch. He gestured toward one of my chairs. "Take a seat. Let's talk."

Callie didn't move. "Those boxes were in there, weren't they?"

Max frowned. "Maybe we should wait until Jayden and Kyle get here."

"Just answer the question, Hunter." Callie's hip jutted out to one side.

"Give it a rest, Cal. It's not Max's fault." Grace sat down next to Angie and crossed one leg over the other. Side by side, I couldn't help noticing that the pair of them looked like they'd stepped out of different eras.

Angie had this killer bad-girls-of-rock-and-roll look with her black jeans and black boots paired with a silky, low-cut emerald-green wrap blouse. The ends of her dark-brown bob were dyed purple. Meanwhile, Grace was all soft fabrics and earth tones with the clean-cut preppy-chic catalog look that she'd been rocking since we were actually in prep school. I had this fleeting thought about interviewing them for an up-coming video before remembering that, after the disaster that was Morgan's party, my career was probably over.

I'd led poor Nigel into a trap, my big break had turned into a battle zone, and the celebrities I'd hoped to interview might as well be auditioning as extras in a live-action *Sleeping Beauty* remake. Unfortunately, I was pretty sure that a kiss from a prince wasn't going to bring anyone back to life. More like the opposite of that was true. The fact that, against my better judgment, I'd given in to temptation and ended up making out with that Dragon Fae had been more or less what had started this mess. Including the part where Silicon Moon exploded.

"It's my fault." I didn't realize I'd spoken the words out loud until everyone turned to look at me.

Another knock at the door saved me from having to elaborate. I turned my back on everyone and checked to make sure it was Jayden and Kyle before letting them inside.

"Oh, good. You're all here." Kyle sighed. He carried a thick leather-bound book tucked against his chest with one hand. The other was intertwined with Jayden's.

"You can relax, Max," Jayden called out as he pulled Kyle inside. "All employees have been accounted for. No one was in the building except for the security guards. The one who was down in the lobby only needs to shower some plaster out of his hair. The one who was on patrol got patched up and sent home by the EMTs."

"What's with the book?" I asked Kyle.

Kyle tipped it away from his body so I could see the cover. "Jay and I found something. We were on our way over to Silly Moon to experiment on one of the boxes, but when we got there..."

The symbol embossed on the leather cover was the same one that had been on the demon protection charm they'd sent for Ved.

"We were greeted with sirens, flashing lights, and the shell of what used to be our beautiful headquarters building." Jayden finished Kyle's sentence. "Good thing we decided to stop for coffee on our way there."

Angie glared at Jayden. She reached over and massaged Max's neck. "It's all right. Everyone's okay. You can relax now."

"I thought that creepy old dude from the bookstore just decided to pack up and move on—like when he disappeared after he gave you that key, Max." Kyle shook his head. "But this is too much of a coincidence. At least we still have the spell book I got from him."

"Thanks, Jay, Kyle." Max took a deep breath. He reached up and set his hand on top of Angie's, where she was attempting to knead his still tense shoulders. Then he looked up to meet Callie's glare. "The building alarm system alerted me of the explosion. I arrived just before the authorities."

Max held up the little transporter device that his engineering team had been working on. "The good news is, thanks to this, I was able to get in and out without them seeing me. The bad news is, while the emergency responders were clearing the lower levels, I confirmed that the boxes were gone. I didn't have time to do a thorough investigation, but I didn't notice anything else missing."

"So, the demons blew up the Silicon Moon building just to get the boxes." Grace picked at the sleeve of her cashmere sweater.

Next to Grace, Angie leaned forward. Her eyes locked with mine. She set her elbows on her thighs and folded her hands. "Why do you think this is your fault, Hannah? What happened at Morgan's?"

Everyone looked at me.

All of a sudden, the room seemed too warm and too small. I gathered my hair at the nape of my neck and pulled it over my shoulder, smoothing my hand down the clump of strands to the end as I tried to summarize. "It's a long story, but basically, Lilium showed up. Ved captured Morgan. He took her and the box that she had back to the Dragon Fae. Then a bunch of Lilium's demon minions arrived, and there was a big fight on the pool deck. The demons lost their heads, and Lilium disappeared with Nigel."

Max tensed. "The Dragon Fae have my sister?"

"Yeah. I think so."

Jayden glanced around the room. "Speaking of Dragon Fae...where is the one who was supposed to be guarding you, Hannah?"

I shrugged. "After Lilium disappeared, he insisted on returning with the Dragon Fae that he brought to fight the demons. He left me with Brianne, who had been guarding Nigel. She brought me back here and then left just after Max and Angie arrived."

"Wait. That birdbrain abandoned you?" Jayden put his hands on his hips. The last time I'd seen that look on his face, he'd been staring down Ved, and I'd had to intervene before fists started flying.

"Temporarily." I cringed, hating that I felt this need to defend Ved when I was still mad at him. If Jayden wanted to give Ved a lecture on teamwork and responsibility, he was going to have to get behind me. Still, despite my response, I doubted we'd be seeing that Dragon Fae's perfectly symmetrical face around here again anytime soon.

"Temporarily?" Jayden raised his eyebrows.

Kyle put a hand on his boyfriend's arm. "Let's put a pin in that and go back to the part where the Dragon Fae captured Morgan and the box that she had."

"Yes. Let's," Max said. "How did that even happen? Did you guys break into Morgan's office?"

I shook my head. "No. I thought I was winning Morgan over to our side, but she was really just using me to get to Nigel. Once Nigel showed up, she called Lilium. Then Lilium wanted to use the box to suck magic from Ved and Brianne, so she sent Morgan to fetch one. Ved was supposed to be rescuing Nigel, but the next thing I knew, he had disappeared with Morgan and the box."

"So, Lilium stole our boxes, and now the demons and the Fae have all the power, and the wizards are once again left defenseless." Callie crossed her arms. "You and your family have made a mess of this, Hunter. It's time for a new family to take over control of the Society."

"Callie, no." Grace shot her girlfriend a look. "Now is not the time—"

"Now is the best time." Callie spread her arms out. "If someone doesn't do something now, that's going to be it for the Society of Wizards. The demons are coming for us next, and you know it."

Max stood. He brushed his hands down the front of his jeans. "You know what? You're right. Let's do this."

Grace leaned forward at the same time as Angie reached up to grasp Max's arm. Jayden took a half step toward Callie, and Kyle tucked the book under his arm so he could pull out his phone. Time seemed to slow down as the tension built.

"Stop it." I pulled water from the vase of flowers on my coffee table and shot it upward, dividing it into two streams. I directed one toward Max's face and the other toward Callie's.

They stumbled back, blinking and sputtering, as they tried to wipe the water out of their eyes and dry off their faces.

"What was that for?" Max asked.

"No fighting in my living room."

Angie's phone buzzed.

Kyle looked up from his screen. "I've informed the Council. They're calling a meeting."

Callie frowned at Kyle. "It's not going to do any good. You know that as well as I do. The Hunters have ruled the Council for centuries. If giving birth to a half demon wasn't enough to persuade the Council to replace Elton and Marcella, then what makes you think *this* will change anything?"

Kyle set a hand on Callie's shoulder. "Because you're right. We're in trouble."

"We're in a *lot* of trouble," Angie said, still staring down at her phone screen.

Max stuck his hands in his pockets. "For the record, Hannah, I wasn't going to fight anyone. I was actually going to agree with Callie. I was going to offer to take her to the Council myself."

"Um, guys?" Angie looked up. Her thumbs hovered over her screen. "Is anyone even listening to me? Eve just texted me. The Fae are retreating. Fiona held a meeting of her High Court to discuss what happened. Eve and Willow have until sundown tomorrow to decide if they're going to remain in the Fae Forest for good or if they're going to return to live among the humans."

"What? Why?" I wasn't sure which was worse. The Faerie Queen had made a deal with Max that the Fae would help the wizards. Going back on that seemed almost as unfair as making Eve and Willow, who were both humans with Fae mates, pick a side.

Angie shook her head. "Arabella says that the Guard isn't ready to take on the demons, especially now that they have three of the magic traps. They aren't going to help us."

Callie, Kyle, and Max exchanged a look. Their parents sat on the council that ran the Wizard Society. I didn't know what they were silently communicating, but based on her reaction, Grace thought she did.

"No." Grace stood up. "If you go, we all go."

"I can't believe I'm about to say this..." Jayden rubbed his chin. "I'm no fan of Marcella or Elton, but I think voting the Hunters out now is only going to make things worse. The Society is all we have. If we can't hold it together, we don't stand a chance against the demons. Especially now that the Fae have backed out of their bargain."

"How is that even possible?" I asked. "I didn't think Fae could back out of a bargain."

"Loopholes." Kyle shrugged. "They're Fae."

Something crashed behind me, and everyone craned their necks to look. When I turned around, Ved was standing just inside my apartment door, staring at the entry table. The tabletop was angled down on the side closest to the door, and everything that had been sitting on top was scattered on the floor, soaking in a puddle, mixed in with shards of my favorite vase and the scattered flowers it had been holding.

"Sorry about that." Ved cringed. "I must have misjudged the coordinates."

WHATEVER I'd been expecting when I transported myself from Fiona's High Court to Hannah's apartment, it wasn't this. No one looked happy to see me, least of all Hannah. It probably didn't help that I'd made a mess and broken her table and some ceramic object in the process.

Hannah waved a hand and the water on the floor evaporated. "What are you doing here?" she asked.

"Some nerve," Jayden muttered. He crossed his arms and jutted one hip to the side as he glared at me.

"I was at Fiona's meeting. I wanted to make sure you were all right, and I only have until tomorrow at sunset. After that, I'm forbidden from having any contact with humans." I really didn't want to have this conversation in front of all her friends.

"I'm fine. Thanks for checking." Hannah tossed her hair over her shoulder. "If you're not here to help, you can go."

"I tried to convince them to help." I took a step forward. My boot crunched on one of the broken pieces of pottery.

Hannah cringed.

One of her friends—there were three there that I hadn't met—pushed up the sleeves of her sweater, then gestured toward the floor with both hands. Bits of ceramic began reassembling themselves under her direction until there was only one empty hole remaining on the curved side of what must have been a vase.

The earth wizard sighed. "Move your foot."

I lifted my foot, and the remaining pieces snapped into place. The broken seams disappeared, and the vase rested, good as new, on the floor among a scattering of flowers. The table legs that had buckled and cracked straightened, and the tabletop leveled out. I watched, fascinated, having only ever seen earth magic used for destructive purposes.

"Thanks," Relieved that I hadn't done any permanent damage, I returned to my explanation. "There was a vote—"

Hannah held up her hand. "It's fine. We'll figure it out. Thanks for your help at Morgan's. You can go. Really."

"Wait!" Max stepped forward. "How's my sister?"

One of the other wizards I didn't recognize exhaled in a huff. "You have to be kidding me."

Max sighed. "She's my sister, Callie."

"She's half demon and working with the enemy, Hunter."

"I don't know. I haven't seen her," I said. Checking on Morgan wasn't something I had considered.

"Aren't the Dragon Fae the ones keeping her prisoner?" Max asked.

I nodded once. "Yes. There's no transport in or out of our caverns, so she'd have to get past our guards and find her way through a maze of tunnels if she wanted to try to escape. But I'm sure they're treating her well."

Damir and Ivo were nothing like Boro. I'd once been Boro's prisoner, and he'd nearly let me die. Even though she was helping the enemy, my wing-mates would make sure Morgan had enough food and water, and medicine if she needed it. At least as long as she behaved herself and didn't try to escape. Though I decided it wouldn't hurt to check on her when I returned, just to be sure.

Max sighed. "Thanks."

"All right." I took one last look at Hannah, wishing there was some way to talk with her alone. "Are you sure there's nothing I can do to help?"

Hannah's eyes widened. "You're joking, right?"

I shook my head. "I have until tomorrow at sunset. I could stay and help until then."

Jayden crossed his arms. "Unless you're planning on staying for the duration, I don't see how you're going to be of any use to us."

I glanced around at each of their faces. Even though the others didn't hold nearly as much hostility as Jayden's, none of them looked particularly welcoming. "What about Morgan's party? I could take you back there so you could finish your work."

Hannah's shoulders slumped. "The party's over, and so is my career. So, thanks, I guess? But it's too late."

"There must be some way—"

"Dude." Jayden shook his head. "You heard her. We don't need your help. Just go."

"Actually, Jay. Hang on a sec." Max set a hand on Jayden's

shoulder. "I don't think it's a good idea to leave Hannah here alone. Callie, Kyle, Grace, and I all need to go talk to the Wizard Council. That leaves you here with Angie and Hannah, unless—"

"No way." Jayden shook his head. "I'll stay with Angie and Hannah, but the Dragon Fae is not staying."

"How about this?" Hannah raised her voice. "It's my apartment, and I decide who stays and who goes. And right now, I'm thinking everyone goes. Everyone. My apartment is warded. I'll be fine. All you Council kids, help your parents gather our forces. Jayden, you bring Angie to Eve—it sounds like she could probably use a friend right now—and then figure out how to get all the underground wizards mobilized. I have some filming to do. I owe my subscribers an explanation, and it's going to take me a minute to come up with something believable."

"I'll leave Salty with you," Angie said, her voice barely above a whisper.

"Great." Hannah put her hands on her hips. Her posture challenged anyone to defy her commands. "Now get going. All of you."

Her eyes locked with mine.

"Good hunting." I nodded at them, then transported myself home.

After landing outside the West Mouth of the caverns, I lingered there, watching Firrag, Sillag, and Tarmog circle the night sky. As their silhouettes slid across the stars, I tried to shake the feeling of disappointment that lingered. I should be satisfied. Content, even.

I'd gone to Hannah's apartment to help but also to say goodbye. She hadn't appeared at all concerned about me taking my leave of her. She'd even gone so far as to insist that I go. That she didn't need me or an explanation. So, why did my chest ache?

I glanced down at my hands in the moonlight. The tips of my fingers were round and fleshy, not long with razor-sharp edges, tapered to a point at the end. She'd touched my claws and hadn't flinched. What would have happened if she'd seen me fully transformed?

It didn't matter. Whatever fun we'd had was over. Just like any visit to the village, I needed to leave it behind me and focus on the future. Especially now that even the village was going to be off-limits to our clan.

I stared up at the faerie dragons and tried to picture a pear in my mind like Grandsire Firewing had instructed me. I couldn't manage it with my eyes open, so I closed them and tried again. Once I held the image of the pear firmly in my mind's eye, the backdrop shifted. The pear glowed a milky white surrounded by an inky-black sky dotted with twinkling stars.

Firrag didn't want to join me inside. Firrag wanted to play in the moonlight with her friends.

I sighed. Even my faerie dragon wanted me to go.

With one last glance up at the sky, I turned my back on the mountaintops and ducked inside, trudging through the safety of the cavern tunnels to find my wing-mates. At least there was a chance they might welcome me with open arms.

I tried to keep an eye out for any sign of where they were keeping Morgan as I made my way to the arena. None of the caves I passed were guarded. I'd been so far gone when Boro's lieutenants deposited me in whatever corner of the caverns they were using as their prison cell, I couldn't remember where it might be, or if Damir would even use the same one. I decided I'd ask him, once I found him, so I could check on Max's sister and reassure myself that what I'd told Max was true.

I entered the arena and crossed to the Alpha's room. The guards outside the door stood at attention when they spotted me, then stepped aside to let me pass without any questions. I ducked inside and shut the door behind me.

"What have you done?" Damir asked as soon as the door closed.

16

AFTER Ved disappeared, the others organized themselves into groups. Max pulled Angie off to the side where they conversed in hushed voices. Kyle gave Jayden a kiss, then he followed Callie and Grace to the door. I hugged each of them to make sure they knew I didn't love them any less even though I'd basically kicked them out.

As soon as I let them out into the hall, they started bickering about which car service would get them across town fastest. Salty leaned against my leg when I shut the door. So, I bent down to pick her up.

I stared at the vase Ved had broken and Grace had repaired. "I guess that's it," I whispered into Salty's fur.

Angie caught my eye and left Max to come over to me. "You okay?" she asked.

I smiled. "Fine. I'm just tired. It's been a long day."

"Yeah." Angie tucked her hair behind her ear. "So, am I right in guessing that you and that Dragon Fae hooked up?"

I sighed. "I told you it was a bad idea."

"Well, I still want to hear all about it…whenever you want to talk. Okay?"

I nodded. I wasn't fine, and I didn't want to talk about it. At least not yet.

"Thanks. Give Eve a hug for me? And Willow if you see her?" I didn't want to think about how I might not get to say goodbye to either of them. I might never speak to either of them again. I certainly wouldn't blame them if they decided to stay with their mates and the Fae.

Angie squeezed my arm. "Of course. Take care of Salty for me?"

"Definitely." I kissed the top of the little dog's head.

"Ready?" Jayden asked.

"Let's go." Angie scratched Salty under her chin, then bent to whisper something in her ear before giving me a quick hug and turning away.

"You going to be okay here?" Jayden asked me.

"Go. I've got a ton of work to get done. Especially if I'm going to be busy helping you all fight demons on top of everything else." I waved them off.

Jayden programmed one of Silicon Moon's transporters while Angie gave Max a kiss goodbye. Then Jayden and Angie linked arms, Jayden pressed a button, and they disappeared.

I shivered. "Ugh."

"Ugh?" Max asked.

"Transporting like that makes me want to hurl every time." I gagged just thinking about it.

Max ran a hand through his hair. "Sorry I never noticed."

Ved had, though. I grinned in spite of the ache that squeezed my chest. "It's fine."

"You're sure you don't need anything else before I go? I really hate leaving you like this." Max glanced around the room like he was checking the corners for demons.

"Go do your thing. Make a plan. Salty and I will be here when you get back." I shrugged. "It's not like my water magic is going to be much help to anyone, anyway."

"That's not true."

"Come on, Max. You know it is—otherwise, why would you have thought I needed a bodyguard."

"Hannah, I love my sister, even now. Even after everything she's done. But I also grew up with her. I know what she's capable of. If I could have managed to get Fiona to assign a bodyguard to every single one of you, I would have done it. It had nothing to do with your magic. You are one of the most talented wizards I know."

I snorted. "A lot of good that talent is in a fight with a demon. You weren't there. You didn't see. Brianne was barely holding them back, and she's Fae."

"If we—" He cut himself off and paused for a moment. "*When* we get through this, I'm going to make Fiona follow through with her pledge to train all the wizards."

I shook my head. "And how exactly do you figure that we're going to manage to defeat these demons on our own?"

"We figured out how the boxes work, right? We figured out where they were. We would have had all of them if I hadn't slipped up and told my sister what we were up to." He paused to look down at his feet. "This isn't your fault, you know. It's mine. I'm the one who took you with me to Italy and got you injured. If Morgan didn't know that you knew about her, then none of this would have happened. You could have gone and done your work, and she would only have me and Angie to focus her wrath on."

"It's not that simple. She attacked me before Italy."

"Did you remember what happened?" Max's eyes widened.

I frowned. "No. But it had to have been her. Who else could it have been? Who else could even get into your office building like that?"

"You have a point there." He cocked his head to one side. "But even if she was the one who knocked you out so that she could get access to everything we'd been working on, she would have still assumed that you didn't know about her demon half. It's not like I was going to tell anyone."

"It wasn't your secret to tell, Max." I crossed my arms. "Morgan should have told me years ago. She shouldn't have hidden this from me. If I'd known, I would have done anything to help her."

"I tried."

"I know you did. It's not your fault that she went to Lilium for help. That Demon Queen manipulated her." Tears welled in the corners of my eyes as thoughts of Morgan and Lilium had me replaying everything I'd seen on the pool deck and remembering Nigel's moans and the pain on his face. "We have to do something to help Nigel. We can't leave him with her."

"I'll send a message to Jayden and get him on it. If any one of us can figure out where Lilium is hiding, it will be him."

Another memory popped into my head. I glanced over at my camera bag, still sitting where I'd left it, safely tucked under my chair. "Actually...I may be able to help with that as well."

"Great." Max grinned. "I'm going to deal with the Council. Okay if everyone regroups here when we're done?"

I nodded, already moving toward my equipment. "Sure."

Max was gone when I turned around with my arms full of bags, but I didn't care. I carried everything down the hall to my room. Salty followed me inside. She hopped up onto my bed and made herself comfortable while I unpacked my camera, set up my lighting, and started up my computer.

Once everything was running, I pulled the storage card out of my camera and slid it into my laptop. It took a moment to copy everything over to my hard drive. Then I scrolled to the very end of the images and scanned through them, working my way backward. I needed to see if I'd managed to get any that showed Lilium's face in enough detail to be useful.

I skipped past several, then went back when a flash of red caught my eye. There. I zoomed in. That was it. I cropped the image and saved it.

Time to crowdsource me a Demon Queen. Or, to put a Fashion Friday spin on it, identify a potential fashion icon from an unknown celebrity sighting.

As I waited for the storage card to eject from my computer, I scanned through the photos I'd taken before Nigel arrived and everything went sideways. There were a few I didn't remember taking. Then there were several of me.

Ved. He was a natural with the camera. I selected the first of a batch of candid shots he'd taken while I was rearranging the backdrop in one of the potential interview locations. It was a cozy corner with good light and two overstuffed armchairs. In the first shot, he'd caught me leaning over the flower arrangement. A few strands of hair curled down to frame my face as I appeared to be inhaling the scent of the lilacs.

The next shot captured me gazing thoughtfully out of the window. In another, I was actually laughing. I remembered the moment. He'd been messing around with Salty who had found an old deflated medicine ball outside on the gym patio. The thing was bigger than her head, but she brought it inside and straight to Ved.

The look of disgust on his face at the dirty, lopsided mess

lying at his feet was priceless. I'd laughed until he'd threatened to toss the ball at me. At some point, he must have taken my picture.

It really was too bad that he was Fae. He was the first guy I'd dated who not only didn't question the legitimacy of my work but also jumped in and offered to help without even being asked. And he was naturally good at it. Who would have thought that a beefy warrior type would have such a natural artistic eye?

There was no point in wishing for things I couldn't have. I'd tried that back when I stopped getting callbacks for auditions. I'd tried it with my magic. I'd even tried it with Morgan. And what did I have to show for it? Nothing.

I wasn't an actress. I was a water wizard with disappointed parents who was moderately internet famous. My friendship with Morgan was over. And the party that was supposed to be the thing that put me back on Hollywood's radar was a disaster. Wishing for a relationship with an immortal warrior who happened to also have the potential to be an asset to my career wasn't going to change any of that. Especially now that said career was probably over.

I needed to film the video that would disappoint my followers and probably result in more angry comments than I had the heart to face. At least it would get a lot of views. I was counting on that because it meant I could use this as an opportunity to locate Lilium. Something good might come out of this disappointing mess, and for that, I would face the nasty internet trolls. They weren't half as scary as facing an actual demon, anyway.

I returned the now empty storage card to my camera and repositioned my lighting. After changing into an appropriately fashionable yet casual—just another movie night at home—outfit, I touched up my makeup and took a seat on what I liked to think of as my vlog chair.

"Ready?" I asked Salty.

She cocked her head at me.

"Quiet, now. It's showtime." I reached out and hit record on what I expected would be my last video.

———

DAMIR and Ivo stared at me from their seats at the Alpha's table, waiting for an explanation. I'd disappeared from the High Court meeting without saying where I was going or why, but why did Damir have to automatically assume I'd gone and done something impulsive and gotten into trouble?

"I went to see Hannah and tell her that the wizards were on their own. No more Fae bodyguard. No more Fae army. Why?" I hadn't done anything wrong.

Damir shook his head and groaned.

I bristled, ready to defend myself, but Ivo spoke first.

"Mir, he didn't know." Ivo leaned his head against the back of the Alpha's chair. He looked exhausted and also like he hadn't moved since we'd left.

"Didn't know what?" I asked, trying to read whatever it was I'd missed off their faces.

Damir tapped his fingers on the table. "This."

I shook my head. "What? The table? I don't get it."

Ivo sighed. "Fiona has a code she uses to communicate with her High Fae kin. Did you notice during the meeting how she was tapping her fingers on the table?"

I nodded. "Sure. But I just thought she was annoyed. I figured that Barrfhionn jerk was getting under her skin. She looked like she wanted to wring his neck. I know I wanted to. Almost did." My fingers flexed at the thought.

"Right. Well, while she was saying 'the Fae will retreat,' she was giving me different orders." Damir crossed his arms.

"Oh." I sank into the third chair.

"Oh, indeed." Ivo grinned.

"So, we're not retreating?" I glanced back and forth between their faces.

Damir leaned back in his chair. "They are. We've been given permission to do as we deem necessary."

"What about that lecture about how we could take Forest Fae as mates and didn't need to rely on women from the village?" I asked. "Are you saying she didn't mean that, either?"

"Oh, no. She definitely meant that. She's hinted at her displeasure before. I've been expecting the discussion to come up at some point. She has a point, but we also don't have much research on what happens when Dragon Fae mate with other Fae. Sure, there's me and Ivo, as she pointed out, but we're both male. We don't really know what happens when a Dragon Fae gives his seed to a Fae female and the resulting offspring is female. All our Elders can tell us is that Dragon Fae are always male. Would a female born of a Dragon Fae and an Elemental Fae pairing, for example, be able to shift into a dragon? Would it be different for the offspring of a High Fae, who already have the genetic ability to shift into the form of a predatory animal? And how would these potential changes impact the future of our clan?"

"I'm so glad I don't have to worry about any of this." I shook my head. "How soon can we assemble a squadron of guards?"

Ivo laughed. "Not so fast, Ash."

Damir grinned. "Yeah. What did you think was going to happen when you offered your seed to the queen of the Fae? That's a High Fae and Dragon Fae pairing. Different from what I have with Seren, and it's going to provide important data. Whatever characteristics develop in that offspring will help us determine the future of our clan."

"But I thought Fiona didn't want my seed. I thought she was still considering who would sire her firstborn."

Ivo waved a hand. "Firstborn or not, she'll take your seed. She is committed to uniting all the Fae factions, and historically, the best way to do that has been to take the seed from at least one eligible male in each faction. It worked for her grandmother, and she intends to follow that model, assuming the demons don't kill off all the Fae first."

"That's where we come in." Damir leaned forward and set his elbows on the table.

"So, this is what you two have been working out while I was stuck staring at the infirmary ceiling and sparring with the Queen's Guard?" I scowled at them. "When were you going to tell me any of this? How long were you going to leave me out, wondering where I stood in the new clan hierarchy?"

Damir's eyes went wide. "You can't be serious. Wing-mates for life. Remember? You didn't really think we would leave you out? You and Ivo are my lieutenants. You've always been."

"See?" Ivo smirked at me over his crossed arms.

I swallowed the lump in my throat. Damir had no idea how much I needed to hear him say that.

"Ash?" Damir blinked at me.

I nodded, still trying to force words past the knot of emotion. "All right."

"All right." Damir set his hand over mine. Then he reached over and set his other hand on Ivo's shoulder. "Fire, Ash, Light," he said, his voice a hoarse whisper.

"Wing-mates for life," we said together.

After a moment, I asked, "Is Ivo also meant to take a Fae mate?"

Ivo raised a finger. "Choose a Fae to take my seed, yes. However, like you, I've made no promises about whom I will take as a mate."

"If you take a mate," Damir challenged.

"It won't be a human." I focused on a groove that had been worn into the wooden tabletop to avoid their eyes.

"Oh, we're down on humans, now, are we?" Ivo teased.

"This has nothing to do with the water wizard." I couldn't even bring myself to say her name.

"Of course not," Damir said. His voice held no hint of either judgment or jest.

Encouraged that at least one of them might understand and sympathize instead of seeing my frustration over Hannah's dismissal amusing, I looked up. Just in time to catch the glance that Damir and Ivo exchanged. So much for thinking they wouldn't tease me.

"Dragon Fae don't take mates." I tried to explain what I thought was obvious, gesturing to Damir. "Except perhaps for the Alphas."

"Yes. Well. I'm sure Seren will be happy to hear that," Damir said, his voice loaded with sarcasm. "Besides, I would have taken her as my mate even if I didn't become Alpha. I knew the moment I saw her. Not to mention, my sire wasn't Alpha, and he took a mate."

"But your mother was the High Fae daughter of the Faerie Queen. That's a bit different." My fingers curled around the armrest on the chair as memories flashed through my mind of those long nights in the infirmary watching over Hannah as she cried out in her sleep or moaned in pain. I looked forward to her gentle snoring because it meant she was finally resting and healing.

She had been so fragile. Now she had her magic to protect her, but she was still mortal. Even with all the power of water at her command and her friends at her side, they would struggle to defeat the united force of the demon clans.

"Perhaps it will become more common. If Fiona has her way, all the Dragon Fae will be encouraged to give up their seed. Some might choose to take a mate in the process." Ivo rubbed his chin. "Still, aside from that pesky problem of mortality, I don't see what would be so awful about taking a human as a mate. Our cousins Liam and Arabella both did, and that seems to be working out all right for them. And as Dragon Fae, we have something they don't. Our male offspring will always be Dragon Fae, regardless of the mother."

Damir tapped his fingers on the table. "Did you know that Fiona gave Liam's mate, Eve, immortality as a way of thanking her for her service to the Fae?"

I stared at Damir's fingers. "What did Eve do?"

"She banished the vengeful spirit that had been plaguing the Forest Fae for centuries. Killing them off until only a fraction remained. The remaining High Fae thought banishing him would put an end to that."

"But it turned out that Lilium got to him first. For nearly a generation, she'd been the one stoking the flames of Edric's hatred of the Fae," Ivo added.

I folded my arms and leaned back in my chair. "Don't think I don't know why you're telling me this. You can save your breath, though. There is nothing between me and Hannah."

Damir hummed as his fingers drummed a beat. "If that's the case, perhaps we shouldn't risk our clan fighting the demons."

I slapped my hand down on top of his, pinning his fingers

to the table. "Enough of that. I know you're using Fiona's code to talk about me. Say whatever it is you have to say, or at least teach me to understand."

"I wasn't. I swear." Damir laughed. "And it's actually Willow's code. She taught it to Arabella who taught it to Fiona, and—"

Ivo cut Damir off. "We'll teach you the code, but not tonight." He stretched and yawned. "If there's nothing between you and your human, then Damir's right. Perhaps we should all get some rest."

"I want to go and check on the half demon first," I said, standing. There were more things I needed to think about, but I wasn't quite ready to face those yet.

The three of us made our way across the arena together, then split up as we each reached the passageway we were heading toward. Ivo, as it turned out, was staying with Grandsire Firewing so that he could keep a close eye on Ivo's recovery. Damir had found himself an empty cavern near the nursery, which he'd moved into with Seren. He gave me instructions as to where I would find Morgan before he headed off in the opposite direction.

The long walk through the empty, winding tunnel that led me to the cluster of caverns designated as isolation cells gave me time to think about what I would say to the guards and to Morgan, if she were awake. Still, when I finally stopped in front of the guards, my tongue stumbled on the words.

I recognized the little anteroom at the end of the tunnel where the guards stood. There were three caverns, but only one was being guarded. I was about to speak when a female ducked out of the cavern and nodded to the guards.

Seren paused when she saw me. "What are you doing here?"

"I could ask you the same thing." I didn't know much about Damir's mate, but I did know that, after she'd been cast out by her kin, she used to fight demons for humans who, in exchange, would give her a warm, safe place to sleep or supplies that she couldn't conjure for herself.

Seren led me back down the tunnel until we were far enough away that even the guards with their sensitive Fae ears wouldn't be able to hear us. "I was testing her. Trying to see what sort of magic we're dealing with. We can't keep her sedated forever."

"Is she asleep now?"

Seren shook her head. "She's awake, but she refuses to speak to me. I managed to get a sample of her blood. I'm hoping that, if we can get it to Gwawr, she might be able to tell us something more. She once used Nigel's and Arabella's blood to locate their sire. If she can do the same for Morgan, it might help us."

"How are they treating her?" I asked.

Seren frowned. "She's chained, but not tightly. The medics healed her broken wrist. She can sit and stretch, but the steel cuffs and the bars of her cell should keep her from conjuring."

I thought of the petite woman I'd met and tried but failed to picture her in chains. "Her brother was asking about her. I reassured him that we wouldn't hurt her, but I wanted to check for myself."

Seren squeezed my arm. "If you go in there, be careful."

I nodded. "I'll be fine."

Seren shook her head. She set one hand on her belly. "Stubborn males. Almost makes me wish for a female. Almost."

"We're not all bad."

Seren raised her eyebrows. "Right. This brutish clan of males makes my kin look like a pack of peace-loving gnomes.

Or live-to-serve brownies. And that's saying something, especially since I heard you met our two finest shining specimens, Wenny and Barr."

"I thought Gwawr was the best of the Elementals?" I asked, confused about why she thought so highly of that pompous red-headed ass.

Seren snorted. "And I thought Dragon Fae understood sarcasm."

"Oh."

"Yes. Oh." Seren grinned. "Wouldn't have hated it if you'd punched him right in his smug little face, you know?"

I smiled at her. "Next time. I promise."

"Deal." She patted my shoulder.

"Do you want me to take that to Gwawr for you?" I pointed at the vial of blood she held in her hand.

She glanced down, then back up to meet my eyes. "You'll have to return to the human lands to do it."

"What? Why? Where is she?"

Seren tugged me farther away from the prison caves. "She went after Nigel."

"Alone?" I asked.

"No. Brianne is with her."

"Does Fiona know?"

Seren nodded. "She told Gwawr to go. Fiona knows that Barr is a festering boil, but Gwawr had to convey the decision made by the Elemental Elders. They aren't the most open-minded group, and several of them are directly related to Wenny, which makes them very easy for Barr to manipulate."

"Are they mates?" I asked.

Seren shook her head. "Maybe? But I doubt it. Last I heard, poor Wenny doesn't have enough power to be more than a plaything. Though, if Gwawr doesn't return, they'll call another Conclave, and that will shift power among the Hands again."

"Where are Brianne and Gwawr?"

"I don't know." She extracted a coin from a pocket in her tunic. "I have this, though. It's keyed to her. So we can find out."

17

Y eyes were tired from staring at my computer screen, but I decided to watch the whole thing through once more before uploading it. I'd spliced in the photos I'd taken of Lexie and her friends. I'd added a clip from karaoke. And then I'd thrown in a cropped picture of a well-dressed "mystery woman" and asked my subscribers to help me figure out who she was and how to find her so I could "interview her for my channel."

It was a tad transparent. Sure, Lilium's signature ankle-skimming red dress was flattering. And her hair and makeup were flawless—assuming demons even wore makeup. For all I knew, she woke up looking that good. But any true fans of my channel would know that I wasn't into the classically elegant look. They might buy into the idea that I was curious about her celebrity potential, though. Regardless, it was worth a shot. I crossed my fingers and clicked upload.

Salty whined, and that probably meant I should take her outside. I'd been hoping that one of the others would return before I needed to do that. I really wasn't looking forward to leaving the safety of my apartment, alone.

I checked my phone. There was a message from Max on the group chat that I must have missed while I was rewatching my video for what felt like the hundredth time.

Council has agreed to mobilize. Jay, any luck locating L?

I checked the upload progress of my video, then added a message to the chat. *Salty needs to go out.*

Dots on my screen indicated that someone was typing. Several messages appeared one after another.

On our way.

Working on getting the word out.

I'm going to stay with Eve tonight.

I frowned at the last message and opened up my direct chat with Angie. *You need anything?*

I posted video teaser thumbnails to my social media accounts while I waited for Angie to respond.

No. Eve is upset, and I'm probably safer here at Lydbury, anyway.

We'd known each other long enough that I understood what she wasn't saying. This might be the last time she ever saw her best friend, and Angie wasn't a wizard. She wasn't going to be any help in this fight.

Make sure Max doesn't do anything stupid? she added.

If he tries, I'll wrap him up in a cyclone and send him home. I added a smiley face.

Thanks. This sucks.

It really does.

She sent an angry-devil-head emoji, plus a confetti cannon and then a few knives.

"Hannah? Where are you?" Grace's voice called out from my living room.

"She better not have gone outside without us," Max said.

Salty jumped off the bed and ran to greet them.

I sent Angie a few heart emojis and added, *Take care. Gotta go. Wizcrew just arrived.*

"Be right there," I called toward the living room.

My upload was nearly complete. I checked my phone to make sure I had comment notifications turned on, then I tucked it into my pocket. Once I made sure that I'd turned off all my equipment and set my camera batteries to charge, I retraced my steps back down the hallway to my living room.

Three faces turned to look at me when I entered. I'd been expecting four.

"Where's Max?" I asked.

"He took Salty out. He'll be right back," Callie said. She had her arm around Grace's shoulders, and they were snuggled together at one end of the couch. Whatever argument they'd been having appeared to have been settled.

"What happened at the Council meeting?"

"It was great," Grace said. She grinned over at Kyle, who was busy flipping through the leather-bound spell book in his lap. "Do you want to tell her what you did?"

Kyle glanced up. "You tell her. I'm looking for something."

My front door opened, and Max stepped inside, followed by our friend Varun, who was carrying Salty.

"Hope you don't mind if I join the fun." Varun let Salty down so she could run around the apartment.

I hurried over to give him a hug. "I thought you were in London on business."

"I was. Until I heard that the Hunters had called an emergency Council meeting." He glanced at Max. "Someone has to make sure we keep our parents in line."

"Though I think Kyle has that covered." Max looked to

Grace and Callie on the couch. "Did you tell Hannah yet?"

"No. You're just in time."

"Oh, do let me tell the story." Varun settled himself in one of my armchairs. "It's a tale for the history books. I think our children's children will still be talking about the time Uncle Kyle faced off against the almighty Wizard Council."

"Assuming we survive long enough to have children," Callie said.

Grace frowned and shifted away from her girlfriend just a bit.

"We'll have none of that, now." Varun wagged a finger at Callie. "Kyle over here has a plan, remember? And it's a good one. And we will succeed, because if I don't give my parents at least three grandchildren, I won't have to worry about demons threatening to zap me into oblivion."

"Is someone going to tell me the story, or what?" I asked.

Max's phone pinged. He checked the screen, then looked over at me. "You didn't."

A surge of adrenaline spiked through me as two thoughts surfaced one after another. The first was that my video must have finally posted. The second was surprise that Max had subscribed and turned on notifications.

Grace's phone buzzed next. Then Kyle's and Varun's, and even Callie's phone chirped. I hoped they were all so busy checking their phones that they wouldn't notice the blush warming my cheeks.

"You guys..." If my eyes could have turned into heart emojis, they would have in that moment. "You're just...the absolute best."

Callie gaped at her phone screen. "And you are a total genius, Hannah." She looked up and locked eyes with me. "This is great!"

I waved her off. "You haven't even watched the video yet."

She held out her phone so I could see the screen where my video was playing silently with captions. "No, I am watching, and you're brilliant."

"Do you really think it might work?" My own phone started dinging with comment notifications. "I guess let's find out."

Kyle looked up from his spell book and stared at us. "What's going on?"

"Hannah used her platform to crowdsource Lilium's location," Max explained, waving his phone in the air.

Kyle shut the spell book, keeping one finger inside to mark his page. "Good. Let's hope it works because I found the spell."

Callie's eyes narrowed at him "What do you mean 'found'? You told the Council that you had it."

Kyle shrugged one shoulder. "I did have it. Here. At least, I was pretty sure I'd seen it in here. It's more complex than I remember from first glance, though. And it takes more than an air wizard. We also need a strong water wizard."

All eyes shifted to me.

"Why are you looking at me? Callie is water, too."

Callie grimaced. "I'm also one of the only doctors. We already promised that I'd help my parents in the med tent. It was the only way we could get them to agree to Kyle's plan."

I crossed my arms. "How about we back up a minute and fill me in on this plan, then."

Max tucked his phone into his jacket pocket and leaned forward. "Kyle has a spell that will open a portal to shove the demons back to their realms. It takes a while to get that going, though, and we need to flush the demons out of hiding so that we can force them through the portal. The idea was to organize a surprise attack. Jayden is rounding up the underground wizards. The Council is mobilizing the Society. We just have to point them in a direction—hence the usefulness of your video—and then lead the attack."

"We're leading the attack?" I stared at him. There were plenty of wizards in the Society with decades more experience than any of us.

"We're the ones who have been working with the Fae and who know the most about the demons," Max said.

"Also, no one trusts Marcella and Elton," Callie added.

Grace elbowed Callie in the ribs. "Be nice."

"But it's true." Callie winced and rubbed her side.

"It is true." Max shrugged. "We'll deal with that after we've dealt with the demons. One thing at a time."

Kyle nodded. "Besides, once the Society sees what the underground can do, it's going to change everything."

"He's right. And they're ready." Jayden chose that moment to make an appearance. "Nice video, Han. Have you checked your comments? Looks like we have a few leads."

I pulled out my phone and started scanning through the replies. "London flat? Old news. She knows that the Fae know about that one. She wouldn't go back there now. Would she?"

"Not that one." Jayden gestured for me to dig deeper.

I kept scrolling. "Oh. This is interesting."

Grace stood and crossed over to where I was so she could look over my shoulder as I pulled up a map. The location was close to LA. It was a warehouse district, which wasn't exactly the sort of place one would expect someone who looked, and dressed, like Lilium to be hanging out. Which is probably why she got noticed.

"That one sounds good," Grace agreed.

"The one in the warehouse district, right?" Jayden asked.

"Looks promising." Varun stood over my other shoulder,

watching me zoom in on the map.

I nodded. "Jay, do you want to check it out while I keep looking?"

"Anyone want to join me?" Jayden pulled up the location on his phone and started entering coordinates into his Silicon Moon transporter.

"How much charge do you have left on that thing?" Max asked.

Jayden scowled at the device. "Good question."

"Jay," Kyle groaned.

"I would have remembered." Jayden turned the transporter over in his hands. "Where's that gauge again?"

Max walked over and plucked the device out of Jayden's fingers, offering his own in exchange. "Take mine. I charged it during the Council meeting and again when we got to Hannah's."

"You carry a charger around with you?" Jayden took Max's device and started entering coordinates.

"The engineering team updated the form factor." He pulled a clear cylinder filled with some sort of blue-green liquid out of his jacket pocket. After unscrewing the cap, he dropped Jayden's transporter inside.

"Gross." Jayden scowled. "That stuff stinks, and if the container leaks, it's going to get all over your clothes. I don't like it."

"Take it up with engineering." Max shook his head.

"Don't think I won't." Jayden finished programming the coordinates for his destination. "Be back in a minute."

Callie stood. "I'm going with, just in case."

Grace tensed at my side. "Be careful. Both of you."

Kyle opened the spell book, but his eyes were on Jayden. "What she said."

With a solemn nod to their respective partners, Jayden and Callie disappeared.

"Okay. About that spell." I handed Grace my phone and shifted closer to Kyle. "What exactly do you need me for?"

He handed me the spell book. "Best if you read through it yourself. And you should probably sit down. It's not short."

I stared down at the two-page spread of text, diagrams, and symbols. Some of them I recognized, but most I did not. I glanced up at Kyle. "Do you understand all this?"

He shrugged. "Enough of it. I'll admit I'm guessing at some things, and I'm curious to know if you come to the same conclusions or not."

I shook my head. "I've never even seen a spell book before."

"Yes, you have," Max said. "Don't you remember back in college when I found that book deep in the stacks of the library? That was a spell book."

I raised my eyebrows. "Oh, I remember all right. You hoarded that thing for weeks, and then when it came time to take it back to the library, you couldn't find it."

"I still think Nate took it. That nosy jerk was always snooping around my side of the room." Max shoved his hands in his pockets. "I keep forgetting that you didn't have Society School on the weekends like us."

"Morgan tried to come up with an excuse that would convince my parents. I think Marcella even tried once, as well." I rolled my eyes. "Yeah. There are definitely some gaps in my wizard education. It just never seemed important or urgent. Just a bunch of fun party tricks that I couldn't even share with anyone outside the Society. Maybe if she'd told my parents I'd need to read spell books in order to defeat a demon army, it might have changed their minds?"

"You'd need divination magic for that, and trust me, I still

haven't found anyone that can help me focus my visions."
Kyle shook his head.

"He's not wrong," Grace added. She had even less understanding about how to reliably use her ability to see possible
futures than Kyle did with the images he accessed by touching objects. And now that the Fae had turned their backs on
us, they might never learn to use those powers.

"Why don't you set that book down on the table over here,"
Varun suggested. "Then we can all read through it together.
Maybe Max and I can help you two figure stuff out."

I moved over to the couch and set the spell book on the
coffee table. Grace removed the flowers and candles from
the tabletop before curling up in one of my chairs. Max and
Varun positioned themselves on either side of me, and Kyle
scooted his chair closer so he could look at the book upside
down from the opposite side of the table. For a moment, it
felt like old times, gathering in Max's dorm room, working
on little Society projects while we tried to hide what we were
up to from Angie.

Only, this time, we were going to war.

WE didn't have to wait long for a response after Seren sent
her blood coin to Gwawr. The Elemental guardian confirmed
she might be able to locate Morgan's sire, but she'd need
something of his in order to do that, and she was busy trying
to figure out where Lilium had taken Nigel. If we thought
locating Morgan's sire would lead her to Nigel, she would do
what she could to help us.

"Something of his?" Seren asked. "How are we supposed
to get something of his if we don't know where to find him?"

"What did Gwawr use to locate Nigel's sire?" I asked.

"A medallion." She glanced down at my wrist. "Like this one. Nearly identical, actually. What is that, anyway?"

"Something to warn me about demons. It's either that or my throat closes up and I break out in hives. If I take the potion the Hands made to stop the allergic reaction, I can't see through demon glamour."

"Interesting." She tapped the blood coin against her lower lip. "I wonder if that's why Nigel's father had one."

"You think Nigel's father might have been allergic to demons?"

Seren squinted at me. "No. But he was being ensorcelled by one. A little warning medallion might be helpful if your brain's been muddled by a lusty succubus you would rather avoid."

"Right." I looked toward the cave where they were keeping Morgan. "I might as well ask her."

Seren followed my gaze. "You think she might have something?"

"It's worth a try." I shrugged. "Wait here. I'll be back."

I started back through the tunnel before Seren could respond. When I reached the cave, the guards stepped aside without any hesitation to let me through.

Morgan looked up from where she sat slumped on the floor against the rock wall. "You. I should have known."

"You may not appreciate this, but you're safe here." I squatted down in front of her, just outside the steel bars that arched out of the stone wall to form a cage around her.

"You mean that you're safe because I'm trapped in here," she sneered at me.

I could sense her heart racing and smell her fear. Her bravado wasn't intimidating. It only made me sad. "You really hurt Hannah, you know?"

Her iciness thawed a bit as she blinked at me. "I guess maybe I was wrong about you two."

"What do you mean?" I asked.

"I was certain that she was faking, but here you are, caring about her feelings. Maybe I owe you an apology." She frowned.

"For what?"

"For not believing that you're really Hannah's boyfriend and not some Fae spy sent to keep tabs on me." She pushed the metal cuff on her wrist up so she could massage the bare skin with her other hand.

"I'm not a spy." I could admit to that, at least. "But I need to ask you something."

Morgan bristled, shoulders tensing. "So? Ask. Doesn't mean I'll answer."

"I thought you owed me?"

"An apology, maybe. But that's all." Morgan scuffed the sole of her boot against the stone floor.

"Fine." It was worth a try. "What do you know about your sire?"

Morgan glanced up. "Why do you care?"

"We may be able to locate him."

"And why would I want you to do that? You'll just kill him before I could even meet him. At least, Lilium promised to—" She pressed her lips closed.

"Promised to what?" I asked. "She told you that she knows who he is? Where he is?"

"I don't have to tell you anything." She focused on rubbing her recently healed wrist.

I knew from experience how much healing bones hurt and how much those cuffs chafed. I also knew that if she weren't restrained, she'd probably blast me with her magic. The best

I could do was keep trying to convince her we were trying to help. "I don't know about you, but I'd take a Fae promise over one from a demon any day. Fae can't lie. And I promise you that if we find your sire, we won't kill him. At least not before you have a chance to speak with him."

Morgan snorted. "What sort of promise is that? You're going to let me meet my sire before you kill him in front of me? Do you think I'm that easily fooled? No. Not going to happen."

"We're not that cruel." The words had barely left my lips before the liars' pains stabbed my side. I winced. "Fine. I'm not that cruel."

"Why do you want to know who my sire is? What does it matter to you?" Morgan glared at me. "*I* don't even care who my sire is, even though everyone seems to think I should. My mother said he was some random incubus who seduced her when she was feeling particularly vulnerable because my father had just broken up with her. Like that's going to make me want to get to know him better."

She had a point. It wasn't like I was in a hurry to find the woman who gave birth to me. My wing-mates were my family.

"Who else thinks you should care? Your mother?"

Morgan rolled her eyes. "Gods no. Lilium said—"

She cut herself off and looked up at me. "Nice try, Fae."

I shrugged. "It doesn't matter to me. I don't really care who your sire is, either. I care *where* he is. We need to find Lilium so we can save Nigel, and I'm pretty sure that, if Lilium knows where your sire is, it's because he's with her. Perhaps willingly, but maybe not. If I had to guess, though, I'd say she probably isn't being nearly as gentle with him as we've been with you."

Morgan stared at me, and I stared back, waiting for her to take the bait.

After a long enough pause, where I was almost certain that she wasn't going to speak, Morgan said, "Fine. You're right. Lilium promised she'd introduce me to him if I did something for her in exchange. She gave me something of his to prove that she could be trusted to follow through."

"What did she give you?" I asked.

Morgan extended her leg and wiggled her ankle. "Take off my boot."

I sighed. So, it was going to be like that. "Are the chains too tight? I can have the guards loosen them so that you can reach to do it yourself."

Morgan laughed. "I should really take you up on that. You're too nice for your own good, you know that?"

"Huh?" Had I misunderstood?

"Just take my boot off. You'll see. It's better if you do it." She waved her foot back and forth again.

I reached through the bars and untied her laces. When my hand wrapped around her heel to pull the boot from her foot, my fingers pressed against something hard. I moved my hand to feel through the leather. Then I reached in and extracted a small dagger with a jewel-encrusted hilt.

"What is this and how did you get it past the guards?" I glanced toward the door.

"I concealed it with my magic." Morgan raised her eyebrows.

I stared at the dagger, then back at her. "No. Nice try. Tell me the truth."

"Not so dumb as I thought." Morgan smiled. She shrugged. "I threatened your guard. Told him that if he searched me, I would curse him so that his nuts would fall off."

"And he believed you?"

Morgan laughed. "You Dragon Fae don't get out much, do you?"

My sire would have made these guards drill until dawn with no dinner for an error like that. I would deal with them later, though. First, I had to find Nigel so I could help Hannah.

"This was your sire's?" I asked.

Morgan nodded. "That's what Lilium said."

"How do you know she wasn't lying to you?"

Morgan frowned. "I don't. She could have been. But even if she were, it might still lead you to her. Or Nigel."

I turned the blade over in my hand. "Why did you decide to be helpful?"

"Did Hannah tell you how long we've been best friends for?" Morgan leaned her head back against the rock wall. She didn't wait for a response before continuing. "I met Hannah just after Max was born. Her family lived near ours. I don't know if she mentioned this, but her parents aren't wizards. They have the blood—otherwise, they wouldn't have been able to pass it to Hannah—but they never figured it out. They're both so grounded and driven."

She paused and shook her head. "Hannah used to love coming to our house because my family was so 'out there' compared to hers. My parents were the ones to figure out that Hannah was a wizard. They traced her lineage. They did that with everyone I associated with because they were both wizard snobs—still are, actually. But, in Hannah's case, it was good because it meant she got to learn magic. Though, I'm not sure she thanks me for that now."

"Why not?"

"I never got the sense that she liked being a wizard. She was happy she had something that helped her fit in with our group, but she knew that the wizard snobs would never accept her as one of them because of her family. And whatever success she had as a wizard, it wasn't anything her parents would be able to appreciate or value. Being a wizard just meant she had to work twice as hard if she wanted to be considered successful in both worlds."

"Why are you telling me all this?" I asked.

"I feel bad, okay? That's what I'm trying to say. I made my best friend's life harder when all she's ever been is good to me. And now she'll probably never forgive me. Especially if Lilium hurts Nigel. Hannah will never forgive herself, even though it's really my fault. So just take the dagger, rescue Nigel, and maybe let me know if you find the demon who sired me and ruined my life, okay?"

"When I'm done with all that, I'll be back to help you, too." I stared at her for a moment longer, waiting to see if she had anything else to say. Then I turned to go.

"Just keep Hannah safe," Morgan added, her voice quiet.

"I'll do my best."

Seren was still waiting for me when I emerged. I handed her the dagger. "I need to gather a squadron. Tell me when you know where we're going. I'll have them ready at the West Mouth."

Seren nodded. "I'll let Damir and Ivo know once I'm done with this."

I didn't wait for her to send the blood coin to Gwawr. I wanted to be ready to fly with a squadron at my back. If Hannah and her wizard friends decided to take on Lilium, they would need help. But if they delayed, maybe there would be time to rescue Nigel and take down Lilium before any of the wizards were put in danger. No matter what, I wasn't going to let Hannah go into battle against a demon army alone. We were a team.

I may have forgotten that in my excitement at being named lieutenant, but Morgan's speech reminded me of the promise I'd made to Hannah. I only hoped it wasn't too late to show her that I really did care and that I wouldn't let her down again.

While the squadron prepared for flight, I paid a visit to Grandsire Firewing.

"I apologize for waking you, Grandsire," I said when he greeted me at the door to his cave.

"Oh, I don't sleep. Sleep is for the young. Like you." He patted my arm and nudged me inside. "What has you awake and about at this hour?"

In the main chamber, a candle flame flickered next to an open book set on the table in front of the hearth. The coals of a small fire smoldered inside, keeping the small room warm. Elder Dragon Fae may not sleep, but they did lose their natural warmth as they aged. I was pleased to see that he had a fire going to keep the damp darkness of the caverns away.

It wasn't until I noticed the curtains covering the alcove at the back that I remembered Ivo was probably trying to sleep back there. Keeping my voice low, I said, "I need to know if it's safe for me to transform."

"You're going to fight, then?" he asked.

I nodded.

"Well, you did it once. I suspect you'll be able to do it again."

"But what if I get stuck? Is there some sort of medicine I can take with me that might help?"

"When you're in your dragon form?" He waggled his fingers. "Claws won't be much good for injections."

"Then what do I do?"

"You fight. And you don't worry." He shrugged.

I snorted. "It's that simple."

He nodded. "It is. How do you think I survived this long in a clan like ours?"

"That's the secret to your success?"

He laid his palms on my shoulders. Even though he was much thinner than me, his hands were still strong, and he could still look me in the eye. "Fight. And don't worry."

I took a deep breath, absorbing his words.

He grinned and pushed me toward the door. "And bring home the girl. I want to meet her."

"Grandsire." I shook my head.

"Good hunting!" he called after me with more cheer in his voice than seemed reasonable given the fact that I was about to take on an army of demons.

18

JAYDEN and Callie returned without much to report. There were lights on at what looked like an otherwise abandoned warehouse, and a few demons had been lurking about in the lot. They'd poked around outside the fence, but it didn't look like Lilium, if she were in there, was expecting any company.

"Good," Max said. "Let's start getting the word out. Jayden, pick a drop point nearby, close enough to use as an operations base, but somewhere that the demons won't notice. Kyle, write out the message with instructions on how to use the portal. I want all wizards ready to go within an hour. Once we confirm that Lilium is there, I don't want to give her enough time to move."

"I'll start the Society comm chain going," Grace said.

"And I'll tell my parents where we can get started on setting up the med tent," Callie said.

"Wait. How are we getting everyone there?" I asked. "That warehouse is in Southern California. There's no way there are enough local wizards down there to take Lilium on, and not everyone has one of your little Silly Moon transporters."

Varun grinned. "Guess we never got to that part. See, that bit right there is why Kyle is going down in the history books as the wizard who saved us all."

Kyle shook his head. "I just found the spell. Anyone could have."

"Do I get to tell the story now?" Varun sat up straight. His eyes sparkled with barely contained glee.

Max gestured for him to go ahead before pulling Grace, Callie, and Jayden into the kitchen.

"I believe it was Callie's mum who brought up the same issue you just pointed out," Varun began. "Up to that point, Max and Callie had been doing most of the talking, convincing their parents and the rest of the Council to work together, etc. When the bit about transportation came up, the pair of them looked baffled. I almost felt bad for them. They'd nearly succeeded. Then Kyle stepped forward and slapped that book of his down on the table."

"You're exaggerating," Kyle said, but the corner of his mouth twitched up in a half grin. "It was just a piece of paper, and I very politely handed it to the High Wizard."

"Oh, do let me tell the story." Varun sighed.

Kyle gestured for Varun to continue.

"Right. Where was I?" Varun rubbed his palms together. "After announcing that he had an answer to that problem, Kyle let the Council review his *sheet of paper.*" Varun rolled his eyes.

"And what was on this sheet of paper?" I asked.

"Only the single most brilliant spell. One that, once it gets out, is going to make it difficult for Max to make much money off that finicky invention his engineers have been perfecting."

I stared at Varun when he paused. "Explain?"

"Oh, go on. Show her the spell." Varun gestured to Kyle. "It's a one-way transport, but in reverse. Pull instead of push, if you will. See, you don't get to just pick where you're going and go there. Someone at the destination has to initiate it."

Kyle turned the spell book to face him, flipped to a marked page, then slid it back toward me so I could read what was written there.

"We thought this wasn't possible." I skimmed the paragraph of introduction and cautionary warnings in order to get to the bit that mentioned how this portal would work. "Wait. You need a water wizard for this one, too?"

"Seems like portals are a bit air and a bit water," Kyle said. "The introduction mentions the other spell, which is why I knew to look for it. They're very similar, but this one is a little easier because we don't have to do any pushing *or* pulling, really. We only have to open the door."

"That's the brilliant part," Varun added. "Any wizard who wants to use the portal, from wherever they happen to be, only has to know the activating ingredient ratios. They sprinkle that at the base of a closed door, and when they open it, they can walk right through to us at the other end."

"One-way portal." I grinned. "You're right. It is brilliant. Where did you get this book from, again?"

Kyle frowned. "Remember how Max had that key?"

I thought back, trying to remember what key he was referring to. It only took a moment before I remembered that night we'd gathered at Max's house, back before the mess with the boxes and Morgan. The night that Angie returned. The last time we'd all been together. "Yeah. I remember."

"I had a vision that night, of the wizard that gave Max the key. What he looked like and a glimpse of where he was—a lead. Max and I talked afterward, and I confirmed the guy's description with him, just to be sure it was the same person. Then I found him. He was running a magic shop in this hippie mountain town. Middle of nowhere." Kyle shook his head. "Jay and I lurked around his shop for almost an hour at the end of the day, waiting for the last of his customers to leave. Then Jay started up a conversation with him."

I nodded. "Sounds about right."

"Guy didn't talk much. Seemed really nervous about something, especially after Jay mentioned the key. He kept looking at the door. Finally gave us this spell book that he had tucked behind the counter." Kyle held up the book. "Then he told us to leave. When I came back the next day, the place was empty. Everything gone. Like we'd imagined the whole thing."

"Creepy." I shivered.

Max walked over to us and set his hand on the back of Varun's chair. "We're just about ready to go. Jay and Grace are working on getting the message out, so the clock is ticking. I'm going to take Kyle and Hannah so they can get set up. Varun, take the other transporter, go with Callie to get her parents, and then help them get the med tent set up. Once I get Kyle and Hannah settled, I'll come back to get Jay and Grace."

I glanced up at Max, then over to Kyle. "I'm going now?"

Kyle raised his eyebrows. "Is that a problem?"

"No. I just..." I looked over at Callie. Her head was bent over one of the transporters as she concentrated on programming in the coordinates of her desired destination. "You really want me to do this? There's got to be another water wizard. Someone with more experience?"

Kyle's eyes locked with mine. "We have experience working together, and there's no one I trust more to do this with me."

"You've got this." Max reached over and patted me on the shoulder. "Besides, think of it like a warm-up for the big event."

Somehow that didn't make me feel any better. The fact that everyone was going to be depending on me to both get them there safely and to get the demons away and keep them away for good only made me more nervous. I glanced around the room at the others, wondering what it was that made them all think that they could go up against Lilium and her demon army and win.

Then I remembered that Lilium had taken Nigel, and despite what anyone said, that was, at least partly, my fault. I owed it to Nigel to do what I could to save him. At least creating portals with Kyle would keep me away from the worst of the fighting. It wasn't like they were asking me to raise cyclones and blind the enemy with blasts of water.

I stood, which caused Salty to get up from where she lay sprawled out on the floor next to the couch and shake herself. She trotted over to me and sat down next to my feet.

"What about Salty?" I asked, bending down to pet her.

"I'd say we should leave her here, but she is a faerie guard dog." Max grimaced. "It's too late to bring her to Angie, and if anything happens to her..."

"Maybe we should leave her, then." I gave Salty one last pat before standing.

As soon as I started to move away, she yipped.

"You can't come with," I tried to explain.

Salty trotted around my legs, panting, like she was definitely not on board with my decision to leave her home.

Kyle bent down and scooped her up. He secured her with one arm while he picked up the spell book with the other.

"Nope. I disagree. We can't just leave her. She's coming with."

"All right." Max shrugged. "Then you two are responsible for her, and you can explain to Angie if anything happens."

Kyle lifted Salty up so that he could nuzzle her head. "You'll be fine, won't you, girl?"

Salty licked him on the nose.

"Well, that settles that, then." Max extracted the transporter from the charging device. He returned the cylinder to his pocket before programming our destination and waiting for the little green confirmation light.

I tensed. "Just warn me, okay?"

"Does that help?" he asked.

I tried to think back to the times I'd transported with Ved. "On second thought, maybe don't? Wait until I'm distracted and then go."

"Hey," Callie called from across the room. "We're leaving."

Max lifted one hand to wave. "See you there."

I turned my head just in time to watch them disappear. Then I blinked and gasped as Max's hand clamped down on my bicep and all the air was sucked from my lungs.

We reappeared in a dark alley, and I bent over with my hands on my knees to suck in air like I'd just been pulled up from the bottom of a lake. "I. Hate. That. So. Much."

"Wow." Kyle released Salty so she could run over and lean against my legs to comfort me. "You do not travel well."

I smoothed a hand over my hair as I straightened up to face them. "I travel just fine. It's transporting that does not sit well with me."

"We should really have one of Fiona's Hands check that out. You know, assuming the Fae ever come out of hiding. I'm kind of worried that I did this to you." Max rubbed a hand against his jaw.

"What? How?"

"Well, the first time you transported, it was with me, right? When I dragged you with me to Italy?"

I thought back to the events leading up to that incident, including the part where I'd been knocked out. It had only been a few hours earlier that I'd first learned about the Silicon Moon transport devices. "I think you're right."

"You were barely functional when we did that transport. I just wonder if maybe that has something to do with why transporting seems to affect you so much."

I looked back and forth between Kyle and Max. "It doesn't bother either of you at all? Really?"

Kyle shrugged, and Max shook his head.

"It's cold, and I can't breathe, but it's not that different than jumping into a pool first thing in the morning." Of course, Kyle, the state champion swimmer, would compare transporting to his favorite sport.

"Sure, except it's more like drowning than just diving into the deep end, isn't it?" I asked.

Max shook his head. "I'm with Kyle on this one. But we can compare notes later. You two should get to work. Are you going to be okay if I leave you here while I go back for Jay and Grace?"

Kyle pulled out his phone and turned on the flashlight function. "We'll be fine. We've got our little guard dog. Right, buddy?"

Max shook his head. "Keep your eyes and ears open. All right?"

I glanced up and down the alley. "Where's the warehouse?"

Max consulted the map on his phone. It took him a minute to get oriented, then he pointed. "Over there. Should be just on the other side of this building."

"Should we go check it out?" I asked.

"No. Definitely not. Focus on getting the portal up. Callie and her parents should be here before we get back. Just try to keep a low profile. If any demons come this way, make sure they don't get away to warn the others."

I glanced over at Kyle, but his head was already down, all his attention focused on the spell book. "Um. We'll think of something?"

Max hesitated. "Are you sure—"

"The faster you get out of here, the faster you'll be back. Go."

He glanced down at his transporter device, then held it up so I could see the green light. "See you in a bit."

As soon as he disappeared, I walked over to Kyle so I could read over his shoulder. "What do we do first?" I asked.

Salty barked once.

I looked up, still jumpy about Max's warning about demons. Luckily, it was a familiar face I found staring back at me. One that I wasn't expecting to see again. "What are you doing here?"

"I was just about to ask you the same thing," Brianne responded.

The Fae with the long red hair standing next to Brianne stared at me and Kyle, then looked at Brianne. "You two know each other?"

THE squadron of thirty Dragon Fae, organized into clutches of five, each with their own commander, circled the dark skies high above the boxy buildings waiting for my signal. I glided through the ocean breeze, back and forth above the spot of heat that marked where Brianne and Gwawr had landed, enjoying the wind on my wings while I waited for Gwawr's signal.

The pair of them were planning on going into the building as soon as they figured out the best way past any defenses the demons had set up. Once they had eyes on Morgan's sire and Nigel, they would send up a signal. It would be our job to create a distraction to lure the demons away so they could free Nigel and capture Morgan's sire.

It wasn't until I banked and started to circle back toward the building that I noticed there were more than just two bodies throwing off heat in the alley. I drifted lower, trying to determine if Brianne and Gwawr were in danger. My dragon sight made it difficult for me to see features in the same way I would if I were in my Fae form.

I couldn't get too close without revealing myself to anyone who happened to be looking up. At the height I'd chosen, the gray-black scales that covered my belly would blend with the night sky. Any lower, though, and the silver streaks on my sides might be noticed.

So far, neither Brianne nor Gwawr had thrown any magic at the other creatures, and the pair of them didn't appear to have horns. I inhaled as I glided over their heads, trying to catch a scent on the light breeze coming off the ocean, and hoping that might help identify any potential danger. But I was too far away to pick up anything of note, even with my enhanced senses.

Concerned, I cut my next loop short and banked back toward the ally. As I turned, more bodies appeared out of nowhere. Still, none threw any magic. They had to be wizards. I considered transporting myself down to the ground, but I wasn't sure if I would be able to transform into my Fae form without issue. While I hesitated, Gwawr and Brianne separated from the others and started toward the warehouse Gwawr's spell had led us to.

The wizards in the ally continued to move around, busy with something, but they didn't follow Brianne and Gwawr, and they didn't appear to pose any threat to our mission. I relaxed a bit, preparing to settle back into my flight pattern and wait, when a familiar scent filled my nostrils.

Hannah. She was down there with the wizards. Even though I couldn't be sure which figure was hers from this height, I knew she was in that alley. Once Gwawr signaled us to attack, she would be in danger. Brianne and Gwawr must have warned them. But if they had, why weren't they leaving? By the time I turned and circled over them again, there were already more bodies than there had been before.

Hold steady and wait for my signal. I sent the thought to the clutch commanders somewhere in the sky above me.

I waited for their confirmations, then swooped down toward the roof of a building with no heat signatures. Once my claws scraped against the concrete, I pulled at my magic and prepared to transform. I needed to go down there and warn Hannah.

It was a risk. If Brianne and Gwawr sent a signal while I was on the ground, I might miss it. And, in my Fae form, I couldn't communicate with my Dragon Fae commanders. I would need to be fast.

Luckily, it only took me two tries to transform. I transported myself down to the alley where everyone was too busy to notice me except Salty. The little faerie guard dog spotted me as soon as I appeared and trotted toward me with her tongue hanging out.

Hannah's eyes followed the dog and landed on me. Her shoulders tensed and her mouth opened, but I closed the distance between us and spoke first.

"You can't stay here. I have a squadron of Dragon Fae up there waiting to attack on Gwawr's signal. I can't keep you safe and fight the demons at the same time."

Hannah raised her eyebrows. "That's fine. You don't need to. We're here to fight as well."

A quick glance tallied up the wizards. "There aren't nearly enough of you to take on the demons in that place. I've seen the heat signature from the building. It's crawling with demons."

"More are coming. We have a plan." Hannah crossed her arms.

"Do Gwawr and Brianne know about this plan?" I asked.

"We told them." She glanced back over her shoulder at a wizard I recognized from her apartment. "I need to get back to work, but basically, we're here to banish some demons and take down Lilium. Kyle and I are going to open a portal so we can shove the demons back to the realms they came from."

I glanced at Kyle. He was one of the three I hadn't met. "All right. Be ready. I'll have my squadron herd them this way once Gwawr gives us the signal to attack."

Hannah cocked her head to one side. "You aren't going to try to talk me out of it and tell me to go home where it's safe?"

The muscles in my jaw tensed. Nowhere was safe for wizards like her. Not with the demon clans united, searching for sources to power their magic traps. And especially not while the Fae hid behind their wards.

My eyes locked with hers. "I let you down, and I'm sorry. We were supposed to be acting as a team. This time, I'll be the one to fight by *your* side, and we will take down Lilium together."

"What about your Dragon Fae?" she asked.

"They are at your service. Gwawr and Brianne will get what they came for, and we will coordinate our attack with yours. Watch for Gwawr's signal."

"What signal?"

"When you see fire in the sky, you'll know. I must return to inform the squadron of our new plan." I lifted her hand to my lips and brushed a kiss across her knuckles. "Good hunting."

Then I disappeared, emerging above in my dragon form. I marked the heat signature of Hannah's body, then turned toward the warehouse to watch and wait.

19

KYLE stared at the sky. "Woah."

"Let's just get back to work. We need to set this end of the portal up so that we can get everyone here."

Max jogged over to us. "Are you two ready?"

"Almost." I glanced up, but the dragon that was most likely Ved was already gone.

"Was that who I thought it was?" Max asked.

"Yeah. The Dragon Fae are here." I pointed up. "They're going to help herd the demons to us once we get the portal up and running."

"I thought the Fae all went into hiding," Kyle said.

"We'll figure it out later. Right now, I'm grateful for the backup. Let's get the rest of the wizards here and get this party started." Max jogged off again before we could respond.

"Are you ready?" Kyle asked.

I took a deep breath. "How long are we going to have to hold this open?"

Kyle skimmed the instructions in the spell book. "We

shouldn't have to hold this one. We just open it and then close it when we're done."

I flexed my fingers. "Okay. Let's do this."

Kyle set the book down, and Salty curled up next to it like a good guard dog.

I waited for Kyle to part the air, creating a void. While he held the space open, and before more atmosphere could rush in to take the place of what he had dispersed, I reached through the void, searching for what the spell book called "the flow."

I had no idea what I was searching for in the emptiness. There wasn't anything there. Then I thought to reach for water. There wasn't any within the space Kyle had made, but there was liquid in the air around me. I drew the molecules together until they formed a visible droplet. The tiny bubble of water floated in the air just outside the emptiness.

Beside me, Kyle started panting from the effort. I needed to move quickly or he'd lose his hold and we'd have to start over. Acting on instinct, unsure if what I was doing was right, I stretched the surface of the droplet to fill the shape of the emptiness, and then I pushed.

That's when I felt it. Some sort of wave rushed the water shield, surging outward, toward me. I pressed it back until it curved inward, then, with a pop, the bubble burst. Water flowed inward from the edges of the opening, like falls cascading over the sides of a cliff, ending in an opaque mist.

"You did it." Kyle bent over his legs, trying to catch his breath. "But how? That thing you did...that wasn't in the book."

"I don't know. It just seemed right." I flexed my fingers.

Beside him, the portal opening glimmered. Wizards began to emerge from the opening. Max hurried over and started directing the new arrivals away from us and toward Jayden and Grace.

At first, I thought it strange that I could see his lips moving, giving instructions, but I couldn't hear anything. Then my vision started to go black. My knees crumpled, and I lost my balance.

A pair of arms caught me. "Oh my gosh! Hannah, is that you? Are you okay?"

I blinked up at a familiar face. One that I'd watched on an assortment of large and small screens, but one I'd never seen in the flesh. For a moment, I thought I was hallucinating. "Selena Luna?"

Brady's former costar laughed. "Not Selena. Not anymore, anyway. Just Kayla, and you have no idea how relieved I am to see that you're okay. You are okay, right?"

"Yeah. I just..." I found my footing as she guided me back to standing. Then I gestured to the portal glimmering beside us.

"It looks like it's working," Kyle said, still admiring our work. It took him a minute before he noticed who had joined us. "Wait. You're Kayla Monroe. No way! I didn't know... You mean, you're really a wizard? You and Brady both? Man, that is wild. I had no idea."

Kayla's long braids slid across her eye when she ducked her head. She flicked them back across her shoulder. "I try to keep it quiet. Only a few people know. But my mom and Jayden's mom are cousins. So when Jayden put the call out, I got here as fast as I could. As soon as I saw Hannah, I just had to come over. Then she looked like she was going to faint— again... I'm seriously beginning to think you're allergic to me or something."

"Again?" I blinked at her, still trying to recover from the fact that the Hollywood wizard I'd idolized was an actual

wizard. I'd been so focused on wondering if Brady was one of
the few who already knew this that I'd almost missed the part
where she implied that we'd already met. There was no way I
would have forgotten meeting Kayla Monroe.

"Yeah. You were waiting for your agent? Remember? I was
in Seattle filming a pilot, and Brady asked me to meet up with
him about some audition. We ran into you. He introduced us.
Then we walked you back to the Silicon Moon office?" She
paused, waiting for some sign of recognition from me.

I stood there gaping at her. I remembered leaving the Silicon Moon office to meet with my agent. After that, the next
thing I remembered was waking up on the office floor. Whatever had happened between those two events was lost. "I'm
so sorry. I...I don't remember."

"You don't remember us walking you back? We were saying goodbye, and Brady went to hug you. Then you just fainted." She shivered. "It was so scary. Brady picked you up and
carried you inside. I asked if he wanted me to stay or to call
nine-one-one, but he said not to worry. He'd get the security
guards to help. I wondered what happened. When I saw you
were making videos again, I can't even tell you how relieved
I was. I just came over to say that I'm glad you're okay."

"Thank you." I had a pretty good idea of what happened after Brady brought me inside, even though I still had no memory of it. What I didn't understand was why Brady didn't get
help. Why did he just leave me unconscious on the floor? It
didn't make any sense.

"Yeah. Thank you." Kyle tapped my arm, then pointed up.
"I really wish we had more time to discuss this, but..."

Above us, the sky crackled with lightning.

My first thought was for Ved. He was up there, somewhere,
with the other Dragon Fae. But the flash of light hadn't come

from above. It appeared to have come from the demon hide-out.

A cluster of enormous dragons swooped down from above. The bright light flashed off the pale-green scales of the one in lead. Four dragons followed the leader in a V formation, all heading toward the warehouse.

"Shit. We haven't even started on the second portal." I searched the nearby faces, trying to locate Max, but he must have wandered off while Kyle and I were talking with Kayla.

"What's going on?" Kayla asked. "Were those *actual drag-ons*?"

I reached out and grabbed her hands. "Find Max. Tell him that's the signal. He needs to get everyone ready to fight."

Kayla nodded, then ran off. I had so many more questions for her, but none of it would matter if I didn't focus on creating this portal to get rid of the demons. Without it, we wouldn't have a chance of surviving this fight.

I turned to Kyle. "We have to hurry. We don't have much time before the demons get here."

"Let's do this," Kyle yelled over the screech of dragons on the hunt. He reached for the spell book. "I just hope the others can hold them off until we're ready."

My heart raced. Judging by the effort needed to craft the first portal, I was nervous about this next one, especially because, even after we had it formed, we'd be facing down an angry horde of demons while we tried to hold it open so the others could force them through.

Kyle flipped to the spell we needed, then held the book up so I could read the instructions with him. Around us, bursts of flame lit the sky, dragons shrieked, and everyone seemed to be speaking at once. I could barely hear myself think.

"This is impossible." I clamped my hands down over my

ears.

Kyle glanced at me, then flicked his wrist. All the sounds disappeared.

"Better?" he asked.

"Better." I concentrated on reading through what we needed to do. The instructions made more sense than they had back in my apartment. Or maybe it was just that I had a bit of practical experience now and knew what they were talking about. "Is it just me, or do the instructions for this one seem... easier?"

Kyle rubbed his chin. "It's weird, right? Almost like we're missing something?"

I skimmed the instructions a second time. "I really hope this works."

"Me, too." Kyle set the book down at our feet. He glanced around us, then pointed to the opening of the alley that led back to the warehouse. "If they're going to be coming from there, maybe we should get closer and cast it at the end?"

"But what if they come around the other side?" I pointed to the far end of the building.

A dragon with a stripe of silver scales running down the length of its side glided low over our heads. *Hurry. They're coming.*

The words in my head confirmed what I'd feared. We were running out of time. "Let's just pick a spot farther away from this portal and the med tent before we cast it. Wherever we are, it will be up to the others to funnel the demons to us."

Kyle picked up the book, and we ran to the far end of the building. Only Salty followed us.

"This seems like a very bad idea," I said, staring back at the others and realizing how far away we were from the protection they offered.

"They'll figure it out once we get it going. And if not, your Dragon Fae have our back, right?"

I locked eyes with Kyle, then took a breath. There wasn't time to get into my level of confidence in Ved's ability to work as a team. I was going to have to trust that he had it figured out this time. "I hope so."

"Then let's do this." Kyle set the open book at our feet where we could reference it if we needed.

Like with the first portal, Kyle sliced through the air. This time, I knew what to expect, and I was ready with my droplet of water, expanding it as I reached out, waiting for a response. Only, what pushed back wasn't a wave. It was a wind, dry and hot like the desert.

Kyle must have felt it, too. He reached farther, pushing more of the air aside, making room for me to stretch my bubble of water inward. I searched for an anchor as he continued to reach and push at the parched air.

Sweat beaded on my forehead, but I didn't dare break my concentration or raise a hand to wipe my brow. Beside me, Kyle was panting. I tried to hurry, casting about for the slightest droplet in what seemed to be a desolate wasteland.

"There." Kyle said the word on an exhale before sucking in another breath.

I followed the lead of his magic, stretching the droplet until I was sure the bubble would burst. The moment the tip of my tunnel touched the tiny bulb of liquid Kyle had found, my magic surged outward, only to slam back toward me. This time, it wasn't like a wave as much as a coiled spring oscillating between where I stood and whatever realm shimmered on the other side.

It was all I could do to hold the wellspring in balance and keep it from slamming me back or sucking me in. Somewhere

I registered Salty's barks, someone skidding to a stop between me and Kyle, and a blast of magic blocking us from the flames roaring over our heads.

Even though I couldn't turn my head to look, I knew the moment the first demons arrived in the alley because the edges of my vision flashed as the wizards we'd assembled drove them toward where Kyle and I struggled to maintain control over the portal we'd created. Then the first unlucky demon slipped over the edge.

Its claws ripped at walls I'd created, trying to scramble back out. Kyle released his hold on the air surrounding the portal, and the wellspring walls recoiled. The demon lost its grip and fell through to the other side, but without Kyle pressing the space open, the oscillations returned and magnified as blasts of hot air buffeted the tunnel from all sides.

"Can you hold it while I push them through?" Kyle asked.

I grunted, struggling to smooth the sloshing waves into something more manageable. The honest answer was that I didn't know if I could. I had no idea what I was doing. All I knew was that we'd only sent one demon through. We were a long way from done.

The rest of the group of demons that had been teetering on the edge of the portal realized that one of their number was gone. They paused their fight to inspect the yawning hole behind them just as the earth beneath their feet tilted up. They stumbled back and fell, scrambling into the void. Only, this time, Kyle pushed with his air magic, flushing them through before they could tear at the walls of the portal.

I sighed with relief, but there wasn't any time to relax before another batch of demons appeared in my peripheral vision.

A flash of light cut through the night sky like a beacon, shining up out of a hole that Gwawr blasted through the roof of the warehouse when she cast her fire magic. Flames licked through the opening as smoke curled up into the darkness.

If the building was on fire, that meant two things. The first filled me with relief. Gwawr and Brianne must have escaped with Lilium's prisoners. The second sent a bolt of adrenaline through my veins. It was time to fight.

Demons hated fire. Even though it couldn't harm them, they were repelled by it. Exploiting that weakness was how we planned to drive them toward the army of wizards who would send them back to their own realm. Any moment now, the demons inside the warehouse would decide to flee. Gwawr should have warded the building so they couldn't transport themselves away. If she succeeded, then they would be forced to come outside, where we would be waiting for them.

Positions. I sent the thought to the clutch commanders, then circled down to check on Hannah and the wizards.

A few of the wizards turned their heads up and pointed as I glided by. At first, I wasn't sure if they were pointing at me or at Gwawr's signal beacon, still lighting up the sky. Either way, they didn't look like they were ready to fight.

I spotted the portal Hannah and Kyle had made as I glided overhead on silent wings. It was hard to miss with more and more batches of wizards stumbling out every moment. But when I noticed there was no second portal, I banked and circled back, this time even closer to the tops of the surrounding buildings.

Hurry. They're coming. I sent the thought to Hannah's mind as soon as I located her among the wizards gathered below.

Then I swept up, higher, over the top of the building that separated the wizards from the demons. My thermal vision flared pinpricks of red where demons dotted the ground surrounding their burning hideout. A cluster of bodies separated from the rest, peeling off to search the perimeter, while the others formed a defensive barrier closer to the building. Everything was going according to plan, and judging from their behavior, none of the horn-headed fools had bothered looking up.

Ready? On my signal. I sent my command to the entire squadron assembled above me.

My Dragon Fae commanders had been instructed to drive the demons away from the building and funnel them toward the wizards. I reached out, sensing the five clutches that made up the squadron as they circled in their assigned positions.

As soon as I was within range of the building again, I pulled up and flapped my wings, sending a crack of sound echoing between the boxy structures.

Below me, the demons looked up.

I roared a warning, then unleashed a torch of flame at the spot with the thickest cluster of demons standing guard, hoping to send them scurrying away from the building. The first clutch would follow my solitary attack with a sweep of flame that would drive the fleeing demons toward clutches two and three, who would land and create a wall of flame that would force the demons to retreat toward the wizards. There was always the chance that they would decide to transport away in the face of our onslaught, but if we'd succeeded in trapping Lilium inside, it was unlikely they would choose to abandon her.

When I'd exhausted my breath of flame, I soared upward, making room for the first clutch that was already advancing and raining fire from the sky. From my vantage point above, I watched the little red dots swerve in panic. Some ran back toward the burning warehouse. Others ran away, searching for cover within the fenced area surrounding the building.

The second and third clutch soared in from the opposite direction, hovering over the fence and releasing a wave of fire before landing just inside the perimeter. Pairs within each clutch alternated driving the demons back with blasts of flame, working together to herd them away from the building and back toward the gate. The fourth and fifth clutches patrolled the flanks, picking up any demons who thought they might escape the net we were forming around them.

I circled up and headed back toward the wizards to check on their progress as the first clutch banked around and returned to rejoin the fight. Gliding over the top of the neighboring warehouses, I spotted Hannah and Kyle working on a second portal in the alley. Beyond the void they'd created, my thermal vision caught brief glimpses of intense heat. Whatever they were doing, I hoped it was working and that Hannah would be safe.

Around them, the other wizards formed small groups. Some moved closer to Hannah and Kyle, likely to take up defensive positions around the portal. It appeared that they were almost ready. We just had to get the demons heading their way.

I banked into the saltwater breeze, now clogged with smoke from the blazing warehouse. The second and third Dragon Fae clutches advanced on the ground, backed by the first, fourth, and fifth in the air. But the demons remained determined to guard the warehouse. Despite their best efforts at squeezing the demons closer to the gate, as soon as the Dragon Fae squadron turned from the building, the demons would transport themselves back to resume their positions, guarding the warehouse and protecting their queen, who was likely still trapped inside.

Frustrated with the stalemate, the first clutch landed and began using teeth, tails, and talons to slice at the demons. A few Dragon Fae in the second and third clutches transformed and took up abandoned battle-axes to fight the demons, in line with our original plan to eliminate them all. If I allowed this to continue, we might succeed in slicing off dozens of demon heads, but Hannah and the wizards wanted to send the demons back to their realms, not kill them.

I'd promised that my squadron of Dragon Fae would assist the wizards with their plan. Even if I hadn't, I agreed with the wizards' approach. After spending time with the Entugs, it didn't seem right to kill demons who were being forced to fight for a cause they'd been coerced into backing. Returning them home might not be what all of them wanted, but they couldn't stay here, at least not if they remained under Lilium's command.

I quickly reassessed our positions. If we couldn't drive them away from the building, then we'd need to carry them off and drop them within range of the wizards.

First clutch, to the sky. With me. Everyone else, form up and hold the perimeter.

Below me, the Dragon Fae on the ground responded, returning to their dragon forms. Some chose to keep their stolen weapons, grasping them with their fore talons as they stepped back into formation. The first clutch took to the sky and flanked me, awaiting my command to strike. But before I could send my thought to them, a fresh batch of demons rushed out of the building, this time carrying long-range weapons.

Our adversaries had reacted to our attack from the air faster than I'd anticipated. There wasn't time to warn the clutches on the ground before the first volley of shots sailed through their wall of flames. Some of their crossbow arrows bounced off dragon scales, but a few pierced hide. I roared my frustration.

Get them away. I sent an image of what I wanted. Then, at my command, the first clutch dove low over the demons who were busy reloading their weapons. They managed to scoop up a few with their talons, then flew off toward the wizards to deposit them closer to the mouth of the portal.

But it wasn't enough. More and more demons rushed out of the building as though Lilium had somehow created a demon factory inside.

I wasn't sure how long we would be able to hold position, especially with the wave of crossbow attacks increasing. I needed to get a message to the wizards. We needed magic on the front lines. Flames and force weren't going to be enough on their own. But I couldn't abandon my squadron.

A flash of light near the gate caught my attention. At first, I thought it was more demons, attacking from a different direction. All five clutches were busy, so I flew closer, determined to take on this new group myself and protect my kin.

Then a wave of Elemental magic surged past me, twisting and manipulating the Dragon Fae flames, shaking the Earth, combining wind and water into fierce storm fronts that cut off the demons from the warehouse they guarded.

As I glided overhead, Damir sent me a thought. *I bring reinforcements.*

Along with the thought came a glimpse of the battle through his eyes. Damir, in his dragon form, glided above Arabella and Seren, who led the Queen's Guard. Fiona, Liam, and Sorcha had taken position on a nearby rooftop. The Faerie Queen and her cousin cast warding magic to weave a net around the demons while their aunt cast illusion magic to isolate and confuse our horn-brained foes.

Just in time, I responded before commanding my squadron to work with the new arrivals.

Below me, Liam shouted something at Fiona, then disappeared. He reappeared moments later at the head of the Queen's Guard, where he fell into stride alongside Arabella. I glided closer to Damir so I could find out what was going on.

"Cover me," Liam shouted to Arabella. "I'm going in after her."

"Not without me, you aren't," Arabella shouted back. "You took down Edric without me. I'm not missing out this time."

They're not seriously thinking of going in there. I sent the thought to Damir.

Guard Seren, he replied. *Keep her safe. I'll go with them. Fiona will never forgive me if anything happens to Arabella and the Faeling she carries.*

I couldn't let him risk himself that way. It was my responsibility to keep him safe. *I'll go. You take command of the squadron.*

Before he could argue, I broadcast a thought to Damir and the clutch commanders informing them of the change in command. Then I transformed, joining Arabella and Liam on the ground. "I'm coming with."

Above us, the first clutch cleared our path to the nearest door. I scooped up a pair of battle-axes without breaking stride and followed the Queen's Guard commander and her cousin into the burning warehouse in search of Lilium.

20

SOMETHING had shifted. The demons were coming faster now, and it was all I could do to hold on. I wasn't sure how much longer I could maintain the portal, and I knew that if I fell and the portal collapsed with me, we would be crushed by the onslaught of demons.

A cold shiver ran down my spine. I didn't want to die. I didn't want my friends to die.

Kyle pressed against my side as he blasted another demon through to the other side. "Lean on me if you need to."

I couldn't lean on him. He was working as hard as I was. What we needed were more of us. More air and water wizards who could help.

Help. The thought echoed in my mind, even as I swayed on my feet, sweating and shivering. The realization that I was going to die here, holding this portal open, hit me.

A moment later, Kyle's magic faltered. Someone nearby sucked in a breath. Small sounds of shock from all around me made the hairs on the back of my neck prickle.

"What's going on?" I didn't dare look or the portal would collapse, and I didn't have enough left in me to start over again.

"The Fae," Kyle panted. "They're here."

His words ignited a flare of hope in my heart. Then heat from dragon flames above us forced another batch of demons closer to the portal opening. Close enough for Kyle to blast them through. And they were gone.

More took their place.

Then someone stepped in alongside me. I allowed myself a quick glance and recognized Brianne. She stretched her magic alongside mine, reaching for the wellspring at the other end of the portal. When she found it, she took a piece of the burden, lightening my load and bringing me a fraction of relief.

A moment later, something landed behind me with a thump and a roar. *I'm here. What do you need?*

More. I recognized Ved's voice in my head but didn't know how to speak to him with my mind, so I just imagined duplicates of myself and of Kyle. A half dozen of each of us, all directing our power at the portal.

They're coming. He sent a wave of emotion that somehow felt like a hug. *Now focus. I have your back.*

He was right—even with Brianne's help, my grip on the portal was slipping. I was exhausted, barely able to stand. And the demons kept coming.

New arrivals. Ved sent an image to my mind. Gwawr standing next to a demon. One with long gray hair that hung in stringy waves around a lined face half hidden by a bushy salt-and-pepper beard. A pair of hooked horns arched from his temples. Even though the demon looked like he'd seen better days, he held himself with a somehow regal posture.

Who...? I asked, unable to finish the question as I struggled to divide my attention between the strain of holding the portal open and understanding what this new distraction meant.

Baylord clan, from the looks of him. There was something more. Something Ved wasn't saying.

"That's...the wizard...who gave us...the book," Kyle managed to say between panting breaths as he continued to flush the demons who came our way through the portal with his air magic. "Except...he's...a demon?"

"I command you to stop," a rich, deep voice boomed over the chaos of the battle.

"Kyle?" I hesitated, assuming whoever had spoken meant for those who were fighting to stop and not me.

"Hold it open." This time, it was Ved's voice, and his hand was on my shoulder. He must have transformed back into his Fae form. "Just a little longer."

"Demon kin, drop your weapons. Bow to me or be banished."

I wanted to turn and look, but sweat dripped down my cheeks. I started to shake from the effort of holding the portal open, even with the help of the Fae. One by one, more demons were swept through until I thought it might never end. Until I was sure that Ved's hand on my shoulder was the only thing keeping me standing.

Then something bound in crackling bands of magic was dropped on the ground in front of me. Two Fae appeared alongside the struggling captive, and a hush fell over the alley.

"Lilium Strum of Clan Cubus, you have violated the terms of your apprenticeship and endangered the safety of those demons who have taken refuge in this realm. I hereby banish you back to your home realm and forbid you from returning to Earth." The owner of the deep voice speaking those words remained out of sight.

Lilium screamed as someone with air magic lifted her off the ground and shoved her into the portal. Once she was gone, the two Fae who had been standing over her turned to face me.

"You've done well." The voice was the same one that had banished Lilium. This time, he was speaking to me. I only knew because his words were accompanied by a hand on my shoulder. "Let me help you."

A strong band of magic wrapped around the oscillating waves and squeezed.

"The Fae must let go first," he said. "The wizard who opened it last."

Brianne withdrew her strength, and I stumbled. Ved's arm looped around my waist, holding me steady until it was my turn.

"It's all right, wizard. You can let go now. I have it," whoever it was with the deep voice reassured me as his magic pressed down on mine, pinching the opening we'd created closed and sealing it off with a pop.

The relief made my knees weak. I slumped in Ved's arms, barely able to keep my eyes open.

A cool hand pressed against my cheek. "Take her somewhere she can rest. She'll need time. Portal magic changes you."

I forced my eyes open and caught a glimpse of the gray-haired demon surrounded by wizards gaping and horned demons kneeling with heads bowed. Then it all disappeared.

———

As soon as the meeting of Fiona's Court ended, I returned to the Fae infirmary to wait for Hannah to wake up. I'd been anxious throughout the meeting, worried that she would wake up before I returned. But my attendance had been required. For two reasons. One I held clutched between my hands as I sat, staring at the floor, thinking. The other was why my thoughts were so muddled.

I didn't have long to wait before Hannah began to stir. The moment that her soft snoring stopped and she groaned, I rushed to her side. But I hesitated before reaching out to touch her. I didn't want to startle her, and I didn't know what to do with the heavy object clutched in my palm. So, I stood there, next to her cot, waiting for her to open her eyes.

As soon as they blinked open, her groan turned into a moan and she pinched her lids shut again. "You have got to be kidding me. Was it all just a bad dream?"

I curled the fingers of my free hand around hers. "Hannah?"

Her eyes opened again. "Wait. You're here. Then it wasn't a dream?"

I laughed. "No dream. You really held that portal open until we forced every last one of the demons who wouldn't surrender through."

"Then what am I doing back here again?" Her eyes shifted to stare up at the wooden beams that spanned the width of the infirmary.

"You collapsed after you released your hold on the portal, and Marcus helped seal it off." I brushed a strand of hair off her forehead. "I was worried about you. So, I took you here."

"Marcus?" Hannah tried to push herself up on her elbows. "Is he the gray-haired demon guy?"

"Yes." I grinned. "He's the missing Baylord king and also, as it turns out, Morgan's sire. It's a long story, and I promise

I'll tell you all of it. But first, there's something I need to tell you."

Her eyes narrowed. "They're not keeping me here again, are they? I can go home when I want?"

I sat down on the edge of her cot. "No one is keeping you here. You had a few minor injuries. Talie healed you and said you could go home as soon as you woke up."

"And Fiona agreed?" She sat up and scooted back until she could rest against the wall at the head of the bed.

I didn't like how she'd moved away from me, but I nodded. "I just came from a meeting with Fiona's Court. That's what I wanted to talk with you about."

Her eyes fell on the glint of metal I still had clutched in my hand. "What's that?"

I opened my fingers so she could see the disk of gold I'd been hiding. "A token of gratitude from the Faerie Queen."

"Fiona gave you a medal?"

I shrugged. "It's a token. She gave one to both of us, actually. Plus Kyle, Seren, and Gwawr. She tried to give one to Brianne, but that stubborn Elemental refused to accept it. She's still beating herself up about what happened to Nigel, I think."

"Is he okay?" Hannah asked.

I swallowed. "He's healing. Gwawr says he'll be fine."

"But Lilium's really gone, right?" Hannah shook her head. "I didn't imagine that? You aren't here to tell me it's not over, are you?"

I set a hand on her knee. "No. It's over. Liam and Arabella captured Lilium. Marcus banished her."

Hannah glanced up. "Is Morgan still being held prisoner?"

"Morgan is still safe with the Dragon Fae. I'll take you to her. Later."

Hannah wrapped her arms around her waist. "You're sure it's over and Lilium's gone? Because I really don't think I can do that portal thing again anytime soon."

I nodded. "Marcus confirmed it. Go on and take your token."

Hannah reached out and uncurled the forest-green ribbon attached to the medallion. "Call it what you want, but it looks like a medal. It even has this thing so you can wear it around your neck."

"Some Fae do choose to wear it but only for official occasions when they want to flaunt the fact that the queen of the Fae is in their debt." I watched Hannah's face, waiting for her to understand the significance.

She looked up. Her eyes locked with mine. "Fiona owes me a favor?"

I nodded once. "Both of us."

"What are you going to ask for?"

"That's what I wanted to talk with you about." I lifted the medallion and set it down on the bed so I could capture her hands between both of mine.

"Me?" She raised her eyebrows.

"Yes." I smiled. "You."

"Why me?" She scooted closer.

"We're a team. Aren't we?" I lifted one hand to brush my fingertips along her jaw.

Hannah cocked her head to one side, leaning into my touch. "It sounds like we accomplished our mission. You don't owe me anything anymore."

"I owe you everything." My eyes dropped down to rest on our joined hands before returning to meet hers. "I want to be on your team, Hannah Vos, water wizard. I want to be on your team as long as you'll have me. But you need to know that I've already promised the Faerie Queen my seed."

Hannah shook her head. "Wait. What?"

"I have been asked to sire the Faerie Queen's firstborn." My body tensed, waiting for her response. "Fiona's Court voted in favor of the decision."

"You and Fiona." She paused. The corners of her mouth pulled down into something that was half pout, half frown. She started to lean back. "Okay. I understand."

I squeezed her hands, silently urging her not to pull away. "I don't think you do. Fiona is not my mate. It doesn't work that way for Fae. She can have my seed without any sort of intimacy between us."

"Oh." Hannah's brow wrinkled.

"I tell you this because as much as I want to be with you, I will understand if you don't want to be with someone who has offspring with another."

Hannah snorted. "That's what you're worried about?"

"I would not want to share my partner with another, so I understand if you also feel that way."

Hannah squinted at me. "Explain to me how this works."

"I give Fiona my seed. She implants it—"

"You just have the one?" Hannah interrupted.

"All male Fae and all Rogues carry only one seed. Dragon Fae are a bit different, though. Since all Dragon Fae are male, we can have Fledgelings with humans, but they are produced according to human biology and only the males become Fae."

"The females have magic, though?" she asked.

"Yes."

"So, even if you give this seed of yours to Fiona, you can still have children...with a human?"

"Yes."

Hannah frowned. "Is that a requirement?"

I tried to read her face but couldn't tell what she was thinking. "No. Why?"

She squirmed and tried to scoot backward, but I wouldn't let go of her. "Ved, I...I never wanted children. You should know that."

I grinned. "Oh."

"So, if that's what you want—"

I leaned forward, lifting one hand to tilt her chin up so I could interrupt her with a kiss.

"No." I whispered the word against her lips when I let her pause to catch her breath. "That's not what I want. I want you."

"Oh." She paused for a heartbeat. "Are you sure?"

"It's not the same for Fae. Our offspring are raised in the crèche. I barely knew my sire except for the time he spent training me and my wing-mates. I've never allowed myself to conceive with any of the humans I bedded because I didn't want any Fledgeling to grow up with our previous Alpha in charge of the clan. It's different now with Damir in charge. But I have only had interest in one human since he became Alpha." I teased her lips with small kisses.

"Is that how it will be for your Fledgeling with Fiona?" she asked.

I sighed. "Fiona insists that she wants to raise her offspring herself. Damir may have something to say about that if she gives birth to a male. A Fledgeling. In that case, he will be Dragon Fae. If our offspring is female, she will be a Faeling, and heir to Fiona's crown, but only if Arabella or Seren don't give birth to a female first."

"I see." The wrinkle that creased the bridge of her nose didn't appear to agree.

"I know it's a lot, but what do you think? Is it too much for you?" I asked.

Hannah's face gave nothing away as she stared at me, considering my question. "I told you that I don't want a boyfriend. I still don't."

"I don't want to be your boyfriend, water wizard." I grinned at her. "I want to be your partner. Your teammate. The person who has your back forever."

"Forever is a lot longer for you than it is for me." She scowled.

I reached down and lifted the Faerie Queen's token. "If you want to change that, say the word and that will be the favor I request."

"You would use your favor for me?"

"I would do anything for you. You should know that by now."

Hannah curled her fingers around my hand and the medallion. "Why don't you take us home, and we can talk about who asks Fiona for what favor later?"

"Not until you answer my question." I pressed a lingering kiss to her lips. One that held all the promise of what she could expect if she accepted my offer. "Hannah Vos, wielder of water and banisher of demons, will you be my partner? My mate?"

Hannah leaned her forehead against mine. "Do you remember when you swooped down to save me during the fight?"

"Yes." I squeezed her hands. It chilled me just to think about how close I'd come to losing her.

"I knew it was you. Even before I heard your voice in my head. I don't know how, but I did. In that moment, I knew. I told myself that if we survived, I wasn't letting you go again." She lifted her hand to my cheek. "I would be honored to be your mate, Vedran Ashwing, hero of the demon war. There is no other creature on Earth who I would rather have as a partner."

Joy surged through my heart as I transported us from the Forest Fae infirmary to the mouth of the Dragon Fae caverns. I held her close and let her take in the view of the mountain peaks.

"This wasn't exactly what I had in mind when I said 'home.' And it's freezing." She shivered as she stared out at the scenery.

"You're not in pain?" I asked, surprised that she expressed no discomfort from the transport.

"No. That's...weird?" Her eyes widened as she wrapped her hands around her body. "Marcus said something about how portal magic changes you. Maybe this is what he meant?"

I pulled her deeper inside the West Mouth, then set my hands on her shoulders. "Don't move. I'll be right back."

I disappeared, returning a moment later with Hannah's bed from her apartment. "Better?"

She laughed. "What are you going to do with that?"

"Drag it and you back to my chambers and have my way with you." I allowed my forefinger to transform and beckoned to her with it. Then I let myself transform fully.

She stared at me for a moment before stepping closer and pressing her hand against the scales that covered my chest. A shiver ran through me at the contact. I held still as she ran a finger over the tip of my wing. But it was too much. I wanted her.

I dipped my head until it was level with hers, and she reached up to place her hand against the side of my jaw.

"You're magnificent." She whispered the words.

I huffed a bit of smoke in response, then stretched my

wings wide in warning. When she stepped back, I leapt into the air, grasping her bed in my talons before soaring deeper into the caverns. *Follow me.*

21

I ROLLED over and stretched, opening my eyes as Ved's arm curled around my waist to tug me closer. Staring up at the stone ceiling, I remembered that, even though these were my sheets covering our naked bodies, and my pillows cushioning our heads, we were not in my apartment.

Firrag, who must have sensed us wake up, chose that moment to soar into Ved's cavern. She settled on the headboard and peered down at us.

"Ved?" I tugged the sheet up.

"Mm-hmm…" Ved's warm lips pressed against my collarbone. His hand skimmed up my side.

"Ved." I shifted away from him. When he opened his eyes to meet mine, I jerked my chin up. "Firrag?"

Ved groaned. He sat up and plucked a note from Firrag's talon.

"What does it say?"

"Fiona's called another meeting. We're to bring Morgan to the Faerie Falls." He squinted at the paper. "And there's something about a viral video? Do you know what that means?"

I shot up, snatching the note from him with one hand as I used the other to tuck the sheet under my arms. A quick scan confirmed the bit about the meeting, but I had to reread the part about the video twice before it made sense.

"Someone caught the battle with the demons on camera. They posted it to the internet." My stomach sank as I glanced up to meet his eyes. "The humans know about magic. And Fae. And demons. All of it."

Ved frowned. "That's...not good."

"No. It is very 'not good.'" I handed him back the piece of paper and started scanning the room for my clothes. Shredded fabric littered the stone floor. That's when I remembered Ved's claws. "Crap."

Ved snickered. "Hang on."

He transformed and flew off, returning a minute later with an armful of clothes. It looked like he'd just pulled everything out of my closet. He transformed back into his Fae form before depositing the bundle of fabric onto my bed, and I was rewarded with an excellent view of his bare muscled chest. My eyes traveled down, absorbing the delicious sight of him, barely able to believe what he'd said about wanting to be with me forever.

Ved leaned forward as if, even though he were no longer in his dragon form, he could sense my thoughts. He set his hands down on the bed, pausing with his lips just inches from mine. "We have some time before we have to leave, you know..."

I shook my head, then reached for one of my sweaters at random and pulled it closer. It was cold in these caverns when there wasn't a Dragon Fae keeping me warm. "Not if I want to talk with Morgan before we go."

"Hmm." Ved grunted. He pushed himself back up to standing and ran a hand through his hair. "Fair enough, I suppose."

I shoved some of the clothes aside searching for the components I needed to make up a comfortable, practical outfit. Even though Ved assured me they were gone, I wasn't going to get caught fighting demons in a sundress again.

"I don't suppose you grabbed any underwear for me?"

Ved glanced over as he tugged trousers over his slim hips. "What's the point? I'm just going to tear it off you again."

I rolled my eyes. "Top drawer of my dresser? Please?"

Ved sighed. Then flew off again, reappearing moments later with the entire dresser clutched in his talons. He transformed and set it against one of the stone walls.

I stared at him. "Vedran Ashwing, is this your not-so-subtle way of moving me in with you?"

He grinned. "Would that be so terrible?"

"We can negotiate the details later." I wrapped the sheet around my body and walked over to where he stood leaning against the dresser. "But I don't think this caveman frat house is going to work as a full-time residence."

When I reached out to open the dresser drawer, Ved tugged the sheet away, letting it drop to the ground. His hands roamed my body as he slid in behind me and kissed my neck.

I glanced over at Firrag. "You know your familiar is watching."

Ved's laugh vibrated against my body. "So?"

I plucked my least favorite underwear and bra from the drawer before shutting it. Then I dangled the pair from my hooked fingertips. "Let me get dressed and give me some time to talk with Morgan, and you can rip these off me as soon as we get home."

His lips curled up where they were pressed against my

shoulder. "Home? Does that mean you'll let me get the rest of your things and bring them back here?"

"Not yet." I was pretty sure they didn't have internet in these caverns, and that was going to be a problem.

Ved released me after one long kiss that had me questioning how much I really wanted to speak with my ex–best friend.

"I told her I'd try to help her," he said.

"Why?" I asked, pulling on my favorite jeans.

"I don't think she meant to hurt you." Ved stood in the doorway, waiting for me.

Firrag led the way through twisty, turning, windowless tunnels that all looked identical to me. Yet another strike against cavern living.

"What time is it, anyway?" I asked.

Ved shrugged. "Morning."

"Dragon Fae aren't big on watches, I take it?"

Ved stopped at the entrance to a short tunnel. A pair of guards stood outside a chamber at the very end. "She's in there."

"Aren't you coming with?" I asked.

Ved shook his head. "You go ahead. I need to find Ivo and Damir. I'll come get you both when it's time to leave."

He kissed me, then waited until I'd made it past the guards before retreating.

Inside the small prison cave, Morgan sat hunched against a stone wall inside a steel cage. She looked up when I scuffed the sole of my boot on the floor.

"It's you." Glowing bulbs of light hovering just below the stone ceiling illuminated her face.

"Who were you expecting?" I asked, walking closer.

She shrugged. "They already brought breakfast. Too early

for lunch."

"Are you okay?" I asked.

"Good enough." Her boots were lying on their sides outside the bars.

I hesitated, suddenly unsure why I'd even bothered insisting on talking with her.

"I've been thinking about what I'd say to you, if I had the chance." Morgan glanced up at me, then back down at her chained wrists.

"'Sorry' might be a good place to start." I picked up her boots and set them upright in a pair beside the cell door.

"It's not exactly what you think." Morgan shifted her body against the rock wall. "She tempted me, sure. She said she'd teach me how to use my power. Told me that she'd introduce me to the demon that sired me. All I wanted was to learn. But not enough to go against the wizards.

"When Lilium first asked me to find the boxes for her, I refused. By then, I'd learned that I could mostly control my power. And I didn't care about meeting my sire. Then she kept putting off arranging for me to meet him. I started to think she didn't actually know him, or she was trying to use that introduction as a bribe. Turned out it was the second one."

"So, what happened when you refused?" I knew how the story ended. She had hurt me. She did end up betraying us. But if it weren't for knowledge, then I didn't understand why.

"Once she figured out that I would do anything for my family, she discovered something that meant more to me than the demon who sired me. And she's a succubus, so..." Morgan cringed.

"No." Puzzle pieces began clicking together in my head. The tension between Morgan and Brady. Everything Kayla had told me about the meeting I didn't remember. What if Brady hadn't been operating under Morgan's direction? "Lilium seduced *Brady*?"

Morgan bent her knees and wrapped her arms around her legs. "Sort of? As far as I can tell, she didn't *seduce him* seduce him, you know? She was toying with him just enough for me to get a sense of what she could do. What she could take away from me, if I refused again."

"That bitch!" My hand wrapped around one of the steel bars.

Morgan sighed. "Yeah."

"I'm so sorry. If we'd known, maybe we could have—"

"Don't." Morgan waved a hand to cut me off. "It all happened so fast. I'd only just figured out what she was up to and confronted her about it when Max told me about the boxes. I wasn't thinking logically. She made sure of that. It was all part of her plan."

I stepped closer and rested my forehead against the bars. "Well, I think you were right when you suspected that she didn't actually know your sire."

"What do you mean?"

"He isn't an incubus, for one."

"They found him?" Morgan asked.

I nodded. "He's the one who got the demons to stop fighting, in the end. Turns out he's some sort of Demon King or something. His name is Marcus. Kyle recognized him as the wizard who gave Max the key that led us to the boxes Emilio made. He also gave Kyle and Jayden the spell book with the directions on how to make the demon-warning charm they gave Ved, and the spells for how to open the portals.

"It's possible that your sire was hiding out, pretending to be a wizard, trying to find a way to defeat Lilium for decades.

He may have even tried to help Emilio escape her. And if your mom was lying about your sire being an incubus who seduced her..."

"Maybe they were actually in love?" Morgan leaned forward.

"Yeah."

"Wow."

Ved's voice called to us from the door. "It's time. We need to go."

The guards followed Ved inside.

He looked at Morgan. "They're going to let you out, but we have to leave the cuffs on."

"Where are we going?" she asked.

One guard unlocked her door, the other stepped inside and unfastened the chains from the wall. They marched her out the door and into the main tunnel. Then, without warning, one transformed and flew off with Morgan secured in his talons.

"Your turn." Ved looked at me.

"Can't you just transport us?"

"Not until we get to the Mouth." He took my hand. "We can walk, or we can fly. Your choice."

"If I say fly, are you going to carry me off like dinner?"

Ved laughed. "Unless you have a better idea."

I grinned. "Transform, and I'll show you."

Ved shifted into his dragon form, and I pictured what I had in mind. A puff of smoke curled from his nostrils, but he bent his head down and lowered his shoulders so I could climb up onto his back.

Once I was settled with my arms wrapped as far around his neck as I could reach, he leapt into the air. Wind rushed at my face as we sped through the cavern tunnels. Then, the pinprick of light at the end of one turned into blue sky and snowy mountain peaks.

We burst out of the caverns and into the sunlight, then disappeared. A heartbeat later, we reappeared above treetops, gliding above the sea of green until Ved angled us toward a clearing. I lifted my head and let out a whoop of joy.

Firrag screeched in response. Then an image of a pear appeared in my mind.

Pears? I sent the thought to Ved.

Ved replied with a vision of Firrag, jaws dripping with pear juice as she tore into the ripe fruit. *They're her favorite.*

I glanced over at the little faerie dragon. *She sent me that?*

I think she likes you, Ved replied.

Before I could respond, we were landing in the last remaining open spot at the base of a beautiful waterfall.. A stretch of grass left open between the enormous outpouring of Fae in all sizes, shapes, and skin tones, united by their devotion to Fiona, and the cluster of wizards. I recognized more than a few faces in that group. My friends waved from their position near the center of the gathering. The only one missing was Max.

Ved interlaced his fingers with mine. I hadn't even noticed that he'd transformed, but he was back in his Fae form with Firrag curled around his neck like a scarf.

"Where's Max? Shouldn't he be here? And Morgan?" I glanced around, searching for any sign of my friends, or of the other Dragon Fae. The one who had brought Morgan.

I spotted Damir and Seren near the edge of the lake at the foot of the falls. They stood with most of Fiona's Court. But Max wasn't there, either.

Then Ved pointed toward the base of the falls. A trio of figures was walking around the far side of the lake. As they approached, I identified two of the three faces. Fiona walked at the center and a little bit ahead of the other two. Max followed at her side.

"Is that...?"

"Marcus. Morgan's sire. The Baylord king," Ved whispered in my ear.

A hush had fallen over the assembled Fae. The wizards stopped talking next. Then Fiona took her place at the edge of the lake. She stood on top of a large, flat rock overlooking the gathering.

"My kin." She raised her hands to the sky. "And the Ancients who guide us. A new era is beginning. An age where Fae and human and demon will coexist in peace."

Murmurs traveled through the crowd.

"I present to you Marcus, Overlord of the Baylord Clan and King of Demons on Earth. He comes before us to swear his loyalty to the Fae and take responsibility for ruling the demon clans who chose to remain among us."

Marcus stepped forward, then dropped to one knee before Fiona. "I swear my Oath of Loyalty to you, Fiona, Faerie Queen."

"Rise, Marcus." Fiona took a bundle from Max and handed it to the Demon King. "As a token to seal our alliance, we give you these six boxes."

Fiona reached into the bag and held up one of Emilio's wizard boxes. I sucked in a breath at the same time as many around me.

"These boxes have been charged with magic and reconfigured so that you and your kin may use them as a source of power. My kin swears to keep them full so long as the demon clans honor their agreements to do no harm."

Marcus took the bag from Fiona. "We thank you, Faerie

Queen, and swear to honor our promises."

Fiona waited while Marcus bowed and moved off to one side. Then she continued. "Next, I present to you Maxwell Hunter of the newly formed Wizard Triumvirate."

Some of the wizards in the group next to me began whispering to each other. A chorus of "Did you know? Did you?" echoed through the clustered humans.

"No longer will the wizards be governed by a hereditary council. From this day forward, a triumvirate will determine wizard law. They will be elected by the wizards to serve three-year terms with one replaced each year. However, the founding three have been selected by me. In addition to Maxwell, the two others who have agreed to serve are Grace Shin and Jayden Reyes. They will be replaced, one per year, starting with Maxwell."

The buzz of chatter from the wizards increased.

Fiona silenced them with her next proclamation. "In exchange for their loyalty, so long as the wizards remain allies to the Fae, the Elementals will be responsible for educating any wizard who wishes to learn. The Elemental guardian has charged Barrfhionn and Anwen with the responsibility of forming and running an academy for formal study."

Max stepped forward and knelt in front of Fiona. "Thank you, Faerie Queen. The wizards renew their pledge of loyalty to the Fae."

After Max stepped back, Fiona continued. "Finally, let it be known that the humans have obtained evidence of our presence. Therefore, I think it is time for us to adjust our way of living. Any Fae caught manipulating humans will be punished. Any humans wishing to reside in the Fae lands may petition my Court for permission. Otherwise, contact between Fae and humankind is no longer forbidden."

The assembled Fae erupted with chatter in response to Fiona's decree.

"Further"—she raised her voice to speak over them—"I have asked our human ambassador, Evelyn Serra, to lead an outreach program to educate humans about magic and test any who think they might have magic.

"Thank you, and I look forward to many centuries of peaceful coexistence with our allies. That is all."

Ved leaned closer to me. "What do you think? Should we officially petition the Court for their blessing on our union?"

"Do you think we'll need to use one of our favors?"

Ved pulled me into his arms. "I have a feeling they're already rooting for us."

"Oh, you think so, do you?"

"I do." Ved stole a quick kiss.

"Then what are you going to use your favor for?"

"I think we can discuss that later." Ved slid his hand up, under my sweater. "Someone promised I could rip her clothes off after this meeting. And I've been very, very patient." His fingers crept up my spine as he punctuated his words with slow, tantalizing kisses.

When I opened my eyes, we were once again standing at the mouth of the Dragon Fae caverns surrounded by mountains. "I suppose I could get used to calling this home."

Epilogue

I HAD really hoped to never spend another minute in the Forest Fae infirmary, but Damir insisted on going, even though we had plenty of medics in our clan. He wouldn't let any of them touch Seren. Not for this. He insisted that the Hands of his mother's kin would be best suited to care for his mate as she labored to give birth to their offspring.

I'd been the one to transport her. Damir didn't trust himself. He was too nervous. And Ivo was still too weak to transport anyone other than himself.

When we arrived, Arabella was already here, occupying one of the beds. No less than three of the Elemental Hands were rushing about as Willow sat holding Arabella's hand.

"Must be the moon," Ioryn said by way of greeting as he passed me on his way out of the infirmary.

Ioryn was one of the Hands, in addition to being the sire of Arabella's Faeling. I also recognized Talie and Eira, who were preparing herbs and ointments on a worktable near the entrance. That left the male sitting near Arabella's bed as the only one I didn't know. I decided he must be Ioryn's mate.

Damir waved at me from the far end of the infirmary. He'd chosen the bed that had been mine when I'd been stuck in here recovering. It seemed like an odd choice to me, but I wasn't about to say anything about it.

Seren squirmed in my arms. "This is embarrassing. Just let me down, and I'll walk."

I glanced down at her. "You know if I do that, he'll have my head."

Her face contorted as a wave of pain hit. "Fine," she grunted.

I carried her down the aisle, nodding to Willow and Arabella, as well as the male I didn't know. By the time I made it to Damir and settled Seren onto the bed, Eira was hovering nearby, ready to take over.

I caught Damir's eye. "I'll just..." I gestured toward the entry, hoping he'd let me retreat now that my job was complete.

"Don't go far. I want you here to meet your kin." Damir looked past me and waved. "Fiona just arrived."

I nodded. "I'll go greet her, then."

As I made my way back up the aisle, I watched Talie fuss over Fiona. Ivo walked in just as Talie placed a hand on Fiona's belly. The two of us exchanged a knowing look. It was my seed growing in Fiona's womb, but we both knew that Talie had claim over her heart. Even though he couldn't yet claim her as his mate. Not officially, anyway.

To keep the Fae united, Fiona had sworn to birth at least seven Faelings, each by a sire from a different one of the Fae factions scattered across the world. As part of her Oath, she'd promised not to take a mate until she'd completed her vow so as not to show favor to any one faction over another. But that didn't mean she hadn't promised her heart to someone already.

Given how long it took Fae females to produce offspring, Talie would be waiting for nearly two decades to take his place by her side, officially. But that was just the blink of an eye for our kin, and he seemed content enough to wait.

Fiona spotted me and smiled. "Greetings, Faesire. How is your water wizard?"

I grinned. "Hannah is well. Thank you."

"If there is anything that either of you need, I do hope you will ask. It need not be an official favor. We are family now." The glow emanating from her practically vibrated with her joy.

I dipped my head out of respect but stopped short of a full bow since we were, as she said, family. "I appreciate that. There is one thing I was hoping you might consider."

"Name it." She rested her hands on her belly.

"I was hoping that you might agree to let Hannah interview you." I paused. Then, in case it wasn't obvious, I added, "For one of her videos."

Fiona nodded. "Yes. I would be honored. Evelyn says that Hannah—and you—are doing quite well smoothing things over with the humans."

"It is more Hannah than me. Though, I hope I'll have more time to help after this." I gestured behind me.

A frown tugged at the corners of Fiona's mouth. "I thought Seren intended to raise her Faeling in the caverns. Won't you be even more busy now that you have to guard them both?"

I laughed. "Seren hates having a guard. I'm certain that she won't stand for it after she's healed, no matter how much Damir insists. But I'll let them sort that out."

"Is Hannah here?" Fiona glanced around.

I shook my head. "There wasn't time to get her before, and

now that we're here, Damir asked that I stay."

"Well, I'll send someone to transport her here. I'm sure she would want to be present for the birth of Damir and Seren's Faeling." Fiona gestured to the guard at the door.

"Thank you. I would appreciate that." I set my palm against my chest, above my heart.

While Fiona relayed instructions to the guard on duty, I turned to Ivo.

"Faeling?" he whispered.

I shrugged. "Sounds like Fiona is hoping that Seren will give birth to a female."

The Forest Fae used the term "Faeling" to apply to female, male, and Rogue offspring. But among the Dragon Fae, male offspring were "Fledgelings." Fiona knew that, so her choice must have been intentional.

"Look who is picking up on the fine points of diplomacy." Ivo grinned at me.

I shook my head. "Don't get too excited. I'm perfectly content in my role as commander of the Dragon Fae Guard."

After she finished speaking with the guard, Fiona stepped toward us.

Ivo bowed to her. "My queen."

"It is good to see you again, Ivo Lightwing. Don't think I have forgotten. I am still waiting for you to inform me of your choice." She raised an eyebrow.

Ivo inclined his head to one side. "Apologies. I have been busy helping Damir. Once he and Seren and their *Faeling* are settled back in the caverns, I promise I will devote my full attention to the list of names you provided me."

"Good." She patted Ivo's shoulder as she slid past us. "I want to check on Arabella, even though I'm sure she won't want me hovering about. Perhaps one of you can find us a deck or some dice to keep us busy while we wait?"

"She is a force." Ivo shook his head. "I can only imagine the Faeling that the pair of you will produce."

I shoved his shoulder. "Fledgeling, you mean."

He laughed. "I'll go check on Damir. You find us some cards and see if Ioryn's mate wants to join us."

A little while later, Ivo, Kal, Fiona and I settled in to play cards while Seren and Arabella labored, and the Hands scurried back and forth between them. Just before dawn, the first wails from new lungs echoed off the high wood ceiling. We had barely set down our cards before another, slightly different cry joined the first.

Fiona and Kal rushed to Arabella's beside while Ivo and I continued past the commander's bed to join Seren and Damir.

As we hurried by, I caught Ioryn's words of greeting to his mate and his queen. "It's a female."

I sucked in a breath. My heart raced in anticipation.

Damir welcomed us with a glowing smile. "She's well. They're both well."

"And?" Ivo asked.

"Female," Seren whispered, cradling her Faeling against her chest.

I stood and stared, watching Ivo and Damir, waiting for a hint as to what they wanted me to do. This had been both a hope of theirs and a fear.

Eira checked Seren and her Faeling one more time, then retreated, leaving the four, now five, of us alone.

"It's all right," Damir said.

"Who was first?" I asked.

"They will both have a claim," Seren whispered. "Tell them what we decided, Mir."

Damir placed his hand on my shoulder. "We would like

to call her Ash, short for Ashley, after you. Ashley Light Firewing."

I blinked, then looked to Ivo, only to find him smiling. He'd known. "You're okay with this?"

He nodded. "It was my idea."

"You're the one who brought us together," Damir said. "And you're the one who led the charge against the demons. If our Faeling has half your strength and courage, she will be a force to be reckoned with."

Hannah slid in beside me and wrapped an arm around my waist. "I think it's an excellent choice."

"She will be a queen to be reckoned with," Seren added, her voice soft as she handed the sleeping Faeling off to Damir.

"And she will have me as her sworn protector," I pledged, leaning closer to get a look at my niece's face.

"Now we wait," Ivo said. "To see what sort of magic our little queen will manifest."

If you enjoyed this book, don't miss the other books in the
Modern Fae series:

Eve of the Fae
Dawn of the Fae
Will of the Fae
Hunter of the Fae
Tales of the Fae

To be the first to know about new books, discounts, give-
aways, and behind the scenes book info, sign up for my
newsletter at
`http://www.tinyletter.com/emenozzi.`

ACKNOWLEDGEMENTS

To all the readers who have stuck with this Modern Fae series from book one, especially my Magic for Mortals subscribers, thank you! You are the reason I write these stories. I am so glad that you enjoy them and that you share them with others. That epilogue is a promise to you. There is always more to the story, and this is probably not the last you'll see of our Modern Fae friends.

Even though I had so much fun writing this book, 2021 was a tough year for writing (at least for me). I definitely would not have been able to finish this book, let alone figure out a whole mess of writing, publishing, and general life nonsense without the support of my Struggle Bus Crew. Thank you for being so wise and generous and supportive. You are all rock stars!

My SJI NaNoWriMo group, especially Pam, Naomi, and Lillie, kept me writing all year long, even when I didn't feel like it. Thank you for being there for our weekly write-ins!

To our fellow geeky local friends, Tony and Zoe, thank you

for the game nights and the bonfires and the rambling chats about life. I'm so glad we managed to build a friendship in the midst of a pandemic.

I am extremely grateful for my little home office, and I am especially charmed that the original owner was also a writer. Paul, wherever you are, I hope a fraction of the magic you created here rubs off on me.

Possibly my biggest distraction while writing this book was my young friend Jude, and his friends Theo and Sean, who introduced me to the Arena and got me hooked on virtual Magic. Even though I probably should have been writing, thank you for drafting with me and putting up with my nonsensical love of goblin decks.

Thank you to my excellent cover designer, Elizabeth Mackey, for another beautiful cover!

And thank you to my fantastic copy editor, Michelle Hope, for helping me make the narrative shine.

Thank you to my all-star alpha readers, Carolyn and Kaitlin. The pair of you are a perfect combo of good cop and bad cop. I don't know what I would do without your feedback and cheer-leading.

For all the years of encouragement and "you can do it" pep talks, an extra big thank you to my mom!

And last, but certainly not least, thank you to my husband for being the best partner I could ask for.

ABOUT THE AUTHOR

ELIZABETH Menozzi is an award-winning writer of science fiction and fantasy with romance. A former Midwestern girl, she currently resides on Orcas Island with her husband. In her spare time she is a competitive swimmer, reluctant runner, and devourer of books.

You can follow her on Twitter (@emenozzi) and Instagram (emmenozzi), or contact her via her website at http://www.elizabethmenozzi.com/.